Rule #1:
A truly improper lady
<u>always</u> surrenders to
her desires . . .

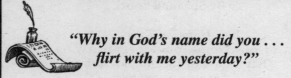

"Why in God's name did you . . . flirt with me yesterday?"

Theresa opened her mouth to retort. The breath of vulnerability in his hard voice, though, stopped her. Of course she'd been flirting with him. She might not have called it that at the time, but as she stood behind him now, alone in the garden, it was obvious. That was *not* how a young lady conducted herself.

"I suppose I may speak with and dance with whomever I please."

"What about what pleases me?" he asked, catching her right hand in his left.

This close she realized that the top of her head just came to his chin. "Let go of my hand."

"Do you think me a charity project?"

"I do not."

"Good." Colonel James pulled her against him. "Because I don't want charity. Yours or anyone else's."

As she opened her mouth to protest that she hadn't considered that he required charity, he leaned in and kissed her.

He felt warm and solid, and unexpectedly electric. For a bare second she felt . . . unbound, as though she wasn't even touching the ground.

Then he broke away. "There," he said roughly. "You flirted, and now I've kissed you. Go back to Montrose."

By Suzanne Enoch

A Lady's Guide to
Improper Behavior

SUZANNE ENOCH

AVON
An Imprint of HarperCollinsPublishers

AVON BOOKS
An Imprint of HarperCollins*Publishers*
10 East 53rd Street
New York, New York 10022-5299

Copyright © 2010 by Suzanne Enoch
ISBN 978-0-06-166221-8
www.avonromance.com

First Avon Books paperback printing: May 2010

For Saundra Stark,
who wanted to appear as a sexy diva villainess,
but unfortunately doesn't have a Regency name.
So instead I give you the book's first page.

A Lady's Guide to
Improper
Behavior

Chapter One

"Being a true lady means making even a mundane topic such as the weather interesting. A gentleman must *want* to approach you, and a gentleman does not want to be bored."

A LADY'S GUIDE TO PROPER BEHAVIOR

.

What do you think of that, Colonel? He's brought in another one."

Annoyed, Colonel Bartholomew James opened one eye. At the far end of the room, beyond the two dozen comfortable chairs and tables, past the billiards table and the generous stand of liquor bottles, the Duke of Sommerset stood speaking with a tall, dark-haired fellow wearing the uniform of a naval captain.

"It's Sommerset's club," he returned, giving up on feigning sleep; clearly Thomas Easton meant to converse with him whether he was awake or not. "I suppose he can invite whomever he pleases to join it."

"Damned navy," Easton grumbled. "Let him try spending a year in the desert like we did, and see how fine his uniform looks."

"I wasn't in the desert."

"Part of India is desert." Easton cursed under his breath. "Damn. They're walking this way. Pretend to be asleep."

"That doesn't seem to be very effective," Bartholomew noted dryly, shifting in the deep chair a little and ignoring the sharp pain jabbing through his left knee.

"This is Mr. Thomas Easton," Sommerset drawled as the two men approached. "He spent a year in Persia to encourage the expansion of the silk trade to Britain. Easton, Captain Bradshaw Carroway."

"Carroway. So now the only qualification to join the Adventurers' Club is what, to survive a rough sea?"

"The only qualification," the duke returned, still cool and unconcerned, "is my say-so. I see you're awake, Colonel."

Bartholomew sent a sideways glance at Easton. "Under the circumstances, there's little else I could be."

Sommerset's mouth twitched. "Captain Carroway, this is Colonel Bartholomew James. Tolly served for a time in India."

Served for a time. Interesting that four words could so completely describe ten years of his life. Bartholomew nodded. "Captain."

"Colonel." The naval officer straightened. "I read about your ordeal. My condolences."

So it was an "ordeal" now. Better than an "incident" or an "unfortunate occurrence" or even an exaggeration, he supposed, and he'd heard it described as all of those things. "Thank you," he said aloud.

"Come, Sommerset," Easton broke in, "you always have a reason for admitting another uncivilized beast into your club. What's our dear Captain Carroway here for?"

"That's for him to tell, if he wishes to do so—just as I only mention the parts of your tale that you've made public knowledge." The duke motioned Carroway to follow, and the two men walked over to greet the Earl of Hennessy, the only other club member present at the moment.

Easton leaned over the arm of his chair. "What do you think it is, Colonel? A shipwreck? Capture by pirates?"

Bartholomew made one last attempt to ignore the blast of hot air that was Thomas Easton. He shut his eyes again. And immediately rocky hills, bone-dry stream beds, twisted trees hanging over crumbling ravines filled his mind. It was nowhere he particularly cared to revisit, but he could never seem to be anywhere else. He deserved to still be there, he supposed. Everyone under his command was still there, beneath the stones.

"We're fifteen now," Easton went on, unmindful of the fact that no one else wanted to talk to him. "Fifteen outcasts, unfit for proper Society. Ah, the tales we could tell, with only us to listen."

"Some of us stopped listening to *you* ages ago," Hennessy commented from across the room. Bartholomew snorted.

"You don't—"

"The Adventurers' Club is supposed to be a damned refuge, Easton," the earl continued. "Not a place for you to torment the rest of us. Leave be."

"I'm talking to the colonel, not you. If he doesn't like it, he can tell me so."

"Shut up, Easton," Bartholomew muttered.

Yes, the Adventurers' Club, established several months ago by the Duke of Sommerset and located in the east wing of his massive town house, was a refuge for misfits. Explorers, adventurers—how had Sommerset put it? A place for those who'd learned to view the world and Society with clearer eyes than the rest of London. That was he, Bartholomew supposed. Because most of the time he couldn't see London at all any longer.

A moment later he heard Thomas Easton rise and wander off, likely to torment Hennessy or the new fellow. Thank God. Perhaps now he could manage a few minutes of sleep, given the way it tended to evade him at night. Then the scent of sandalwood touched his nostrils, and someone else settled into Easton's vacated chair. "Sommerset," he drawled.

"Hervey tells me you've been here for three days now," the duke said, pitching his voice lower.

Inwardly sighing, Bartholomew opened his eyes again and straightened from his current I'd-rather-not-speak-with-you slouch. The movement twisted his knee again, but he hid his flinch. "I don't feel like going out," he admitted aloud.

"And you don't have to. That's why the Adventurers' Club provides spare rooms for whichever of us requires one. If I'm not mistaken, Tolly, didn't your sister and brother arrive in Town the day before yesterday?"

He didn't recall that Sommerset had ever been mistaken about anything. "Hence me being here rather than at James House." Bartholomew cocked his head. "You're using my nickname. What do you want?" Lifting his cane, he twirled it idly in his hands. Somewhere in the past few months it had become another limb, an extension of his body. He required it and hated it all at the same time.

"I recall you speaking fondly of your siblings," the duke countered, ignoring his question.

"I am fond of them. But Stephen and Violet are very . . . chirpy. I'm not." Not any longer, anyway.

"Just keep in mind that I won't have them here. Nor do I want them searching London for you and raising all sorts of alarms that point here."

"Ah. So that's what you want." It was the first rule of the Adventurers' Club. Members only. As far as Bartholomew had been able to determine in the six weeks he'd been a member, no one else in London had ever heard a word about its existence. "I'll go see them tomorrow and let them know I'm staying elsewhere."

"Do it today. They're already asking around for you."

A murmur of uneasiness went through his gut. Sommerset made the rules at this club, however, and Bartholomew had no desire to be asked to leave. It was, after all, the only place where he seemed able to close his eyes for more than a few minutes at a time. Apparently there was something to be said for being surrounded by people who knew how to manage themselves in a crisis. "I'll have my horse brought around, then."

The duke stood again. "I'll see to it."

Drawing a breath and clenching his jaw, Bartholomew braced both hands against the arms of the deep chair and muscled himself upright. He'd gotten better at it; when he'd first begun, he'd ended up on the floor more often than not. Now, however, with another sharp, lingering stab and grind in his left knee, he stood. The end of the cane clicked against the polished hardwood floor, his third leg. One short of a horse.

He didn't have to go at that moment, he supposed. Sommerset had only told him to take care of it today, and going by the longcase clock in the corner, it was barely eleven. The sooner he saw to it, though, the sooner he could return to the refuge of the Adventurers' Club.

Outside the well-hidden entrance of the club, Harlow held the reins of his big, dark gray gelding, Meru. The groom had already circled the gray so Bartholomew could mount from the right side—a damned shame, but the only way he could make it into the saddle these days. Thankfully Meru had caught on quickly and stood still as a rock while he slid the cane into the straps that would normally have held a rifle or a sword, then swung up into the saddle.

With a nod to the groom, Bartholomew sent Meru down the Ainsley House drive and out onto the streets of Mayfair. It was odd; he'd grown up familiar with these streets, attending parties, recitals, whatever his parents could drag him to first as a lad and then as a very naive young man down from Oxford. Even later there had been an army leave here or there when he'd returned, visiting family and friends, attending parties, but not quite seeing it any longer as the raison d'être his less-traveled fellows seemed to think it.

Now it all seemed foreign. As he turned onto Davies Street a pair of cart drivers stood arguing and throwing produce at one another over some slight or other. Smashed peaches littered the street, attracting a slew of dogs, pigeons, and street urchins. Bartholomew leaned out and caught one of the fruits as it soared by, then dropped it into a small girl's outstretched hands. She fled back into an alley, skittish as the dogs.

Once he reached the white, multi-windowed front of James House he stopped. For the past few weeks since his return from India he'd been living more or less in the family home, though most nights he seemed either to end up riding the streets or sleeping in one of the back rooms of the Adventurers' Club—or one of the chairs in front of the fireplace there. Now that the Season had begun in earnest, of course Stephen and Violet would have come to London. He supposed he'd just been pretending ignorance of that fact—until he'd received Stephen's letter four days ago.

Blowing out his breath, he urged Meru up the drive and around the side of the house to the stable. As soon as he appeared two grooms hurried out, Harry to take the gray by the bridle, and Tom to gingerly pull Tolly's left foot from the stirrup and then circle around to take Bartholomew's weight as he dismounted.

As his left foot settled on the ground the sharp, familiar pain shot from his toes all the way up his spine. For a moment he held still, not so much waiting for the pain to subside as allowing his body to adjust to it again. If he could live on horseback, he would hardly mind the injury at all. Unfortunately, Meru couldn't manage the stairs at James House. Even more unfortunately, Bartholomew couldn't, either.

"Thank you, Tom," he said, reaching over to free the cane and shifting to settle his weight on it.

"Lord and Lady Gardner and Miss Violet arrived the day before yesterday, Colonel," the sturdy groom said, taking a step back, out of the way. "They've been inquiring as to your whereabouts."

"Yes, I know. I'll see to it."

He'd just reached the front of the house when the door swung open. "Tolly!"

Black-haired Violet flew down the steps at him. Bartholomew braced himself, digging the tip of his cane into the dirt and clenching his jaw against the pain that he knew would come. Just short of colliding with him, though, Violet skidded to a stop.

"Stephen said you'd been hurt," she said, looking up at him with concerned brown eyes. "You're still hurt, aren't you?"

"I heard you've been looking for me," he said gruffly.

"Of course we've been looking for you! May I hug you, or should we shake hands?"

Bartholomew didn't quite know how to answer that. Thankfully, before he could decide, Stephen, Viscount Gardner, descended the front steps, as well. "Stephen," he said, nodding. His gaze lifted to the young light-haired lady following his older brother outside. "And you must be Amelia."

She nodded. "I'm pleased to finally meet you, Colonel."

Knowing what he must look like, he had to give his new sister-in-law credit for not shrieking. He couldn't remember whether he'd shaved that morning or not, and his brown hair was badly in need of a trim. And then there was the cane. At least his cravat hid the marks around his throat. "Call me Tolly," he returned, and offered his free hand to Stephen.

His brother shook it. "Where the devil have you been?"

"Staying with a friend," Bartholomew hedged.

"But this is your home!" Violet exclaimed, finally stepping in to wrap her hands around his left arm. "Do come in. Do you need assistance? I can fetch Graham."

Bartholomew shrugged free of her grip. "Leave be, Vi. Graham and I already have an understanding."

"Which is?" Stephen prompted as Bartholomew limped past him.

"He opens the door and then goes away," Bartholomew returned, clenching his jaw as he reached the first of the three shallow steps. It wasn't so much that he minded looking ungainly as he didn't want to appear weak. He glared at the step, willing it to sink into the drive.

"Violet, Stephen," Amelia's too-sweet voice came from the doorway above, "why don't we sit in the morning room? The Colonel—Tolly—can join us when he pleases."

He glanced up at her. At least someone understood that he didn't want to be stared at. She was fairly pretty, he decided, blond-haired and green-eyed, with that cheery look that suited Stephen's own manner. He wasn't certain he would have given her a second look under other circumstances, but for this moment he was grateful for her presence.

"Right." Stephen collected Violet and the two of them pranced up the steps with no noticeable effort and vanished into the house behind Stephen's new wife.

Once left to himself, Bartholomew reached out to hook the door frame with the cane's handle. Gripping the shaft with both hands, he pulled himself up, one slow, painful step at a time. When he reached the foyer a light sweat covered his brow. Wiping it away impatiently, he shrugged out of his overcoat and set his hat onto a hook. Then, shaking himself, he walked three-legged into the morning room.

"You should sit down," Violet said immediately, bouncing to her feet to make room for him close by the door. She'd been out for a year now, and by his count would be nineteen by the end of the month, but she still flounced and chirped like the child he remembered.

If he sat, he would have to stand again. "I'm fine," he said, moving across the room to lean against the fireplace mantel.

"You knew we were coming to London, didn't you?" Stephen asked, taking Amelia's hand and drawing it across his knee. "I wrote you nearly a week ago."

"I knew."

"Then why have you been missing for the past two days?"

"I haven't been missing. I've been elsewhere."

The viscount cocked his head. "Are you angry with me?"

"No."

"Good, because I'm quite happy to see you. It's been three years, nearly, since you were last home."

"I'm aware of that." Bartholomew took a breath. "I'm poor company these days. You're newly wed, and I know that Vi has never missed a dance in her life. So proceed with enjoying the Season, and I'll be about."

"But we're your family," Violet protested. "We're supposed to hold you close in your time of need."

Good God. That was actually almost amusing. "My time of need was eight months ago," he said aloud. "Since then I've come to prefer my own company." Bartholomew straightened again, heading for the door.

"Where can we reach you?"

"You may leave messages for me at the Society Club."

Stephen stood up behind him. "At least say you'll join us for dinner this evening. It will be family only. Amelia's cousins Theresa and Michael, and us."

He didn't want to. He wanted to return to the Adventurers' Club and the quiet of his own thoughts. Somewhere he didn't have to be polite, or answer any questions, or have anyone crowd him.

In the foyer Graham inclined his head, pulled open the front door, and headed away down the hall. Descending the stairs was an even trickier ordeal than climbing up; he had nothing to hold on to. Leaning forward a little, he planted the cane on the second step and then stepped down, bad leg first.

"Tolly."

Damnation. "Not now, Stephen. I'm occupied."

"Then let me help you, damn it all."

Before he could protest, his older brother had grabbed his free arm. Pulling Bartholomew's arm across his shoulder, the viscount swiftly descended the remaining two steps. As soon as his feet were on the ground, Bartholomew shoved his brother away. "Hands off," he snapped, stumbling backward until he could catch his balance.

"Apologies. But I don't understand what's—"

"Just don't touch me." Not only did it physically throw him off, but the memories of being grabbed, held down . . . It was still too fresh.

Whether he read the upset on his brother's face or he recognized that Bartholomew had gripped the cane like a weapon, Stephen raised his arms and backed away a step. "Very well."

"Good. I have to go now."

"Tolly, I read the newspaper account of what happened in India, and I received your letter. I know what you've been through. And I understand. We only want to help you recover."

A shiver ran down Bartholomew's spine. "You may know what happened, but you don't know what I've been through, Stephen. And I'm as recovered as I will ever be." He motioned at Tom as the groom peered around the corner. "I truly only wish to be left alone."

"After tonight. Come by at seven o'clock."

"I'll consider it."

"Not good enough. Be here, or I'll come looking for you."

And then Sommerset would likely boot him out of the Adventurers' Club altogether. "Seven o'clock," he grunted. "And then you'll leave me be."

"I'll consider it."

Bartholomew abruptly understood why his brother

had thought that an unsatisfactory answer. All he could do at the moment was appear for dinner, and then either convince his family that they wanted nothing to do with him, or disappear. Either one would do, he supposed.

"Theresa, do stop preening," Michael Weller said with a grin as he descended the stairs of Weller House. "You're already the embodiment of perfection. And we know everyone attending tonight."

Theresa looked away from the foyer mirror to frown at her older brother. "The point is to look one's best, no matter the company."

"You're quoting your booklet at me again, aren't you?"

"I knew you read it. You said you hadn't." She flashed him a smile, trying to picture him reading *A Lady's Guide to Proper Behavior.*

"Because it's for chits."

"Well, thank you, anyway." She finished putting on her hat. "And we don't know everyone attending tonight. The other brother will be there. Amelia sent over a note."

"The colonel?" Michael spent his own moment in front of the mirror adjusting his cravat.

"Yes. He was wounded, wasn't he? Do you have to purchase a new uniform if the old one is ruined in battle, or does the army provide it for you?"

"How the devil should I know? He's retired on half pay, anyway. The uniform is only for large soirees and people he wishes to impress. And I doubt he'll worry about impressing us." Michael collected his hat from Ramsey. "See that Mooney has my riding boots cleaned, will you?" he asked the butler. "I'm to go riding with Lord Gardner in the morning."

"Very good, my lord."

Offering her an arm, Michael walked outside with her to their waiting coach. "You did tell Grandmama we're leaving, didn't you?" he asked.

Theresa nodded. "Of course I did. She said you should mind your language, and then she went to find some strawberries." She looked over at her brother as he took the seat beside her. At six-and-twenty he might have been three years her elder, but he seldom acted like the more mature sibling. That responsibility fell to her. "Whether the colonel wears a uniform or not, he was the lone survivor of an attack. We must show compassion."

"I'm always compassionate. And I imagine I can find something other than uniforms to chat about," he said dryly. "If I settle on an unsafe topic, you may kick me beneath the table."

"Gladly," she said, offering him another smile.

"You didn't have to agree to that quite so swiftly."

"Hmm." She straightened her gloves. "By the way, have you spoken with Lord Montrose lately?" she asked as casually as she could.

"I saw him this afternoon at White's. Why do you ask?"

Theresa made a face. "Why do you think I ask?"

Michael lifted an eyebrow. "So you've settled on him?"

"I'm not certain yet," she hedged. And that was the truth. Whether everyone else thought she was being coy or not, she simply wasn't certain—about Montrose, or any of her other suitors. And mostly, about herself.

"You only wanted to know, then, if he'd gone off and found someone more interesting?" her brother asked skeptically.

She sniffed, shaking herself. "I was only curious as to his whereabouts. You're his friend, Michael, so you should know. I can't very well send a note over to his house to ask his health."

"I do know all about him. Which is why I'm fairly certain his only illness is that he's still pining after you."

"I told him not to do that. I simply need more time to make up my mind."

"The trouble, Tess, is that you have so many to choose from. His odds make him nervous."

"That's not actually my fault."

Whatever her brother teased, in truth the Marquis of Montrose *wasn't* her only prospect. In fact, the only difficulty should have been in narrowing down her choices. But she didn't quite feel ready for that, yet. The more choices there were, the more time she could be expected to take to choose. And that suited her quite well.

Chapter Two

"It is easy to relax one's manners in private, with family. The ones with whom you are the most comfortable, the most intimate, however, are the ones who most deserve a pleasant countenance and a modest reserve."

A LADY'S GUIDE TO PROPER BEHAVIOR

As Theresa stepped down from the coach, Amelia gave her a warm hug and a kiss on the cheek. "I need to speak with you," her cousin whispered, then released her to greet Michael.

Amelia had never been a great gossip, but her tone was certainly conspiratorial. Her own interest piqued, Theresa made her way through the greetings of her cousin's husband, Stephen, Lord Gardner, and his delightful younger sister, Violet. No other guests seemed to be in attendance.

They went into the morning room just off the foyer rather than upstairs to the drawing room, but since they were all family now, she supposed there was no reason for formality. Before she could take a seat,

Amelia grabbed her by the arm and hauled her back toward the hallway. "Theresa and I will be back in a moment," her cousin said.

"Whatever are you up to?" Theresa asked as they continued down the hallway toward the back of the house.

"Nothing. I just wanted to chat with you in private."

With a grin, Theresa followed Amelia into her husband's office. "Grandmama Agnes is after another cat," she said conversationally. "A black one this time. That's why she begged off dinner tonight; she thinks Lady Selgrave knows the location of a 'prime litter,' as she put it."

"Good Lord. Black cats? She's not tinkering with witchcraft now, is she?"

"That hadn't occurred to me." Laughing, Theresa sank into one of the guest chairs in the small room. "She says it's because she has all the other colors, but you never know."

"Well, keep an eye on things. She's your responsibility now that I'm married." Amelia settled into the opposite chair. "I met Stephen's brother this morning."

"Did you?" It seemed an odd topic for a secret conversation. "What was he like?"

"Not at all what I expected. I told you he was wounded, didn't I?"

"Yes. And I already told Michael to behave himself tonight. So don't worry; we will be calm and compassionate."

"Very calm, I hope."

Theresa looked again at Amelia. They'd been raised together since Amelia's mother had died when Amelia was eight and Theresa's own parents when she'd been ten, more like sisters than cousins. And something—whether it was Colonel James or something else—was clearly troubling her cousin. "I'm very good at conversation," she said aloud. "And at being charming. You know I won't leave you to chat with a soldier unassisted."

Finally Amelia smiled. "I know. And thank you. On our first meeting, he seemed rather fierce." Amelia stood, offering a hand to Theresa. "Oh, and Stephen's purchased me a horse," she continued, returning to the hallway. "Can you believe it? Me, with a horse."

"I'm certain he chose a gentle animal for y . . ."

As they looked toward the foyer, Theresa's voice trailed off. At first glance she thought that Stephen had come looking for them, but almost immediately she realized that the man standing there was *not* Lord Gardner. For one thing he was taller by a good three or four inches. And the viscount's brown hair was short and orderly, not the collar-brushing uneven mess of rich mahogany that belonged to this man.

And then there were the eyes. Stephen's were kind and brown, crinkling at the edges with humor. Not whiskey-colored and gazing straight through her as though she'd already been catalogued and dismissed. She cleared her throat. "Hello."

He didn't move. A moment later Amelia stepped between them. "Oh, good. You've come," she said warmly, though she didn't approach him. "Tess, this is Colonel Bartholomew James. Tolly, my cousin, Theresa Weller."

"You look like your cousin," he informed her in a low voice.

Theresa blinked. "Do you think so? Leelee's hair is so much prettier than mine."

With a chuckle, Amelia gestured them both to the morning room. "Don't expect me to disagree with that. We're all in h—"

"I like your hair," the colonel interrupted. "It reminds me of sunshine." He glanced at Amelia, and then his gaze caught Theresa's again. "Where is dinner being served?" he asked.

"Oh, we decided to eat in the breakfast room, so you wouldn't have to climb the stairs."

The gaze left Theresa again, and she blinked, feeling almost as though she'd been dragged forward against her will. Or not against her will, rather. His gaze, his bearing—they spoke of raw, barely contained power. Mesmerizing.

"I'll wait there, then." Not until he turned away did she realize that he held a cane in one hand and that he had a terrible limp. Moving further into the shadows, he disappeared through the neighboring doorway.

Realizing she'd been holding her breath, Theresa exhaled sharply. "*That* is your brother-in-law?" she whispered.

"Yes," Amelia whispered back. "Much less like Stephen than I ever expected."

"He's very . . . intense." But it was more than that. In the moments she'd gazed at him, it seemed as though everything not absolutely necessary for him to be alive had been done away with. She nearly felt that she'd seen straight through to his soul. It had been a very dark place.

"Don't be afraid of him, Tess. Come along," her

cousin said, taking her arm. "I'll tell Stephen that he's arrived."

She shook herself. "I'm not afraid of him. He merely wasn't what *I* expected, either." Not at all.

His brother and sister were charming and chatty and amiable. Colonel James, however, seemed their exact opposite in every way. She shook herself. It wasn't as though a wild beast had been let loose in London. It was merely that he was . . . outside of her usual experience. Far outside. Theresa glanced over her shoulder in the direction of the breakfast room doorway. Outside was rather more exciting than she'd expected.

"He's here?" Lord Gardner said, standing as she and Amelia walked back into the room.

"Yes. He went to sit in the breakfast room."

The viscount gave a brief frown. "I suppose I should apologize in advance for Tolly," he said in a low voice. "He's had a rough go of it."

Michael patted him on the shoulder. "No need for that, Stephen," he said warmly. "No one could expect your brother to dance a jig after his unit was massacred."

He couldn't dance a jig, regardless, from the look of that cane. Theresa kept silent, only nodding as they all decided to join the colonel in the breakfast room. It seemed a shame about his leg and his fear-some demeanor, because the more she considered it, he was actually quite handsome in a dangerous sort of way. But he needn't worry about his welcome; he was a wounded hero, and there were oh-so-many rules about how one addressed a hero. Luckily, she knew them all.

* * *

Bartholomew took the seat nearest to the door. Family dinners had used to be one of his favorite activities; Violet alone always had enough gossip and anecdotes to keep them laughing for hours. But now he couldn't remember the last time he'd laughed, and he didn't give a damn what anyone else in his old circle might be up to.

He accepted the glass of wine one of the footmen provided for him, and downed it at one go. This was the room where he'd been taking all his meals since his return from India, but it irked that his family had decided they had to accommodate him by serving dinner on the ground floor. Especially when they'd invited guests, and especially when he meant this visit to be as brief as possible.

At least once this was done he could retreat to the Adventurers' Club. And behaving according to his mood would only help his cause, since he needed to convince Violet and Stephen not to attempt to track him down. That had been the first thing Sommerset had said upon inviting him to join the club: No one else was allowed to know about it. The reason the club served as a haven was that no one else clamored for entry or came by to sample its services.

"You might have stuck your head into the morning room and said hello," Stephen commented from the doorway. The rest of the family and guests shuffled in behind him.

"Hello," Bartholomew returned, halfway through his third glass of wine. The servants were accustomed to his drinking, but he didn't need any particularly acute skills of observation to see that neither Stephen nor Violet was pleased to see the bottle in front of him and the glass in his hand.

"Tolly, this is Amelia's cousin Michael, Lord Weller, and his sister, Theresa. Michael, Tess, Colonel Bartholomew James."

He nodded, his gaze on the chit. Staring was rude, he recalled, but he stared anyway. Her hair was the color of rich churned butter, and though he could detect no flaw at all in the soft curls bound by pins, he would have preferred to see it loose. It looked long, perhaps down to her waist. And her eyes were pretty, too, a grayish green that reminded him of the ocean.

"Tolly."

He shook himself, breaking his gaze to glance at his brother. "What?"

"You haven't given us the name of the friend you're staying with."

"No, I haven't."

The chit, Theresa, took a seat across the table and down at the far end—well away from him. That fact didn't escape his notice. He'd frightened her, then. And it had only taken a dozen words and making eye contact. And his general appearance, of course.

"I heard about your battle with those Indian bandits," the other cousin, Lord Weller, commented, sitting beside Violet.

"Oh, really?" Tolly set his glass down with a clank and leaned forward. "What did you hear?"

"I . . ." The fellow cleared his throat. "That your unit engaged a group of highwaymen the locals had taken to calling the Thuggee, and you were the only survivor."

"Well, that sounds fantastic." He emptied the bottle

into his glass. "I must be a bloody hero." He snorted. "Imagine that."

"You're a damned drunk, is what you are," Stephen grumbled.

"Then stop talking to me. Christ. What do I have to do, begin throwing things?"

Everyone stared at him.

Well, not everyone. "I'm certain I would never have had the courage to go to India," Theresa Weller said smoothly. "Much less fight anyone there."

He glared at her. Sympathy? He wanted them to be angry and to ask him to leave, damn it all. "Then we should all be grateful they don't let chits into the army," he shot back.

"Tolly." Stephen's expression tightened.

Miss Weller, though, waved at the viscount. "I take no offense, Stephen. In fact, I strongly agree with Colonel James."

"Oh, you do? You agree with the most basic tenet of warfare in the last thousand years? How startlingly mundane of you, Miss Weller." Somewhat to his surprise, he was disappointed. It was likely too much to expect that the prettiest chit in the room would have any sense.

A scowl crossed her face, then smoothed away again, to be replaced by a determined smile. "No doubt I'm an easier target than an armed attacker, but I certainly bear you no ill will."

"Well said, Tess," her brother put in.

"This is damned disappointing," Bartholomew said aloud. "Not a bloody one of you has any spleen. It's bad enough that you have a chit wagging her tongue because you're all afraid to do so."

Her frown reappearing, Miss Weller stood. "Please mind your manners, Colonel. There's no call for such language."

Ah, finally. "I bloody well disagree."

She slapped her palm against the tabletop. "Ooh, yes, we're all very frightened of you," Theresa Wheeler stated, this time not attempting to hide the frown that drew her fine brows together. "Can't you tell?"

"If you had any sense at all, Miss Weller, you would sit down," he growled. She would do, although he preferred a fight with family. They were the ones he wanted to avoid, after all.

"You obviously don't wish to be here," she continued forcefully. "As you were invited, in the future I would suggest that you merely decline to attend. It will save on the arguing."

"Tess," Stephen's wife whispered. "Don't argue with him. He's—"

"He's what?" Bartholomew broke in, grabbing onto the table and awkwardly shoving himself to his feet. "He's damaged? I think we all knew that."

"I didn't notice until your little tantrum," Theresa retorted, lifting her chin. "Clearly, though, your manners *are* damaged."

"I'll just let those of you with undamaged manners enjoy your dinner, then," he snapped, levering his cane around and stalking for the door.

"Tolly, where the devil are you going?"

"Back where I came from."

"I want to see you tomorrow."

Damnation. At least the chit had enough sense to know that he wanted to be left alone. "You know how to reach me."

"Yes, but—"

He hooked the door handle with his cane and slammed the door closed behind him. A sharp pain ran up his knee, but he wasn't about to stop and see to it now.

Swearing, he staggered sideways into the hall table. *Do not fall down*, he ordered himself, reaching out to steady himself against the wall. Drinking on an empty stomach in enemy territory—Lucifer's balls, he'd been an idiot.

The door opened behind him. To the hushed sound of "Theresa, don't," and "leave him be," muffled footsteps tromped up behind him. And then she grasped his arm.

He jerked around to face her, and nearly lost his balance again. "Do not put your hands on me," he hissed.

She looked up at him, gray-green eyes steady and completely unafraid. "Don't be an idiot. They might all be terrified of hurting you or your feelings, but I'm not."

"You're the damned reason I'm leaving."

"No, I'm not. *You're* the reason you're leaving. And when there's no one about for you to offend, curse all you like. Damnation. You see? I can curse, too. It's only that I choose not to do so because it's terribly lowbrow."

"What happened to you being so polite?"

"You made me angry."

"It took bloody long enough." He stumbled again.

"Yes, well now I'm attempting to apologize for my behavior." She ducked beneath his arm, drawing up against him. "Do you have a coach, or are you riding?"

"Riding," he grunted. Whatever the devil was afoot, he certainly didn't like it. And he didn't like the way she put her free arm around his waist, as though someone as slender and delicate as she was could keep him on his feet. "And I don't want your apology."

"You have it, regardless. So argue with yourself." She reached out to pull open the front door and held on to him while he hobbled out to the portico. "Your horse is waiting; you never intended to stay."

Her tone was accusing, but considering that she was correct, he didn't see any reason to deny it. "No, I didn't. Hence me not caring about your apology."

"With those manners, I'm surprised you were invited here at all."

Bartholomew scowled. "They had to ask me; they're family."

"And thank goodness for that, or someone would have punched you."

He sent her a sharp glance. "I don't find you the least bit amusing, you know."

She gazed straight back at him. "Well, you shall have to improve your sense of humor. Why don't you spend a few minutes at the Haramund soiree tomorrow night?" she returned, taking his cane as he grabbed onto the saddle horn. "I do like to dance, Colonel."

"I don't dance." With a stifled gasp he swung up on Meru and settled his bad foot into the stirrup. "Clearly."

"I didn't say I wanted to dance with you. You have no manners." Shoving his cane into its straps, she stepped back. "I meant that you can watch." With that she turned her back and returned to the house.

"That little . . ." Bartholomew stopped. He had absolutely no idea how to finish the sentence. As far as he was from being a virgin, Theresa Wheeler in a matter of five minutes had set him so far back on his heels that he'd nearly fallen over. Literally.

He'd set out to be curt and uncommunicative. What he hadn't expected was to be called on his poor behavior. The last time he'd been so unsure of his footing had been when he'd literally had his legs cut out from under him. He didn't like the sensation any more now than he had then. This time, though, he could do something about it. Something simple. He could avoid the Haramund soiree.

The other members of the James family weren't terribly pleased with her, Theresa realized, but compared with how she viewed her behavior, their opinion of her actions couldn't possibly be worse than her own. Conversation throughout dinner remained stilted and far too cautious. Even Amelia sent her glances of veiled annoyance whenever no one else was looking, and considering that she'd promised conversational compassion, she couldn't blame her cousin for her annoyance. Yes, the colonel had overstepped, but he didn't pride himself on his manners. She did.

"What were you thinking?" her cousin finally demanded, wrapping both hands around her arm once they left the men to their cigars and port.

"I was thinking that he was rude," Theresa whispered back, watching as Violet pranced upstairs to the drawing room ahead of them. "I tried to keep my temper, but . . . well, there's no excuse for my behavior. Should I leave?"

"No. Of course not." Her cousin frowned thoughtfully. "You're generally so much more careful about what you say."

Yes, she was. "I apologized to him." Well, she hadn't, precisely, but at least she had helped him down the front steps. If he'd fallen, she would have been worse than mortified. "If you and Stephen and Violet wish to be angry with me, then do so. Heaven knows I deserve it."

"Tolly didn't used to be rude like that," Violet put in unexpectedly. "When he last came back on leave three years ago, he was funny and warm and kind, just as he always was. He was awful tonight. Much worse than you were."

Now she felt even more terrible. "I'm never rude like that, Violet. I'm so sorry if I drove him away." Even though she hadn't. The fact that he'd been attempting to goad someone into snapping back at him, however, didn't excuse her. She should have been the last one to lose her temper. She *never* lost her temper. Not in thirteen years.

Amelia hugged her sister-in-law. "Everyone's more than likely been prodding at him for months. Perhaps he just needs a bit of fresh air without being smothered."

"I can hardly smother him if he won't even tell me where's he's staying." Violet shrugged free and plunked into a chair. "He is very mean now."

"He's hurt," Theresa offered. "He deserves compassion."

"At least you made him think about something aside from his injuries." With a grimace, Violet looked away. Then the eighteen-year-old faced her again. "I've changed my mind," she announced. "I'm glad you spoke up, Theresa. I wish I'd done so."

With a forced smile, Theresa sat beside her. "I'm glad you didn't. I suppose this way he can know you're not happy with his behavior, and he can be angry with me instead of you. I'm more than willing to take that upon my shoulders." She deserved to have it there.

Amelia was looking at her again, her cousin's expression more concerned this time, but Theresa pretended not to notice. The last thing she wanted was for Amelia to begin comparing her outburst tonight to the one that had inspired her concern with propriety, her booklet on proper behavior, and everything else she'd done over the past thirteen years.

Once Michael and Stephen rejoined them, Lord Gardner evidently realized that with Violet and Amelia no longer annoyed with her, he'd best give in as well. By the end of the evening they were all the dearest of friends once more.

That was just as well, because Theresa didn't quite feel up to further explanations, or even apologies. In fact, she felt unusually distracted with trying to decipher why she'd allowed herself to be goaded into snapping back. She wanted to blame her odd behavior on the very provoking Bartholomew James. At the least he'd set her off kilter from her very first view of him.

It was quite late when she and Michael boarded their coach to return to Weller House. With a sigh, she settled into the corner, happy to have a moment to sort through her thoughts.

"What the devil happened to you, Tess?" Michael asked abruptly, pressing the toe of his boot against her slipper.

"Stop that." She sat upright. "I've already attempted to explain myself to Violet, and no one's angry with me. Leave be."

"I don't mean your upset of our in-laws, Troll. I mean you lost your temper."

Theresa scowled, as much at the use of his old pet name for her as his words. "I don't know what happened. I've been trying to figure it out, and I can't."

"I'm actually relieved to know you still have a temper." He leaned forward to pat her on the knee. "Still, you might have chosen your target a bit better."

"Yes, I know. Colonel James is a wounded hero."

"Not just that. Rumor is, these Thuggee don't take prisoners," he returned. "They ambushed his unit and killed everyone they could. Then they hunted down the survivors."

"And Colonel James escaped."

"That's one story."

She looked at her brother. He had a definite flare for the dramatic, and he did torment and tease her on occasion, but he sounded serious. "What's another story, then?"

"That *he* hunted *them* down."

"Oh." If she asked, Michael would no doubt regale her with every gory detail, real or fantastical, but she could imagine it well enough herself. And she knew what he meant, now. That she'd begun an argument with a man who killed people, and one who clearly wasn't . . . balanced. "That's only a story, though, yes? You don't know for certain what happened."

"Not for certain," he conceded, clearly reluctant to do so. "Stephen wouldn't say. He may not know, either. Colonel James doesn't seem to be very communicative."

"Violet said he didn't use to be that way."

"If I saw everyone under my command slaughtered and then either ran from or killed the men who'd done it, I wouldn't be chatty, either."

"No, you'd be chatty, regardless."

"Ha-ha. Don't antagonize him, Tess. That's tonight's lesson."

Don't antagonize him. Theresa turned her gaze out the window at the darkness of Mayfair. Just to herself, without taking into account what she *should* be feeling, she could admit that she'd rather enjoyed unseating the colonel. And she half hoped she would have another chance to do so. Where no one else could overhear and be appalled, of course.

It didn't seem at all proper, but it had been very . . . interesting.

Chapter Three

"If a gentleman you favor is late arriving at a party, save him a dance—but not the waltz. Save him a country dance, because you won't mind missing one of those if he should fail to appear."

A LADY'S GUIDE TO PROPER BEHAVIOR

Bartholomew awoke with a start, springing out of bed before his body remembered that his left leg would no longer support him in such an athletic move. With a sharp gasp he fell to the floor.

"Damnation," he growled, shifting to straighten his leg, concentrating on taking short breaths to avoid shrieking like a chit.

In one sense, the pain was welcome. It roused him from an endless night of gunfire and screaming and the more muffled sounds and sensation of choking. He leaned back against the side of the bed. At least he could tell even in the pitch dark that he wasn't back in India. The air was too cool, and faintly smelled of cigar and chimney smoke rather than forest and earth and dust.

Knuckles rapped faintly against his door. "Colonel?"

Scowling, Bartholomew glanced over his shoulder up at the bed. The very high bed. "Come in, Gibbs."

The door opened. The Adventurers' Club morning caretaker slipped into the small room. Wordlessly the stout fellow stepped forward and bent down, grasping Bartholomew beneath the arms and lifting.

"Thank you," Bartholomew grunted, as he pulled free to sit on the edge of the bed again. "Sommerset doesn't have you listening at my door, does he? This isn't precisely the club."

"It is a part of the club, Colonel. And no one is in the lounge, so I thought to take a bit of a stroll." He gestured at Bartholomew's bad leg. "Want me to have a look at it?"

Tolly started to refuse without even considering his answer; he could barely stand to look at it himself. That was one of the reasons he wore a pair of old trousers to bed; so he wouldn't have to see it. The other reason was habit. Over the years he'd become accustomed to having to rise in the middle of the night. The army didn't precisely keep regular hours. "No." The pain had begun to subside, and he didn't think his leg could get much worse without falling off completely.

"I'll see you in the morning, then." With a nod, Gibbs turned on his heel.

"Gibbs."

The servant stopped. "Yes, Colonel?"

"Do you know how I might go about obtaining an invitation to a soiree?"

Gibbs pursed his lips. "Which soiree?"

"It's at Haramund House. Tomorrow night. Or tonight, rather."

"Haramund House. Lord and Lady Allen. I'll see what I can come up with."

"Thank you again, then."

Tolly lay back as the servant left the room and closed the door quietly behind him. He had no idea why the devil he was even considering attending the damned party. Hopefully Gibbs would turn out to be less resourceful than he generally seemed to be, and no invitation would be forthcoming.

If he did attend, however, Theresa Weller was not going to have the last word. He wouldn't even watch her dance. In fact, he would make a point of not watching her dance, and of making certain she knew that he wasn't watching.

For a time he attempted to return to sleep, but the memory of the dream provided very little incentive to succumb. Finally he sat up again, threw a shirt on over his head, then grabbed his cane and left the bed chamber for the main sitting room of the Adventurers' Club. The back wall was lined with books and maps. Most of them were Sommerset's taste, but in his favor at least the duke was well traveled and an avid collector.

Settling for a silly and highly erroneous history of the Indian Sikh, no doubt written by an accountant who'd never left the protection of Fort William, he lit a candle and sat close by the fireplace. As Gibbs had said, no one else was about—which was pleasant for a change. The club never closed its doors, and he wasn't the only member who didn't sleep well.

He glanced toward the door in the far corner. It led into Ainsley House proper, Sommerset's London residence. Whatever had possessed the duke to create a very exclusive club in his front rooms, Bartholomew at least was grateful for it. Here no one gave a damn who was rude or who wasn't, and no chits teased him about dancing.

"The Sikh Mystery?"

His eyes shot open, his fingers instinctively reaching for the rapier hidden inside his cane. Sommerset sat in the chair opposite, eyeing him. Judging by the light pouring in through the set of generous-sized east-facing windows, he'd missed daybreak by at least an hour. "Damnation," he muttered, lifting the book from across his chest.

"I purchased that book for a laugh," the duke continued, taking a swallow of steaming tea from a delicate china cup. "Glad to see it's served a purpose other than for kindling."

"A cure for sleeplessness, yes." Bartholomew motioned at the tea. "Is there more of that?"

"Mmm-hmm." Sommerset gestured, and Gibbs appeared a moment later, carrying another cup and saucer. "Thank you, Gibbs."

"I live to serve, Your Grace."

The duke lifted an eyebrow as the servant vanished again into the shadows. "I would say he's become high in the instep, but he might well have been serious just then." He took another swallow of tea. "That reminds me. Here." Producing a folded note card from one pocket of his coat, Sommerset handed it over.

Bartholomew opened it. Embossed and complete with a small blue ribbon dangling from the bottom edge, it was an invitation to the Haramund soiree. "This has my name on it," he said aloud, then sent a glance around the large room.

"It's just you and me in here for the moment," Sommerset commented, following his gaze. "And it's not a crime to attend a party."

"But this is addressed to me."

"I am a duke, you know. If I can't perform a miracle here and there I might as well be a butler in expensive clothes." He brushed at the sleeve of his well-tailored brown coat. "And butlers don't get to dance with attractive women."

"I don't dance," Bartholomew returned, considering that he'd twice in the space of one day had to inform people of that fact. It should have been damned obvious. Fleetingly he wondered if Gibbs had mentioned the circumstances under which he'd made the request for the invitation, but then he decided that he didn't care. It wasn't the first night he'd awakened screaming. And Sommerset, he'd observed, tended to be very well informed. "Thank you for this."

"You're welcome. And I presume you've put a stop to your family asking after your whereabouts?"

"Yes. If they want to reach me, they're to leave word at the Society."

"Good." Sommerset finished off his tea and stood. "And while I don't give a damn what our club members choose to attire themselves in, you're getting blood on my Persian carpet."

With a curse, Tolly straightened. His bare left foot was spattered with blood, while more of the stuff soaked his trouser leg up to the knee. "Apologies."

"Don't bother with that. I've sent for Dr. Prentiss. And it's been better than eight months since you were wounded, has it not? Shouldn't you have healed by now?"

There were a great many things that should have been, and weren't. "Infection," he said stiffly. "Mostly gone now, but it wouldn't knit. And I fell on it last night."

"Speak to Prentiss about that. He's saved the lives of at least two other club members since their return to London."

Ah, the do-this-and-be-cured conversation. He'd had them before, but hadn't expected to hear such nonsense from the Duke of Sommerset. "Thank goodness. I'd wondered when the miracle would occur. I should be dancing by midnight, don't you think?"

The club door opened, and Lucas Crestley, Lord Piper, walked in. The duke nodded at the morning's first arrival, then returned his gaze to Bartholomew. "What I think, Tolly," he drawled, "is that yesterday you would have been skeptical about walking by midnight." He tapped the Haramund invitation with one finger. "Someone's got you thinking about dancing."

As the duke walked back toward the private door leading to Ainsley House, Tolly silently reminded himself that the Duke of Sommerset, even at the relatively young age of two and thirty, was one of the most brilliant men he'd ever encountered. Clearly Tolly was going to have to work harder if he wanted to keep his affairs to himself.

On the other hand, what did he care if Sommerset discovered that some chit had teased him about dancing? The answer was that he didn't give a damn, of course. Clenching the Haramund invitation in his fist, he pushed upright. Grabbing the cane with his other hand, he stood for a moment until he was sure of his balance, then headed through the back door to his small, borrowed room to shave and dress, and to wait for the miraculous Dr. Prentiss.

And yes, damn it all, he was thinking about dancing.

Theresa looked from the black cat on her lap to the black cat curled into the one sunny spot on the window sill. "If that one is Blackie, then who is this on my lap?"

Grandmama Agnes, Lady Weller, chortled as she spooned another lump of sugar into her morning tea. As she told it, in her day she'd been a diamond of the first water, while today she'd faded to a mere emerald. With her bright green eyes and vivacious smile, she looked like one. Her wit, however, remained diamond-sharp, if a bit eccentric. "He's Midnight," the family's matron said.

"How do you tell them apart?"

"Blackie has one white back paw, and Midnight has one white front paw. I do believe that Millicent had her eye on Midnight, but I was far too clever."

"Of course you were. I've yet to see Lady Selgrave best you in a cat negotiation." With a grin, Theresa finished off her own tea and put Midnight off her lap. Then she had to stand quickly; she'd discovered that if she remained seated in her grandmama's part of the house for longer than a heartbeat, she would have a cat on her lap. "Are you certain you don't wish to go walking with Leelee and me this morning?"

"Oh, no. Mrs. Smith-Warner and I are going to visit Lady Dorchester. She has a terrible case of the gout, you know. I've told her to take the waters at Bath, but she refuses to miss any of the Season even for the sake of her health."

"Give her my best wishes, then," Theresa said, leaning down to kiss her grandmother on the cheek.

"You are a dear heart, Tess."

"As are you, Grandmama." Halfway to the door, she paused. "You are still attending the Haramund soiree tonight, aren't you?"

"Lord Wilcox has promised me a waltz," Lady Weller said with a chuckle. "Since he's been attempting to learn the dance since last Tuesday, I must attend."

"I would like to see that myself." Especially considering that Lord Wilcox had only given up wearing powdered wigs two years ago. "He's become very progressive, hasn't he?"

"I think he's smitten with me, and you know how progressive I am."

"Indeed." Smiling, Theresa slipped out the door into the main part of the house.

Some gentleman or other was always smitten with Grandmama Agnes, though Theresa suspected if they knew how many cats the dowager viscountess owned, they might be less enthusiastic. Or perhaps they wouldn't be, considering how much property her grandmother owned thanks both to her blue-blooded parentage and to her marriage to the late Viscount

Weller. Plenty of room for cats, when a fortune came along with them.

Ramsey opened the front door to admit Amelia just as Theresa finished tying on her bonnet. "You're ready, Tess," her cousin exclaimed, after greeting the old butler.

"Of course I'm ready. You said ten o'clock."

"But I'm five minutes early."

Theresa deepened her smile. "A lady should take the time to put herself together well, but neither should she lessen the affect of her appearance by being tardy."

"Ah. I seem to remember reading that somewhere."

Of course Amelia had read it. Even though her cousin had seemed a little hesitant to assist in any way with the booklet's publication, once she'd realized that Theresa meant to do it anonymously, she'd read every word of it. At least Theresa supposed that had been the reason for Leelee's hesitation—the worry that Tess would be looked at askance for publishing. "Did you hear that Gilroy's has their new hats on display this morning?" she asked aloud, shaking herself.

"Oh, heavens. Come along, then."

Once they were well on their way, Theresa slowed a touch and wrapped her arm around her cousin's. "Now, you must tell me. What do you know of your husband's brother?"

"Tolly?" Amelia sent her a shocked look. "You're not interested in him, are you?"

"I admit he's very handsome, but heaven knows he could stand to acquire some manners."

Amelia stopped so quickly that Theresa nearly lost her balance. "No."

"What do you mean, 'no'? I made a mistake at dinner, and I wish to correct my error. There is a way to draw anyone into polite conversation, and I should never have lost my temper."

"Colonel James is a very troubled man who was lucky to have survived his ordeal in India. He nearly lost a leg—and from what Stephen says, he may still do so. He's not . . . social enough for you, nor is he concerned with such things. Leave him be."

No, he wasn't social. There was something else entirely about him, something she couldn't quite put her finger on. And that was more than likely what intrigued her. And it was more than likely why her own poor behavior where he was concerned troubled her. She wouldn't make the same mistake a second time.

"I didn't say I wished him to court me, or any such thing," she said aloud, forcing a chuckle. "I only want to know about him. Single gentlemen are so rarely deliberately rude in polite company. Especially in my company. Even if I hadn't worked so diligently at knowing the rules of proper behavior, I do have a dowry of two thousand a year."

"You are incorrigible."

"That has nothing to do with it. Most single gentlemen know by now that they have nothing to gain by rude behavior. Not in my presence."

Amelia laughed reluctantly. "I heard Olivia Grey referring to you as 'the paragon' the other day. And she meant it."

"Then you know I have no ulterior motive. Tell me about your brother-in-law."

"Very well, but you're going to be disappointed, because I don't know very much."

"You know more than I do."

Her cousin took a deep breath. "Tolly is twenty-eight, three years younger than Stephen. He's been an officer serving in Europe and then in India for ten years. Just over eight months ago he and his company were escorting a local zamindar or chieftain or whatever they call him, to Delhi. They'd been sent to accompany the fellow because of a rash of robberies by highwaymen. There was some sort of altercation, and Tolly was the only survivor. He arrived back in London just a month ago, and that's only because the weather was favorable on his return voyage."

"Violet said his nasty temperament is new."

"I never met him until yesterday, so I couldn't speak to that. I will say that both Stephen and Violet have always seemed very fond of him." Amelia waved at Miss Traynor across the street. "Does that satisfy your curiosity?"

Not a bit. "Yes. Thank you. That wasn't so painful, was it?"

"No, it wasn't. But I thought you would want to know his favorite music, or which game bird he prefers, and whether he enjoys reading."

Theresa chuckled. "I told you that I wasn't smitten with him. I'm only curious because of his lack of manners."

That wasn't quite true. It wasn't only his lack of manners that intrigued her. And Amelia's tidbits had only served to whet her appetite for more information about Colonel Bartholomew James. She had no idea why, because he had been brusque and rude and antagonistic. In the past, she'd actively avoided anyone with a questionable reputation, not wanting to be connected with such nonsense even by association. And yet she'd been thinking about Tolly James—and when she would next see him—all morning. Perhaps it was her own need to improve. One's manners could never be too perfect.

"Are you going to tromp down the street all the way to the Thames, or should we shop?" Amelia asked.

Shaking herself, Theresa stopped. They were three shops past Gilroy's haberdashery. "Oh, dear. My apologies. I suppose I was thinking about what I should wear to the Haramund party this evening."

"Oh, you should wear that new green and gray silk from Madame Costanza's dress shop. You'll receive at least half a dozen proposals because of that dress alone."

"It's not the quantity of marriage offers that count, Leelee. It's the quality." With a laugh and a quick look about to be certain no one else had heard her comment, she towed her cousin back to Gilroy's. "You know that I'm not waiting for a proposal, my dear. I'm waiting for *the* proposal."

"Then we can only hope that Hercules or Achilles or perhaps Apollo are still about and seeking a wife."

"They're all too violent and bloodthirsty." Theresa sent her cousin an amused scowl. "And even if they weren't they are all a bit old for me."

Finally Amelia joined her in laughing. "You are utterly incorrigible."

"I'm completely corrigible, except when I'm with you. And I apolo—"

"Don't you dare." Her cousin's smile faded, and Amelia put an arm across her shoulders. "It's not poor behavior when you jest with your family and friends. And I'm glad and honored that you still jest with me. Saying something unexpected doesn't always make it the wrong thing to say."

Well, Amelia was in error about that. After the way Theresa had lost her temper last night, she needed to be especially careful not to do so again. No matter that the thought of another argument with Bartholomew James made her heart beat faster or not.

Bartholomew handed his invitation over to the Haramund House footman. The man didn't bat an eye, so apparently wherever Sommerset had acquired it, the paper was legitimate.

"If you'll wait here, Colonel," the servant said, "the butler shall announce you in turn."

Glancing at the short line of notables awaiting the fanfare of an announcement before they entered the ballroom, Bartholomew shook his head. "I know who I am," he muttered, "and no one else gives a damn." Not waiting for either a protest or an agreement, he limped through the milling crowd and slipped into the main room.

He took a seat in the first vacant chair he sighted. Only one poor soul had offered assistance to help him up the stairs, and that fellow wasn't likely to do so again. Drawing in a stiff breath, he sent his gaze around the room. Before he could demonstrate to Miss Theresa Weller that he didn't give a damn about either her or dancing, he needed to find her.

"Colonel James," a round fellow greeted him, stepping out of the crowd. "Didn't expect to find you at a soiree."

"And why is that, Mr. Henning?" Bartholomew asked, barely sparing the man a glance.

"Well, you . . . because . . . you know." Francis Henning backed up a step as he blustered.

"No, I don't know. Humor me."

"It's . . . well, you've a bit of a limp. And you ain't exactly been social since you came back from India. I wouldn't even have known you was in Town if I hadn't read about it in the newspaper."

Finally Bartholomew eyed him. "And yet I apparently am being social."

"I suppose."

"Go away, Henning."

"Oh. Very well, then."

As Henning sped away, Tolly spied Theresa Weller—and the breath that he'd drawn to sigh, instead caught in his chest. *Good God.* Her spun gold hair curled about her temples and coiled onto the top of her head, while the gray-green of her eyes matched the colors of her gown to such perfection that the silks might have been made expressly with her in mind.

Because he saw her an instant before she saw him, he had the opportunity to watch her pretty eyes widen a little, and the tip of her tongue swipe quickly at her lower lip as their eyes met. She wasn't quite as collected as she pretended, then.

Apparently he remained enough of a gentleman to wish to stand as she lifted her chin and approached. At the same time, stumbling to his feet wouldn't precisely strengthen his position, and so he forced himself to remain seated. "Miss Weller," he said, nodding.

She stopped in front of him. "Colonel James. How pleasant that you came to watch me dance."

A slow smile touched his mouth. Clearly she wouldn't believe him if he claimed to have made an appearance for some other reason—and it would be a lie, anyway. He'd made a fair living at turning disadvantage into advantage, however, until that one, last time. "I did," he drawled. "I shall watch you every moment. Try not to disappoint me, will you?"

Miss Weller tilted her head, examining his expression. "I think I shall save a dance for you," she announced.

"That would be a waste of a quadrille," he retorted. If she was attempting to injure his feelings, he'd been cut by a far sharper blade than her tongue.

"Well, if you can't dance, then we'll have to find something else with which to amuse ourselves."

For a heartbeat he was tempted to tell her precisely how he could imagine the two of them amusing themselves. It would involve smooth, bare skin glowing softly in candlelight, and the sound of her moaning beneath him. His cock twitched, and Bartholomew blinked. It had been a while since that had happened.

"Cat got your tongue, Colonel?" she prompted, still gazing at him. "It's polite to respond when someone converses with you."

"I was just considering what you would do if I agreed to us going somewhere to amuse ourselves," he said after a moment.

"As long as your suggestion is polite and respectful, I am at your disposal."

"Then, Miss Weller, perhaps we should take a stroll in the garden during your first available dance."

She glanced down at her dance card. "Ah, the second country dance." This time she smiled. "That would be acceptable."

Chapter Four

"Though it is considered forward to shake hands with a man if he is not a close friend of the family, in this I disagree. A touch, palm to palm, is demure enough. And by that small gesture I can know if a mutual attraction exists."

A LADY'S GUIDE TO PROPER BEHAVIOR

First Theresa had wanted Tolly James to attend the party, then she'd decided it would be best after all if he didn't. Then she hadn't been able to stop thinking about what she would say to him under either circumstance.

And then he'd appeared. Those whiskey-colored eyes had already been gazing at her when she first spied him, and she wondered how long he'd been looking at her. That seemed significant, especially after he'd said that he intended to watch her all evening. A delicious, excited shiver ran down her spine.

She had suitors aplenty, but no one who spoke so directly or made so little effort to be charming. Why she found that attractive she had no idea, but in all honesty it might have had at least a little to do with his appearance. Even so, it wasn't a question of over-looking his manners because his other qualities compensated.

Rather, it was the whole of him that just felt more . . . interesting than anyone else of her acquaintance. More interesting, and more real. Not a predetermined set of witticisms and observations she'd heard a hundred times before. She merely needed to remember her own rules, and they would end the evening with her having proven that last night was only a misstep, and that he could gain more respect and empathy from people by minding his manners.

Theresa glanced over her shoulder at him again, to find him still watching her, sitting back with a glass in one hand. Even just sitting there, he was unlike everyone else in the room. It was as if he'd been marked by whatever it was he'd been through. Not on his handsome face or even his leg, but deeper inside where it only showed in his eyes.

A hand brushed her arm. Startled, she turned around. "Alexander," she said, smiling as she recognized the tall, golden-haired man standing before her.

Behind his back they called him "Alexander the Great," though Alexander Rable, the Marquis of Montrose, more than likely wouldn't have minded hearing it said to his face. He sketched an elegant bow. "Tess, you look absolutely ravishing this evening."

"Ah. For that compliment, you may have a waltz."

"Good. I was worried that I'd arrived too late to claim any dance, much less a waltz."

"I was about to give it away."

"But you didn't." He took the dance card and

pencil from her fingers. "You were about to leave me with nothing but a country dance, weren't you?" A slight scowl drew his arched brows together, and he lifted his head again. "'B. James'?" he read.

"Yes. Colonel Bartholomew James. My cousin married his brother."

"I know who he is." The marquis's gaze moved past her to where she knew Tolly still sat, no doubt watching the entire exchange. "My cousin is with the East India Company, you know. And there are some rumors that James deserted his men, and that's why he's still alive. More or less."

All she had to do was look into Colonel James's eyes to know that he hadn't deserted anyone. Except for his own family, of course. Arguing about a man whom she barely knew, however, wouldn't be seemly. "I believe we're at a dance, Alexander. That means we should discuss only pleasant topics."

"How pleasant would it be for you, then, to limp about the floor with him? There are a multitude of less sought-after chits available tonight to offer him charity. Cross out his name."

"I could never do such a thing." Not even if she wanted to, which she didn't.

"Don't frown at me, Tess," Montrose said smoothly, returning her dance card to her. "I'm only saying that you needn't put yourself out when there are others who would be happy to do so. As far as anyone else knows he's a wounded hero, after all."

She did not need anyone to tell her what her duties and options might be. For heaven's sake, she had literally penned a booklet on the subject. And so she also knew when a lady could—albeit delicately—allow her displeasure to be known. The fact that she'd rarely ever done so before didn't even signify. "Whatever your opinion of him, Alexander, I have agreed to dance with Colonel James, just as I've agreed to dance with you. If I decline one, I shall have to decline them all."

He blew out his breath. "I see. I'm going to fetch myself a drink, then, and desist from any further arguments with beautiful women. I'll be back for my dance." Bending down, he collected her hand and drew it up to kiss her knuckles.

While she took a moment to settle her thoughts, he strolled back into the crowd. Yes, he'd done the proper thing by leaving, but it wasn't very . . . satisfying. "Coward," she muttered, then turned around—and stopped abruptly. "Colonel."

Bartholomew James stood directly in front of her, close enough to touch. The way her heart jumped, she almost felt as though she *had* been touched. For a long moment he gazed down at her in silence, his whiskey-colored eyes seeming to see straight through her skin and into her soul.

"Is there something you require?" she finally demanded, folding her arms across her chest and lifting her chin to reduce the difference in their heights.

"You have no idea what I require."

"Which is why I asked."

His mouth pinched at one corner, then relaxed again. "I want my dance now." He turned on his heel. "Out in the garden."

"I am not going out into the garden with you," she returned, keeping her expression easy despite the sudden rush of her heartbeat.

"Coward," he said over his shoulder, in the exact same tone she'd used against Montrose.

Oh, he was aggravating. Blowing out her breath, she tromped after him. "Very well. I imagine I can outrun you," she said stiffly.

"I imagine you can."

"You know I actually have a partner for this dance."

"Then go dance. I'm going out to the garden."

She saw Elliot Pender making his way toward her, and she smiled at him. "I cannot be impolite, Colonel. It's not seem—"

Colonel James was halfway across the room and out of earshot already, despite his game leg. Damnation. If she stayed and danced, he would still call her a coward, even when she had a perfectly legitimate reason for remaining behind.

"Tess," Elliot said with a bow as he reached her. "Our country dance?"

"Elliot, I've a pebble or something in my shoe." She made a show of shaking her right foot. "Would you give me the country dance after the waltz in place of this one?"

"I . . . Certainly. I'll just go find—"

"Oh, thank you," she interrupted, and hurried away.

She felt a bit silly following behind a badly limping man who hadn't even checked to see whether she was still there. If it would keep him from calling her a coward again, however, she would tolerate it.

The colonel shouldered open one of the full-length windows and rather ungracefully stepped out into the Haramund House garden. Torches lined the curving stone pathway, dimmer than the bright chandelier light inside, but still nearly enough to read by.

"Are we going to march all the way around the house?" she asked. "Because I didn't wear my walking shoes. And I told Mr. Pender I've a pebble in one of my slippers."

He stopped, his back still to her. "Montrose is courting you."

"Yes, he is."

"Then why in God's name did you . . . flirt with me yesterday?"

Theresa opened her mouth to retort that she hadn't been flirting with him at all. The breath of vulnerability in his hard voice, though, stopped her. She had the sudden impression that no one had flirted with him in some time. And of course she'd been flirting with him. She might not have called it that at the time, but as she stood behind him now, alone in the garden, it was obvious. She wouldn't have come out there if she hadn't felt an attraction. Elliot Pender was a perfectly acceptable fellow, after all, and yet she hadn't thought twice about leaving him standing there, mouth open. That was *not* how a young lady conducted herself.

"I am not married to Lord Montrose," she stated belatedly. "And until I *am* married to someone, I suppose I may speak with and dance with whomever I please."

He turned around, faster and more graceful than she expected him to be. "What about what pleases me?" he asked, catching her right hand in his left.

This close she realized that the top of her head just

came to his chin. Her brother had always said she was a tall chit, and indeed she was accustomed to being eye to eye with a dance partner. Not tonight, however. Not with Bartholomew James.

Realizing he was still gazing at her, Theresa rose onto her toes. "Let go of my hand."

"Do you think me a charity project?" he demanded, keeping his grip firmly around her fingers.

"I do not."

"Good." Colonel James pulled her against him. "Because I don't want charity," he stated. "Yours or anyone else's."

As she opened her mouth to protest that she hadn't considered he required charity, he leaned in and kissed her.

He felt warm and solid, and unexpectedly electric. *Good heavens.* She lifted up, drawing her free arm around his shoulders. For a bare second she felt . . . unbound, as though she wasn't even touching the ground.

Then he broke away, taking a stumbling half step backward. "There," he said roughly. "You flirted, and now I've kissed you. Go back to Montrose."

She wanted to demand another kiss. Theresa took a steadying breath, blinking to try to pull her scattered wits back into place. "I don't believe you're allowed to order me to do anything," she retorted. "And you're . . . you're not allowed to kiss me like that."

"How should I kiss you, then?" Abruptly he closed again, taking her mouth in another hot, lingering kiss. "Like this?"

Oh, good heavens. "I—stop that!"

"Or were you only antagonizing me because you thought I was nothing but a cripple? Or a eunuch? I'm not. A eunuch, that is. You'd best figure out what you're about, Tess." He turned around, heading for the front of the house. "You know where to find me."

Actually, she had no idea where to find him, since he evidently wasn't staying at James House. She stood there as he limped out of sight, still unable to decide whether she was more offended or intrigued. Clearly he'd been attempting to make a point of some sort, but considering that she still couldn't quite catch her breath, she wasn't certain what that might have been.

"There you are, Tess." Lord Montrose strolled up the pathway. "Very well, be angry with me if you must. But don't deprive all the other poor gentlemen the pleasure of a dance with you."

"I'm not angry with you," she returned, taking his arm and practically towing him back to the ballroom.

Tolly James had been correct about one thing. Handsome as he was, she hadn't considered more than the fact that she enjoyed the look and sound and intrigue of him. As of that kiss, he'd made one thing very clear. He made her forget herself. And that was very troubling, because she hadn't lost her hold on proper behavior since she'd been ten years old. And that was the last time she'd ever done so.

Bartholomew stepped down from the hired hack at the edge of the Ainsley House drive. His leg felt like it was bound with saw blades, but he tried to ignore that as he made his way up to the west wing of the house. Beneath a vine- and flower-covered archway the plain, unobtrusive doorway waited, locked and unattended.

Pulling out his key, he opened the door. Inside the large main room of the Adventurers' Club lay before him, all dark-paneled walls and bookcases and bits and bobs from foreign lands. Four other club members were already in attendance, two of them playing whist, one reading, and the fourth one making his way through what looked like an entire bottle of whiskey.

"Colonel," Hervey, the club's other caretaker, butler, footman, and nanny said, approaching from the direction of the extra rooms. "Good evening."

"Hervey."

"Cook's just pulled a roast chicken from the oven. Might I interest you in a plate?"

"Yes, thank you." Refusing to grimace, Tolly took a seat at one of the empty tables scattered through the large room. From what the Duke of Sommerset had said, before he'd turned it into a gentleman's hideaway the room had originally been a morning room and an office. However much the renovations had cost, it gave Tolly an otherwise nearly impossible privacy.

That was fortunate, because at the moment he didn't feel very communicative. He shouldn't have kissed her. It had been weakness, frustration over hearing the dazzling Lord Montrose calling him an object of pity and charity. He'd easily defeated that bastard at every game of skill and sport they'd ever engaged in at Oxford, and now the damned earl called him pitiful.

Since his return to London, every look and every whispered comment had reminded him that his worth as a man related directly to unsubstantiated rumor and the mere fact of his survival. It had practically struck him between the eyes that Tess Weller was the first entity in eight months and two continents able to make him forget . . . everything—even if only for just a moment. And then with her teasing, flirting manner—he hadn't been able to stop himself. He hadn't wanted to stop himself.

The servant set a steaming plate of roasted chicken in front of him. "Thank you, Hervey. Some of that Polish vodka, too, if you please."

"I'll see to it, Colonel."

For the first time in months, he was hungry. And that was a good thing. He damned well didn't wish to end up an invalid again, particularly when he'd just flung a challenge at a very sharp-tongued chit.

The front door of the club opened again. Apparently several Adventurers were feeling less than social this evening. Tolly wondered whether anyone else had kissed a lady and then fled.

"Well, if it ain't the man and his monkey," Thomas Easton exclaimed from across the room, and Bartholomew looked up.

He'd seen the imposing Captain Sir Bennett Wolfe on a handful of occasions over the past few weeks, and witnessing the uproar that had accompanied the explorer's return from Africa had made him exceedingly thankful to have been more or less ignored, even with the whispers over the reason for his survival.

"Left your lady love at home all alone, did you?" Easton continued with a grin.

"I would say you're less of a fool when you're sober, Easton," the captain returned, heading for the wall of bookshelves at the back of the club, "but I've never seen you sober."

"I spent a bloody year in Arabia being sober," Easton returned. "Never again."

Sir Bennett searched the shelves for a moment, then pulled a book down. As he turned around his gaze met Bartholomew's, and he changed direction. "Colonel James," he said, offering his hand as he stopped at the table. "You've been asleep or drinking most times I've seen you here, sir."

Tolly shook his hand, eyeing the young vervet monkey perched on the captain's shoulder as it eyed him in return. In the month since he'd arrived back in London very few people offered to shake hands with him. It was a social, human gesture, and he frequently felt like neither of those things. "You've been chasing disaster, most every time I've seen you."

With a brief grin, Wolfe inclined his head. "I think I've finally got it on the run," he returned.

"I heard you were on your way to Greece."

"Next week, as a matter of fact." Hefting the book, the captain backed a step toward the door. "If Sommerset asks, I'll have this back tomorrow. Just verifying some Latin etymologies."

"You're writing another book?"

"Eventually. This is actually to settle a wager I made with my wife." The captain gave a mock scowl. "I have the sneaking suspicion that Phillipa is going to win. She generally does."

Bartholomew settled for nodding as Bennett Wolfe left the club again. There wasn't much he could say in reply other than "good luck," but from his expression the captain seemed perfectly content with the idea of losing.

Perfectly content. On occasion, in the past, he'd felt that way. Like sleep, it was something he imagined he'd never find again. He allowed himself to feel envious for a brief moment, then returned to his dinner.

Theresa Weller enjoyed dancing. Aside from that, she was a favorite among her fellows, and her feet seemed barely to touch the floor even when she was standing still. If nothing else, *he* was irretrievably earthbound.

It had only been a kiss, anyway. Two kisses. If he hadn't surprised her, he more than likely wouldn't have managed it. And if he'd been solid on his feet, he imagined that she would have kicked or slapped him for taking such a liberty.

He rubbed at his temple. If he could capture some sleep for a damned change, at least his mind would be more solid. And then he would realize that he had already spent too much time contemplating a bloody kiss, that before his last assignment in India he'd been a quite competent and sought-after lover, and that perhaps he'd only needed that one last kiss to bid his old life farewell.

Belatedly he remembered that he'd neglected to stop at the Society Club for any messages. He wasn't likely to have any, however, so it could wait until tomorrow. Simple enough—except that he then had to wonder if Stephen would invite him again for dinner, and if the cousin of Stephen's new wife would be attending.

With a curse he downed the dregs of his glass and

shoved to his feet. A little temptation served him right. Some of his men—his dead men—had left behind wives and children. Those soldiers wouldn't be dreaming of kissing or holding anyone again. Which made him what, lucky? He limped to the club's rear door and shouldered it open. If he didn't get his left boot off now, he would have to sleep in it again.

Yes, that was him—lucky. And cursed. Under the circumstances, the one deserved the other. And neither left any room for the temptation of a sharp-tongued, kissable chit.

For someone who could barely put both feet on the ground, Colonel Bartholomew James was exceedingly elusive, Theresa decided. A pair of stolen kisses and then . . . nothing. For two days, it was as if he'd never existed at all.

"Whatever are you thinking about?" Lord Lionel Humphreys asked from beside her. "I've never seen you so quiet."

That was only because she always had to carry the conversation when Lord Lionel came to call, and she hadn't felt up to it this morning. "I was only wondering how long this fine weather will last," she improvised. "What say we go for a drive and enjoy it?"

"I—well, I rode to Weller House. On a horse."

She bounced to her feet. "Even better. I'll have Cleopatra saddled while I run upstairs and change." She summoned Ramsey and gave the butler her instructions.

"But I—that is, I thought we might chat a bit. You and I."

Oh, dear. "We can chat while we ride," she said over her shoulder, not slowing her flight through the door and to the staircase. At least out of doors she would have something else with which to distract herself.

"But I—I had something particular to say to you, Tess."

Her maid, Sally, who'd been sitting unobtrusively in the corner of the morning room, made a choking sound but didn't look up. Keeping a smile pasted on her own face, Theresa stopped and turned around. So Lionel had chosen this morning to deliver his marriage proposal. As if she could seriously consider marrying anyone who could barely put three syllables together without having to stop and re-measure his words.

"I'm sorry," she said quickly, "but it's Wednesday. I never have serious conversations on Wednesdays."

"Yes, you do."

For heaven's sake, she was attempting to spare the man's feelings. He was attractive enough, and wealthy enough, she supposed, but as far as she was concerned he lacked a bit in the brain area. And that would be difficult to look past—as would be the fact that she didn't love him. The thought of marrying him had never seriously crossed her mind.

"Well, I don't today," she returned, hurrying on up the stairs. "It's far too pretty outside to remain in here for any reason."

"Oh. Very well."

Stifling a sigh, Theresa returned to her bedchamber. As she dug through the wardrobe for her forest green riding habit, she heard Sally enter the room behind her. "You're not supposed to laugh when a gentleman makes to propose to me."

"I apologize, Miss Tess," the maid said, pulling out the dressing table chair for her. "But I wasn't laughing; I was only surprised. I thought Lord Lionel and Lord Montrose were friends."

"So did I. Perhaps Lionel only means to deduce my feelings toward Alexander."

She took a moment to consider that. It was possible; Lionel was definitely more of a follower, so if Alexander had asked him to be an intermediary, he would likely do so. On the other hand, Lionel could be suitor number five to propose to her this Season.

"If I'm not being too forward, Miss Tess, have any of the handsome young gentlemen caught your eye yet?"

"You *are* being too forward, Sally, and they've all caught my eye. Montrose dances well, John Kelly has a very sharp wit, Lord Lionel is very handsome, Richard Bromford has a superior stable and, well, you see? They're all quite acceptable. It's just that none of them are exceptional." She hid a frown. It wasn't their fault. Any of them. "Or perhaps I'm simply not ready yet to decide."

"It is better to have too many choices than too few, I think."

Theresa shook herself. "Indeed it is." There was that third trail of reasoning, of course, the one she traveled alone; they all thought they knew her, and she didn't agree. Laughing, chatting, dancing, dressing prettily—that was all they saw, and all they required. And all they expected.

No one other than her immediate family members even challenged or argued with her. That was the way she wanted it. She paused as she stepped into her riding habit. Tolly James argued, and he kissed. The question remained, though, whether that made him challenging or merely unpleasant. And that was only one of the questions she had about him.

For instance, if he liked her enough to kiss her, why had he then disappeared for two days rather than come calling? That was not how things were done. Theresa blew out her breath, straightening her spine as Sally came around to button up the back of her dress. Why the devil did she even care if he made another appearance or not? He'd been rude and forward, and he had yet to say anything nice to her except for the pedestrian comment about her hair.

"There you are, Miss Tess. All set."

"Thank you, Sally. Have my lavender gown pressed for this evening, will you? I think it and those silver hair ribbons will show well at the Ridgemont soiree tonight."

"Oh, yes! I'll see to it right away."

Lord Lionel seemed to have given up on the idea of speaking with her privately, because when she returned downstairs he was already out on the front drive waiting with the groom and her bay mare.

"Thank you, Wallace," she said, as the groom handed her up and then mounted his own horse to accompany them. "What do you say to St. James's Park, Lionel?"

"Why not Hyde Park?"

"Oh, it's so crowded at this time of day."

The Marquis of Quilby's second son swung up on his chestnut gelding. "As you wish, Tess."

So now he was humoring her, more than likely because he was annoyed that she hadn't given him the chance to ask her about marriage. She was only attempting to save his blasted self-respect. Of course he had such an overblown sense of his own—or Montrose's—irresistibility that he had no idea she was actually being kind. Of course she could never allow him to realize either of those points.

Theresa smiled. "And you will now tell me the names of everyone you know who will be attending the Ridgemont soiree tonight."

His expression lifted a little as they trotted down the drive. "Everyone?"

"Absolutely everyone."

She almost immediately regretted making the request, but it did give him something to say. And it therefore allowed her to enjoy the ride and the remainder of the morning without having to fish about for topics of conversation. Theresa smiled and returned the wave of the trio of Parker-Lyons sisters in their barouche.

Once they reached St. James's Park she started Cleopatra along the hard-packed earth path that ran beneath the tall stands of oak and ash trees. Yes, this was much more fun than sitting on a sofa and dashing the hopes of a likely suitor before he could realize on his own that they would never, ever suit.

Ahead of them someone on a big gray horse rode across the path at a breakneck pace, winding in and out of the trees with a speed and precision that only the finest of riders could manage. It wasn't a particularly safe endeavor considering the number of carriages and pedestrians about, but horse and rider avoided them all with little apparent effort.

"He's going to break his neck," Lionel said from beside her.

She'd forgotten her would-be suitor was even there. "Who is that?"

"Bartholomew James. It's his gelding, anyw—"

"That?" Theresa pointed at the rider, her jaw nearly dropping. "That is Tolly James? He can barely walk!"

Lionel shrugged. "He ain't walking."

She returned her gaze to the rider. "No, he isn't," she mused.

As they drew closer she could make out what looked like a tightly wrapped sheath of leather around his left knee, from mid-thigh to mid-calf. Considering how much a rider used his knees, especially on twists and turns such as those he and his horse were engaging in, Colonel James must have been in extreme pain. And yet he continued his bruising ride.

"Maybe he's been looking for sympathy and he's not as crippled as he pretends." Lionel stopped half in front of her, blocking her view of the colonel. "The East India Company don't like stories of men getting murdered, regardless. He'd best watch himself."

Theresa had seen enough. "Let's go, shall we?" Clucking at Cleopatra, she turned the mare away.

A heartbeat later Colonel James and his splendid dark gray horse thundered up on her—then came to a sliding, grinding stop. "Good morning, Miss Weller."

For a bare second she felt breathless, quite unable

to remember what she was supposed to say. Hatless, his too-long dark hair tossed by the wind, his great-coat flared out behind him, his whiskey gold eyes alight, he looked absolutely mesmerizing. She shook herself. "Colonel."

"Were you out looking for me?"

"I should say not." For a second she glared at him. Clearly he was attempting to unsettle her. "Though I am forced to observe," she continued aloud, "that if you can ride this well, surely you can manage a dance. Or at least a social call."

Before he could respond to that, she sent Cleopatra into a trot. She hardly noticed when Lionel caught up to her and resumed his recitation of the evening's guest list. That should do it. She couldn't think of a way to make it more obvious to Bartholomew James that he interested her without standing straight up and saying it. And ladies did not do such things.

Chapter Five

"I have seen many a young lady, swayed by pretty words and pretty eyes, fall from Society's favor. Think hard on this, ladies: Is one kiss, no matter how perfect or heartfelt, worth the risk?"

A LADY'S GUIDE TO PROPER BEHAVIOR

Tolly stared after Theresa as she and the lumbering Adonis known as Lord Lionel Humphreys trotted away. A heady mix of heat, lust, and pain seared through his muscles, rendering him taut and speechless at the same time.

Sweet Lucifer. All she'd done was appear, and all he could think of was bare skin and sweat and sweet moans of pleasure. While it might have been his fault for being unable to resist riding her down and then teasing her, he hadn't expected that the impossible chit would still want to dance with him—even after he'd mauled her the last time she'd saved him a dance.

Still breathing hard from the morning's exercise,

Tolly patted Meru on the flank. "That's enough for today, I think."

Taking a more sedate pace mostly because Mayfair's late morning traffic demanded it, he headed back to Ainsley House and the Adventurers' Club. His knee felt on fire, but at least on horseback he could move the way he used to. For an hour or two, for a handful of miles, he could forget that he'd allowed fifteen men to die while he'd lived.

Except that he never forgot. Not until today. Today he'd been thinking about Theresa Weller—and then she'd appeared twenty feet away from him.

"He looks winded, Colonel," Jenkins observed as he gripped Meru's bridle. "You had a good ride, then?"

"Yes," he answered, as he always did. The Ainsley House grooms had proved to be as helpful as those at James House, and without waiting to be asked the second groom, Harlow, carefully pulled his boot from the stirrup, then stepped around to help him to the ground.

Tolly swung his leg over, and Harlow helped support his weight until he could free his right foot. The second his bad foot touched the ground, though, white-hot agony shot all the way up his spine into his skull, where it exploded. Before he could do more than gasp, everything went black.

A cut-off scream, and then the worse sound of absolute silence. A quiet filled with murder and death. Then screams that broke through, first one, then more, all around. Shouting, gunfire, a burst of flames and the glint of steel. Being choked—

Tolly roared upright, wrapping his hands around the throat of the man leaning over him. A heartbeat later an arm snaked around his neck and shoulder from behind, pulling him down again.

"Colonel! Tolly! Let him go!"

He blinked, the present crashing back into his mind. "Gibbs," he rasped, and released the servant. The man staggered backward, coughing.

"He was untying your cravat." The arm pulling him back onto the bed relaxed and vanished, and the Duke of Sommerset stood to straighten the sleeve of his fine gray jacket.

"Apologies," Tolly grunted, rubbing his own throat. "You startled me, Gibbs."

"I'll try not to do that again, then, Colonel."

He was in the small room he'd commandeered at the club, and in addition to Sommerset and Gibbs, Dr. Prentiss and Harlow the groom were packed inside, as well. With a scowl Bartholomew pulled himself into a seated position on the bed.

"Did someone convene Parliament when I wasn't looking?" he asked stiffly. "And where are my damned trousers?" His frown deepening, he adjusted the blanket thrown across his middle.

"Ruined, I'm afraid," Dr. Prentiss answered, indicating a ripped pile of dark cloth on the floor.

"I fainted. The devil knows I've done that before. You didn't need to strip me. So thank you for carrying me off, and now leave me be."

"About that," Prentiss continued, clearing his throat. "You've been using your leg a bit hard, lad."

"It's my leg. I've been using it as necessary."

"Mmm-hmm. Who tended it in India?"

Tolly looked from Sommerset to the physician. "Arnold. The company's head groom."

"A groom."

"The company's doctor was traveling with my unit. He was killed." He watched, seeing the looks of mingled sympathy and supposed understanding on their faces. "It was some time before I could reach Arnold. He did what he could. I have nothing to complain about."

"The bone just below your knee was broken in what looks like two places," Prentiss said. "I took the liberty of examining it while you were unconscious. It was never set properly. Every time you walk on it, it shifts. Luckily, your activity has kept the upper break from healing entirely. Unluckily, it keeps tearing the wound open and causing infection."

"And?" Tolly prompted after a moment.

"The pain must be excruciating."

"And?" he demanded again.

The doctor folded his arms across his barrel-shaped chest. "And so I can either cut it off, or break it again and set it properly, in which case I might, if you're lucky, be able to avoid cutting it off."

For a long moment Tolly regarded him. "So the one is supposed to frighten me into doing the other? Arnold offered to hack the thing off for me in India. I declined. I decline again."

"And the other? You'll probably lose it regardless, but if I don't reset it soon you'll be permanently subjected to that pain, and you'll never gain more use of it than you've got at this moment."

Tolly looked down at his bare leg. They'd not only cut off his trousers, but they'd removed his damned boot and the tight leather brace he'd fashioned to hold together his knee while he rode, plus the bandage underneath all of the other clutter. "If I say I'll consider one offer or the other, will you leave and let me put some blasted clothes back on?"

"I'll even dress that mess in a fresh poultice and re-bandage it."

"In a moment, Dr. Prentiss." Sommerset angled his head at Gibbs, and almost immediately the two servants and the physician were gone from the room.

"You don't frighten me, either, Sommerset."

"I know that. Misguided of you, but I haven't the time at the moment to change your mind."

"What do you want, then?"

The duke narrowed his steel gray eyes. "Outside of this club, I expect you to address me properly."

Half hoping this would end in a brawl no matter how poor his odds of winning were at the moment, Tolly nodded. "Outside the club."

"Secondly, this *is* a club. Not an infirmary. I don't mind Gibbs having to pick someone off the floor from time to time, but this place is attached to my house. If Dr. Prentiss keeps calling here, the wags will begin speculating over whether I'm on my deathbed or not. With my stocks and myriad public investments, I can't have that."

The breath Tolly took shook a little. Sommerset was booting him out. Panic touched him with cold, familiar fingers. He could rent a small house or an apartment in Town, but that would mean hiring servants. Hiring a keeper. Because however damned little he wanted to admit it, with his leg like this there were things he simply couldn't do for himself.

"Is that understood?" the duke pressed. "You're welcome here at any time, but not while you require medical assistance."

Tolly leaned over to grab his cane and swing his legs off the side of the bed. Without the bandage on, that motion alone nearly brought him down again. "You might have waited to tell me until I had my damned trousers on," he growled.

"I'm not your wet nurse." Sommerset walked to the door. "And whatever you think you deserve, Colonel, killing yourself by inches is a bit time-consuming. If you mean to commit suicide, use a pistol."

"You may have traveled the world, Sommerset, but you've never walked in my boots."

"True enough."

"Then cease advising me. And someone else decided what I deserve. I'm only living with it."

"You're dying with it, but I suppose that's semantics." The duke pulled open the door. "I'll send in Prentiss."

As the doctor put fresh bandages around his knee, Tolly reviewed his options. Stephen would never ask him to leave James House if he returned there, so he supposed he could make it clear that he wanted to be left alone—or as alone as he could be, considering that half the time he couldn't pull off his own boots.

As for the rest of it, he wasn't ready to see his leg gone. Nor was he certain, though, that he wanted to risk additional time in a sickbed for the same eventual outcome. Whatever he truly did deserve was likely to come about with or without his assistance. At the same time, he couldn't help thinking if he did take another chance, a certain irritating young lady would want to dance with him.

"I don't know what you're talking about, Grandmama," Theresa said, not bothering to hide her grin. "That hat is absolutely magnificent."

Grandmama Agnes reached up to finger the brim of the ostrich feather-topped monstrosity, then reached across the carriage to rap Michael on the knee. "Your sister is a much better liar than you are."

"Clearly not, if you didn't believe either of us. Why did you purchase the silly thing, anyway? It looks like a mossy, half-sunk schooner."

"I think it more resembles the chimney tops of Hampton Court," Theresa countered, laughing outright now.

"I bought it because I saw Lady Dalloware fondling it, and I can't abide that woman and her wagging tongue."

"Well, I hope she attends the party tonight, or you'll have to wear it a second time." Michael pulled out his pocket watch and flipped it open. "Tell me again why we're stopping at James House? We won't all fit in one carriage, anyway, so I don't see the point."

"We're going because Amelia wants to borrow my pearl ear bobs," Theresa replied, "and she can't very well put them on after she arrives at the Ridgemonts'."

"Ah. As long as it's something vital."

"Young man, you have no idea," their grandmother noted. "Will I finally get to set eyes on the viscount's younger brother, do you think?"

Theresa's heart accelerated for a beat or two. "I doubt it," she supplied, keeping her voice light and uncaring. "He doesn't reside with them."

"Damned unpleasant fellow, anyway." Michael frowned briefly. "He was crippled in India, you know."

"I'd heard something about that. Poor man. Young Violet always seemed very fond of him."

"He's not dead, for heaven's sake," Theresa put in. "He's merely injured and a bit . . . direct."

"Direct like a musket ball." Her brother squinted one eye at her. "Why are you defending him, Troll?"

"I'm not. You described him incorrectly, and I corrected you. Aside from that, you shouldn't gossip about someone behind his back."

"Is that in your guide?"

"I'm going to write a second one, I think. It's going to go in there."

The coach stopped in front of James House, and a footman and the butler emerged to help them onto the drive and see them into the drawing room upstairs. "Lord and Lady Gardner will be with you shortly," the butler droned, and exited.

"He seems in a lather, doesn't he?" Grandmama Agnes observed.

"If Leelee takes as long to dress now as she used to when she resided with us, I can see why." Michael strolled over to the liquor tantalus to pour himself half a glass of brandy.

"Ha ha." Theresa dug the pearl ear bobs out of her reticule. "I'll be back in a moment."

"If she hasn't selected a dress yet," her brother

drawled after her, "send down a shout and I'll go out to White's for dinner while we wait."

"I think I'm going to tell Amelia how many cravats you and Mooney ruined tonight attempting that ridiculous knot around your neck."

"It's the new fashion, Troll."

Laughing, Theresa climbed the stairs and turned down the hallway leading along the north-facing wing of the house. She went slowly; she'd only been in James House a handful of times, and she would feel foolish if she became lost.

Stopping outside the closed doors of the master bedchamber, she hesitated. Her cousin was a married lady now. Heavens, her husband might be in there, as well. Tess certainly didn't wish to interrupt them. They'd only been married for six months, after all.

"So you do have common sense."

She jumped. Immediately she recognized the deep voice across the hallway behind her, but it was too late to pretend she hadn't been startled. *Blast it all.* "Common sense *and* the good manners to make my presence known so I don't frighten anyone half to death."

When she turned around Colonel James stood in the doorway of the room opposite. As usual he had a cane gripped in one hand, his long, lean body canted slightly to one side as he attempted to keep weight off his bad leg.

"*You* startled *me*," he returned, regarding her evenly. "For the second time today, I might add."

"You didn't sound startled," she retorted defensively. "Either time."

He ignored that. "You know, that's the first time I've seen you hesitate at anything." Golden eyes trailed from her face down to her toes and back again.

Warmth crept up her cheeks. "Well?" she demanded, when he didn't say anything. She was accustomed to men scrutinizing her, but a compliment on her appearance generally followed.

"The color of the gown makes your eyes look more gray than green," he said, still studying her face.

"Is that your idea of a compliment?" She scowled to cover the fact that both his gaze and his direct words continued to unsettle her. It was almost as if he didn't see the gown or the hair ribbons, but rather noticed only . . . her.

"It was an observation." Swinging the cane forward, he limped into the hallway, directly up to her.

Theresa lifted her chin to keep her gaze on his. "Are you visiting?" she asked, attempting to keep her attention away from his wickedly sensual mouth and the thoughts of the kiss in the Haramund garden.

"I've moved back in. For the moment." His gaze momentarily broke from hers, letting her breathe again. "My former host didn't appreciate the frequency with which I lost my footing."

"That's rude of him."

"I didn't say it was a *him*," the colonel replied. Leaning toward her a little, he knocked the end of his cane against the closed master bedchamber door beyond her. Then, with the first grin she'd seen him wear, a wicked, humorous expression that made him look younger than his twenty-eight years, he turned and headed toward the back of the house and the narrow servants' stairs there.

She opened her mouth to retort that no one residing with a woman—not in the way he implied—would have kissed her the way he did. Before she could utter a sound, though, the door in front of her opened.

"Tess!" Amelia exclaimed, her faced flushed and a smile on her face. "I—we were—"

"Here," Theresa said, handing over the ear bobs. "I'll be downstairs." Without a backward glance she strode off in the direction Colonel James had taken.

She found him four steps down from the top, his hands braced against either side of the narrow walls and his cane hooked over one thumb as he swore under his breath.

Arguing with him or not, she didn't like seeing him in such obvious pain. Grimacing, she caught up to him and pulled the cane out of his fingers. "You are n—"

With a breath-freezing hiss he whipped around. Before she could react he had a forearm across her chest shoving her against the wall, the other hand fisted and headed for her face. Gasping, she squeezed her eyes closed.

The blow never came. She opened one eye to see his fist lowered, his mouth inches from hers, breath warm on her lips. "Apologies," he said roughly. "I don't like anyone coming up behind me."

Theresa nodded. "I can see that. Would you please release my bosom?"

He stayed where he was, his hard body pressing her against the wall, close enough to kiss but not doing so. "I don't want to," he murmured.

Her heart skittered. "Do so anyway, Colonel," she ordered.

"Call me Tolly."

"You are . . . not behaving," she bit out, realizing both that she could fairly easily push him down the stairs and that she had no intention of doing so. He might act like a wild creature who went about grabbing women by the bosom, but she would not misbehave in turn.

"I've never found much benefit in following the rules." He raised his free hand again, this time to brush his fingers against her hair. "I haven't heard a woman say my name in a long time, Theresa. Say my name."

She pulled in a hard breath, pretending to be annoyed rather than unsettled and excited by the intimacy. "Very well. Tolly. Better?"

"Infinitely." Slowly he ran his fingertips along her cheek, making her shiver. "So many handsome gentlemen courting you, Tess," he whispered, "and yet here you are." Finally he brushed his mouth against hers, lightly at first, making her ache, then hotter and more insistently. He shifted his confining hand to join the other at her shoulders.

The cane clattered onto the step and then down to the small landing below. She noted the sound distantly, every ounce of her immediate attention on where Tolly touched her. Mouth first, expert and delicious and breathless, then his hands tugging her hips forward against his. The immediate, insane desire to put her hands on his bare, warm skin seized her, making her moan.

"Tess? Where the devil are you?" Amelia's voice echoed from the hallway just above them.

With another hot, openmouthed kiss, Tolly broke the embrace. "I can't run," he murmured, brushing a fingertip down the front of her throat. "You should."

For a heartbeat she didn't want to move. She wanted more kisses, more touches. His cynical gaze, though, brought her back to herself. He expected her to flee. She could even guess what he was thinking. Why would she want anyone to know that she'd been compromised at all—much less by *him*?

Theresa narrowed her eyes. No one had seen them, and she refused to be intimidated. Not by some aggravating man who thought none of the rules applied to him. "I'm on the stairs, Leelee," she called. "With Tolly."

He blanched as she lifted an eyebrow at him. "You little . . ." With a curse he grabbed her hand and placed it around his waist, sliding his free arm across her shoulders and turning back down the stairs as Amelia came into view above them. "I lost my balance," he grumbled, his eyes glinting.

Amelia made a sympathetic sound. "Oh, dear. Shall I call for Stephen?"

Even through his clothes Theresa felt Tolly's spine tense. "Oh, no," she said aloud, waving her free hand up at her cousin. "We can manage. We'll meet you around front, shall we?"

"Of course. Thank you for the ear bobs. I'll see you in a moment."

As soon as Amelia's footsteps faded from hearing, Tolly jerked halfway around to face her. "I'm not meeting anyone around front. Go to your own damned party."

With him down a step, they were eye to eye. His expression could likely melt glass, but she didn't feel in the mood to be trifled with, either. "You're dressed for it," she noted, meeting his furious, frustrated gaze squarely. "And I think we've established that you have a thought for at least your own reputation. So yes, you are going with us to the Ridgemont soiree."

Whatever the condition of his leg, she knew without a doubt that Tolly James was not a man to be bullied into something he didn't wish to do. When he uttered another curse and continued down the stairs, she felt both relieved and thrilled. He wanted to go. With her.

"I don't need your damned help," he growled, shrugging out of her grip.

"You're the one who put my hand there."

"Only because I was in error about you having common sense. You don't have the sense God gave a kitten."

She frowned again, brushing past him as they reached the landing and retrieving his cane before he could regret his short-sighted rejection of her assistance. Clutching it, she proceeded down the remainder of the stairs to wait at the bottom.

"What, no response to that?" he jibed, a little out of breath as he hitched himself down toward her.

"Is it my lack of sense or the grayness of my eyes this evening that compelled you to kiss me, then? Or was it perhaps your parting from the imaginary woman with whom you claimed to be living?" she retorted, glaring up at him.

That compelling mouth of his twitched before it dove back into a scowl. "The eye color."

"Oh, really?"

"Yes. I'm partial to gray."

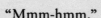

"Mmm-hmm."

She didn't believe that, of course. It was entirely possible, however, that he was as mystified by his attraction to her as she was by the effect he had on her. No good would come of it; Colonel Tolly James was an angry, defensive man who'd in three seconds gone from nearly striking her to kissing her. But something had kept her thinking about him for the past two days, even while she danced and drove and rode and chatted with a half dozen other gentlemen who'd already made their intentions toward her very clear, and who knew how to behave themselves.

When he finally reached the level floor just outside the kitchen, she held out his cane to him. "Thank you," he said, not sounding grateful at all. "And don't ask me to dance with you tonight. We both know that that's an impossibility. Nor is it particularly amusing."

"I have no intention of asking you to dance," she said, falling in beside him as they left the house through the servants' entrance and slowly made their way up the carriage drive to the front of the house. "From now on you will have to ask me to dance."

"I will not do that."

With a quick smile she left his side and climbed into her brother's carriage. "Yes, you will," she returned, leaning out again. "I'll save you a place on my dance card."

Chapter Six

"A young lady should be sensible and serene, and if lucky will find herself attended by a man of similar temperament. If she is *very* lucky, he will also be possessed of passion and wealth. But of the three, I must rank passion last. Passion does not pay the bills."

A LADY'S GUIDE TO PROPER BEHAVIOR

"I'm so pleased you're living at James House again," Violet gushed, taking the chair beside Tolly's and grabbing his right hand in both of hers. "I've missed you terribly, you know."

"You've only seen me for two months or so every two or three years as it is, Vi," he returned, freeing his hand as swiftly as he could do so without dumping her off the chair in the middle of the damned Ridgemont ballroom.

"Yes, but you always stayed with us the entire time you were on leave. This time we had to come to London just to find you, and then you still wouldn't come near us."

What could he tell her about that? That he'd become

more comfortable among strangers he could watch with suspicion than with friends and family he was expected to trust? *Trust.* That word had certainly taken on new significance in the past year.

Of course his obsession with that word in no way explained his immediate fascination with Theresa Weller. Even with his gaze on his sister he knew precisely where Tess was in the large ballroom, and with whom she was dancing—currently stocky, round Francis Henning. Apparently she enjoyed dancing so much that she would partner with anyone.

Except him. He shifted a little, though it had been months since he'd found something close to a comfortable position. Bartholomew glanced at the dance floor again, catching a glimpse of violet gown and hair the color of morning sunshine.

"Stephen's letter said he met Amelia at the Hutchings recital last year," he commented, making a final attempt at distracting himself.

Violet snuggled in against his shoulder as she used to do, and he steeled himself as both her arms wrapped around his. "Yes. He complained about going, you know, but my good friend Celia was going to play the pianoforte, and so I forced him to escort me."

"Love at first sight?"

His sister chuckled. "Most definitely. We only realized later that Tess had forced Amelia to go because she reckoned Stephen might be there. She thought they would suit."

With a slight scowl he looked again at the lavender butterfly floating elegantly across the dance floor. "Amelia and her cousins do seem very close."

"They were all raised together by their grandmother. That's her," Violet said, gesturing with one forefinger. "The Dowager Viscountess Weller. She's very nice, too. And quite funny. She's obsessed with cats. She asked us all to call her Grandmama Agnes."

Bartholomew glanced over at her—and blinked. Grandmama Agnes wore a hat topped with three brightly colored ostrich plumes, the thing so enormous he was somewhat surprised she didn't topple over. Despite her advanced age she looked bright-eyed enough, with an open, friendly countenance very like all three of her grandchildren.

But his curiosity had little to do with grandmothers. "What's your opinion of Amelia's family?" he pursued. "The cousins, I mean."

"Well, I think Michael is excessively handsome," she said, and sighed. "Extremely excessively handsome."

"Mmm-hmm." He wondered whether Stephen knew of their sister's infatuation, but then Violet had had a new beau for every letter she'd written him since she'd turned fifteen. "And the sister?"

"Tess is wonderful. And very witty. And she knows a great deal about how to encourage or deflect the attentions of a gentleman. So I hope you don't hate her simply because she spoke a bit harshly to you the other night."

Hate wasn't the word. "Confounded by" fit much better. And "infatuated with." He shook himself, realizing that his sister expected a response. "I spoke harshly first," he decided. Then he blinked. "What does she know about encouraging the attentions of a gentleman?"

"Oh, a great deal. She's already published a booklet on proper behavior. Anonymously, of course, but Amelia told me it was Tess after she saw me reading it."

"Really?" He doubted some of the things she'd said to him were in that booklet.

"Truly." The cotillion ended, and Violet bounced to her feet as a young man approached. "Hello, Andrew," she chirped, and took his arm without a backward glance at her brother.

Tolly stopped her with his cane. "Introductions, Vi," he said. This fellow might be known to Stephen, but as Violet had already noted, *he'd* been away. And he was not a damned sack of potatoes, for God's sake.

"What? Oh. Apologies, Tolly. Andrew, this is my brother, Colonel Bartholomew James. Tolly, Mr. Andrew Carroway, Lord Dare's third brother."

With a nod, Tolly dismissed the pair of them. He couldn't very well tell Andrew that he'd met his older brother, Captain Bradshaw Carroway, at the Adventurers' Club, unless he wanted to be asked to leave it.

"How's the leg?"

Alexander Rable, the Marquis of Montrose, sank onto the chair beside him. Alarm bells immediately began ringing in Tolly's skull; the two of them hadn't spoken more than a dozen words together over the past five years, and there was a quadrille being played thirty feet away. "I still have two of them," he returned.

"I heard you lost everyone under your command. And by 'lost' I mean they died."

The hostility didn't surprise him; they'd never been on friendly terms even at Oxford. He did not, however, appreciate the path this little conversation was taking. "They were murdered," he corrected, keeping his voice level.

"But you weren't."

"Are we playing a game of state the obvious? You should have told me, so I could mention that you're acquiring that hanging jowl that runs on your father's side of the family." He gestured at the base of Montrose's jaw.

"If you weren't a cripple, I would flatten you for that."

Bartholomew sent a quick look toward the dance floor. Theresa was on the far side of the room, well out of earshot. For some reason that was important. "Don't talk to me about India, and I won't mention your wobbling jowls."

"I actually only came over here to tell you to stop staring at Tess Weller. You're embarrassing yourself, and if you keep it up, you'll embarrass her."

He could explain his attention away, he supposed, mention that her cousin had recently married his brother and that he was attempting to become acquainted with the family. It would be a lie, though.

"Thank you for the advice," Tolly said coolly. "Have you warned away everyone who looks in her direction, or is it just the cripple you feel threatened by?"

"I'm not threatened by you," Montrose shot back. "I told you, you're an embarrassment. You carry damned rumors with you, and she won't want them touching her."

"I suppose I'll wait for her to tell me that."

"If you want to appear that pitiful, then by all means." The marquis stood. "I was only trying to be kind."

"Ah. Then you've changed."

With a cold smile, Montrose nodded and vanished into the large, festive crowd. Tolly curled his fingers around the brass handle of his cane so hard his knuckles turned white. He should be gratified, he supposed, that anyone had taken enough notice of his presence to warn him away, but mostly he was angry because Montrose was correct. He didn't have much to offer, and he'd heard the rumors, too. Both the ones about his cowardice and the ones that he'd manufactured the entire incident with the Thuggee. They couldn't possibly help his reputation, or his standing with Tess Weller.

Was he actually in pursuit, though? Yes, in her presence he tended to forget the blackness and pain of the last months. And she was definitely pleasant to look at. But she also made him want things, made him feel things he wasn't certain he had the right to enjoy any longer.

Dancing, first and foremost. And sex. As he considered it, he would place sex first, with dancing a far-following second. At least he could still manage sex, though it hadn't been much on his mind until he'd crossed Theresa Weller's path.

She twirled into view, shimmering in the light of a hundred candles. She laughed and spun, happy and safe amid her large circle of friends and admirers, while he crouched, steeling his thoughts against the creeping, silent dark that threatened to overwhelm him every night. The worst of it was the knowledge that the horror was real, because that one night, back when he'd thought that kindness and vigilance and honor would be met with the same, it had caught him.

At least he'd learned the lesson and accepted the pain and punishment that had been dealt him. Sommerset said that he didn't deserve either, but it wasn't about what he deserved. His men couldn't change their circumstances. It was wrong of him to attempt to alter his.

The quadrille finished. Amid the chatter and the applause, a swirl of rose-scented lavender gown dropped into the chair Montrose had vacated. "Well?" Theresa prompted.

"Well what?"

"I told you that I wouldn't ask you to dance again. I left a space open on my card later in the evening because you're somewhat dim-witted, but you still have to ask me."

That was bloody enough of that. Keeping his gaze sightlessly somewhere three or so feet ahead of him, he clenched his jaw. "Tease and prod at me as much as you please, Theresa, as long as you stay out of my damned reach," he uttered in a low voice.

"I—"

"Because while I am slow-moving," he continued, ignoring her interruption, "I am not a simpleton, and I believe I mentioned already that I am not a eunuch. I have some pride, and I must still have the remains of a gentleman about me, or I would tell you precisely what I would like to do with you right now. And it has very little to do with dancing."

He heard her sharp intake of breath, waited for her to scream, faint, or stand up and stalk away. She had spleen, but he'd become well enough acquainted with her to know that she didn't like being spoken to that way. And now she knew that he didn't like it, either.

"Don't you have a dance?" he demanded when she neither spoke nor fled.

"What, exactly, happened to your leg?"

Tolly flinched. That hadn't been on his list of her possible reactions, blasted chit. "You don't want to know. Leave me be."

"I asked because I do want to know, and no, I won't leave you be. Not until you answer my question."

For a moment Theresa thought he might refuse to say anything. With her next dance partner hovering at the edge of her vision, she didn't have much time to convince the colonel to talk to her. What she did have, though, was a very fresh memory of a kiss on the servants' stairs. A kiss that had positively curled her toes. And quite possibly his, as well. He didn't want her to walk away. He couldn't want that. And so she asked an improper question, one that a lady wouldn't ask. At least she'd made certain that no one but Tolly had heard her.

"Very well, Tess," he said in a low, toneless voice, his gaze lowering to the floor. "I was stabbed and shot and thrown into a deep, damp well, and the corpses of my men were dumped in after me. That is what happened to my leg. Now go waltz with Lord Lionel."

Theresa couldn't breathe. She'd known it would be something awful. She'd even steeled herself against a tale of a battle and bloodshed. But this—no matter what she imagined, the reality must have been much, much worse. Shaking, she clasped her hands tightly together against her thighs. "Bartholomew," she whispered, willing him to look at her.

He didn't. "Will you go away now?"

She nodded. For heaven's sake, she wanted some fresh air. A strong wind out in the open, in the sunlight, and preferably on the top of a hill. Grabbing onto the back of her chair, she stood.

As Lionel approached, though, Theresa stopped. She could fill her mind with other things, push the images that Tolly's words conjured far away from her. He couldn't. And she'd asked the question because she'd wanted to know the answer. Taking a deep breath, she faced him. "Look at me," she murmured.

Golden brown eyes lifted to meet hers.

"I wasn't teasing," she continued in the same low voice. "I wanted to dance with you. What you just told me is horrific, but it is not my fault. And I would still like to dance with you. I would settle, however, for you coming to call on me."

"Would you, now? You would settle for a social call?"

At this moment, she could recall the exact passage she'd written in her lady's guide about how a lady did not ask a gentleman to call on her. And that wasn't even the first of her own rules she'd broken where Tolly James was concerned. He intrigued her mightily, and though the reasons for that were still madly baffling, she couldn't seem to stop thinking about him. And she wanted to figure out why.

"Since you haven't managed a social call yet, I think that would be a good beginning." She favored him with a slow smile, excitement tingling down to her toes. "And we both know you'll be stopping by." Before he could reply to that, however, she took Lord Lionel's arm and pulled him onto the dance floor.

"That fellow always seems to be about, don't he?" the marquis's second son commented as they turned about the floor.

"Everyone's about all the time during the Season," she returned with a brisk smile. She wanted a bit of time to sort through her thoughts, and thankfully Lionel didn't tax her mind too severely.

"Yes, but he's always about you."

Theresa stifled an annoyed sigh. At times, dancing was quite overrated. "Shall I name all of the gentlemen who are about me all the time? Your name would appear on that list, my lord. And you and I don't have a close familial connection as Colonel James and I do."

"But Montrose don't mind me being about you. He ain't so fond of Bartholomew, there."

"And why is that?"

"You'd have to ask Alexander. I ain't a wag."

Theresa just barely restrained herself from pointing out that Lionel had done nothing but gossip since the moment they'd met. Instead she glanced again in Tolly's direction, as she'd been doing all evening. His chair was empty.

Keen disappointment touched her, in herself for ignoring the rules of politeness and decorum and quite probably saying the wrong thing, and in him for taking the excuse of their conversation to leave when he hadn't wanted to be there in the first place.

After those blasted kisses he had best manage to pay a call and say hello properly, or she would be forced to track him down and find out why. And that was something that would never appear in her *Guide*.

Bartholomew stepped down from the hired hack and stopped on the street for a moment to gaze at the modest Cheapside home. Every instinct he possessed yelled at him to climb back into that carriage and return to James House posthaste. Instead he dug the tip of his cane into the hard ground and limped forward.

With his free hand he swung the brass knocker against the door. At ten o'clock the hour was still fairly early for the peerage during the Season of balls and parties, but this wasn't the home of a nobleman.

The door swung open. A stern-looking woman in a voluminous night rail and a robe, a lit candle in one hand, peered out at him.

"This house is closed for the evening, sir," she said, her voice softer than he expected.

"Yes, I know," he returned. "I wondered if I might have a minute of the good doctor's time."

"Well, come into the sitting room, and I shall inquire."

More walking and sitting and standing again. "I'll wait here," he decided.

"Your name, sir?"

"Colonel James."

With a nod she shut the door on him. Bartholomew

clenched his jaw against the growing urge to run—or rather, to hobble away at his best speed. There was a damned war raging in his mind. To one side his own resolve to accept what misfortune fate had dealt him, to . . . honor his men by continuing to suffer from the attack that had ended their lives. That ongoing pain of the last months pushed and shoved against a woman's words; Theresa Weller wanted him to call on her, wanted him to dance with her. And he quite simply wanted her.

The door opened for the second time, and the more familiar figure of Dr. Prentiss stepped forward. "What can I do for you, Colonel?" he asked. "Did you manage to tear that wound open again?"

"No." He swallowed. "I wondered whether you might call on me at James House tomorrow. I . . . want you to break and reset my leg."

Prentiss eyed him for a long moment, then nodded. "Is noon acceptable?"

Fourteen damned hours to contemplate how large a fool he was to intentionally risk losing a limb altogether. "Yes. Thank you."

"Don't thank me yet, Colonel. I imagine you'll be hating me tomorrow."

He was more likely to be hating himself by then. With a nod Bartholomew turned and made his way back to the waiting hack.

He knew he was being foolish, because he'd been driven to this moment by hope. Hope that he might in a few weeks be able to limp without excruciating pain. And hope that if everything went far better than he deserved, he would be able to waltz with Tess Weller. The only problem with all of that was that he and hope had had a very poor relationship for the past eight months.

"I can't approve of this, Tolly."

"I didn't ask you to." Wishing his brother would give up the argument, Tolly continued to pretend to be interested in the stack of calling cards on the hallway table. None of them were for him, but that didn't signify.

"Who is this Dr. Prentiss, anyway?"

Bartholomew went through the stack for a third time. "I met him through a . . . friend." Not that he considered the Duke of Sommerset to be a friend, precisely, but he wasn't certain how else to describe him without revealing the entire Adventurers' Club business. "And he'll do as well as anyone, don't you think?"

"No, I don't! You have both legs. You need simply to thank God for that and leave it be."

Bartholomew gazed levelly at his older brother. "I do not have both my legs. I have one leg and one anchor dragging and clanking with me wherever I go. As I said, I didn't ask your permission. I informed you because I'll be off my feet for a time. If you prefer that I do this elsewhere, I w—"

"Don't even begin throwing that garbage in my direction." Stephen jabbed a finger at him. "You are not going anywhere. And whatever you think of my opinion, this is too risky."

"I've been thinking about that, myself," Bartholomew said slowly. "I need to risk this. I just wanted you to know."

"Thank you for that, at least."

"You're welcome."

When Stephen still showed no sign of going away, Bartholomew muttered a curse and limped to the base of the stairs. The narrow, closed-in servants's stairs were easier to descend, but he needed to hang on to the railing of the main staircase to climb up.

Three steps up from the bottom, he heard Stephen start after him. As soon as his brother's arm closed around his shoulders, he shoved backward. "No!" he growled, panicked at being grabbed from behind even though he knew damned well who it was. He'd known before, too, eight months ago.

"I don't understand," his older brother grumbled, returning to the foyer. "You never used to behave like this."

"No, I don't suppose I did." Wrapping his hand around one of the balustrades, he hauled himself up another step. "He'll be here at noon. I'm going to have a drink."

Stephen stood back, watching his stubborn, fearless, athletic younger brother hitching himself up the stairs step by painful step. They'd received word from the damned butler that Tolly had returned to England. No word from Tolly himself, and still no explanation about what, precisely, had happened in India.

All he knew for certain was that Tolly had been injured, and badly. And he knew that his good-humored brother didn't smile or laugh any longer, that he was curt and angry and on edge. If Tolly had decided to risk the loss of his leg by having it intentionally rebroken, there was clearly nothing anyone could do to change his mind.

That did not mean, however, that he could stop himself from worrying. And from wondering—if Tolly with an injured leg was unpredictable and barely civil, what might Tolly with only one leg attempt?

With a shudder Stephen returned to the morning room to explain to his wife and his sister that Tolly had not been joking and that they all might very well have just seen him on his feet—both his feet—for the last time.

Chapter Seven

"Making a match is always to be left to the man. If he is so occupied with being manly and adventurous that he doesn't consider affairs of the heart, well, then he is a man whom I would not wish to marry. Setting your cap for such a man is both futile and foolish."

A LADY'S GUIDE TO PROPER BEHAVIOR

Your cards this morning, Miss Tess." Inclining his head, the butler held out the silver salver piled with calling cards.

Theresa wiped jam off her fingers and lifted the cards. "Thank you, Ramsey."

"Those are all for you?" Michael asked as he strolled into the breakfast room. Planting a swift kiss on Grandmama Agnes's cheek, he came around to rest his hands on Theresa's shoulders and read the cards over her head.

"Let's see," she said, looking through them one by one. "Lord Lionel, Montrose, Bertle—oh, goodness, you may have him."

"Thank you, no. He has a very particular odor about him."

She looked up at her brother. "You should attempt a dance with him."

"Let's put that one aside," he said with a grin. "Who else?"

"Harriet, Lord Hayverton, Lord Wilcox . . ." She stopped to slide that card across the table to their grandmother. "A caller, Grandmama?"

"Hmm. Apparently that hat was even more impressive than we thought." Chuckling, Agnes read the note scrawled across the back of the calling card, then set it aside. "Wilcox has invited me to go for a stroll this afternoon. How very nice!"

"Don't wear the hat," Michael advised. "You'll have the poor baron suffering an apoplexy of lust."

While her brother and grandmother bantered about the state of Lord Wilcox's health, Theresa looked through the remaining cards. As she finished and stacked them all together again, she frowned. Nothing from Tolly James. Not a card, not a note, not a flower or even a bare stem.

"What's amiss, my dear?"

Swiftly wiping away her scowl, Theresa looked up. "Nothing's amiss, Grandmama. I have three invitations to luncheon."

"I foresee two gentlemen with broken hearts." Releasing her shoulders, Michael went to the sideboard to select his breakfast.

One luncheon companion, two broken hearts, and one broken head, if she had her way. She'd done everything she could think of to make Colonel James aware of her interest. And judging from a trio of supremely exemplary kisses, he was interested, as well. And yet he refused to call on her.

Perhaps he kissed so many women when no one else was looking that he simply hadn't yet made his way to her particular door. This was unacceptable. It was maddening. Didn't he realize that firstly she was considered a catch, and secondly he was rotten and unpleasant and was not considered a catch?

She pursed her lips. Honesty made her admit to herself that he wasn't entirely unpleasant—not the way he looked at her sometimes, anyway—and that considering what had happened to him, he was perhaps entitled to be a bit . . . prickly from time to time. On the other hand, the heated kisses and horrific personal secrets with which he'd favored her, together with him otherwise completely ignoring her, was too much to bear.

Turning her annoyed, irritated growl into a cough, she pushed to her feet. "I forgot, I already made luncheon plans with Amelia," she stated.

"Ah. Three broken hearts, then," Michael amended with a grin. "You're a cruel, cruel girl, Troll."

Theresa paused in the doorway just long enough to stick her tongue out at her terribly amusing brother. Then she hurried upstairs to scribble out her regrets to her three would-be luncheon hosts, collect her maid and her hat, and attempt to figure out how she could accidently run across the colonel at James House and make certain he knew just how displeased she was— all without causing a stir.

Of course all of that would make her appear desperate for his attention, which she was most definitely not. Hmm. Perhaps she could accidently stumble across him and then ignore him. That would show him how little his kisses and his pretty eyes and his obvious courage impressed her.

By the time the family coach stopped at James House, she was ready for battle. After all, she had a dozen beaux trailing after her, and she'd had her fill of showing interest and kindness and empathy where none was returned. She'd never encountered the like before. Someone needed to teach that man a lesson.

Generally Graham opened the front door for her before her feet even left the coach. Today, though, she had to rap the brass, lion-shaped knocker against the door twice and then wait before it finally opened.

"Miss Weller," the butler said, inclining his head.

"Good afternoon, Graham. Is Lady . . ." She paused, belatedly noting the butler's pale complexion and the thin, straight line of his generally amiable mouth. "Is something amiss?"

A strangled male yell of pure agony ripped through the interior of the house. The sound froze her to her very bones.

"Good heavens!"

She practically flew up the staircase, Graham and Sally on her heels. Clearly something was dreadfully wrong, and the image that immediately came to her mind was of Tolly. Had he fallen? Had those awful Thuggee somehow invaded Mayfair and come to finish him off?

At the end of the same hallway that led to Lord and Lady Gardner's master bedchamber she found them—Amelia and Stephen and Violet and a half dozen servants, all clustered around the door from which Tolly had startled her the other evening.

Her heart clenched. "What's happened?" she asked, her voice shrill.

Amelia jumped. "You should go," she whispered, her face pale and one hand over her mouth.

Oh, no. "Is it Tolly? What's wrong?"

Another muffled yell cut through her. Her breath catching, Theresa pushed forward. Whatever the devil it was, whatever the rules said about minding her own affairs and letting men be manly, she needed to know.

Stephen's broad chest blocked her path. "No lady should see this," he said, his own voice tight. "My brother is being tended by a physician."

"Yes, one who's breaking his leg," Violet sobbed, sinking to the floor.

"Oh, Vi." Amelia sat down beside her, taking the younger girl's hands in hers. "It will all be well."

None of them looked as though they believed that. Theresa didn't much believe in trusting to hope, anyway. She hadn't for a very long time. Taking her skirt in one hand, she slipped through the distracted group and into the room. And stopped dead in her tracks.

Tolly James lay on his back in a large bed, his face very nearly the same coloring as the white sheets. His nightshirt was askew and soaked with sweat, his fingers clenching into the folds of the bedsheets. He wore tan knee-length breeches, the left leg torn open up to the thigh. A stain of red spread around the awful mess that was his left knee.

"My God," she whispered.

The stout, balding man leaning over Tolly's leg and with what looked like a pair of pliers dug into the wound, looked up at her. "Are you squeamish?" he barked.

She tore her gaze from the mangle of Tolly's knee. *Good heavens.* He'd walked on that. He'd ridden on it. She'd teased him about dancing on it. "No. No, I'm not," she managed.

"Then come here and hold his leg still so I can pull out the rest of the damned lead ball." He shifted to look down at Tolly's face. "Your horse doctor didn't find it all."

Bartholomew, though, was gazing at her. "Get out of here," he rasped.

Oh, she wanted to. "Nonsense." She stepped forward, pulling off her gloves and dropping them to the floor. "You're a physician?"

He nodded. "Prentiss. Put your fingers there. Press hard, no matter what damned thing he says."

"Theresa Weller," she returned, hoping conversation would keep her from contemplating precisely what she was doing. She'd wanted to touch his bare skin, but this wasn't remotely what she'd imagined. "Why don't you have someone here to assist you?"

The doctor jabbed his chin toward the half-open door. As she looked in that direction, she spotted the figure crumpled against the baseboard behind it. "He fainted? I'm sorry, but he can't be much of an assistant."

"Ha. He didn't faint, did you, Clarke?"

The man moaned.

"Colonel James here kicked him in the . . . in a sensitive area. I told Clarke to hold him still. Hopefully next time he'll listen."

"If it's not too damned much trouble, would you get the bloody hell on with it?" Tolly growled.

"We are. Hold still and don't injure Miss Weller."

Amber eyes held hers for a brief moment. "I won't."

Dr. Prentiss twisted his hand and pulled. With a wrench the fragment of lead came free, prompting another strangled yelp from Tolly. Her fingers pressed just above his knee, and she felt the muscles there tighten and then relax again.

"Well, that makes things a bit easier," Dr. Prentiss commented, brushing his forearm across his forehead. "Lad should have passed out ten minutes ago."

She looked at Tolly's face again. His eyes were closed, the color of his skin still alarmingly pale. "Violet said you needed to break his leg again," she said, swallowing.

"I already did. That's where I lost Clarke and found the lead fragment. Now I need to set it and bandage it again. Are you up for that, Miss Weller?"

"Yes," she heard herself say. "Of course."

Theresa preferred not to remember the next twenty minutes, the twisting muscles and the blood and the popping of bones shifting reluctantly back into place. Finally the doctor pointed her at the wash basin. She cleaned Tolly's blood from her hands, then sat on the upper corner of the bed leaning against the headboard while Dr. Prentiss finished stitching the jagged wound, dashed it with whiskey, then began wrapping it in a thick cloth bandage with the help of the mostly recovered Clarke.

Gently she stroked her fingers through Tolly's damp, too-long dark hair. "Will he be able to walk now?"

"I don't know. What I did today should have been done months ago. The bone kept trying to knit, but it wasn't set straight. It's damned unhealthy for a wound to be open and aggravated for this long. My guess is that he'll still lose it." He glanced over at Clarke. "And do not drink all of that blasted whiskey. I warned you to hold him still, so this is your own bloody fault."

"He was supposed to be an invalid," the doctor's assistant grumbled. "Not kick like a mule."

"Mmm-hmm. Go tell the family he's resting quietly."

Prentiss leaned closer to Theresa. "That man is an idiot," he whispered. "If my sister hadn't married his brother, he would be out selling oranges on the street corner."

She chuckled, then looked down again as warm fingers closed over her free hand—the one that rested on Tolly's chest. Whisky-colored eyes dulled by shock gazed at her.

"It's finished now except for the rest of the bandaging," she said quietly, more moved than she expected. She'd had his blood literally on her hands, but it was more than that. Seeing the state of his leg—he might very well have died in India or on the ship sailing him back to England, and they never would have met. That thought left her inexplicably saddened.

"What are you doing here?" he asked thinly.

Why had she come by? Oh, yes, to make a point of ignoring him because he wouldn't call on her. It seemed silly and petty now. "I came to ask Amelia to luncheon." At least that was partly true. "Does your leg hurt?"

"You are far too bright a chit to be asking that question."

"I'm making conversation," she retorted.

"I'm leaving laudanum and instructions for administering it," the doctor interrupted. "That should help some with the pain."

"Don't need it," Tolly grunted.

Theresa glared at him. "Don't be silly. Of course you do. You just allowed someone to break your leg, for heaven's sake." She squeezed his fingers.

He closed his eyes again. "You like to dance," he murmured. His fingers relaxed as he drifted off once more, either to sleep or to unconsciousness.

His family shuffled into the room, but Theresa barely noted them. He'd done this for her? Because she'd teased him about dancing? That was . . . She didn't have the words.

This sort of thing—a man she barely knew, and one who intentionally aggravated her, subjecting himself to such agony on her behalf—just didn't happen. She'd read all the books. At the request of her many friends, she'd written a guide, herself. Women suffered silently, doing their duty without complaint, while men went on as they always did.

After a few moments of the family hovering and whispering, Amelia tugged on Theresa's sleeve. "Do you have a moment?"

Nodding, Theresa settled Tolly's hand beneath the blanket Dr. Prentiss had pulled over him. Amelia led her out into the hallway, then faced her. "What was that?" her cousin asked.

"What was what? You know I helped Lawkins

deliver foals every spring. This was no worse than that." It had been much worse, actually, but she wasn't about to admit it.

"You were holding his hand. I'm his sister-in-law, and he's never so much as shaken hands with me."

Theresa frowned. "He was in pain. Of course I offered him comfort."

Her cousin continued to eye her. She'd been a master at fabricating tales as a child, so she had no idea what Amelia thought she might detect by staring at her face. There wasn't even anything to detect. At all.

"Well, it was grand of you to step in," her cousin finally acknowledged. "I couldn't have done it, and Stephen and Violet were too overwrought."

Privately Theresa thought that being overwrought should wait until after a given emergency was finished with. Oh, that could go into the second edition of her *Guide*. "I'm glad I could help." She took a breath. "In fact, I'd like to call on my patient tomorrow to see how he's recovering."

Amelia smiled and squeezed her arm. "You know you never need to wait for an invitation. You're always welcome here."

"Thank you. And since I imagine that you are not free for luncheon today, I will leave you in peace."

She wanted to stay until he awoke again, and she wanted him to reach out to hold her hand as he had done before. And both of those were very good reasons for her to take her leave immediately. Because according to what he'd said to her, he'd put himself through this hell for her. That required some contemplation far away from his company. That wasn't what someone did as part of a mild flirtation.

"Sally," she said, spying her maid. "We will take our leave now."

The maid curtsied. "Yes, miss."

By the time she passed through the foyer, the butler had summoned her coach, and she swiftly climbed in. As soon as the maid was seated opposite her, they rolled into the street. For a moment Theresa closed her eyes.

Yes, she was deeply, deeply moved that a man as . . . compelling as Colonel Bartholomew James would take such a risk for her. But what if it went wrong? Dr. Prentiss had said quite clearly that Tolly would likely lose his left leg altogether.

She had suitors for every day of the week, and extra ones for Sunday. In the past three years she'd received nine proposals of marriage, three from the same gentleman. The death of her parents had made her a considerable heiress, which more than likely had at least something to do with the quantity of her beaux. Their deaths were also why she remained unmarried, but she didn't care to contemplate that at the moment.

Nothing like this had ever happened before in her experience. By calling at James House today, by deciding that no man in his right mind should have been able to ignore the rules of civility, had she obligated herself to one man? "Oh, dear," she muttered under her breath. She wasn't prepared for any of that.

"What is it, Miss Tess?"

She shook herself. "I forgot my gloves," she improvised.

"I'm certain Lady Gardner will send them back to you."

"Yes. Yes, of course she will."

As soon as they returned home, Theresa retreated to the solitude of her bedchamber. Two questions troubled her more than anything else—was she truly the reason Tolly had subjected himself to such pain, and did she truly want—could she even manage—such a complicated soul in her life? She couldn't think of a single sentence in her *Lady's Guide to Proper Behavior* that came even close to describing or explaining Colonel Bartholomew James. Or the way she behaved when she was around him.

She gazed at herself in her dressing table mirror. From the moment she'd first set eyes on Tolly James she'd felt electric, lightning coursing down her spine and out to the tips of her fingers. And those kisses, and the way he looked at her sometimes, heated her from the inside out. But she'd teased and flirted, and then by his actions today he'd all but declared himself. And now she was the one who needed to find her footing.

A knock sounded at her door. "Come in," she said, hurriedly moving to the chair by the window and picking up a book so she wouldn't be caught admiring herself in the mirror.

The door opened, and an orange cat slipped through the opening and darted onto her lap. "Hello, Caesar," she said, scratching the big tom between the ears. "Hello, Grandmama."

Agnes followed the cat into the room and closed the door behind her. "Caesar insisted on joining me," she said, taking the seat Theresa had just vacated. "Though he's a very poor escort."

"I thought you were going for a stroll with Lord

Wilcox," Theresa commented, setting the unread book aside to scratch Caesar with both hands.

"He's downstairs waiting for me. I'm being coy."

"Grandmama!"

"Oh, it'll do him good to have a sit-down before we go. You were to join Amelia for luncheon."

"Yes. We had a change of plans. It's no matter; I have some work to do on the second edition of my *Guide*."

" 'It's no matter,' is it? You are aware by now that servants gossip, I hope. Particularly when a female member of the household goes visiting and ends up assisting in a surgery."

Dash it all. She hadn't asked Sally to exercise any discretion, though, so she supposed the subsequent gossip was her own fault. "I did what I could," she said aloud.

"I hear you were quite distressed when you learned who the doctor had come to see."

Theresa looked sideways at her grandmother. "Do you have a question for me, or are we going to make observations all afternoon while poor Lord Wilcox wastes away downstairs?"

Agnes's fingers wandered through hair clips and hat pins and combs spread across the dressing table. "Yes, I have a question. While I have never known you to be missish or retiring, pushing your way into a man's bedchamber and then voluntarily getting his blood on your hands isn't precisely your . . . usual cup of tea, as they say."

Keeping her gaze on the purring cat, Theresa hid a scowl. "That still isn't a question."

"That was the preface, being that my question is only one word: Why?"

Why indeed? "I think he might have risked losing his leg because I teased about wanting to dance with him."

"You—"

"And if he did do this because of my jests," Theresa pressed, unwilling and unable to stop now that she'd begun, "then everything that follows is my fault. I behaved improperly."

"Nonsense."

"It's not nonsense. Actions have consequences." An unbidden image of her parents touched her, and she mentally brushed it away. "I can't turn my back on him now."

"Do you want to turn your back on him?"

"No. I think I might find him intriguing. But if he loses his leg because I was inappropriate and flirted with him, I'll be doubly obligated to remain with him, regardless. No dancing, no long walks in the evenings, and probably no riding horses because how could he do that with one leg cut off above the knee? I don't even know if he can have children, and you know I've always wanted children, and—"

"I thought it was his knee that had been injured," her grandmother interrupted.

"That's what I've been talking about."

Grandmama Agnes's expression softened into a brief smile. "Then he can very likely father children."

Theresa's heart jolted. "You think I should marry him, then."

"Has he asked you?"

"No, but—"

"Is Colonel Bartholomew James a weak-minded man?"

She frowned. "No. Not at all. I think he's very likely at least as stubborn as I am."

"Then why do you think you caused him to risk his leg?"

"Because he looked at me and said he wanted to dance with me, and then he fainted." That hadn't been precisely what he'd said, but it was close enough.

"I see." Agnes gazed out the window for a moment. "Colonel James wants to dance with you."

"It's more than that, Grandmama, and you know that perfectly well."

"You met him what, a week ago?"

Had it only been seven days? "I believe so."

"Then, my dear, I would suggest that you become acquainted with Colonel Bartholomew James. Decide whether you like him before you plan a marriage with him."

"I—"

"Because if you like him, truly like him, while he has two legs, then I believe you'll like him when or if he has only one. But you need to discover that now, or you'll never know for certain."

"But what he said was—"

"Tess, do not take all the world's burdens and tragedies onto your shoulders. As I've said before, simply because someone brings up your name in regard to an event, doesn't make what follows your fault."

"I find it difficult to believe that he was attempting to mislead me. I'm not very trickable."

Her grandmother stood. "No, you're not. Perhaps he merely wasn't thinking clearly." She strolled over, kissed Theresa on the forehead, and collected Caesar.

Theresa sighed as Grandmama Agnes left the room and closed the door quietly behind her. As usual, her grandmother was correct; she couldn't plan her future without deciphering her present.

And that meant that tomorrow she would have to break another of her own rules and pay a visit to Bartholomew James.

Chapter Eight

"A brush of fingers is a satisfactory and sufficient means of demonstrating affection. But even this must be done cautiously, with a thought toward reputation. Self-restraint, ladies. Always exercise self-restraint."

A LADY'S GUIDE TO PROPER BEHAVIOR

Bartholomew awoke with a start, his hands half raised to ward off an attack. The bedchamber around him, though, was silent and lit with muted light peering around the edges of the heavy window curtains.

Nine months had made quite a difference. He still fought the same injury, but this time he lay propped up by pillows in a comfortable bed. No climbing up steep, crumbling walls using only three limbs, no stealing damned ponies to follow anyone, no riding in the backs of wagons on rutted roads, no fearful questions and angry, disbelieving arguments. At least none of those so far. Not directly to his face.

He lifted up on his elbows. They'd bent his leg over a pillow, bandaging it so that it was held at that angle. While he would have preferred it remain straight, which made hobbling easier, it was too late to do anything about that now. He'd wagered everything he possessed on this strategy, and now all he could do was await the outcome.

His door opened quietly. "Good," Stephen said, stepping into the room. "You're awake."

"More or less." Bartholomew eyed his brother. This was the moment he'd dreaded. Now he had to admit that he was as helpless as a babe in swaddling rags, and now he had to ask for help. "I—"

"Being that you've never been home long enough to employ a valet of your own," his brother interrupted, "and being that I rather like my Gernsey and don't intend to see him run off by your foul temper, I took the liberty of hiring you a man." He gestured behind him, and a short, barrel-chested fellow with a porcupine's backside of brown hair atop his head entered the room. "This is Lackaby."

"Colonel James," the stout man said. And then he drew up his spine, pushed out his chest, and saluted. *Splendid.* "I'm retired," Tolly grunted. "Don't salute me."

"Apologies, Colonel. A habit, don't you know."

"Lackaby served in India, as well," his brother explained. "Fourteen years ago, was it, Sergeant?"

"Yes, my lord. I was on Wellington's personal staff, except he was Major-General Wellesley back then."

"See if you can manage opening the curtains then, will you?"

"Yes, sir." Turning smartly on his heel, Lackaby marched to the windows and began pulling open the dark blue material, flooding the room with welcome sunlight.

"How long did it take you to find a former soldier who'd served in India?" Bartholomew asked his brother in a low voice.

Stephen moved closer. "All of last evening and most of the damned morning. So don't you dare refuse having him here."

"I can't put on my own boots," he muttered back, pushing against the responding sense of helplessness. "I'm not in a position to refuse."

"Good."

The relief on his brother's face was unmistakable. Stephen had been genuinely concerned that he would refuse all assistance. Bartholomew lay back once more on the pile of pillows. Finding a former soldier in need of employment was easy enough these days; they were everywhere now that Bonaparte had surrendered for the second time. Hence the new flood of adventurers and those seeking their fortunes in India and elsewhere. But tracking down a former soldier who'd served in India as an aide-de-camp—that must have been a challenge.

"Thank you, Stephen," he said aloud.

His older brother smiled, his shoulders easing. "You're welcome."

With daylight in the room the fog in his head began to clear. The ache in his leg sharpened as well, but he set his jaw and ignored it. Prentiss had left him a generous supply of laudanum, but he disliked the fuzzy thickness that clogged his mind when he took it. Aside from that, muzzling the pain seemed wrong.

After a few minutes Stephen left him in Lackaby's care, and while he lost what little dignity and privacy he had remaining, he couldn't have done it on his own. When Lackaby approached him with a shaving razor, though, Tolly's chest tightened. "No."

The valet stopped. "You need a shave, Colonel. And if I may say so, your beak is a bit more in proportion than is the duke's. Difficult to make that turn, it is, when the snout juts out further than Gibraltar, but I mastered it. So don't worry; I'll give you a nice, close shave."

The abrupt image of daggers and ribbon-thin garrotes glinting red in firelight struck him with almost palpable force. "No," he repeated more forcefully, sitting up and dragging himself to the edge of the bed. Christ. His foot felt half-numb as it was. All he needed was to rattle the damned thing off.

"But Colonel, the—"

"Don't you fu—"

"Good morning, Tolly."

At the sweet feminine drawl emanating from the open doorway, Bartholomew stopped the black curse he'd been about to utter. "Tess," he said, a sudden sharp elation replacing the bleak fear of a moment ago.

Strolling into the room, she smiled at Lackaby and held out her hands to the servant, palms up. With a puzzled glance between her and Tolly, the valet handed her the razor and shaving cup. "I'll get a cloth then, shall I?" he commented.

"Please do." As soon as the valet left the room, Tess approached the bed. "You looked as though you were going to punch that man," she said.

Tolly settled himself on the pillows again and made an effort not to grimace. "He's my valet. Stephen hired him this morning."

"You didn't have a valet?"

"I had an aide-de-camp in India." And he declined to say where Freddie was now. At least the lad had company. "I generally borrowed Stephen's valet when I was in Town."

She nodded. "So you don't trust this fellow with a sharp blade to your throat."

He watched her expression, waiting for a hint of ridicule or pity. He saw neither. "I prefer to know someone for more than an hour before I give him the opportunity to kill me."

"You've known *me* for more than an hour."

"You want to give me a shave?" Bartholomew asked, attempting to sound dubious but not certain he'd managed it. He liked her touch. When he'd opened his eyes to her stroking his hair, the peace he'd felt had nearly convinced him that he'd died—with her the angel to escort him to St. Peter. Or elsewhere. In her company, the destination hadn't concerned him overly much.

"I'll give it a go, shall I? Sit up a bit." Setting the shaving bits and bobs on the nightstand, she shifted pillows behind him until he was close to upright and they were eye to eye.

"That doesn't inspire much confidence," he said belatedly. "You've never done this before, I take it."

"When would I have? Just tell me the basics. I'm fairly clever at figuring things out."

Surprisingly, even knowing that Tess Weller more than likely represented a larger risk to his health than did Lackaby, he felt less trepidation at the prospect of her shaving him. It was odd, actually, considering that in the past he'd fared better with strangers than with friends. Tess seemed to be in a different category altogether, though—one of her own making.

"Shave downward, in short strokes, and don't lop off my head." He leaned his head back, half closing his eyes as she began brushing shaving soap over his cheeks and down his throat.

Her fingers hesitated. "Good God," she whispered, touching fingertips to the base of his throat. "What happened here?"

Damnation. For a moment he'd actually forgotten about those scars. "One of the Thuggee attempted to strangle me. I got loose; hence the gunshot."

"Are you wounded anywhere else?"

Nowhere that showed. "A few holes and slices," he said aloud. "It's all healed." Bartholomew cleared his throat. "I didn't expect to see you after yesterday," he offered, trying to find something else about which to converse.

"Why? Because I've seen some of your insides? Or because you said you wanted your leg re-broken because you wished to dance with me?"

Tolly sat bolt upright, ignoring the resulting stab of pain in his knee. *"What?"* Oh, good God. He hadn't actually said that aloud, had he?

She nodded, as if hearing his silent question. "A lady doesn't forget when a man says something like that to her." Calmly she set the cup aside and experimentally opened the razor.

"I—if—you know I might well have been delirious from pain and blood loss."

"So you didn't mean it?" The blade paused.

A very uneasy wrench of panic touched his gut again. Swiftly he reached out to block her hand. "That's enough," he muttered, scowling. "I'll see to it." A damned day or two of beard wouldn't hurt anything. It wasn't as if he was attempting to impress anyone.

Immediately her expression dropped into concern. "I apologize, Tolly. I was only bamming you. You were nearly strangled, and here I am, saying those silly things while holding a sharp blade."

"You were teasing," he repeated, studying her gray-green eyes. Considering that she'd been much on his mind yesterday before she'd actually appeared, he might very well have said something that idiotic.

"Yes, I was teasing. Shall we proceed?"

At this point, however compelling he found her presence, he would rather have shaved himself. The current shake of his hands, however, made that a poor idea—especially since he clearly *was* attempting to impress someone. And whatever his reasons, he didn't want her to see him as lacking courage and character. "Do your worst."

"I will do my best, but thank you for lowering your expectations."

An unexpected grin touched his mouth as she leaned forward. "Get a cloth first."

"Stop talking. And no smiling."

Lackaby returned a moment later. He handed over the cloth without protest and went to find a clean nightshirt. At least the valet wasn't prissy about his duties. Bartholomew had never precisely been conventional, and he'd become less so over the past months. "Very well."

He kept his gaze on her as she leaned in again. Steel slid flatly down his cheek toward his jaw. Her lips pursed, her elegant brows knitted in concentration, she wiped off the razor and then repeated the motion. She clearly had little skill, but he would have been more surprised to find otherwise.

For a long moment the only sound in the room was the quiet whoosh and scrape along his cheeks. Tolly began to relax by inches, forgetting the blade as he gazed at her. When he'd returned to London, intimate female companionship had been the last thing on his mind. That wasn't so any longer.

With every stroke she made layers of his darkness fall away. His blood heated, and if not for the sharp blade he would have seriously contemplated pulling her into his arms until she regained her senses and pushed him away. Something broke loose in his chest as her face twisted to match his.

"Do this," she said, elongating her upper lip.

"I don't think I can equal that, but I'll certainly try."

She pinched his nose, apparently determined to wrench it out of her way. "Now who's teasing?" she muttered. "And don't answer that."

From across the room the valet made a sound that might have been either amusement or allergies. Other than noting Lackaby's location, Tolly ignored him.

He had other things to consider. If he hadn't said anything about wanting to dance with Theresa, had such a thing been in her thoughts? Her comments, teasing or not, had come from somewhere. Aside from that, one of the most celebrated beauties of the Season wasn't supposed to be spending her morning shaving an invalid.

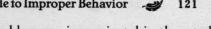

Before she could come in against his throat, he lifted his hand to block her approach again. "Since we both know that I didn't say anything about dancing with you, what are you doing here?" he asked.

"I operated on your leg," she returned.

"You assisted."

"You were unconscious half the time, so you wouldn't possibly know what I did. You're my patient now, and I intend to oversee your recovery."

"And you have nothing better to do?"

She pushed his hand away. "Apparently not."

Before this mess he'd been something of a gambler, a devil-may-care, even a rake. For a few minutes he was going to have to remember who he used to be, and let the chit and the razor have access to his neck. Resolutely he lowered his hand, clenching his fingers into the bedsheets. Then he lifted his chin and closed his eyes. In for a penny, in for a pound, as they said.

After yesterday, Tolly clearly had an excuse to be a bit unsteady. If Theresa had given into fainting and hysterics then, she could have claimed the same thing now. She hadn't done so, however, and at this moment she needed to have very, very steady hands.

Still, she hesitated. The hard-muscled man sitting in the bed beside her clearly had some difficulties with allowing himself to be vulnerable. And she did not want to injure him further. Especially in view of the uneven scars banding his throat—despite what he'd said, she wasn't entirely convince that someone had attempted to choke him to death rather than slice off his head.

The valet by the wardrobe caught her eye. "Shall I?" he mouthed.

She shook her head. Tolly was trusting her. And that trumped the rule about the impropriety of physical contact. With a deep breath she rotated her wrist to loosen the tense muscles there.

"The soap's beginning to dry," Tolly said abruptly. "My face itches."

"I told you not to talk. Now hold still."

"I have been."

Putting her fingers on his warm cheek to steady her aim, she held her breath and scraped the blade down from his chin along his throat. His eyes closed; she didn't know whether that meant he was accepting his fate or preparing for the worst.

If she hadn't been so worried that she would injure him, Theresa was fairly certain she would have enjoyed such intimate contact with him immensely. It was so different from dancing with a man. She shifted her grip so that her finger brushed his skin, following along behind the blade. Smooth, damp, and warm. Heat hummed through her. After this, she would never be able to smell a man's shaving soap without becoming . . . excited. Aroused, even, though she would never admit such a scandalous thing aloud.

She'd wanted to call on him today to determine whether her actions had caused him to act, and therefore rendered her responsible for his current . . . situation. Instead she found herself sinking deeper into his life, into him. Every time they met she did something even less proper, and she enjoyed it more. Surreptitiously she stroked his skin again. Trouble, trouble, trouble.

Finally she had to concede that she was finished. Slowly she wiped the remaining soap from his face with one corner of the cloth. Golden brown eyes opened, gazing into hers. The urge to kiss his slightly smiling mouth seized her so strongly that she had to turn away, busying herself with handing the shaving accouterments over to the valet and hoping the rush of exhilarating madness would pass.

"Thank you, Tess."

"You're welcome, Colonel," she returned, still pretending to dry off her hands and not quite ready to face him. "I'm glad I could help."

"I would have had no idea that you spent your mornings going from house to house, assisting invalids with their morning ablutions," he continued.

So now he wanted to tease her. She turned around. "Well, in this instance, at least, shaving has improved your temperament," she said, lifting an eyebrow at him and still seeking her lost equilibrium. "I can't imagine what miracles might occur if a barber managed to trim your hair."

He didn't even blink, though his eyes darkened with clear amusement. The effect was astounding; handsome before, the warm humor in his gaze now stole her breath. Then he shifted his gaze past her shoulder. "Dr. Prentiss. I'm not dead yet, so my compliments."

"Hold on to those; it's early yet."

As Theresa turned around, the physician approached the bed. "Doctor," she said, inclining her head and not certain whether to be annoyed or grateful that he'd interrupted wherever it was her mind had been going. She knew better than to fall deeper into this . . . morass of impropriety. What was wrong with her?

"Miss Weller. How fares our Colonel today?"

"His hands are unsteady, but his disposition has somewhat improved."

"Good. Will you give us a moment, Miss Weller?"

For a heartbeat she nearly protested that she'd dipped her fingers in the man's blood and she wasn't going anywhere. On the other hand, she had no idea whether Tolly might be naked beneath the sheets. She wished she'd considered that earlier. Ah, well. She couldn't very well be present then, no matter how abruptly curious she might be. Breaking the rules of propriety seemed to be rather more . . . exhilarating than she'd thought. "Certainly."

She sent Bartholomew a last glance that more than likely told him exactly how reluctant she was to go, then retreated into the hallway.

Bartholomew watched her out of the room. Abruptly his semi-pleasant mood fled, and the ache in his leg doubled. He scowled. "How long do I have to stay in this damned bed?"

"If this is an improvement of your disposition, I'm pleased I wasn't here earlier." Prentiss untucked the sheets and shoved them aside, exposing his bandaged leg.

At least it was still there—for now. "How does it look?"

"Your knee and calf are swollen, which I don't like. Can you feel this?" Without warning he jabbed a fingertip into the bottom of Tolly's foot.

"I can feel it."

"Really?" Prentiss lifted his hand again, showing off the pin he held in his fingers.

"I felt something," Tolly growled, uneasiness rising again in his chest.

"Prove it; wiggle your toes."

Bartholomew did so. It took more effort than he expected, as though the distance between his head and his foot had gone from a bit over six feet to a hundred. A sharp spear of pain ran all the way up his leg and clenched into his spine. "Bloody hell, that hurts," he rasped.

"More or less than before?"

So now they were judging degrees of agony. "Well, I hadn't been stabbed in the foot before, but I think it's nearly the same." He considered for a moment, then shifted his toes again. "There's no grinding in my knee now," he admitted.

The doctor nodded, producing a scissor to cut into the thick bandage and peel it off. "That is good, anyway." He grimaced. "Others of my profession would disagree with me, but with the bleeding stopped I'm going to leave this mess open for a day or two." He produced an odd-looking wire tripod and sat it carefully over the knee. "Good. It fits. This should keep the wound from sticking to the sheets."

"That sounds pleasant."

"You've been through infection once. I don't think that knee will withstand it again." Moving with more care than such a large man should have possessed, Prentiss slid a thick cloth beneath the knee, then motioned Lackaby to approach. The valet handed over a bottle of whiskey. "Which is why you're also going to have to go through this twice daily," he continued, and dumped at least half a pint of the stuff over the raw wound.

Bartholomew yelled, lifting half off the bed and yanking the bottle from the physician's grip. "Damnation," he panted, light-headed from shock and pain. "You might have given me a drink of it first." He lifted the bottle to his lips and took several long swallows.

It didn't help, but he supposed it didn't hurt anything, either. Halfway through another drink, Theresa charged back into the room, and he nearly choked. Apparently the sharp-tongued damsel had somehow fashioned herself as his knight-protector. It would have been amusing, except he apparently needed her for that very reason.

"What happened?" she gasped, her cheeks paling.

"The damned doctor tried to murder me," Tolly returned, managing to keep his voice fairly level.

"Mmm-hmm. I hope not," she returned, "or I wasted a great deal of time yesterday."

"As did I," Prentiss seconded, wrestling the bottle back and handing it to Lackaby. "Every twelve hours. Can you manage that?"

The valet nodded. "Yes, sir."

"Good." The physician gently probed around the knee again, then blew out his breath. "I'll be by tomorrow. If you completely lose the feeling in your foot or if your toes stop moving at your command, send for me."

Tolly cocked his head. "And you'll do what, precisely?"

"If your leg dies, Colonel, I'm going to cut it off

before it takes the rest of you to the grave with it." He settled the tripod back in place, then with a nod at Tess, left the room.

Theresa stood staring at his leg as though she expected it to crawl off on its own and beat him over the head. He couldn't mistake the expression in her gray-green eyes; beyond the dismay, she was concerned. Genuinely so. For him.

Apparently one person now cared what happened to him. His family didn't count in that, because they were obligated. And they were also good people. He cleared his throat. "Don't you have another barber appointment somewhere?" he asked. Considering the likely outcome of all this, the best way to keep from further troubling Tess Weller would be to have her go away. Even if he liked having her there. Even if she lightened his soul just a little with her presence. Because he wasn't certain he was prepared to have his burdens all lifted away. Being without them troubled him.

"I'm quite exclusive," she answered easily, sitting in the chair Stephen or someone had placed at his bedside last night. "So the remainder of my afternoon is free."

He regarded her for a long moment. "You're the one who keeps mentioning propriety, Theresa. Which means I have to ask, what are you doing here? Truthfully."

Her gaze lowered briefly to her hands before she looked up at him again. "I don't know why I'm here. I just am. So unless you ask me to leave, I suppose for the moment I'll stay."

She tilted her head, a strand of her summer-colored

hair escaping from its pins to glide softly along her cheek. Absently she brushed it back again. He followed the motion, his fingers twitching with the abrupt desire to perform that service, himself.

"Do you want me to go?" she pursued, a half smile on her face as if she knew that any man in his right mind would never send her away.

No, I don't, he acknowledged. "Yes," he said aloud. "Thank you for your assistance, but I'd prefer to sleep."

"Then sleep. I think you're attempting to appear to be a stoic loner, and you're upset because I'm denting your facade."

A laugh erupted from his chest before he could stop it. At the surprised delight in her eyes, he abruptly felt better—despite the fact that his knee throbbed and he hadn't laughed in so long that that almost hurt, as well. "That might be part of it," he admitted.

"And what is the other part of the reason you wish me gone? Because propriety doesn't seem to concern *you* at all."

He gazed at her. There were so many things he could say, and yet he sensed that if he said the wrong thing, the flip thing, she *would* leave. "You make me feel . . . lighter," he stumbled. "I'm not certain I'm comfortable with that."

Color touched her cheeks as she nodded. "Perhaps you could put it to fever and delirium. That's what I intend to do. Because if you were sound, I wouldn't be able to visit with you here."

Abruptly she stood and walked away. Before he could protest her departure, though, she stopped in front of the bookcase. He had no idea what she might be looking for, but asking questions seemed to encourage her to do the same. Nor did he want to delve into when he'd gone from wanting her gone to needing her to stay.

"Ah. This should do," she said after a moment. Theresa pulled a book from the middle shelf and returned to his bedside. Gracefully she sank into the chair, her light blue muslin skirts draping around her legs.

Tolly flexed his toes. The pain seemed to be the only thing that could keep the wire tripod as the only tent of his bedsheets. "Are you intending on reading to yourself, or to me?"

"Reading to myself would be rude." Her eyes dancing, she cleared her throat. "*Golden Sun of the Serengeti*, by Captain Bennett Wolfe." She looked up as she opened the cover. "He's actually Captain Sir Bennett Wolfe now," she said. "He was knighted because of this book."

He knew that. He'd also both met the man and read the book. "Hmm," he said aloud. "That sounds impressive."

"I am not ignorant of the fact that this book comes from your bookshelf, you know. And fall asleep if you wish. I intend to remain here until four o'clock, regardless."

"What happens at four o'clock?"

"I need to return home and dress. The Saunders dinner is at seven."

Theresa flipped past the title page and the nonsense about the publisher, while he reminded himself that he wouldn't have been invited to or attending the Saunders dinner even if he hadn't been confined to bed. The distinct jealousy creeping through him was therefore both uncalled for and ridiculous.

"Ready?" she asked.

Tolly settled into the pillows. For effect he should probably close his eyes, and in fact he could barely keep them open as it was, but for at least a few minutes he wanted to watch her read. "Ready. Transport me to Africa."

Her lips curved in a soft smile, and she began to read. And for the first time in better than eight months he fell asleep thinking of something other than India and regret.

Chapter Nine

"A lady never pursues. It is the gentleman who decides whether to pay a call, who decides the nature of any outing, and who ultimately declares himself. All we can do is comport ourselves so as to attract the right gentleman."

A LADY'S GUIDE TO PROPER BEHAVIOR

Theresa played the two of hearts, then feigned a frown as Jane Redmond and her partner proceeded to thrash her and Grandmama Agnes at whist. Yes, she should likely have been paying more attention to the game, but she happened to be more concerned with other things. At the moment her main worry was the relentless way that Sarah Saunders was flirting with Michael.

Her brother generally knew better than to be impressed by batting lashes and compliments to his broad shoulders, but tonight he'd scarcely looked at anyone else in the room. Under different circumstances the idea that her brother might be intrigued by someone wouldn't overly trouble her, for she would be more than happy to add a sister-in-law to their small family. But quite simply and quite uncharacteristically of her, she didn't like Sarah Saunders. Not one little bit.

They were of nearly the same age, but Miss Saunders had somewhere decided to become a horrible gossip. And the information she most enjoyed hearing and repeating was the bit with sting. Theresa had never been the recipient herself, but then she made being proper the main focus of her life.

She drew a breath. "Grandmama, I seem to be utterly destroying any chance for victory. Shall I see if Mrs. Wingate would care to replace me?"

Grandmama Agnes snorted. "If we weren't blood relatives, my sweet, I would have cast you aside thirty minutes ago. Yes, for heaven's sake, find Jenny."

Grinning, Theresa excused herself from the game. Jenny Wingate had been sending the players glances all evening—Lord Saunders's sister was an inveterate gambler. In less than a minute Theresa found herself replaced and utterly forgotten. And that, thankfully, left her free to meddle.

At least that was the plan. When she reached Michael's side, she wrapped her hands around her brother's arm. "What are you up to?" she asked with a broad smile.

He glanced down at her, his gaze surprisingly serious despite the grin he bore. "Just attempting to decipher the mystery of the ages—why Sarah Saunders remains unmarried."

Sarah giggled. "It's because I am so very particular."

"Well, it's certainly not for lack of beaux," Theresa

added with another unfelt smile. "Might I steal my brother away for a moment?"

"Certainly." Sarah sketched a curtsy. "Pray don't go too far, Lord Weller."

As soon as she and Michael crossed the room to stand beneath the pretty garden window, Theresa pinched the back of his hand. "What are you doing?"

"Ouch," he exclaimed, jerking his hand free. "Stop that, Troll."

"That didn't hurt."

"It hurt that you thought I needed to be rescued." He sent a glance at Sarah, already busily chatting with another trio of her friends. "That chit is dangerous."

Theresa stopped her frown. "Why? What did she say?"

"She said that her maid heard third-hand from someone at James House that Colonel James tried to kill himself yesterday."

For a moment, she stared at her older brother. "That's ridiculous."

"That is what I was attempting to imply when you dragged me away." He tapped the tip of her nose with one forefinger. "I am not, contrary to your thinking, a complete imbecile."

Finally she gave a genuine smile. "I never thought that. It's only that you frequently baffle me."

"Mmm-hmm." He took a step closer, looking out the window to cover the motion. "We need to speak with Amelia. Whatever the colonel's troubles, the family doesn't need their servants bandying tales about London."

Her smile faded. "Michael, Bartholomew James

did not attempt to kill himself. He asked a physician to re-break his leg, so it would have a chance to heal correctly." She folded her arms across her chest. "And I know that for certain, because I was there. In fact, I assisted with the surgery."

Michael whipped back around to face her, his expression startled and his complexion paling. "What?"

"You heard me."

He continued to glare at her. "Thank God Sarah hasn't heard about that. Troll, you cannot go about assisting surgeries willy-nilly. You're a viscount's sister, and a duke's granddaughter."

"I never do anything willy-nilly," Theresa protested. "Captain James is our cousin-in-law."

"There's no such thing." Michael blew out his breath. "Isn't it enough for you just to enjoy the Season?" he said more quietly. "You've been out for nearly five years. If you're bored, agree to one of the million proposals you've been handed, and marry someone."

Bother. It always boiled down to marriage, lately. "It's closer to a dozen proposals, and several of those were from the same men. And I imagine I'll settle down and marry once I begin to have less variety from which to choose." Lifting her chin, she walked away from him.

She supposed she might have mentioned that he was three years her elder and hadn't married, either, but truthfully she didn't feel much like having that argument tonight. As long as he wasn't seriously flirting with Sarah Saunders, he could do as he pleased. With three of her current suitors in attendance she could likely do some flirting herself, but flirting well took concentration, and tonight her thoughts remained rather scattered.

Tomorrow she would have to inform Tolly that at least one rumor claimed he'd attempted suicide. He wouldn't much like that. In fact, it might make him wish to withdraw even further from Society—if that were even possible. But from what she'd learned of him, he would prefer to know what was being said behind his back to remaining blissfully ignorant. Not that she could imagine him being blissful about anything.

"Tess, Tess," Miss Harriet Silder called as she fluttered up, "there you are. Do you have any idea how many men have stopped me tonight to ask whether you would like to go riding tomorrow?"

Theresa grinned, taking her friend's hand. "They might ask me that question and save us all a bit of bother."

"Yes, but if they ask me, then they haven't been turned away by you." Harriet pulled her in the direction of the open balcony doors, and together they made their way through the crowd.

The air was much cooler outside, and Theresa took a deep breath as she leaned her elbows on the railing to look across the Saunders House carriage drive. "How long do you think we could remain out here before we're missed?" she asked, slipping one foot half out of her shoe and flexing her toes.

Harriet shook her pretty dark curls. "I think it might be more worrisome not to be missed."

With a laugh, Theresa kicked out of her other shoe. "It might be worth experiencing."

Her friend leaned beside her, knocking into her elbow. "I called on you this afternoon. Ramsey said you'd gone to visit an ill friend. Who's ill?"

"Oh, drat. My apologies, Harriet. I shall make it up to you." Theresa studied the outline of the stable for a moment. This morning she'd crossed out two paragraphs of her new guide and rewritten another. Whatever was afoot, she didn't like it. Well, she wasn't supposed to like it, anyway. "I was actually visiting at James House. You know Amelia's brother-in-law is crippled."

She felt rather than saw Harriet looking sideways at her. "So Colonel James is the ill friend?"

For a second she hesitated, and then was angry with herself for doing so. Yes, he was far from being one of Society's favorites, and yes, he was abrupt and occasionally insulting. But he'd done nothing wrong. Nothing other than being the subject of Sarah Saunders's latest gossip, anyway. Nothing other than kissing her—but no one else knew about that. "Yes. Amelia said he wasn't feeling well, so I decided to stop in and cheer him up." Not quite the truth, but Tolly might very well not wish anyone to know the particulars of his recent injury. Re-injury, rather.

"I heard that he—"

"He didn't," she cut in. "Please don't tell me you actually listen to Sarah's gossip."

Harriet sighed. "I do try not to, but she's so very good at it." She smiled. "So, what is Colonel James like? I saw him years ago, and I thought I glimpsed him at the Ridgemont soiree the night before last, but I can't say we've ever been introduced."

"He's . . . interesting. And very witty, which I have to say surprised me a bit."

"And handsome. I did notice that."

For a second Theresa reflected that she didn't much like other ladies—even good friends like Harriet Silder—noticing how handsome Tolly was. Then she decided she was being absolutely ridiculous. "Yes, he is very pleasing to the eyes."

"Do you . . . Hmm. Speaking of pleasing to the eyes," Harriet muttered, leaning forward to look more closely at the horse one of the grooms was leading from around the front of the house, "isn't that Montrose's animal?"

"Yes, it is. Topsy. I hadn't realized Alexander would be attending tonight."

"Well, he's certainly missed the dinner. I wonder what the lure could be?" Harriet grinned at her.

"Very amusing. If he's here, it is because Sarah or her parents invited him. I had nothing to do with it."

"Ah. So he's pursuing Sarah, then, is he?" Harriet elbowed her again. "What's troubling you?"

Other than rumors that a hero for whom she felt a very troubling attraction had attempted to do himself harm? "Nothing," she said aloud. "I'm a little surprised at myself for coming here, I suppose."

Her friend straightened, taking Theresa's arm to return her to the drawing room. "You're here because your grandmother asked you to come," she said with a smile. "Now be your usual charming self, and Montrose will never know you're less than pleased to see him."

"It's not that," Theresa protested. "For heaven's

sake." All she needed was to gain a reputation for being some kind of disapproving ice queen. It was only that tonight she felt as though there was something else she would rather be doing.

"Then I shan't set my cap at Montrose," Harriet whispered, grinning.

Theresa didn't think she would mind all that much if anyone else did pursue the marquis. Not that she didn't like Alexander—she liked all of her suitors. It was just the feeling that they shouldn't be wasting so much of their time waiting for her.

"Tess," Lord Montrose said, grinning warmly as he met them in the middle of the drawing room. "And Harriet. How pleasant to see you here this evening." Glancing at the scattering of guests around them, he deepened his smile. "If I'd known how many lovely young ladies would be present tonight, I most certainly would have put my estate manager off until tomorrow."

"Everything is well at Montrose Park, I hope," Theresa responded, taking his arm when he offered it.

"Yes. Just a few questions about which fields to plant. Thank you for your concern."

"Well, you've told me several times how lovely it is there. I would hate to learn that it's been overrun by rabbits or squirrels or something."

The marquis laughed. "That might ruin the crops, but it would improve the hunting." He placed his free hand over hers where it rested on his sleeve. "You could be Montrose's mistress, you know," he continued in a lower voice. "All you need do is tell me yes."

A nervous flutter touched her stomach. Then she

set a smile on her face. "You are very kind, Alexander. And you know I'm simply not yet quite ready to marry."

He nodded, his expression not altering a jot. "Knowing the eventual outcome, I remain patient." His fingers tightened briefly, then released hers. "Though you do realize that at least announcing our engagement would save me from invitations to dinners like this one. And it would save you from having to dance with the likes of Francis Henning."

"Suffering builds character," she returned, then had to push away the unbidden image of Bartholomew James lying pale and unconscious in his bed. By all rights he should have the most character of anyone she'd ever met. "Speaking of which," she continued aloud, freeing her hand from his arm, "our hostess didn't invite you here to flirt with me."

With a mock scowl he sketched a bow and retreated across the room. For the remainder of the evening Theresa wandered from group to group—not so much to avoid monopolizing anyone, but rather because she couldn't escape the restlessness beneath her own skin, the sensation that she would much rather be elsewhere. Finally she couldn't stand it any longer. The moment her grandmother finished a game, and before they could begin another round, she hurried forward.

"Grandmama," she leaned down to whisper, "I've a terrible aching head. Would you mind horribly if—"

Grandmama Agnes slid approximately two pounds' worth of coins off the table and into her palm. "I am being a scoundrel," she announced, standing, "taking my winnings and leaving."

"You're a cruel woman, Agnes," Lord Wilcox returned with a grin. "Promise me a chance to win back my losses."

"We shall have to see about that."

She took Theresa's arm as they went to find Michael. "You are so coy," Theresa whispered with a smile.

"In all these years I'd like to think I've learned how to entice a man," her grandmother returned. "Michael? Michael. Escort us home. Your sister doesn't feel well."

Dash it all. At her grandmother's pronouncement everyone began crowding in, asking whether she felt ill and if they might call on her tomorrow. Generally she would have felt guilty for pulling attention away from the party's hostess; she'd never been much for petty dramatics. Not since she was ten, anyway. Tonight, however, what she most felt was impatience—she was impatient to be home with her own thoughts, and she was impatient for tomorrow when she could go chat with Colonel Bartholomew James again.

"I'll have Mrs. Reilly send you up some tea," her grandmother said, giving her a brief hug as they walked into the Weller House foyer.

"I don't think she needs tea," Michael put in, stooping to scoop up one of their grandmother's newest acquisitions, a fluffy white kitten they'd named Cotton. "I think she was trying to separate me from my new beloved, Sarah."

Theresa grimaced at him. "Please don't even jest about that. She's horrid."

"She is my dear friend's niece," the family's matron put in, plucking an additional cat, brown Mr. Brown, from the hall table. "Though truthfully I don't think Jenny is terribly pleased with Sarah's wagging tongue, either." She eyed the butler. "Why are my cats all over the foyer?"

Ramsey bowed. "Henry went up to feed them, my lady, and he claims they ambushed him in order to escape."

"They missed me, no doubt." Grandmama Agnes retrieved another of the purring animals. "Come, my dears," she cooed, climbing the stairs, "Mama Agnes will find you some cream."

A trail of cats ascended the stairway behind her. With an amused snort Michael set Cotton down, and the kitten clambered up after them. "How many are there now?"

"At least a dozen." Theresa sighed. "I'm going up to bed."

Her brother stepped around her to block the stairs. "What's got you so melancholy?"

"I'm not melancholy. I'm thoughtful."

"Also unlike you," he countered with a teasing grin. "You know I would never seriously consider marriage to Miss Saunders."

"I know that. I would kidnap you and lock you in the cellar if you attempted it."

He grinned. "Now you sound like yourself. Proper, but fearsome." Michael lightly pinched her nose as he moved out of her way. "Good night, Troll."

"Perhaps you *should* marry Sarah," she decided, shaking her head at him. "You would certainly appreciate my kindness and graciousness more in comparison."

"Mmm-hmm. By the way, I'm going riding with

Gardner in the morning, if you want me to escort you over to see Leelee."

Her breath caught, abrupt excitement coursing through her. "At what time should I be ready?"

"Nine o'clock. Frightfully early for you, I know, so I'll understand if you—"

"I'll be ready." She'd thought to have to conjure an excuse to visit James House and the colonel therein, and now one had been handed to her. Little as she cared to trust in providence, this did seem rather lucky. Not for her fondness for proper behavior, but definitely for her tumbling mind.

"The physician said you were to remain in bed, Colonel." Lackaby paused halfway through opening the bedchamber's curtains and turned, frowning, to face the bed.

"I take anything a damned sawbones tells me with a grain of salt," Tolly replied, shoving aside the sheets and pulling himself backward, toward the headboard. "And I'm still in bed. I'm merely sitting up in it."

The valet squinted one eye, then returned to opening the room. "That was Arthur's way, too. 'No one on this damned continent outranks me, Lackaby,' he'd say, and 'I bloody well don't follow anyone's orders but my own.'"

Bartholomew lifted an eyebrow. "You called the future Duke of Wellington, Arthur?"

"Not to his face. But I suppose I can tell the story however I wish to."

"I suppose you can."

With a nod, Lackaby went to the dressing table

and gathered all the neatly arranged shaving items there. "Since your lady isn't here, I reckon I can hold the mirror if your hands are steady enough to do the shaving."

"Yes," Tolly agreed, somewhat relieved that he wouldn't have to have that argument again today. Then he frowned. "But she's not my lady."

"No? It looked . . . well, never mind that, then. Whose lady is she?"

Bartholomew was fairly certain that servants weren't supposed to pry—at least it had been that way the last time he'd been in England. Even so, he didn't precisely give a damn. "She's her own lady, I'm fairly certain. And my brother is wed to her cousin."

"Ah. So she's family."

Oh, she was definitely not family. At least he had never for an instant thought of her as a relation. In fact, persons who thought about their family members the way he continually thought about her could be arrested for it. "Yes, family," he said aloud, deciding he didn't care to explain how or why the broken, battered weed was lusting after the Season's fairest flower.

He flexed his toes again, as he had been doing every ten minutes or so during every waking hour. The motion still hurt, but less sharply now. Either that or he was simply becoming accustomed to the new pain, as he had to the old.

Lackaby leaned in to eye his knee. "I think the swelling's gone down a bit," the valet observed, handing over the brush and soap. "Your brother the viscount means to purchase you a wheeled chair."

Anger stabbed through him. "Does he now? Why doesn't he purchase me a damned headstone and be done with it?"

"A headstone's less maneuverable at soirees," the valet returned, holding out the cup of soapy water and the brush.

"You have a very clever tongue, Lackaby," Tolly snapped. "Keep it between your teeth."

With a slight bow, Lackaby angled the mirror so that Tolly could begin shaving. "Yes, Colonel."

The process took longer than usual, but then his arm kept becoming fatigued and succumbing to the shakes. By the time Lackaby collected the razor and handed over a towel, Bartholomew was ready to lie down for a rest again. Clenching his jaw, he kept his seat.

"Dr. Prentiss says you are to have only tea, a beef broth, and toasted bread," the servant commented as he replaced items on the dressing table. "What shall I fetch you for breakfast, then?"

"Tea, toasted bread, and a poached egg or two." He didn't have much of an appetite this morning, but he had no intention of remaining in bed for a second longer than he had to.

"Very good." The valet didn't bat an eye. "I'll be back in a moment."

Once Lackaby vanished, Bartholomew swung his good leg over the edge of the bed and reached over for the cane someone had left behind a chair. "Damnation," he muttered, glaring at the polished stick of stout, scorched ash. His third leg, decidedly out of his reach.

"You even curse when no one else can hear you?" the cheerful female voice came from the doorway. "That's very dedicated of you."

He lowered his hand. Warmth eased through him, from his shoulders down to his toes. It felt as if the room had suddenly become bathed in sunlight. "I've already shaved," he said, as Theresa Weller swirled into the room, all sparkling eyes and yellow muslin gown. "Apologies, but I didn't know how far afield your services to the wretched might take you."

"Hmm." With a coy smile she walked up to the side of the bed and leaned in to run her forefinger along his cheek. "Very smooth," she said, her voice oddly pitched.

That was bloody well enough of that. Bartholomew grabbed her hand. "I think I warned you about teasing me," he murmured.

"Don't kiss me; it's not seemly," she returned, placing her free hand on his shoulder and leaning in to brush her lips against his.

And he'd thought to be the aggressor. Bartholomew drew her forward to sit across his thighs, lifting his hands to cup her pretty face. Whatever the devil was wrong with her, she seemed to like him—and he hoped with an odd fierceness that nothing would happen to alter her opinion.

She moaned softly, the sound spearing through him. Abruptly the ten months he'd been celibate felt like years, and he shifted. For a great while he'd never expected to want anyone ever again, but Theresa Weller decimated that thought with no more than a sigh and a kiss.

A male throat cleared from the doorway. With a stifled yelp, Theresa leaped off his lap. Pain tore through his knee as he tried to catch his balance. "Damnation," he rasped.

"Oh! Oh, I'm sorry!" Tess, her cheeks flushed, clutched her fingers into his shoulder as though she thought he would fall out of the bed. "I forgot."

His attention immediately arrested, Tolly looked up at her. "So did I."

Her smile drove away every shadow in the room. "Then I take it back. I'm not sorry."

"Should I go out and come in again?" Lackaby asked. A large tray of food in his arms, the grinning servant looked from Tolly to Tess.

"No. And stop bloody grinning, you cheeky bastard," Bartholomew ordered.

"One thing's been clarified," the valet said, coming forward to fold down the tray's short legs and set it across Bartholomew's vacated lap. "You ain't family."

"I'll see to feeding him, Lackaby," Tess commented. "Will you fetch me some tea?"

His satisfaction with the kiss fading, Tolly frowned. "I'm not helpless. Not today, at any rate."

"Then pretend you're making me feel helpful." She gave him an assessing look, then reach out to tug on a lock of his dark hair. God, he hadn't been so intimate with anyone in months.

Bartholomew glanced at Lackaby. "You heard her. Get some bloody tea for the chit."

Lackaby saluted and vanished out the door. "You know," she said immediately, brushing a finger along the edge of the mattress, "if you weren't bedridden I wouldn't be able to sit here with you."

He swallowed. "Seems a shame, then, to waste the moment." Reaching out one damnably unsteady hand, he gripped her wandering fingers. "You are rather compelling, Theresa," he murmured, "even to a man half dead."

Her cheeks darkened. "Thank you." Clearing her throat, she eyed Bartholomew's overflowing breakfast tray. "That looks . . . ambitious," she commented.

It was. "I requested eggs and toast, which was more than Dr. Prentiss recommended. I can only assume that Lackaby is attempting to kill me." He gestured at the chair still resting beside the bed. "I don't suppose you'd care for any of this."

Tess grinned again, the expression lighting her gray-green eyes. "I thought you'd never ask."

So she wouldn't take the hint and kiss him again, but she would share his plate. That was something, anyway—though he wasn't quite certain what it all meant. At the moment he was more than willing to take the time to figure it out.

As Lackaby returned with a tea tray, Amelia and Violet appeared in the doorway. He knew they weren't there because of the kiss, since neither of his female relations looked ready to shoot anyone. At least Lackaby knew when to hold his tongue, then. Perhaps he and the valet would make do, after all.

"Tess!" Amelia exclaimed. "Lackaby said you were here."

"Oh, yes," she said, around a mouthful of sweetbread. "I came with Michael. I didn't think you'd risen yet."

"Of course," Amelia said, in a highly skeptical voice. "Might I have a word with you, cousin?"

Theresa nodded. "Certainly." As she stood, she placed a hand on the headboard and leaned closer to Tolly. "I have some news for you, as well," she whispered, her voice pitched so that only he would be able to hear it. "And you won't like it."

As long as the news wasn't that she'd decided to stop calling on him, he didn't much care what it might be.

Chapter Ten

"As young ladies we are taught embroidery and the pianoforte, decorum, and hopefully French. I have never encountered a circumstance where one of those things hasn't served to save an evening or a conversation or a reputation."

A LADY'S GUIDE TO PROPER BEHAVIOR

Theresa followed Amelia into the upstairs hallway of James House. "What is it?" she asked.

"What are you doing?" Her cousin glanced toward Tolly's open bedchamber door and retreated a few additional steps. "Aside from sharing breakfast with my brother-in-law."

"I'm not doing anything." Theresa shrugged. "I think Tolly is interesting, and quite witty when he's not spitting profanity at everyone. And he's stuck in bed. Shouldn't he have some friends to keep him company?"

"Yes, he should. But you aren't one of them."

Theresa frowned. "I have to disagree. In fact, I've

likely exchanged more conversation with him than you have, and you sleep across the hallway from him."

"He doesn't want to talk to me," Amelia returned, her jaw tight. "And frankly, I find him a bit frightening."

"Well, that's the difference, then. I don't find him frightening."

"You should."

Resisting the urge to stomp her foot and fold her arms across her chest, Theresa gazed at her cousin and dearest friend. "Are you asking me to leave him be? Because if you are, I hope you have a better reason than the fact that a man who's fought and been wounded for his country gives you the shivers."

"It's not that. For heaven's sake." Amelia took a breath. "People talk, Tess. You know that. And with even a hint of . . . peculiarity about the incident, people stay away from him. You, however, are balancing how many suitors now?"

"Oh, I don't know. Several."

"You're quite popular, and you're generally so careful of your reputation. But you're not married yet. If you stand too long with Tolly, all of your beaux will go elsewhere. What will you do then?"

A slight shiver of uneasiness ran through her, and she shoved it away again. She'd worked so hard for so long at behaving. She'd never been tempted before to kiss rogues. Why did Tolly have that power over her? "You're being ridiculous," she said aloud. "I enjoy jesting with your brother-in-law. No one will hold that against me. In fact, you should be thanking me. Heaven knows he could stand to recall some manners."

"Something which most everyone has noted."

She didn't mention the kissing, or the fact that while she did feel like they were becoming friends, it wasn't friendship that had her waking up with her first thought being that she would see Tolly James that day. "I think I know what's acceptable and what isn't," she said aloud. "In fact, sitting with a wounded soldier is much more admirable than ignoring him. This is practically a duty."

Amelia looked at her skeptically. "Who are you attempting to convince?"

"I'm already convinced. And perhaps I'm just a bit . . . tired of frivolity. Tolly's not overly concerned with the state of his cravat, for example." That was a large part of his attraction, in fact, now that she considered it. Lionel or Francis might see picking the Derby winner as the most telling moment of a lifetime, but Tolly's world was much larger than that. His experience colored their every conversation. And their every kiss.

"So you've operated on him, shaved him, and now you intend to feed him?" Amelia was saying, her expression still unconvinced.

"Yes."

"He has a valet."

"He doesn't trust anyone else to hold a sharp implement close to his throat."

"But he trusts you?"

Blood rushed just beneath her skin. "I suppose he does."

"Why?"

Theresa shrugged. "All I've done is speak plainly to him. Perhaps he appreciates honesty."

"I don't think that's all he appreciates."

"What do you mean by that?"

Her cousin took a deep breath. "Men adore you, Tess. Why shouldn't he be one of them? I know he's handsome, but as I recall you've been keeping a journal on proper behavior for the past thirteen years. This doesn't seem to fit into any chapter you've published."

"Then perhaps I need to put it into my new booklet."

Amelia had a very good point, whether Theresa meant to acknowledge it or not. She didn't go about feeding and shaving and bantering with other unacceptable men. How was she supposed to reconcile this . . . obsession with Tolly James to the generally accepted rules of proper behavior? Because spending time with him didn't seem proper, but it did feel very exhilarating.

"Do as you will, then. But keep this in mind. Stephen invited Lord Hadderly over for dinner the other night. He thought having the London head of the East India Company thank Tolly for his service and sacrifice might help his brother become more social, and it might halt those awful rumors. Hadderly declined to attend."

Oh, dear. "Does Tolly know that?"

"No. And please don't tell him."

She had enough ill news to deliver. "I won't."

"So what I'm saying, I suppose, is be cautious, Tess."

Before Amelia could conjure a further argument, Theresa stepped back into the room where Bartholomew sat up in bed, his breakfast still across his lap. For a moment, she paused. This morning, and with this man, she couldn't seem to keep in mind that there was a possibility of disaster—much less that she might be waltzing straight into it. And that was very unlike her.

Bartholomew eyed her. "Had some sense talked into you, then?"

Theresa favored him with a mock frown. "If I listened to every bit of advice given me, I would at this moment be married to the Earl of Lorch—or rather, I would be the deceased Lady Lorch, because he's sent two wives to the grave already in his pursuit of fathering children every other damned day."

"I'll give you a point for the appropriate application of profanity," he commented.

"Thank you." And thank goodness Leelee hadn't heard her swearing. If it took a few curse words to put Tolly more at ease and to make her feel a bit rebellious, then so be it. She sat in the bedside chair again to finish her sweetbread and the tea at her elbow.

"Why *aren't* you married?" Bartholomew asked abruptly. "Discounting Lorch, from my observations your suitors numbered altogether could guard the gates of Thermopylae against the invading Persians."

She snorted. "I do not have three hundred suitors, but thank you for the analogy."

Soft amusement touched his whiskey-colored eyes, then fled again. A few days ago she would have been hard-pressed to believe that he possessed a sense of humor, though Violet had insisted that he used to have one. Whether it was pain or guilt or something else that had kept it mostly at bay, she, for one, was pleased to see and hear even the hint of a laugh in him. It seemed vitally important that she help him find his smile.

"You didn't answer my question," he prompted after a moment.

With a shrug she dusted crumbs from her fingers while she decided what to say. Her world was smaller than his, but he wasn't the only one with topics he didn't wish to discuss. "With Amelia married and moved away, my family consists of my brother, our grandmother, and me," she finally offered. "We're quite wealthy—and I'm not bragging; it's merely a statistical fact. Michael has promised to support me even if he marries a shrew and I become an old spinster, so I don't feel the need to barge wide-eyed into matrimony."

A grin made his eyes dance. "Very nice foresight, to factor in the shrewish sister-in-law."

"Yes, I thought so, though I don't intend to allow him to marry anyone disagreeable." Theresa weighed her next question. Best, though, to know the lay of the land before launching an all-out assault. She lifted an eyebrow. "Why aren't *you* married?"

For a heartbeat he gazed at her. "I'm broken."

"Your mouth isn't broken. It kisses quite well, actually, if you were to ask my opinion."

"Thank you for that, but we both know that's not what I meant."

Theresa folded her hands neatly in her lap. "How, then, are you broken?" she finally asked.

"Other than the obvious?"

To her relief he didn't seem angry, and she let out the breath she'd been silently holding. How far she

could push him this morning she had no idea, but
if the reward was more kisses or at least a grudging
smile, she was willing to attempt it. There was something thrilling about being smitten with someone.
She'd certainly never felt this way before. "Yes, other
than your leg."

He looked away, toward the window.

She gazed at his profile. "You already told me about
being flung into the well."

"And that's enough."

"I need to tell you something that will make you
even less happy." Theresa paused, somewhat put out
that he wouldn't confide any further in her. "There
are some rumors going about that you attempted to
take your own life. I suppose it's because Dr. Prentiss
came calling."

"It's because people would rather I wasn't here," he
said, his mouth flattening.

"That's a rather broad statement."

"Step in my shoes, and see how you view things."

Theresa narrowed her eyes. Not only did he not
trust her with his tale, but he dismissed her opinion altogether. Didn't he realize she was risking her
reputation simply by associating with him? "Clearly
we have had different experiences. I suppose I could
make guesses about what troubles you, but I will
assume that this will make you sullen again. After
all, I can't possibly understand what it's like to be
responsible for someone and then survive while they
perish." Her voice shook the veriest bit, but she didn't
think he noticed.

Bartholomew sent her a sharp glance. "I'm not
looking to be soothed, Theresa. But I don't appreci-

ate being cut at again, either. Not by you." He sent his gaze back to the window. "Go find one of your suitors and jest with him."

"Tolly."

He ignored her.

Slapping her palms against her thighs, Theresa stood. "That," she said quietly, "is what I meant by sullen. I suppose you should be thankful that you have the luxury to be so." With that she left the room, collected Sally, and called for her coach.

Clearly she'd pushed too hard. He had no intention of trusting her, after all. And she wasn't as taken with him as she'd imagined. That last conversation hadn't been the least bit amusing. Theresa blew out her breath as she sank back in the coach. Perhaps, though, that was the point. For several years now she'd been working quite hard at being amusing and pleasant and proper. It all seemed to be wearing a bit thin.

Lackaby looked around the emptied bedchamber. "I don't suppose you'd like me to help you finish off that lovely repast then, Colonel?"

"No. I wouldn't." Bartholomew continued the long line of profanity he'd begun muttering under his breath. Tess might think she knew some curse words, but she'd never been in the company of soldiers during combat.

"Finished eating?"

With another glare at the valet, Bartholomew nodded. Their conversation had been proceeding well; hell, he'd even made her laugh. And then she'd . . . what, exactly? She'd given him ill news, then called him sullen, which he undoubtedly was. In fact, he had little objection to that description. No, Theresa Weller had said, whether jestingly or not, that she understood what he'd been through. As if a wealthy, well-born chit with a million suitors could understand anything about pain and fear and death.

The valet removed the tray from the bed. "Might I fetch you a book or something?" he asked, apparently unaffected by the continuing stream of profanity.

"Hand me my cane, and make yourself scarce."

Lackaby drew a breath in through his nose. "I can certainly depart, Colonel, but I'll be sacked if I hand you that stick."

"I'll sack you if you don't."

"You don't pay my salary."

Bartholomew narrowed his eyes. "Then fetch me my brother."

"Gone riding, sir."

This torture was all beginning to seem very intentional. "Violet?"

"Walking."

Bartholomew took a breath of his own. "My sister-in-law, then."

"I'll fetch her, Colonel." Turning smartly on his heel, the valet marched out of the room, more than likely devouring the remainder of his master's breakfast as he went.

As soon as the man was gone, Bartholomew pulled himself sideways to the edge of the bed. The cane was well out of reach now, at least ten feet away. Matched against how badly he wanted to be out of the house and at least free to hobble about the garden, though, it seemed worth the effort.

He swung his good leg over the edge of the bed and placed his bare foot solidly on the floor. For just a second, he closed his eyes. Of course it would hurt; it always hurt. That hadn't stopped him thus far.

"Don't you dare!"

The sharp voice actually froze him for a moment, and he looked up, feeling for a heartbeat like a boy caught with his hand in the biscuit jar. "Lady Gardner."

Stephen's petite, blonde wife stalked into the room. "Get back into that bed at once!"

He could of course ignore the order. As he fully expected to end up crawling on the floor until he could reach his cane, however, he would certainly appear more pitiful than defiant. Narrowing his eyes for effect, Bartholomew swung his good leg back onto the bed.

"Thank you." Visibly squaring her shoulders, the viscountess continued forward more calmly. "Now. What is it I may do for you?"

"I've changed my mind," he grunted. "Apologies. Good day."

"I see." Glancing about the room, her gaze settled on the book Tess had left on the bed stand. "Perhaps I'll just sit here and read for a bit. I like to mumble, you see, and that's considered very poor manners. Here I can pretend I'm reading to you, and no one will be the wiser."

"And what did I do to merit this bit of charity?" Bartholomew asked, beginning to wonder if insanity ran through Lord Weller's family.

"You ran Tess out of the house."

That stopped him for a moment. "You don't like

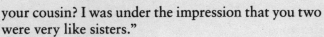

your cousin? I was under the impression that you two
were very like sisters."

"Oh, we are."

"Then what—"

She settled on the chair and opened the book to the
page Tess had marked. "Nothing oversets Theresa.
Not since she was ten. No one corners her, no one
outsmarts her, no one shocks her, and nothing baffles
or unsettles her." Lady Gardner glanced up. "Until
you, apparently."

Hmm. "So I'm supposed to be . . . proud of the fact
that I flummoxed an unflappable chit?" Splendid. No
one else ever upset her, and yet he'd managed to do
so. And quite easily.

"It's good for her. She's not as invulnerable as she'd
like to think. No one can build a wall that sturdy."

Abruptly this conversation was becoming very interesting. Bartholomew settled himself into a seated
position against the headboard. He could fish about,
he supposed, but if Amelia was half as direct as her
cousin, she would not appreciate being led all about
the countryside. "What happened when Miss Weller
was ten?" he asked.

Her lips tightened. "We were at a country party in
Cheshire, about five miles from Weller Abbey. It was
raining frightfully, and my aunt and uncle decided to
stay the night. Tess wouldn't have any of it, though.
She'd left her favorite doll at home, and refused to
stay. Threw an absolute tantrum. Michael and I remained at Reynolds House to spend the night with
our friends, and she and her parents drove home. The
river bank washed out beneath them, and the coach
overturned into the water. The driver managed to

get Tess out, but my aunt and uncle didn't . . . they drowned."

Bartholomew looked down at his leg. A great deal of his last conversation with Tess made sense now. She did have a better sense of what he felt than most everyone else who'd attempted to hand him their sympathy and pity. And she'd called him sullen. She'd come close to accusing him of luxuriating in his self-imposed sulk. "What happened with the doll?" he asked after a moment.

"The doll?"

"The doll she refused to sleep without."

Amelia gazed at him thoughtfully. "No one's ever asked that question before." She took a breath. "Two days after the funeral, Tess threw it into the fireplace. She hasn't spoken of it since."

And then she'd likely begun the process of becoming the diamond that everyone called her. Pretty, pleasant to be around, delightful in company, and surrounded in the hardest shell known to mankind. He cleared his throat. "Lackaby mentioned that Stephen wanted to purchase me a wheeled chair."

"Yes. Your valet informed him of your dismay."

"Well, I changed my mind. I'd like to be able to get about while my leg mends."

She smiled, the expression warming her green eyes. "That is very good news."

Yes, well, he had some apologizing to do, to a very outspoken chit who had clearly reached out to a kindred spirit only to have her hand slapped away. He didn't like to use the word hope, since he didn't believe in it any longer, but something was bumbling and stumbling to life in his chest. And he only felt it when he thought about Tess.

As soon as Sally entered her bedchamber to throw open the curtains the next morning, Theresa rose. And thank goodness the night was done with; what a waste of time that had been. "Have you seen Michael?" she asked the maid as she pulled on her green and white sprigged muslin gown.

"No, miss. He made mention last night of going riding early."

That made sense; Parliament began late this morning, and he wouldn't have an opportunity later. "Thank you."

"Will we be visiting Lady Gardner again today?" Sally questioned as she finished pinning up Theresa's hair.

"No. Not this morning. I want to find a hair ribbon to match my new burgundy dress." She actually didn't care much about that at all, but if she stayed indoors she would only pace and wish herself elsewhere. "We'll be going out in an hour or so."

The maid curtsied. "Very good, Miss Tess."

Halfway downstairs to the breakfast room, the butler caught her eye as he stood in the foyer. "Good morning, Miss Weller," he said, inclining his head.

"Ramsey. I'll be needing the coach after breakfast."

"Very good, miss."

"Thank you." She paused on her way to the breakfast room as she spied a pretty spray of white carnations and daisies on the side table. Taking a step closer, she leaned down to read the sentiment with them. Apparently Lord Wilcox *was* infatuated with Grandmama Agnes. The sight of the posies sparked an idea, and a flutter of nerves went through her. "Ramsey, if I wanted to send a bouquet of flowers to a sick friend, how would I go about doing that?"

"I would see to it, miss. If you wished to write your sentiment on a card, I would send that on to the florist along with the address for delivery, unless you wanted one of the household to carry it personally."

"I see." She pursed her lips. It would be easy enough to say that she was sending the flowers to Amelia, but it wouldn't be her cousin's name on the outside of the card. Whether a florist or one of the various households' servants saw it, any ensuing scandal would be both her fault and out of her hands.

"Shall I make the arrangements?"

Theresa closed her eyes for a heartbeat, unable to conjure any sort of rule that would allow her to send flowers to a man who wasn't part of her immediate family. "No. Thank you," she said aloud. "It was just a question."

"Very good, miss."

She ate a peach and some toast, then took a seat in the morning room and picked up her embroidery while she waited for Harriet to come by and join her for shopping. Tolly didn't deserve flowers, anyway. He owed *her* an apology, the more she thought about it. After all, he had kissed her first.

"Who's ill?" Michael asked, strolling into the room.

With a strangled yelp Theresa snapped the blue thread she was using. "Good heavens. I nearly jumped right out of my shoes."

"Wouldn't be the first time." He continued forward. "If you're sending flowers, you should do it in the morning, before the day's pick at the shops begins to wilt."

"I told Ramsey I'd changed my mind."

"Ah." Abruptly his eyes narrowed. "You are *not* sending flowers to Colonel James."

Damnation. "I just finished saying that I wasn't."

"Good. Because you're not."

"I know I'm not."

"You do not need those looks and those muttered conversations behind your back."

Frowning, Theresa set down her embroidery. "I agreed with you, nick ninny. Stop arguing."

Her brother blinked. "Oh. Well, I wanted to make certain you understood."

"I do."

"Mmm-hmm." He rocked back on his heels. "Why were you considering sending Colonel James flowers, anyway?"

"I—"

"Are you setting your cap at him?"

"I don't know." She frowned.

"Because that's what everyone wou—"

"Quite possibly," she interrupted.

Her brother snapped his jaw closed. "Quite possibly what?"

"It's quite possible that I'm setting my cap at him. He's not like everyone else, and I find him rather . . . interesting."

Michael fell backward into a chair. "I'm done for," he groaned. "Send for Grandmama Agnes and Great Uncle Harry and recruit the pall bearers."

"Oh, stop being so melodramatic," she returned, twisting in the chair to face him. "And what, precisely, is your objection?"

"Have you considered why it is that you find him . . . interesting?"

Her humor began to retreat. "He's quite handsome."

"Tess. You know what I mean."

He would never say it, of course. Neither he nor Amelia nor Grandmama Agnes had ever blamed her—at least not out loud—for anything regarding the death of her parents, because apparently she'd been a good child until that night. And ever since. She stood up. "Perhaps you have it backward. Perhaps it's not that I see a kindred soul, but that I want to pursue where I can't possibly be successful."

"It's a poor idea, either way. If you want a husband, marry Montrose. He'll treat you well. You're allowed to have a good husband."

"Don't counsel me, Michael. You know I always do what's correct."

"To this point."

Theresa jabbed a finger toward the door. "Out. I'm occupied."

Michael shoved to his feet again. "Very well. I'll leave. But I'm going to tell Grandmama that you nearly sent flowers to a man and that you're setting your cap at Colonel James. You'll listen to her."

With that threat, he left the room again. "Drat," she muttered, sitting back at the desk.

That was all she needed, for Grandmama Agnes and Michael to lecture her on proper behavior. She knew what was proper. For once, though, she was tempted to do just one improper thing. And that actually frightened her a little, because she hadn't been tempted in thirteen years.

Someone knocked at the door. "Come in," she called, scowling at the wall opposite. But instead of Grandmama Agnes or Harriet, the butler stepped into the room.

"Miss Tess, you have a caller."

She didn't have a drive or a walk or a brunch scheduled with anyone this morning, because she always checked her calendar in the evening before bed. "Harriet? She's early."

"A man. He didn't give his name. In fact, all he did say was that he was here to see Miss Weller, and that he would be out on the drive."

"Out on the drive?" she repeated. That was unusual. Generally they wanted to come in. Standing again, she headed for the curtains at the front of the morning room. With a breath she took hold of the edge of the material and pulled it back an inch. A man sat in a chair in the middle of the short, half-moon drive, another fellow standing directly behind him. "Goodness," she whispered, loosing the curtain and striding for the foyer.

Bartholomew James had finally come to call on her.

Chapter Eleven

"Beware a man who does not declare his interest. A few simple words don't equate a proposal of marriage, but any gentleman who cannot at least say 'I am looking about for a wife' is not likely to ever make a more formal declaration."

A LADY'S GUIDE TO PROPER BEHAVIOR

The front door opened, and Bartholomew held his breath. The odds were fairly even as to whether Tess would emerge or it would be the butler telling him to go away.

But it was Theresa. She appeared in the doorway and without hesitation descended the shallow front steps. "This is a surprise," she said, lifting an eyebrow as he let out the breath he'd been holding. "Does Dr. Prentiss know you're prowling the streets again?"

He liked the description; "prowling" sounded much better than "completely relying on one's valet and unable to stand." Bartholomew shifted. "No. He doesn't know I'm out of bed," he said aloud. "I wanted to apologize."

"I see. Lackaby, there are fresh-baked biscuits in the kitchen. Please tell Cook you are to have as many as you like."

The valet saluted. "I'll see to it at once." Before Bartholomew could protest, Lackaby vanished into the house.

"Damned sapskull," Bartholomew muttered.

Her lips twitched. "Ramsey," she called toward the front door, "I'll be out in the garden."

The butler continued to stand in the doorway. "Shall I fetch Sally?"

"No need."

With a nod and a last suspicious glance at Bartholomew, the butler shut the door. The front drive wasn't precisely private, but at least she hadn't refused to see him at all. Because he'd discovered something over the past day; previously he'd found Tess Weller intriguing, amusing, and not a little baffling. After what he'd learned about her yesterday, he also admired her.

Clearly she blamed herself for the death of her parents, and just as clearly she viewed herself and Society differently because of that. No one viewed their own behavior more seriously than someone who'd broken the rules once and paid for it.

"Do I have dirt on my face?" she asked.

"No."

"Then why are you staring at me?"

For a moment he contemplated telling her that he knew about her parents and that he thought he had the key now to her behavior. That hardly seemed fair, though, given that she knew only the barest details of what had happened to him and he'd refused to tell her more. "You're pretty," he finally stated, his voice more brusque than he liked, especially since he'd told her he was there to apologize.

"So are you." Sending him a quick smile, Tess stepped around to the back of the chair.

Bartholomew scowled. "Don't push me about."

"I've sent Lackaby away, and I don't want to stand here on the drive to be gawped at by everyone passing by."

With a lurch the chair rolled into motion, bumping across the cobblestone drive. The pace jolted his knee, but he clenched his jaw and kept his silence. The entire morning had literally been torture, both with the pain of descending the stairs at James House and with someone he couldn't see pushing him from behind and dictating where and how far he was able to go.

Once they reached the small Weller House garden, Theresa rolled him beneath a wide-reaching oak tree and then sat on the small stone bench facing him. Folding her hands together in her lap, she gazed at him expectantly. "Well?" she prompted after a moment.

"Well, what?"

"Apologize to me. It's why you came here, I believe."

"I did apologize."

"No, you didn't. You said you *wanted* to apologize. You haven't actually done it yet."

With anyone but her, he would have changed his mind right then, stated that fact and wheeled himself the devil home to James House. As usual, however, where Theresa appeared everything else went by the wayside. "I apologize, then, for being sullen and cross."

"I accept your apology."

"Thank you."

She tilted her head. "And I apologize to you, for being nosy."

And there he sat, guilty of the same damned thing. "I don't—"

"In fact, I was considering sending you a bouquet of flowers to apologize," she continued, smiling brightly. "You may have saved me from scandal."

Bartholomew looked at her. "What game are you playing, Theresa?" he finally asked.

"Well, if I haven't already made my intentions apparent to you, then I apologize again," she said primly. "I want to better our acquaintance, Tolly."

He cleared his throat. "I haven't precisely gone about kissing random women over the past months," he ventured slowly, fighting against the very strong feeling that he didn't deserve to be having this conversation, or to be in this circumstance. But her lovely gray-green eyes held his, and he continued. "I would like to better our acquaintance, as well."

Her shoulders lowered. "Thank goodness. Because I couldn't sleep at all last night, wondering how I would announce that I wish to court you." Abruptly she blanched. "If you were thinking about courtship. Which I don't expect, of course, because we only met a short time ago, but—"

"Do you always talk this much?"

Theresa blinked. "I hadn't really considered. I'm very good at idle conversation, though."

Surreptitiously Bartholomew wriggled his toes. It

hurt, so he wasn't dreaming. That didn't rule out possible delirium, but any fever-induced fantasies would have featured the two of them naked—not her offhandedly declaring that she perhaps wanted to court him. "I have to ask, what in the world makes you think of me as marriageable? I'm something of a wreck."

"I find it rather troubling myself," she returned, "because I've never even considered setting my cap at anyone. It's not at all proper, really. But I find you very . . . compelling, and I would like to understand why that is."

This wasn't supposed to be happening. His luck had failed him months ago, along with any hope for happiness. And yet she seemed as interested in him as he was in her. He cleared his throat. "I have to agree that I would seem to be an ill choice for a courtship, Theresa. Especially for you."

"I don't—"

"That said," he pressed, wondering when heavenly lightning was going to strike him dead for having the audacity to want her, "I am here. Calling on you. You seem more tolerable than most other chits of my acquaintance. Especially now."

"I'll take that as a compliment, I suppose." She smiled.

A return grin touched his own mouth; he couldn't help it. "You really should run, Theresa."

She tilted her head at him. "Are your attentions not honorable, then?"

"I don't know yet." Grabbing the edge of the bench with his fingers, he hauled himself closer to her. "Kiss me again, and perhaps that will help."

"Not so fast. I've been asking you to call on me for weeks, and this is the first time you've done so."

"You can't count the days where I was unconscious."

"Even so."

"Well, I'm here now," Bartholomew reminded her. "I can't escort you to a dance, and I don't enjoy gabbing about the weather, but I'm here."

She sent him a thoughtful glance. "All of my other suitors say they want to become better acquainted with me. To see if we would be compatible. They invite me to the theater, take me for drives, and stand about smiling while I shop for silly little knickknacks I don't even need. And of course they want to chat as much as possible, and dance." She gazed at him, her expression an alluring mix of amusement, excitement, and genuine nervousness. "What do you offer?"

He'd thought himself finished with risk and adventure—and with life in general. Fate and Theresa Weller clearly had other plans for him. "I can sit with you in a damned carriage," he finally said, his voice lowering as he realized how little he did have to offer at the moment.

"Then I think you should take me driving tomorrow," she said.

He nodded. Pragmatically, the only way she would realize they would never suit was to spend more time with him. He might even be able to make himself believe this was for her benefit, if he could make his heart stop pounding so hard for a damned minute.

That afternoon, Theresa sat forward on the curricle's leather-covered seat to wave at Mariana Hopkins. "That's a very nice color on Mariana, don't you think?"

Alexander, the Marquis of Montrose, glanced across the edge of Green Park. "Yes, lovely." He expertly tooled them around a stopped barouche. "Parliament doesn't meet until two o'clock tomorrow. Allow me to take you out to brunch. Eleven o'clock, say."

"I'm engaged tomorrow," she returned, her stomach turning butterflies as she thought for the hundredth time about the look in Bartholomew's eyes when he'd appeared on her front drive only a few short hours ago.

"Beg off. You know you prefer spending time with me."

"Don't ask me to be rude, Alexander."

"Who is it, then? Not Lionel."

She folded her arms across her chest. "I'm not playing this game. Talk about something else, or please take me home."

He subsided, but continued sending her sideways glances. "If it was Henning or Daltrey you would tell me, because they're nothing but your silly friends. It's someone you fancy, isn't it? Now you have to tell me."

"It's a family to-do," she stated, crossing the fingers of the hand he couldn't see. "I simply don't like the way you demand to know every detail of my every day."

"Consider me chastised, then," the marquis said easily. "But don't expect me to stop being jealous. Not when you've received at least nine other offers of marriage."

"All of which I've turned down."

"You turned me down, as well. And yet here we are."

"Tess!"

Starting, Theresa glanced up the pathway to see Lord and Lady Gardner riding toward her. "Stephen, Amelia," she exclaimed, smiling. "I daresay I underestimated you, my lord, if you've managed to get my cousin on horseback."

Amelia grinned back at her, eyes dancing. "Stephen has amazing powers of persuasion."

"Clearly."

Stephen chuckled. "She didn't resist at all. By the way, your patient has allowed me to purchase him a wheeled chair. He actually went outside this morning."

Theresa's cheeks warmed. She knew quite well where Tolly had gone this morning. "That's excellent," she said aloud. "I'm so glad his leg is healing."

"Do you think your brother would make me a loan of his barouche?" the viscount continued. "Tolly mentioned wishing to take some air when his leg improves."

So Bartholomew hadn't informed his family about their odd arrangement, either. "I'm certain he will. I'll mention it to him."

After another few minutes of conversation, Lord and Lady Gardner rode off through the park. On the outside, Lord Gardner and his younger brother looked very similar. On the inside, Stephen was a true gentleman in every sense, whereas Bartholomew was rough as the sea on a stormy day. Stormy weather had never much appealed to her—until now.

When she realized she was daydreaming again, Theresa shook herself and looked at Alexander. He was gazing at her, an unreadable expression on his face. "What is it?" she asked.

He shrugged. "Nothing. Let's look at the bonnets for sale on Bond Street, shall we?" With a cluck he sent the team forward again.

She flashed him another smile, rather relieved that he'd decided against another argument over her various other appointments. Of all her suitors, Montrose was the most persistent, and the one she took most seriously. If Tolly did mean to take her driving, and if he was serious about seeing her, she would eventually have to tell Alexander that her affections had been engaged elsewhere.

A low uneasiness stirred through her. Montrose was definitely the safer, more reliable proposition. But she'd had better than two years to accept his suit, and five years since she'd had her debut, and she remained unmarried. Was Bartholomew then a new path, or a last lesson for herself on the perils of impropriety?

By the time she returned home, she was more than ready for an hour or two of solitude before she had to dress for an evening at the theater with Michael and Grandmama Agnes. As soon as she stepped through the front door, however, she noticed her grandmother standing at the top of the stairs.

"Come see me, Tess," she said, and vanished toward the back of the house.

With a frown Theresa followed the family's matriarch into feline-occupied territory. She found her grandmother in the large upstairs sitting room that had been converted into a cat heaven. Dodging the strands of yarn hanging from floor to ceiling and the faux mice made of ox hide and the tufts of tied-together feathers on the floor, she made her way to the back of the room. Grandmama Agnes sat on the settee beneath the window. On her lap, on either side of her, and curling up on her feet, were cats.

"What is it, Grandmama?"

"I was quite the minx when I was your age, you know," Lady Weller said, stroking the gray and black cat, Pebbles, that sat on her lap.

"Yes, I know. I've heard your stories many times."

"I've never told you the tale of how I once sent flowers to a man, have I?"

Theresa blinked. "No, you haven't."

Agnes set Pebbles aside. "That is because I would never do such a scandalous thing!" she exclaimed. "There is a difference between skirting rules and putting musket balls through them. And while I'm pleased you're finally . . . stretching your boundaries, I do not—"

"But Grandm—"

"You will not do such a thing, either, Theresa Catherine. And stomping your feet and pouting won't do you any good."

"I do not pout or stomp my feet, Grandmama." Not since she'd been ten. And she would never do so again, no matter the provocation. "And I told Michael I'd decided against it. It was only a passing whimsy. I don't know why the two of you think I've suddenly gone mad."

The older woman's expression softened. "Perhaps it was hope," she said so quietly Tess wasn't certain she heard it correctly.

"Beg pardon?"

"I know you don't throw tantrums, dearest," Agnes said more clearly. "It was only an expression."

"There's no need for sending flowers any longer, anyway. He came by, and I spoke to him in person. We're going driving tomorrow." She had no intention of saying any more than that. Not until or unless she and Tolly came to an understanding or she came to her senses again. Above everything else, her family deserved proper, correct behavior from her. A cold wave of guilt washed over her. She shouldn't be embarking on this trail. But seeing Tolly again . . .

"You're going driving with Colonel James?"

Theresa took a deep breath. "Yes. He asked to use our barouche, though, because Gardner doesn't have one."

"Very well. He seems an interesting man, Tess. More so than most of the milksop bucks chasing after you. Is he romantic?"

Romantic. He certainly kissed like it, but that was another topic she meant to avoid. "I don't think romance has been much on his mind," she said instead.

"That's understandable. But if he's asked you to go driving, he must have some thought of romance."

"Perhaps."

Agnes nodded. "Only one more question from your old grandmama, then. Are you ready for the trouble being seen with him could stir? There are other men more admired than he is, and they won't like you showing him favor. And there are the rumors, as well, that these Thuggee don't exist and that he lost his command because he is utterly incompetent. Or worse, a coward."

The image of him lying in bed while Dr. Prentiss dug into his leg made even the sound of that accusation ridiculous. "He is neither of those things."

"I'm only telling you what will be said. Being a bit naughty and being associated with someone else's scandal are two very different things, Tess. And while I'm happy to see you embark on the former, I don't wish to see you hurt by the latter." Grandmama Agnes lifted Mr. Brown onto her lap. "Now go away, and if Michael asks, tell him I scolded you into submission."

Theresa grinned. "Yes, Grandmama."

For the rest of the day and through the evening, however, it wasn't Bartholomew James's questionable character that kept her unsettled and nervous. It was her own. She'd told her family that she didn't need to be reminded to behave. This was the first time in thirteen years, though, that the proper thing and the thing she wanted to do couldn't both be found in her booklet.

"Colonel, the buckskin trousers will not fit over your knee. The boots will look sterling with the breeches, anyway."

Bartholomew ignored his valet for the moment, instead concentrating on shaving. He hated to admit it, but compared with remaining in bed, the wheeled chair in which he currently sat was a bloody godsend. "The buckskins," he said. "Cut the seam up to the knee."

"I don't see the sense in ruining a very fine pair of trousers, but I suppose it isn't up to me."

"I suppose it isn't."

At least in trousers he would look like a gentleman of modern sensibilities. Because if Theresa wanted to be seen with him, he would do his damnedest not to embarrass her. Once she came to her senses, he could take himself back to the Adventurers' Club and disappear from Society again.

"What about that horse's mane on your head?" the valet asked, as he sat down in the chair by the window and began pulling stitches from the seam of the buckskin trousers. "Miss Tess did mention that you needed a trim." He snapped the scissors open and closed. "I can see to it if you like."

"Are you certain you worked for Wellesley?" Bartholomew asked, beginning to wonder whether he was more annoyed or amused by his valet.

"I most certainly did."

"Well, you're not getting near me with those things. Not today." The fresh pain of his knee—and the distraction of Theresa—might be keeping his demons at bay for the moment, but they were never far away.

"Very well, Colonel. I've braided many a horse's tail. I could attempt that."

"You're sacked, Lackaby."

"No, I'm not."

"Keep your sarcasm to yourself, or I'll see to it."

The valet cleared his throat. "Yes, Colonel."

It took twenty minutes, but with some swearing and more pain, the two of them got him into his buckskin trousers and his Hessian boots. Bartholomew glanced at the clock on the mantel. She would arrive at James House in the next ten minutes or so.

Lackaby followed his gaze. "Wait here a moment,

Colonel. I'll fetch some help to haul you and the chair downstairs."

As he waited for the troops to assemble, he took a moment to look at himself again in the dressing mirror. A fortnight ago he could not have cared less about his appearance. And yet there he sat, dressed in a well-fitting black jacket and tan waistcoat, freshly shaved with a neat if simply-tied cravat, and his ragged, overlong hair at least combed.

It was a damned muddle, knowing he was ill-suited to courting and still looking for any excuse to be close to Theresa. Was it selfish to ignore his poor qualifications until she noticed them herself and put a stop to . . . whatever this was? The answer was simple, but before he could contemplate it, Lackaby returned with two footmen and Stephen's valet.

After yesterday they'd decided it was easier to tilt him nearly flat on his back and carry him downstairs, chair and all. He didn't like the extreme feeling of vulnerability, but as of two days ago he'd found a reason to at least give his leg a chance to heal. The better he could fit into Society physically, the better for Theresa while her short-sighted interest in him lasted.

With a last, wrenching jolt they set him upright again at the foot of the stairs. "There you are, Colonel," Lackaby said. "Simple as boiled potatoes."

Bartholomew glanced over his shoulder at the valet. "Thank you for the comparison. Fetch my cane, will you?"

Saluting, Lackaby trotted back up the stairs. The remainder of his assistants disappeared back to their duties. Bartholomew sat alone just short of the foyer. He took a deep breath, unaccustomed excitement running just beneath his skin for the first time in months. If she was wise, Theresa would send her regrets and go off shopping with her friends. And he sincerely hoped that she wouldn't be wise today.

"Your cane, Colonel," Lackaby said, descending the stairs again with an ease Bartholomew couldn't help envying. "Though we'll need more than a stout stick to get you up into a carriage."

"A carriage?" Stephen repeated, emerging from his office. "You're going out?"

Wonderful. "Yes."

"I didn't know Michael had already sent over his barouche."

"I'm waiting for it now." There. And that wasn't even a lie.

"So soon? Does Dr. Prentiss know you're out of bed again, then?"

"You're the one who purchased me the chair. You didn't mean for me just to lie there and look at it, did you?"

"No, but I'd hoped you would demonstrate a touch more patience before you jumped into a carriage."

"I—"

The front door knocker clanked against its brass plate, and he forgot what he'd been about to say. By God, she'd come.

Graham appeared from the direction of the kitchen and hurried past them to pull open the door. "Good morning, Miss Tess," the butler said warmly. "You'll find Lady Gardner in the morning room."

"Thank you," her voice came, a smile in her tone, "but I'm here to collect Colonel James."

While the butler looked baffled, clearly unsettled by her choice of words, Bartholomew motioned at Lackaby to wheel him forward. "Let's be off, shall . . ."

He trailed off as she came into view. She wore a blue muslin decorated with small green flowers, the sleeves short and puffy, and the low, swooped neck and waist overlaid with a delicate ivory lace. The colors turned her eyes gray, and filled him with the immediate . . . need to kiss her.

Her smile deepened. "You're ready?"

Bartholomew shook himself even as Lackaby rolled him into the doorway. "I try to be prompt."

She gazed at him for a long moment, and he wondered what in the world she saw to make her want both to spend time with him, and to get to know him better. Whatever it was, she lifted a hand to shift a strand of her sun-colored hair behind one ear. If he'd been on his feet, he wouldn't have been able to resist touching her.

"What's all this?" Stephen asked, frowning.

"Colonel James and I are going for a drive," Theresa returned. "I brought the barouche as you suggested, since it has the lowest step."

With its bright red trim it was also going to be one of the most noticeable vehicles on the streets. Clearly she wasn't worried about being seen with him. Considering that Stephen now looked as baffled as the butler had a minute ago, it seemed a good time to leave. Carefully he stood, ignoring the jab of pain as he flexed his knee a little. "Lackaby."

The valet came around beside him, and Bartholomew slung an arm across his shoulders while Lackaby braced him around the waist. Lifting him half off the floor, the stocky servant hauled him down the shallow trio of steps to the drive. "Lighter than Arthur in his cups, you are," Lackaby grunted. "But not by much."

Theresa snorted, but stepped forward to open the carriage's low door. Bartholomew handed her the cane as he levered himself up the step and into the seat. Her maid sat opposite him looking vaguely horrified, so the servant likely knew what her mistress was up to.

"Tolly?" Stephen descended the steps behind them.

"I'll have him back by two o'clock. Earlier if he tires." Theresa handed back the cane and clambered in past him, careful to avoid his outstretched leg, and sat beside him. "I've a pillow, if you want it beneath your foot."

"No need." Mostly he wanted to be off before Stephen attempted to interfere.

"Tess," his brother said, with the timing of a clock, "what are the two of you doing? I only asked to borrow the barouche. I didn't mean you had to give up your day for—"

"We're going for a drive." She leaned forward. "Drive on, Andy."

The driver flipped the reins, and the fine pair of matched bays started off. As they left the drive, Theresa sat back again, laughing. "Oh, goodness," she said. "That felt very scandalous."

"It was," he pointed out. "No good can possibly come of it."

"And yet here we are."

"Yes. I think we should clarify something." Bartholomew held her gaze. "I'm not much of a gentleman any longer, but if you're foolish enough to agree to spend time with me, Theresa, I will attempt to follow the rules." From far away he could almost hear the sounds of battle and massacre, mocking him. "But before I step into the middle of your Season," he continued, pushing back against the memories, "I think we should begin with a friendship."

She sat still for a long moment, then nodded. "This is a bit different for both of us, isn't it?"

Relieved, he grinned. "I can safely say that I've never spent a day like this before." Bartholomew shifted a little so he could face her more fully. "Where are we off to?"

"I thought a grand tour around Hyde Park, to begin with."

"Good. I'll purchase you a lemon ice."

"But I invited you. And you can't get out of the carriage."

"I can wave a shilling in the air and bellow as well as anyone," he retorted. "You may have said the word courting first, but I'll be doing it, thank you very much."

Soft color touched her cheeks. "Very well," she said slowly, smiling. "Perhaps you might purchase me a lemon ice."

Bartholomew nodded. "That would be my pleasure."

Chapter Twelve

"Rules a female must not break: being caught kissing a man in public, walking about inappropriately dressed in public, betraying a trust or a friendship. There are additional rules, of course, but I believe these three to be the basis of all the others."

A LADY'S GUIDE TO PROPER BEHAVIOR

Whether Tolly could read minds or merely had a good sense of timing, Theresa was grateful to him. He'd stated that he would do the courting, which made her feel both thrilled and considerably more easy. She didn't need her guidebook to know that ladies did not court gentlemen.

In other ways, however, this infatuation was troubling. She'd never dreamed of being naked in Alexander's arms the way she did Tolly's. In her visions his nether regions had been a blur, which was both understandable and annoying, but she was thinking about them—and him—with almost alarming regularity, and she wasn't accustomed to such . . . carnal, highly improper thoughts.

Propriety dictated that a man and woman be married before she ever saw beneath his clothes, but for heaven's sake, she'd already seen his leg. And his blood. In a sense, she couldn't actually fault herself for imagining the rest.

She glanced at the small clock on one of the sitting room's side tables—not even noon yet. Amelia had suggested they have tea at James House this afternoon, and so she'd begged off shopping with Harriet this morning. Any other time her day would be filled to brimming, but becoming acquainted with Bartholomew James required all of her concentration. Much more so than chatting about the weather with dull, handsome Lionel.

Her cousin undoubtedly knew something unusual was afoot, and so did her grandmother. Michael seemed to think she was merely teasing him, thank goodness, but that still left Tolly's brother and sister. And Tolly. His mood seemed to have improved, but she had the feeling that was partly because his leg was also beginning to mend. If it became infected or if he fell and injured it again, the angry, abrupt man she'd first met might prove to only be a taste of his temperament. She couldn't very well court him if he refused to see her.

Her own footing wasn't precisely certain either, considering that she'd promised to be good and proper evermore. Her parents were likely scowling and shaking their heads at her even now just for having rebellious thoughts. But this felt like a chance at . . . at something, and she simply wasn't ready to give it up. Not yet.

She heard the front door knocker and then Ramsey

speaking, but she didn't look up from her sketching. She'd begun with the idea of rendering one of Grandmama Agnes's cats in charcoal, but then she'd become fixated on drawing cat's eyes, and now the eyes gazing back at her seemed rather familiar, even without their whiskey-colored decoration.

"Miss Tess," Ramsey said from the doorway of the upstairs solarium, "Lord Montrose is—"

"I'm here," Alexander finished, walking past the butler into the room. "Apologies for not waiting to be announced."

Damnation. Hurriedly Theresa set down the charcoal and came forward to meet the marquis, wiping her hands on a cloth as she approached. "Alexander! I didn't expect you this morning."

"Since you were occupied on Tuesday, and I had a previous engagement yesterday and the day before, I thought I might offer my company today," Alexander returned, taking her black-streaked hand and bowing over it. "If you're free, of course."

"Don't you have Parliament this morning?" she asked, motioning for Ramsey to fetch Sally for her. While she would rather not have a chaperone in Tolly's company, here with Alexander the Great she wanted everything to be proper.

"I begged off. Some drivel about canal expansion. I'd be asleep in my chair anyway if I'd attended."

"I have a luncheon engagement, but I suppose I'm free until then," she returned, pushing aside her impatience at having her morning interrupted. What the devil was wrong with her? If she knew one thing, it was how to be pleasantly social.

"Good." Taking off his gloves, he set them across the back of a chair and sat. "What are you working on?"

"That?" She glanced back at the easel. "Nothing. Just practicing."

"If you need a subject, I would be happy to sit for you."

Theresa sent him an assessing look. "I'm not quite proficient enough for people," she said, smiling. "Vases and fruit are my specialty of the moment."

"How long have we known one another, Tess?" he asked abruptly, as Sally hurried into the room, nodded at her, and took a seat beside the door.

"Nearly four years, I think," she answered, her muscles tensing just a little. If he was going to hand her another proposal, he'd picked a poor time for it.

"Do you trust my judgment?"

"I suppose it would depend on the subject." She frowned. "Is something amiss, Alexander?"

"I followed you the other day."

A chill went down her spine. "You followed me? Where?"

"On your so-called family outing. When you took your barouche and went driving with Colonel James for three hours."

Theresa snapped to her feet. "I believe we've already discussed my dislike of you wanting to know my entire calendar each day."

The marquis stayed seated, his pose relaxed despite the alert in his light blue eyes. "I was suspicious. And rightly so."

"I'm not betrothed to you, Alexander, so I suppose I may visit with whomever I please."

"But you lied about it. Why is that?"

Yes, why was that, Tess? Had it been to spare Tolly from Alexander's ire? Or to spare her from any stickiness such as that she seemed to be mired in at that very moment? "I'm not certain why," she responded after a moment. "But my friendship with Tolly James remains my own affair."

"As long as it's only a friendship. If he's after you, then I have to disagree."

What would Lord Montrose say, she wondered, if she informed him that Tolly had announced his interest in her at approximately the same moment she'd confessed to her fascination with him?

"I had breakfast this morning," Montrose said conversationally.

"As did I," she returned a bit dubiously, debating now how to have him leave without making him more out of sorts about Tolly. "Peaches and toast."

"I dined out at the Society," he continued, "with Lord Hadderly. The head of the London offices of the East India Company."

"I'm acquainted with him. Grandmama doesn't like his dogs." Casual as his voice was, something set her on edge. More on edge. Any mention of India seemed to have more significance to her now. And Hadderly had declined to dine at James House.

"Yes. Evidently there have been some gathering rumors about a murderous cult in India, called the Thuggee, who prey on innocent travelers and merchants."

That did it. Theresa sat directly opposite the marquis, her hands clenched stiffly in her lap. "If you intend on doing something . . . underhanded to damage Colonel James's reputation, you will stop it at once. I won't have it."

He lifted an eyebrow. "You won't, will you?"

"No. I won't."

"Mmm-hmm." Light blue eyes gazed into hers for a moment. "The reason I mention this, Tess, is because the Company has been working diligently to stop the rumors and discredit anyone carrying them. It's bad for business." Abruptly he stood, so that she had to lift her chin to look at him. "I tell you this because of our friendship. I know how highly you regard propriety. No one carrying tales about mythical bandits is going to be terribly popular after tomorrow."

"What happens tomorrow?"

"The East India Company publishes their views on the outlandish rumors and calls everyone who has claimed to have encountered the Thuggee cowards, traitors, and liars."

"What?" All the blood drained from her face. "But what does the Horse Guards say about this? Surely they won't stand for it. They've lost men to these brigands."

He shrugged. "I haven't heard how or if the Horse Guards means to respond. But I do know how much money the Company drops into their coffers." Montrose inclined his head. "And now I imagine you'll want to be elsewhere—unless you would care to go driving with me after all."

Theresa shot to her feet. "Um, no. I need to—"

"I thought so," he interrupted. "I'm not your enemy, Tess. And I didn't give you this information for anyone's sake but yours."

She hardly noted what he was saying. Her ties to

Tolly might be tenuous by Society's standards, but all she could think was that he needed to know—at once—that both the East India Company and the War Office were about to call him a liar, and the entire ordeal he'd faced, a coward's tale.

"Go on, Tess," Montrose said, heading for the door. "I'll see you tonight at the Fallon soiree. I hope he appreciates that you're willing to go speak to him in person." He shook his head. "I never much liked Tolly James, but now I almost feel sorry for him. Once the report comes out, he'll go from wounded hero to overmatched and failed officer."

With a nod he excused himself from the sitting room. For a long moment Theresa stood there in the middle of the floor. Alexander Rable had impeccable manners. He'd politely informed her that the fellow who'd caught her eye was about to be very unpopular. He'd done it without asking her to make a choice, or even requesting an apology from her for making such a silly error in judgment. To keep her own reputation and standing safe, all she had to do was . . . nothing.

He'd even made the suggestion that she play the heroine and ease her own conscience by giving Tolly the news herself. And then she could go on tonight and dance with her beaux, and tomorrow she could shop and flirt and pretend she'd never befriended the poor, misguided colonel.

She pulled off her smock. "Sally, tell Ramsey to have the coach readied. I'll be down in a moment."

Bobbing in a curtsy, the maid hurried out of the room. Theresa went across the hallway to her bedchamber to fetch her gloves and bonnet. As she did so, she caught sight of her reflection in the dressing mirror.

Yes, she'd promised to be good. Thirteen years ago she'd sworn that she would never give her family a moment's pause, that everything she said and did would be proper, and correct, and honorable. And in thirteen years she'd never so much as stumbled. But then again, this was the first time she'd found the ground beneath her feet to be uncertain.

Theresa took a steadying breath. She would call on Tolly. Anything beyond that she would decide when the moment came.

Bartholomew glanced toward his valet as someone knocked at the bedchamber door, but Lackaby continued muttering to himself while he pulled out the left leg seam of the black trousers he held.

Well, Lackaby hadn't precisely been hired for his grasp of etiquette. "Come in," he called. Going back to the simple knot he was tying into his cravat, Bartholomew leaned forward in his wheeled chair. Whether it was the twice-daily dashes of whiskey over his knee or the fact that he hadn't put any weight on his leg in nearly a week now, he felt . . . better. Sounder, inside and out. More alive.

Of course the main ingredient to his recovery was one witty, lovely female with hair the color of sunshine and eyes the changeable color of the sea. Because of Theresa Weller, his heart persisted in its return to life, despite the fact that his mind knew he didn't deserve the opportunity.

"Good morning," his brother said, stepping into the room.

"Stephen."

"I'm going to White's for luncheon with Masey and a few others, if you'd care to join me."

Hmm. His disposition *had* improved, if Stephen was now inviting him places. "I've a previous engagement with Tess and your wife, but thank you."

His brother closed the door behind him. "Yes. About that."

The muscles across Bartholomew's shoulders tightened, but he finished the cravat. He very much doubted that Stephen could say anything about his pursuit of Theresa that he hadn't already considered, himself. Even so, he had no intention of encouraging criticism.

Stephen cleared his throat. "Lackaby, give us a moment."

The valet stood.

"Stay," Bartholomew countered, moving from the cravat to buttoning the last few fastenings of his waistcoat.

The valet sat again.

"Very well." The viscount walked across the room to look out the window. Either something extraordinary was taking place in the garden, or his brother was working very hard to choose how he wanted to say something unpleasant. "Tess Weller is a delightful young lady," he finally said.

That wasn't so bad. "Yes, she is."

"You're not the . . . sort of fellow I generally see about her."

"So she told me."

Stephen faced him. "She said that to you?"

"Several times. She thinks I'm sullen."

"I— Do you like her?"

Bartholomew shoved backward from the dressing table, muscling the chair around to face his brother. "I just told you that she said I was sullen."

"Then you don't like her."

"It's complicated."

"Yes, I can see that." Stephen frowned. "Tolly, you've just returned from a nightmare. It makes sense that you would be attracted to someone with such a sunny disposition, but I want to make certain you know that she has other suitors. Men who've been in pursuit for far longer than you have. And—"

"I might be crippled, but I'm not blind."

"You are not crippled," his brother retorted. "You're injured. But your wound does make competing with Tess's beaux even more problematic. I don't want to see you hurt again. That's—"

"I appreciate your concern," Bartholomew cut in again, "but I haven't required your advice or your opinion since I turned seventeen." He held his brother's gaze, touched by the compassion and worry he saw there. Stephen had certainly never done anything to hurt or trouble him. "Do you have an objection to my . . . interest in Theresa Weller?"

"No! God, no. But—"

"So your objection is that you don't think I am capable of winning her hand, not that winning her will add her to the family."

"No. Yes. No."

"Mmm-hmm. I'll manage my own affairs then, Stephen. Thank you for your concern."

The viscount jabbed a finger in his direction. "Just don't send your surly self against Violet and Amelia and me if the world doesn't turn your way. We're family."

"The world doesn't turn my way. And whether you believe it or not, my main concern is that I not hurt you."

"I—"

The door rattled again. With a glance at the seated Lackaby, Stephen returned to the doorway and pulled it open himself. The butler stood there, a silver salver laden with a calling card in his hand.

"My lord," Graham intoned, "Major-General Ross is here to see Colonel James."

"Ross? Do you know him, Tolly?"

Bartholomew gestured for the card. "Yes. He's with the Horse Guards." The card didn't contain a note or a sentiment—nothing but "Major-General Anthony Ross," printed in very unimaginative style across its front. Not a very friendly greeting from someone he'd once saved from a bayoneting at the hands of Boney's Imperial Guards. "Tell him I'm not up to visitors today."

The butler nodded. "Very good, sir."

"Graham, my boy," Lackaby spoke up, "muster the lads to move the colonel down the stairs, will you?"

Graham's stony face could have cracked granite. Not only had the butler more than likely never been called "my boy" before in his life, but being ordered about by an inferior—Bartholomew was rather surprised he didn't drop dead on the spot. "Lackaby, go find our own damned troops," he ordered.

"Aye, Colonel." With a jaunty grin the valet slipped past the butler and down the hallway.

"That . . . man is trouble, my lord," Graham announced, and vanished as well.

"I've tried to sack him thrice already," Bartholomew told Stephen, "so good luck."

His brother snorted. "I've surprised myself with the amount of chaos I'm willing to tolerate in exchange for having you home." He reached out a hand as if to touch his brother's shoulder, then lowered it again. "I won't warn you to be cautious, because I know you don't require my advice. All I'll say, then, is to enjoy your luncheon."

"Thank you."

As his brother left, Bartholomew favored Ross's card with one more glance before he placed it on the dressing table. Eventually, he supposed, he would have to agree to chat about the weather with old friends and acquaintances. Not yet, though. He'd allowed only one exception to disrupt his virtual hermithood. And as he'd discovered, she was also the most likely person to understand what he'd become.

"Colonel." Lackaby strolled back into the room, his quartet of assistants with him. "Your lady just turned up the drive."

"She's early." Bartholomew flipped open his pocket watch to make certain. Tess was nearly an hour early. Each day he saw her, the sight left him surprised; because each night he expected her to come to her senses and change her mind. "Get me downstairs," he said aloud.

Huffing and puffing, Lackaby and the other ser-

vants set him back on his wheels in the foyer just as
Graham opened the front door to admit Tess and her
maid. At least she didn't have to see him tumbling
headfirst down the main staircase.

"Tolly," she said, hurrying past the butler before
he could even acknowledge her presence. "I need a
private word with you."

His stomach muscles clenched; so she'd come to her
senses after all. "Lackaby," he said, gesturing toward
the door just off the foyer.

Theresa led the way inside. "Sally, please wait in
the kitchen," she told her maid as she took over the
short handles of Bartholomew's chair. "And Lackaby, go away."

The valet sketched a bow. "With pleasure."

Once they were alone in the room, she pushed him
close by the hearth. "What's amiss, Tess?" he asked,
craning his neck to keep her in view.

"Oh, I don't even know how to tell you."

For a short moment he watched her pace. And
whatever news she meant to give him, he couldn't
help noticing the soft sway of her hips, the flash of
shoe and ankle as she crossed the floor. It served
him right for hoping; he knew better. Now that he'd
done so, being rejected by the enchanting Tess Weller
would hurt more, but it was no more than he deserved. "Just tell me," he said. "There's little chance
you can wound me, my dear."

Finally she came to a stop in front of him, then
she clenched her fists and tucked them beneath her
chin. "I don't believe in passing on gossip," she said,
her voice unsteady, "but I have no reason to think

any of this is untrue. Tolly, tomorrow the East India Company will be publishing a report. They're going to say that the Thuggee threat is imaginary, conjured by cowards who couldn't perform their duties. The Horse Guards is apparently going to remain silent on the issue, though I'm not certain about that."

Bartholomew stared at her. The information was so far from what he'd expected to hear from her that for a hard beat of his heart he thought he'd imagined it. Then it all crashed into him with the force of a brick wall. And he had to sit there in his damned wheeled chair with his damned mangled leg and take it.

"Tolly?" she said quietly. "Bartholomew? I believe you. I want you to know that. But I also thought someone should . . . warn you about what's coming. The—"

"Thank you," he said stiffly. "Good day."

She blinked, though he scarcely noted it. "Good . . . That's all you have to say? This is terrible news! What are you—"

"I don't need you to tell me what sort of news this is, Miss Weller. Thank you for informing me. You should leave now, before someone connects your name to mine. We both know you don't want that."

Theresa put her hands on her hips. "And what is that supposed to mean?" she demanded. "I have done nothing wrong, so I see no reason for you to be angry with me, Colonel."

He grabbed the arms of the chair and shoved, lifting himself into a standing position. From there he could look down at her, remind her that he was more than a cripple and an object of pity. "I am going to ask you one last time to get the devil away from me. Because if you don't . . ." He reached out, grabbed her arm, and yanked her up against him. Roughly he kissed her, knowing it was for the last time and refusing to dwell on how sweet her mouth was or how her touch warmed him inside.

"Save yourself from scandal, Tess," he said, and pushed her away. "Get out. Now."

Chapter Thirteen

"Propriety must be more than a word. I could claim to be proper all day, for instance, but unless I behave in that same manner, I might as well save my breath."

A LADY'S GUIDE TO PROPER BEHAVIOR

Miss Tess," Sally said, leaning out of the coach's open door, "are we going?"

Theresa, arms folded across her chest, continued to glare at the closed front door of James House. "He threw me out," she muttered to herself.

Yes, his emotions were high, but no one—*no one*—had ever treated her in such a manner. It wasn't as if she was the one who'd decided to call him a liar, for heaven's sake; she actually believed him. How could anyone look into his eyes and not understand that something extraordinary and awful had happened?

And yet there she stood, round cobblestones beneath her feet and her coach waiting behind her. And now returning home, not speaking of him, and continuing on with her Season as if they'd never met would take absolutely no effort whatsoever. Every opportunity, every choice to be . . . other than her usual, proper self had been removed, by Montrose, by Tolly, by everyone.

Everyone but her. She'd done nothing. No disruption, no upset, no harm. With a last look at the closed front door she turned and climbed into her coach. "Take me home, if you please."

For the remainder of the day and all through the evening, while she chatted and danced and played her usual charming self, she half felt she was still standing out on the James House front drive. It was as if that moment had been something pivotal, something vital, and she'd let it pass her by.

"That was a fine evening," her grandmother said, as they left Fallon House with the last dance of the evening still going on behind them. "Did you see Wilcox? Wearing lavender like some man a third his age. I can't decide if he's attempting to recapture his youth, or if he's gone completely mad."

Michael chuckled as he handed Theresa into the coach behind Agnes and then climbed in, himself. "I hope you were flattered. Clearly he views you as a youthful spirit."

"So I am." Agnes took her granddaughter's hand. "And you were the belle of the ball, Tess, as usual. Half the men there couldn't take their eyes off you."

"Thank you."

"Didn't Leelee say they would be attending?" Michael asked, sitting back as the coach rolled out into the dark streets of Mayfair. "Did she say anything to you, Troll?"

Theresa shook herself. "No. I imagine Tolly told

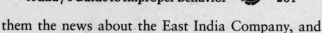

them the news about the East India Company, and they decided to remain at home."

"What news? What are you talking about?"

She glanced at her brother, then faced out the window again. They needed to know; Amelia's marriage connected them to the James family. "The rumors about the Thuggee murders are hurting the Company's business, apparently, so they're putting out a statement tomorrow that the Thuggee don't exist."

Both of her companions stared at her. "How do you know this?" Grandmama Agnes finally asked.

"Montrose told me this morning. He wanted to give me advance warning so I could distance myself from Tolly. His reputation will be utterly ruined, you know."

"Oh, my goodness. Did you speak to Amelia?"

"No. I told Tolly. He threw me out of James House." She attempted to shrug, but her shoulders were clenched up so tightly that they ached already. "Thank goodness I didn't send him those flowers after all. Can you imagine what people would have said about me once it became known that Colonel James is a liar?"

"Christ. That's a bit cold-blooded, don't you think?" Michael muttered.

"She doesn't mean it."

"Of course I do." Theresa kept her gaze out the window, taking in the darkness punctuated by the occasional gas lamp or candle-lit window. "That's who I am. Everyone knows how propriety-minded I am. I may have forgotten for a moment, but I certainly remember now."

For a moment she saw her grandmother's hazy reflection gazing at the back of her head, until the dowager viscountess faced forward again. "Michael, we must call on James House tomorrow, to show our support of the family."

"Certainly, Grandmama."

"I can only hope that Lord Hadderly's greed causes him as much pain as it does those around him. Never trust a man who breeds wolfhounds, I've always said."

Theresa doubted that Bartholomew James would want anyone gathered around him for any reason. She'd attempted to . . . well, at least to tell him that she believed him, and he certainly hadn't appreciated that. "Or one who's sullen," she added.

"Tess, I don't like th—"

"Leave her be, Michael," their grandmother interrupted. "She knows how she wishes to live her life." She shifted. "You needn't come with us tomorrow, my dear. Amelia will understand."

Settling for a nod, Theresa stayed away from the subdued conversation filling the coach for the remainder of the drive back to Weller House. Amelia *would* understand her wish to stay far away from any scandal—or even any sideways glances or muttering.

As soon as they reached the house she said her good nights and went upstairs. Sally had already set out her night rail and made down the bed, but Theresa didn't much feel like sleep.

"Are you ill, miss?" the maid asked, as she helped Theresa remove her deep blue evening gown. "I could fetch you a peppermint tea."

"No, thank you. I think I might read for a bit. Good night, Sally."

"Good night, Miss Tess."

Once alone in her bedchamber, Theresa went to the window that overlooked the carriage drive and pushed it open. Cool, damp night air rushed into the room, putting out the candle on the bed stand and making the low fire in the hearth spit and hiss.

Logically and practically, she'd done nothing wrong today. She'd even performed a good deed of sorts by going out of her way to inform a friend of impending ill news. After that, she'd only done as he asked— ordered—and left him to himself.

And every proper chit was supposed to distance herself from scandal. Any scandal. Even when it involved someone of whom she seemed to have become fond. Theresa touched her lips with her fingers. His kisses had been . . . electric. Nearly heart-stopping. They had certainly stopped her breath and her mind.

She could easily count the number of times her other beaux had kissed her—because they hadn't done so. She hadn't allowed such liberties. Not even from Montrose. Bartholomew touched her in ways she'd never expected. But now that trouble had found him—again—she could no longer spend time with him.

Theresa clenched her fingers into the base of the window sill. This was the first time that following the rules of propriety made her feel like a coward. For heaven's sake, if she could do whatever she pleased, she would march straight over to James House, stomp up the main staircase, shove open Tolly's bedchamber door, and punch him flush in the nose.

He'd sent her away just before she could make her excuses and leave—and both of them knew it. But so what if he had? She didn't owe him her allegiance. Reddening her fingers with his blood and shaving him when no one else was allowed to touch him and encouraging those naughty, exhilarating kisses didn't obligate her to stand by him. But what nerve, to assume that she wouldn't do so.

Except that he'd been utterly correct. Tolly James wasn't the coward. She was.

"Did you see this?" Michael waved the newspaper at Theresa as she walked into the morning room just after nine o'clock.

Dash it all, she thought she'd stayed in her bedchamber long enough to miss both Michael and her grandmother. And yet there they both were, clearly discussing the very thing she'd hoped to avoid this morning. "Of course I haven't seen it," she returned aloud, "but I told you it was coming."

Agnes stirred her tea so vigorously it sloshed over the side of the cup. "I'm going over to James House at once," she stated, rising. "This is even worse than I imagined. If I know Amelia, and I do, she's smiling on the outside and rattling about like a broken teapot on the inside."

"I'm going with you," Michael said, sending a pointed glare at Theresa as he, too, pushed away from the table. He shoved the newspaper across the table's surface in her direction. "Some new silks have arrived from Egypt. That's on page four."

Yes, her family understood her dismay over impropriety, but they clearly didn't like it. And she couldn't blame them. She didn't much like it, herself. "Please have some tea and toast sent up to my room," she said to the waiting footman, then picked up the newspaper and headed upstairs again.

The *London Times*'s coverage of the "Official Report of the East India Company to the Crown Regarding the Alleged Threat of the Thuggee in India" was quite thorough. She doubted that very few readers would feel the need to look farther and delve into the report itself.

According to the newspaper's interpretation of the report, Thuggee was the name assigned by the ignorant native population of India for everything from chicken thefts to the occasional, unfortunate native death. The Indians used the name in an attempt to drive up prices of product and to encourage the hiring of locals as guards for every well-heeled English traveler.

The report quoted governors, rajs, generals, Company officials—anyone who had any authority over anything, to all say what could be boiled down to the same basic ingredient. The Thuggee were nonsense.

Theresa sat back in her writing chair and sipped at her tea. Peppermint—evidently Sally thought her still out of sorts. Which she was, but not because of anything the tea could cure. The worst part about a report that promised safety and profitable enterprise and ridiculed danger was that everyone wanted to believe it.

She wanted to believe it. If not for Tolly's wounds

and scars and more tellingly the haunted look in his eyes, she would be tempted. With a frown, Theresa read the article's final paragraph again. Of course it didn't directly challenge the recollections of any Englishmen who claimed to have encountered the Thuggee, themselves. It didn't call them liars, cowards, or traitors to the fattening purses of all *good* Englishmen, but it certainly implied it.

Slowly she rose and walked to her window. It was a lovely morning; a few white, picturesque clouds deepened the blue of the sky around them, and a pair of wild finches perched in the tree just outside where they chirped musically.

And there she stood knowing that all was not well. Safe in her bedchamber with its yellow curtains and white and green walls, pages of her favorite fashion plates and a sketch of just the most darling hat tacked up beside her dressing mirror.

Nothing untoward ever came through her door; it wouldn't dare. Theresa glanced back at her writing table. Even that awful article was, in its neat black print, full of optimism and opportunity. The fresh shadows in the room, then, weren't from what she'd read. They were from her.

"Damnation," she muttered, using Bartholomew's favorite curse. The curses she chose weren't anything terrible, either. Yes, they might cause a lifted eyebrow or two from the silver-haired set, but otherwise they were very nearly fashionable.

No, the problem was her. Definitely her. She'd spent so long being good. It had never failed her before. Today, in fact, was the first time she could recall that

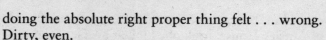

doing the absolute right proper thing felt . . . wrong. Dirty, even.

She knew what others might say to her dilemma. If it seemed to be the thing she should do, then of course she should step forward and denounce the article, or at the least claim Tolly as a friend. What was the worst that could happen?

Except that she knew the worst penalty for being contrary and acting badly. The last time she'd made a scene, two people—her parents—had died.

So what could she do now? She needed to behave properly. Which meant no Tolly. Not ever again. No matter how much she wanted to do otherwise.

"Miss Tess?" Sally called, knocking at her door. "Miss Silder and Miss Aames are here to go shopping with you."

"I'll be right down." Yes, she still had shopping. Just nothing that meant anything. Nothing that actually mattered.

The difficulty with belonging to a secret club, Bartholomew decided as he held on to the door of the hired hack with one hand and jammed his cane into the hard-packed earth with the other, was that it was a damned secret. Half stumbling, he made it to the ground with the grace of a headless chicken.

"You certain you know what you're about?" the driver asked, watching him skeptically as he disembarked. "I'll throw ye over my shoulder and carry ye to the bloody front door for a quid."

"Drive on," Bartholomew ordered. "Bastard," he added under his breath.

Harlow, the groom, appeared from around the side of Ainsley House, took one look at his face, and vanished again. At least someone knew what they were about.

Riding Meru from James House would have been easier, but he hadn't wanted to hear the questions about where he was going, and he hadn't wanted the assistance of Lackaby or the groom that Stephen would have pushed at him. If and when he moved out again he would make the announcement, but not before.

He made his way to the half-concealed door mostly by willpower and stubbornness, then dug the key from his pocket and let himself into the Adventurers' Club. At least they hadn't changed the lock—though it was early yet. There was even the chance that no one had yet read the morning's newspaper.

He'd read it, of course. Whatever he thought of his decision to encourage Tess to abandon him, he was grateful to her for alerting him to the coming storm. The story had actually sounded very convincing, though they'd gotten some of the facts wrong. For a moment he'd actually been . . . thankful to have been wounded. The hole in his leg and the scar around his neck at least provided evidence that something had gone awry.

Easton was of course inside the club as Gibbs came forward to close the door after him. So were five other members, though he only recognized two of them.

"So you had your leg nearly shot off by a chicken thief?" Easton said, guffawing and clearly amused at himself. "It's no wonder they retired you, James."

Bartholomew ignored him, instead keeping his attention on Gibbs. "I need a word with Sommerset," he said to the valet. "Didn't think I should call at the front door."

Gibbs nodded, his expression as impassive as always. "I'll inquire."

Taking the closest chair, Bartholomew half fell into the seat. The grinding agony had gone from his leg, but it hurt enough that he knew damned well he shouldn't be walking on it yet. Considering that his main goal in seeing it mended was so he could dance with Theresa, he supposed he could mangle it again now as he liked.

Thomas Easton rose from the table across the room and ambled over to him. Whatever Bartholomew thought of the man's character, the fellow wasn't shy about arguments. "Go away," he said, before the former silk importer could pull out the neighboring chair.

"Newspaper says only one attack on travelers occurred in India last year," the fellow commented, sitting anyway. "If we suppose that one attack was yours, then you've been exaggerating, Colonel. One man wounded and one man killed ain't nearly the same as one man wounded and eight men killed."

"Fifteen men," Tolly corrected flatly. "The zamindar's son and his attendants were murdered, as well."

"I was only counting Englishmen."

"Count whomever you damned well please, Easton," Bartholomew snapped. "You didn't have to write the letters to their families. I did. And I know how many men I lost. Nor am I likely ever to forget, whatever Lord Hadderly and his gaggle print."

"You've read it, then," the Duke of Sommerset said

as he crossed the room from the door that opened to his house proper. "Good. That saves me breaking the news to you."

"I didn't know you allowed victims of chicken thieves into the Adventurers' Club, Your Grace. My uncle's stableboy might—"

"Go away, Easton," the duke interrupted.

Scowling, Easton picked up his glass of vodka and returned to his former seat. As tempted as Bartholomew was to ask Sommerset why he'd decided to invite the bag of hot air that was Easton to join the club, he kept his silence. He was on shakier ground than Easton at the moment.

"Thank you for seeing me," he said instead.

The duke nodded. "I thought I might have to call on you, actually."

That didn't sound promising. Little as he cared to admit it, he respected the opinions of Sommerset and the men the duke had gathered here. They'd seen their way through things that would leave most members of the peerage quaking in their Hoby boots, if not dead. Being asked to leave their company . . . well, if they thought he deserved the ridicule and condemnation heading his way, he wasn't likely to be able to convince *anyone* otherwise.

"How fares your leg?" Sommerset asked.

Bartholomew looked at the duke for a short moment. "I'd prefer to head straight for the end of this conversation, rather than meandering about the beginning."

Steel gray eyes met his levelly. "I very rarely meander. How is your leg?"

"Mending, I think. I can feel my toes now. Thank

you for asking. Do I turn in my key to you, or to Gibbs?"

"I didn't invite you to join this club because of the East India Company's recommendation, so I don't feel obligated to ask you to leave it because of their condemnation." He sat forward. "On the other hand, if you mean to hide here until everyone forgets you were in India, I won't allow it."

"I won't forget India," Bartholomew retorted. "I don't give a damn what anyone else remembers."

"You're welcome to take a room here again once the scandal ebbs. Give it a week. Perhaps a fortnight."

"Yes, and then the next scandal from India will be about some lord's son who goes looking for his fortune and ends up dead or missing." He clenched his fist. "I don't understand how the Company can turn its back on the memory of brave murdered soldiers and send others to join them when they know the cause of it."

"Because the deity they worship has drawings of the king across it and is made of sterling silver." Sommerset sent a glance at the open space around them. "What do you intend to do about this, Tolly?"

"I imagine I might find a few other Englishmen acquainted with the Thuggee and see if I can persuade them to corroborate my story with theirs."

The duke smiled. "Perhaps I shall make a few inquiries along that line. There are some in the Horse Guards offices who owe me favors. Perhaps a look through the records would be helpful."

"That would make you rather unpopular with the East India Company," Bartholomew noted. Another pair of eyes and ears could be useful, but he refused to have anyone involved who didn't know the full measure of what they faced.

"Hmm. I believe I can look out for myself." Sommerset moved his chair closer. "To my surprise, I find myself curious about the chit who had you thinking about dancing. How goes the hunt?"

Bartholomew shrugged, keeping his face carefully blank. "She likes to dance. She does not like scandal."

"That is a shame," the duke commented. "She seemed to improve your mood."

"Yes, vain hope will do that. Now, however, you will find that my feet are firmly on the ground. Or my foot is, rather."

"If that is the case, I recommend not tripping. If I discover anything of interest, I'll contact you."

"Thank you, Your Grace."

Sommerset stood. "One bit of advice. Don't remain buried in your den, Colonel. The less everyone sees of you, the easier you will be to discount. And whether the Company likes it or not, you are a walking—limping—contradiction to their assertion that all is well in India."

All was not well in India. Nor, however, was London turning out to be any safer.

Thankfully Lackaby arrived out the front door of James House at the same time as the hack Bartholomew had hired after he decided he couldn't extend his luncheon at the Adventurers' Club any longer.

"What the devil do you think you're about, Colonel?" the valet asked, coming forward to half lift his employer to the ground.

Bartholomew pushed free as soon as he had his

balance. "I think you meant to say, 'Welcome home, sir, may I fetch your chair for you?' To which I would then reply, 'Yes, thank you.'"

"Well, you've said all my bits, so I'll go fetch the chair."

No sooner had the valet pushed back into the house past the rather offended-looking Graham, however, than Stephen appeared. "Where the devil have you been?"

Everyone seemed to be singing the same tune. "I've been out. It's called luncheon."

"And didn't you consider that we would be worried about you today and that you should have left word?"

"No, it didn't," Bartholomew said, blowing out his breath. "Apologies."

"Then I . . . Oh. Accepted. Let me help you into the house."

"I don't need your help."

Stephen nodded even as he grabbed Bartholomew around the waist and helped him up the front steps. "I wasn't asking."

Bartholomew untangled himself from his brother, eyeing the viscount. "You have a great deal of spleen today."

"Well, you weren't here, but we had several callers who came by to express their support of and belief in you. It was something of a pity we couldn't trot you out to say thank you."

He didn't feel in the mood to be trotted out, but that wasn't what had caught his attention. "Who, precisely, came to express their support?" For a moment pretty ocean-colored eyes and hair the color of sunshine played across his thoughts. If she'd changed her mind, then she was the one. And he wanted so much for her to be the one.

"Humphrey, Lord Albert," his brother began, "Mr. Popejoy, the Wellers, Aunt Patr—"

"The Wellers?" he cut in.

"Yes. Very kind of them, considering they've only known me for a year, and you only for a fortnight or so. Grandmama Agnes seems to have a very keen dislike of the East India Company."

"Ah," he ventured. "And Theresa?"

"She wasn't feeling well this morning. I've noticed over the past year that she tends to avoid . . . upheaval."

Upheaval. That was a good, polite word for it. But though he understood the reason Theresa disliked upheaval, and though he sympathized strongly with her sense of responsibility for her parents' deaths, he would still rather have had her there.

"Are you going to stay about now," Stephen asked, "or do you intend to vanish again?"

Bartholomew knew quite well what Sommerset had advised, but the duke had also practically banned him from the Adventurers' Club. "I will leave that up to you, Stephen," he finally said. "I intend to defend my reputation and that of my men, so this is likely to become unpleasant. And if I stay here, I won't be the only one affected."

His brother glanced toward the depths of the house for a long moment. At least he was taking this seriously, Bartholomew noted, whatever his answer would be.

"The more I read about the so-called frivolousness

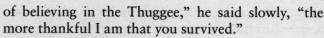

of believing in the Thuggee," he said slowly, "the more thankful I am that you survived."

"Stephen, you—"

"If you'd been killed, or simply vanished, and the Company put out that nonsense of a report, I would be out for blood. As it is, I can only imagine the . . . outrage of the families of the men who didn't return." The viscount took a breath. "You are staying here, Tolly, if I have to remove every stair railing, cane, and wheeled chair from this house. Is that clear?"

Thank God for family. They stood by him, even if a witty, forthright chit of impeccable manners chose not to. "Very clear," he said aloud. "Thank you."

"Do you have any idea how you'll fight these accusations?"

"Not yet." A heavily breathing Lackaby arrived at the foot of the stairs with his wheeled chair and three footmen. Lackaby, who'd served in India as the personal valet to the future Duke of Wellington.

The valet swallowed, eyeing him. "You've got a bit of a . . . a look about you today, Colonel."

"Do I? I was just thinking that you and I need to have a little chat." As he sank into the chair, he shot another look at Stephen. "You're going to a party tonight, are you not?"

"We were. Under the—"

"I'd like to go with you."

Montrose walked up to Theresa before she even had time to relinquish her wrap and procure a dance card. "Tess, you put the sun to shame," he drawled, bending over her hand with an exaggerated bow.

Whether the action was meant to inform her that

all was well and friendly in the ballroom or if it was a mere flirtation, she found it immensely reassuring. All day she'd been nervous about the Clement ball. What would she do when someone made a comment disparaging Tolly? She couldn't laugh and go along with the defamations, because that was wrong. If she said something in his defense, though . . . Oh, what a blasted rat's nest.

"I suppose I must grant you the waltz in exchange for your compliment," she said aloud, shaking herself and forcing a smile.

"I think that's fair enough," Montrose agreed. His gaze took in the crowded room. "Any word from your fr—"

"Oh, is that Harriet?" Theresa interrupted. "That lavender is so lovely on her, don't you think?" She waved. "Harriet!"

For forty-three minutes, it worked. By paying close attention, she deflected at least nine references by her friends that might possibly have been about Tolly. But then, in the middle of stopping another rumor by speculating over whether the wind might pick up tomorrow and give a chance for kite flying, she glanced toward the main ballroom doors.

Oh, my.

He'd worn his uniform. Evidently Colonel Bartholomew James didn't mean to sit quietly at home and wait to be forgotten. As she watched, he rose from his chair and stood to shake hands with the Duke of Sommerset. Chair waiting behind him or not, he looked . . . magnificent. A lion among sheep.

Her heart twisted in her chest. He could be hers.

The striking man in that striking red coat wanted to be with her, wanted her, and the only thing keeping them apart was those rumors, and her. Her and a set of rules she'd made for herself because of something that had happened thirteen years ago.

Tolly half turned in her direction, and Theresa quickly took a step behind the Marquis of Montrose. If Tolly met her gaze everyone would know she was a coward. And at the moment that seemed even more significant than accusations of impropriety. It all meant the same thing, though—she couldn't be anywhere near him.

"Shall we take a stroll?" Alexander asked, his light blue eyes flicking a gaze between her and Colonel James.

"Oh, yes." She grabbed onto his arm. "That would be splendid."

In no time they were out of the ballroom and down the hallway to the quiet and thankfully deserted library. How was she supposed to avoid conversation about Tolly now? He was just a few doors away, and so . . . imposing. People might avoid insulting him to his face if they had any sense of self-preservation at all, but the chatter behind his back would increase tenfold.

"If you continue pacing like that, you'll wear a hole into the breakfast room ceiling," Alexander noted.

She hadn't even realized she was pacing. "Apologies," she said, stopping in front of him. "I seem to be a bit distracted tonight."

Montrose tilted her chin up with his fingers. "Perhaps I can help." Then he leaned down and kissed her. Smooth, warm, and skilled, it caught her completely off guard. Slowly he straightened again, looking down at her. "Any better?" he asked.

"I—stop that."

"Marry me, Tess. Say yes, and you'll be a marchioness in a fortnight."

Theresa blinked. It was such a simple request. Three words. A few weeks ago, that kiss and those words might have been enough to convince her. Suddenly everything seemed plainly, painfully clear. She wasn't going to marry Alexander Rable and be the Marchioness of Montrose. She wanted to be with Bartholomew James.

And Montrose still stood there, gazing at her. Expecting an answer, this time. "As I said, Alexander," she began, "I'm not ready to marry." Her voice shook, but not because of the handsome man standing before her. Rather, she felt all shivery inside because of the man just down the hallway.

"Mmm-hmm. You're not ready to marry, or you're not ready to marry me?"

"Clearly they both mean the same thing, Alexander."

"No, they don't. I have no qualms over protecting your sensibilities if, in the end, doing so is to my benefit. Holding your hand while you decide to screw up your courage enough to approach him again, however, is something else entirely."

"Alexa—"

"You have one week to overcome your infatuation, Tess. If you choose not to, I will take myself elsewhere. It shouldn't be all that difficult for you, considering you don't even want to be seen looking

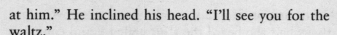

at him." He inclined his head. "I'll see you for the waltz."

With that he left the library.

Theresa looked at the closed door. Of all the mean, manipulative things to say. Except that it was plainly the truth. After a moment, realizing that her hands were clenched, she strode to the window and back again. She knew she had a reputation for propriety. She knew that everyone else knew it. But this—

Just when had people begun using her . . . her squeamishness against her? Had other people aside from Montrose made plans *counting* on the fact that she could be relied upon to act in a certain way? That was simply too much.

"Bloody hell," she blurted, then clapped both hands over her mouth. The bad curse. She *never* used the bad curse.

And yet, nothing happened.

Lightning didn't streak through the closed window to strike her. No one ran into the room and began calling her a hoyden. She certainly *felt* precisely the same, except . . . better.

"Bloody hell," she repeated, allowing the words to roll along her tongue. It felt oddly satisfying. After all, she was quite fond of a man who had very bad manners, no sense of convention, and who was at the beginning of a very unpleasant fight for his reputation. And another man had just all but called her a coward and delivered her an ultimatum.

"Bloody hell," she said for a third time, beginning to understand why some men were so fond of the curse. It was magnificent, really.

The liquor tantalus caught her eye. How many times had she heard the stuff called liquid courage? Well, she could certainly use a bit of that.

Tentatively she tugged on the latch holding up the piece of wood that locked the bottles in place. It fell open with no effort at all. Well, that smacked of providence. Sending a look over her shoulder, heady excitement coursing through her, she picked up one of the pretty decanters, pulled out the stopper, and poured a small portion of the amber liquid into a waiting glass. Still no punishment rained from the heavens or through the closed door to stop her.

Theresa lifted the glass. Then, holding her breath, she took a long, deep swallow.

Fire poured down her throat, raw and burning up into her nostrils, making her eyes water and setting her gagging. "Bloody hell," she choked. Then, pinching her nose shut, she finished off the glass. Liquid courage, indeed.

Chapter Fourteen

"A lady may occasionally imbibe a glass of Madeira or ratafia. A lady who drinks whiskey or any of the stronger spirits, even with little finger delicately poised in the air, is no lady at all. She may as well light up a cigar."

A LADY'S GUIDE TO PROPER BEHAVIOR

The moment Lackaby rolled him into the ballroom, Bartholomew's gaze went to the large, chatty group standing to one side of the dance floor.

Of course she'd be at its center. Theresa Weller was the sun around which all lesser planets circled. But then the sun had hidden behind the damned moon that was the Marquis of Montrose the moment she'd glimpsed him and his very obvious chair. Then she'd fled the blasted room with the man.

"No one's so much as glancing in our direction," Stephen commented under his breath.

"Yes, they are."

"Well, they aren't approaching. Why the devil did you have to wear that damned uniform?"

"It made me the man I am today."

Stephen leaned over him, something which Bartholomew had swiftly realized he disliked. "Do not send your sarcasm my way, Tolly. I am on your side, if you'll recall."

"I know that," Bartholomew retorted, keeping his voice low. "If *you'll* recall, I informed you that standing by me would not be pleasant."

"At least Sommerset shook your hand. The man has a great deal of influence. At the least, everyone's afraid to cross him. To his face. But unless he stands beside you all evening, th—"

"Which he has no reason to do," Bartholomew cut in. The duke had already made it more than clear that his support wouldn't for the most part be public.

There was no reason for it to be otherwise. And in truth, tonight he wouldn't have cared if everyone present turned his or her back on him—save one. She, however, had already fled the room.

Lackaby leaned over his other shoulder. "Whatever you're looking for here, Colonel, you ain't going to find allies. Never seen so many noses pointed in the air."

"I'm not looking for anything," Bartholomew returned. "I'm reminding them that I'm here."

"Well. That seems to be working, then."

It was, at that. The East India Company could claim that India was safe as kittens, but he had a rather obvious limp. They could call him incompetent, which he could almost sense coming, but they couldn't deny that he'd been wounded. In India.

The music for the evening's first dance began.

Montrose reappeared to take a petite, dark-haired chit by the arm and lead her forward. Other than noting that nearly everyone seemed to want to dance tonight, Bartholomew didn't pay them any mind.

Of much more interest was the lad, Lord Biskell's second son, as he recalled, standing just to the side and looking from Theresa's grandmother to the dance floor as though he'd lost something. Bartholomew could guess what it was. Tess hadn't reappeared from wherever she'd gone off to with Montrose. A few moments later Biskell's son gave the room at large an uncertain smile and wandered off in the direction of the refreshment table.

Theresa Weller would not leave a dance partner standing without excuse or explanation. "Lackaby."

The valet stood behind him, tapping his toes to the rhythm of the quadrille. "Aye, Colonel?"

"Push me over there." He indicated the door on one side of the room through which Tess and Montrose had vanished.

"How do I get one of them sugared orange peels?"

"You don't. Push."

With a jolt he and the chair moved. He saw the looks and the swift glances away. He'd seen them since he'd entered the room. He didn't care; tonight was only about making his presence known. In the next day or two he would begin pushing back.

"Stop here."

The chair stopped. "Well, this seems much nicer over here," the valet observed, sarcasm thick in his tone.

Bartholomew held up one hand. "Cane."

"Colonel, you keep walking on the damned leg and it's likely to give up and fall off."

"Cane."

The valet blew out his breath. "Don't say I didn't warn you." With exaggerated care Lackaby handed over the stick of scorched ash with its very sharp rapier hidden inside. The valet's warning was a good one; whatever Bartholomew wanted to accomplish, he had to weigh whether he wished to do it with one leg, or two.

Any sense of self-preservation, though, paled in comparison with his desire to find out where Tess had got to. Whether she wanted him to find her or not.

He pushed upright, hiding his wince as the movement pulled at healing bone and muscle. Leaning on his cane much more heavily than he liked, Bartholomew left the ballroom behind. The half dozen doors to his right and to his left were all open, with the exception of one.

Despite his inclination not to trust his instincts any longer, he headed down the hallway toward the closed door. A pair of servants caught up and passed him, continuing on toward the stairs that would be at the rear of the house.

Sending a quick glance up and down the now-empty hallway, he gripped the door latch and pushed. The door opened silently before him. He moved quietly, not certain what to expect or even completely convinced she would be there.

"Bloody *hell*," he heard from across the room in Tess's distinctive voice.

He knew in an instant that something was awry. Theresa stood near one of the bookcases that lined the left wall. In her hand was a glass. As he watched, she took a delicate sip.

"*Bloody* hell," she said again, making a face.

Christ. As swiftly as he could, Bartholomew shut the door behind him. "Theresa."

Visibly jumping, she faced him. "Vodka is a vile drink," she said. "I prefer whiskey."

"Then why are you drinking vodka?"

"I had to try it, you know. Otherwise, how could I judge?"

Something had definitely happened. Reaching behind him with his free hand, Bartholomew threw the bolt to lock the door. Whatever was amiss, he certainly knew enough about Theresa Weller to realize she would be mortified if anyone caught sight of her now.

"Tess," he said slowly, keeping his voice low and level, "what's troubling you?" What he wanted to do was grab her and shake her and ask if Montrose had done something to harm her. If he had, the marquis was a dead man.

She blew out her lips. "Do you know what I am?" she asked.

Several answers came to mind, among them *lovely* and *inebriated.* "What are you?" he asked aloud.

"I am two things." She lifted two fingers at him, looked at the V she'd made, then giggled and covered the gesture with her other hand. The glass fell to the floor, but she didn't seem to notice it. "That was naughty, wasn't it?"

"Only if you meant it to be. Which two things are you?"

"Oh, yes. I almost forgot. I am predictable, and I am a coward."

He cleared his throat. "I must say, I don't find you predictable at all."

Theresa clapped once, then jabbed a single finger in his direction. "No, you don't," she exclaimed. "I am not predictable around you. It's *your* fault."

"Hmm. Don't expect me to apologize for that."

"I knew you wouldn't."

"And *I* know you're not a coward, Theresa."

"But I am. And everyone knows it. Alex, Alexander the Great, gave me a week to decide whether to marry him or not. And he *knows* what I'll say, because he *knows* I can't be around you." She stepped closer and lowered her voice. "Because of the scandal."

The scandal. He'd actually forgotten about that for a moment, the way he seemed to forget everything dark when she was about. And he wanted so badly to kiss her that he was almost willing to pretend that nothing outside that room even existed. Almost. "I should be going, then."

"No! You should stay." Theresa hurried forward.

Before he could put out a hand to stop her, Tess hit him in the chest. The cane slid out from beneath his grip, and he went down on his backside. Theresa fell with him, landing across his chest with a thud that knocked the air from his lungs.

For a dozen heartbeats he lay there, trying to recover his breath and assess whether his leg remained attached to the rest of him. Petite though she was, Theresa packed a punch. "Tess?" he rasped, putting a hand across her back.

Abruptly she lifted her head, looking down at him from mere inches away. Disheveled blond hair framed her face, her gray-green eyes as surprised as his likely were. "Don't seduce me," she ordered, her gaze lowering to his mouth.

He wanted to. If she hadn't been drunk and upset, he wouldn't have been able to stop himself. "I'm not."

"Oh." Slowly, almost as though she was being dragged forward against her will, she sank down along his body again and kissed him.

She tasted rather strongly of spirits, but Bartholomew didn't give a damn about that. Her mouth molded against his, warm and soft and perfect. He drew his arms around her hip and shoulder, holding her close against him. Desire twitched into his bones.

Fingers began plucking at his neat, military-style cravat, pulling at the knot there. With a silent curse and a very clear understanding that he would very likely regret the next few moments for the rest of his life, Bartholomew broke from her mouth.

"Anywhere but here, Tess," he said softly. "And any time but now." He shifted to put his hands over hers, between them, to stop her from undressing him.

"But this is what you want," she breathed, frowning.

"Yes, it is. But not so you'll hate me for it tomorrow."

She scowled down at him. "You'll miss your chance, Bartholomew. Tonight I am cursing and drinking. I'm almost certain I won't do either one tomorrow. And that means I won't do this, either." She lowered her mouth onto his again.

He sank into the kiss for a moment, then pushed her shoulders, lifting her off him. "Then I suppose I will do without."

"But—"

"You won't want me tomorrow, Tess. You made that clear. And I'd prefer that you simply avoid me rather than hate me."

"I hate you a little bit at this very moment."

"I hate myself more than a little at this moment." He gave her one last, close look, then set her away from him so he could sit up.

"It isn't fair, you know," she said, blowing a strand of her hair from her forehead. "I meant to be a paragon of virtue."

Good God, was he ever falling for the wrong woman. "You still are. We've only kissed."

"I wrote a booklet on proper behavior. It's widely circulated."

"I heard that you had."

"I like kissing you, very much. And I keep thinking about how much I would like . . . everything else with you."

"I think about that, as well." He glanced around them. The most likely object to be able to support his weight was the wall, and that was several feet away.

"Perhaps if you told me that you mean to live quietly until some other scandal takes everyone's attention away from the East India Company nonsense, then we could . . . kiss again. I might even be able to pretend to visit Amelia and come see you instead." She brushed her fingers through his hair. "You do need a trim, you know."

"Yes, I know. The problem, sweet Tess, is that if I agree to be labeled an incompetent and a coward, I've doomed the reputations of my men. No one else can speak for them."

The butler inclined his head. "I will see to it at once."

Michael's office was two doors down the hallway from the breakfast room. Theresa knocked at the closed door, then pushed it open at his reply.

"Thank you for rescuing me last night," she said, before he could begin chastising her.

"You're welcome." He closed the ledger book in front of him. "I've done enough . . . questionable things that I'm not going to yell at you, but I am a bit curious, Troll."

She sighed. "About what?"

"Why after all this time did you decide the Clement soiree was the place to go completely mad? Aside from the fact that Lord Brasten keeps a fine wine cellar."

She set her tea on his desk, then dropped into a chair. Immediately she regretted the motion, and pressed her fingertips to her temple. "Oh, heavens."

Michael sat forward to nudge her tea closer to her. "You'll be feeling better by noon, I imagine."

Three more hours of this. Well, she'd done it to herself, so she would live with the consequences. "Alexander proposed to me again."

He nodded. "He asked my permission. I told him that he needed yours."

"He had this odd idea that I'm infatuated with Tolly James, but that I won't dare go near the colonel because of the scandal. That apparently means that I must make a final decision, and he wants it in the next week."

"Mmm-hmm. That seems an . . . understandable stance for him to take."

"Oh, you think so, do you? I considered it completely underhanded. Counting on my cowardice is just mean."

Her brother gazed at her for a long moment. They were only three years apart, and generally she considered them to be on fairly even ground. Today, though, his light green eyes were full of compassion and sympathy, and even wisdom. And despite her aching head she felt very—well, not young, but unsure. She'd never walked this path before, and she wasn't certain if she should.

"If you don't wish to marry Montrose, all you need do is say so. You don't need to set yourself three sheets to the wind and risk being ruined."

"I didn't do that because I'm upset over Alexander. I did it, I think, because I never do anything."

"My dear," came from behind her, as Grandmama Agnes swept into the room, "while I can't condone your sudden interest in liquor, I am very pleased that you haven't completely done away with that spirit that's always filled you."

"You're happy I misbehaved?"

"All I will say about it at this moment is that indulging oneself should be done sparingly. Because if you go looking for trouble, it will find you."

"That's not terribly helpful." Theresa swallowed. "And what about scandal? If I am seen speaking with Tolly, the—"

"I suggest one step at a time," Agnes interrupted.

"And no more drinking," her brother added.

She looked from one to the other of them. Of course she'd been the one to be obsessed with propriety, but even so their . . . cavalier view of what a few weeks ago would have had her weeping in shame continued to surprise her.

As Tolly had noted, suffering a few sideways glances was far easier than living through the tragedy she'd known. Clearly he felt the same, or he wouldn't have worn that magnificent uniform of his last night. And so if she wanted to have another chat with her friend who happened to be at the center of a possible maelstrom, then she supposed she could give it a try.

Chapter Fifteen

"Which of us hasn't wished to throw back her bonnet and feel the wind on her face? The sensation is lovely, but your red, raw cheeks will be the mark of your carelessness. Reckless pleasure has a price."

A LADY'S GUIDE TO PROPER BEHAVIOR

How long do I need to push you back and forth here?" Lackaby grunted, reversing direction again. "I'm getting blisters."

Bartholomew snapped open his pocket watch. "According to you, Wellington's generally prompt. I'll give him another twenty minutes. If he doesn't appear, I'll either have to find another way to get to him, or I'll have to go to the Horse Guards to have a look for allies."

"They won't give you anything if the East India Company's already lining their pockets. Which it is."

"I know. They may have the records to prove my argument, though."

"Which will prove them liars."

"I didn't say I would go through the front door," Bartholomew returned.

"Seems like they'd be happier if you were dead, Colonel."

The thought had actually occurred to him before; it was another reason for him to make his presence in London known. He didn't want to be able to disappear without commentary.

Bartholomew glanced up at the gates of Apsley House again. A few weeks ago he'd been halfway to wishing the Thuggee had succeeded and he was still down in that damned well rotting with his men. By calling him a liar, the East India Company had forced him into action.

A pair of liveried grooms ran out to the ornate Apsley House gates and pulled them open as a grand black coach rolled down the carriage drive and onto the street. *Damnation.* He hadn't expected Wellington to be on foot, but stopping a carriage hadn't been a part of his plan, either.

"Push me out," Bartholomew ordered.

"Beg pardon?"

"*Push me into the street.*"

"You'll be killed."

"Now, Lackaby."

The valet gave him a hard shove. He rolled forward, coming to a stop directly in front of the looming coach-and-four. The valet dove out of the way, but Bartholomew stood. He'd faced death; nothing else much impressed.

The coach skidded to a halt. "Move aside, you bloody fool!" the driver bellowed at him.

Bartholomew took a limping step forward. "That's Colonel bloody fool to you," he returned. "I require a brief word with His Grace."

"His Grace does not stop to chat with every supposed soldier who steps into his path. Move a—"

"That's enough, Smith."

The coach door swung open. Hurriedly the tiger seated beside Smith jumped to the ground and flipped down the trio of steps spanning from the coach to the ground. A booted foot emerged, and then the blue- and gray-clothed Duke of Wellington himself stepped onto the street.

"My driver is cautious," he said, keen eyes taking in Bartholomew and the chair behind him. "In the past, men have tried to kill me."

"Men have tried to kill me, as well. That's actually what I wanted to speak to you about."

"I know who you are, Colonel James. And I won't be pulled into a dispute with either the army or the East India Company. I have found them both to be invaluable allies in the past. They may prove to be so again."

Bartholomew understood that. "They say politics is a dangerous battlefield, Your Grace."

"And with fewer victories. I—" The duke stopped, his sharp-eyed gaze moving beyond Bartholomew to the edge of the street. "Lackaby, you old dog. Is that you?"

The valet came forward. "I hardly recognize ye, Your Grace. You've more medals and titles now than I can count."

"You're serving Colonel James now, I presume?"

Lackaby puffed out his chest. "I am, and proudly.

Colonel James holds the reputations of his fallen men in his hands, and he ain't about to let them be remembered as anything less than heroes."

Cool gray eyes shifted to regard Bartholomew once more. "Well, then. You're not likely to find many others with whom to compare stories, Colonel. In fact, your experience may well be unique." He frowned a little. "You're residing at James House?"

It was more a statement than a question, but Bartholomew nodded anyway. "I am."

"I may have some old notes you might find informative, though I don't know how helpful they'll be. I'll send them by this evening."

"Thank you."

"You're on the verge of making some very powerful enemies, Colonel. Consider carefully before you proceed. Not many men could stand against that onslaught. And you've only got the one good leg to begin with."

With another look Wellington climbed back into his carriage and knocked on the roof. Lackaby pushed the chair out of the street, and the big coach rolled into motion once more. Bartholomew limped aside and watched as it turned the corner and vanished.

"Well. Looks like you've got a bit of help, after all."

"A bit of help. If his old notes mention any Thuggee attacks. If they don't, I'm back to being alone again."

"I find that somewhat troubling, myself," Lackaby commented, moving the chair behind Bartholomew. "No other survivors means no one to talk."

"Means no proof of how they were actually killed. I am aware of this." Bartholomew sat, handing his cane back to the valet. "If it was easy to prove the Thuggees' existence, the East India Company wouldn't have discounted them. Let's go, shall we?"

"Where to now?"

"I thought I might return home for a pistol, and then take luncheon at the Army Club."

"They'll murder you there, Colonel."

Bartholomew gave a grim smile. "I'm a member. And if I'm fortunate enough to find another member who served in India, I might find an ally." He doubted it, and he wouldn't trust anyone who did come forward, but any additional evidence, stories, or rumors would add to his collection of evidence.

Six streets later, Lackaby was complaining that he was about to lose his own feet, and the left wheel of his chair was beginning to squeak. Apparently it would be a hack and the cane for his luncheon engagement. They turned up the drive to James House.

"Stop," he said, his breath catching before he could cover it.

"Thank God."

Bartholomew shared very nearly the same sentiment. The Weller barouche stood in front of the door, Amelia leaning on the side to talk with its seated occupant. A pretty yellow bonnet swept back from her face, one hand resting on her cousin's, sat Theresa.

"Go."

"I'm thinking we should figure a way to harness a pony to the front of this contraption," Lackaby said, grunting as he pushed the chair into motion again.

Theresa turned as Bartholomew rolled up the drive. On a lesser man the bumping and weaving of the chair might have looked silly, but the resigned, faintly amused expression on his face told her and everyone else who might chance to see him that he could manage on his own perfectly well and that he was only humoring the people around him.

He stood up, limping with his cane to the barouche. Whatever she'd said to him the night before, it hadn't driven him off. Then again, she'd never seen anything to make her think he frightened easily.

"Good morning, Theresa," he said, gripping one hand over the door of the carriage.

"Tolly." She swallowed, trying to settle the butterflies in her stomach. "I wondered if you might care to go driving this morning."

He held her gaze for a heartbeat, then straightened, shaking his head. "I need a haircut. Interested?" With that he nodded at Amelia, and went to haul himself up the steps and into the house.

"What was that about?" Amelia asked, watching him disappear inside.

"He doesn't trust anyone with sharp implements," Theresa offered. "You know that." Her heart beat even faster. She stood up, unlatching the door of the barouche and stepping to the ground. Sally scrambled behind her to catch up.

"He seems to trust you," Amelia observed, falling in beside her. "Sally, see about fetching us some tea and biscuits, will you? For the morning room."

Theresa had no intention of sitting in the morning room when Tolly had just challenged her again, but the request did free her from Sally for the moment. Everything felt topsy-turvy this morning, and she wasn't even certain her feet touched the ground. She imagined others would say it was the result of putting aside a burden she'd carried for a very long time, but she thought it was more about forgiveness. They'd said it all along, but for the first time she believed that her family didn't blame her for the accident. She glanced again at Amelia. Or most of them didn't, anyway.

"I thought you were avoiding Colonel James," her cousin noted.

"I came here, didn't I?"

"Clearly." Amelia took her arm, stopping her just short of the steps. "And why is that? I don't recall that you ever recommended assisting a gentleman with his toiletries in your booklet."

"It never came up."

"Theresa. What's happened?"

Tess took a deep breath. "I'm . . . looking for a new path, Leelee. I've been wondering, though, if I have the right to do so." A tear ran down one cheek, and she swiftly wiped it away. "I think I need your permission. If you say no, I won't be angry. I promise. I just need your per—"

"Oh, for heaven's sake, Tess. Get in the house." Amelia threw her arms around Theresa, giving her a tight hug. "Go on."

They were happy for her. Her family was actually pleased that she'd decided to reassess her obsession with rules—if she could. Thirteen years of perfect, proper behavior was a great deal to consider. It wasn't as though she meant purposely to misbehave, anyway. It was only that she didn't have to stay away from Tolly just because he might be in for a bit of trouble and raised eyebrows. She'd probably been exaggerating the scandal, anyway.

She climbed the staircase. For a man with a bad leg, Tolly moved fairly quickly. "Tolly?" she called, leaning around his half-open bedchamber door. "I'm not here to play hide-and-seek."

"At the risk of sending you fleeing again," his low voice came from directly behind her, "what *are* you here to play?"

She tried to hide her start as she faced him. "I wanted to apologize for my behavior last night."

"Ah." He moved around her into the bedchamber. "For the drinking, or for when you threw me to the ground and attempted to have your way with me?"

"I did not—" She snapped her jaw shut, her cheeks heating. She did have some rather vivid memories of kissing him. "For both things."

"Come in here." He faced her from halfway across the room. "I refuse to yell."

Her fingers just a touch unsteady, Theresa closed the door and threw the bolt. "You said something to me that night. It made sense."

"Yes? What was that?"

So he wouldn't make it easy for her. She couldn't precisely blame him; after all, here she was just under a day after she'd said she didn't wish to be around him any longer. "The part about both of us having already faced our worst moment." Theresa tilted her head. "I assume that means someone told you about my parents."

He nodded. "I was looking for puzzle pieces. You are rather fascinating."

Everyone else upon learning about the death of her parents said they were sorry, which always made her wonder why they were apologizing when it had been her fault. Or they implied that they could sympathize, when of course they had no idea.

"So have you put together my puzzle now?" she asked aloud.

"Clearly not, because I didn't expect to see you here this morning." Setting his cane aside, he gripped the nearest bedpost to approach her again. "If you merely felt the need to be sober while telling me off, you could have saved yourself the trouble."

"As I said, your advice to me made sense. That's why I'm here."

Bartholomew moved another step closer, his amber eyes studying hers very, very intently. She kept forgetting how tall he was when he rose from his chair. What she had been unable to forget, what she craved, was the arousal that flitted through her when he gazed at her as he was now. "So I'm back to courting you again? Or is it your turn?"

"I mean to let you court me. If you'll answer a question."

The fingers of his free hand lifted to brush along her cheek. "What question is that?"

"What happened in India?"

His hand dropped again. "Tess, you don't need to know that."

Despite her abrupt panic that she'd gained his attention once more only to lose it just as swiftly, Theresa stayed still. "I killed my parents through my own selfishness," she said quietly, her voice shaking. "You know my tragedy. It's only fair that I know yours. Especially if I'm to stand there beside you while you're called a liar."

Uttering a quiet curse, Tolly limped to the window. He stood still for a moment, then clenched his fists and pounded them into the sill. "I was wrong."

"About what?" She could think of several things, and then several more she *didn't* want to think about.

"That we're the same."

"I—"

"You threw a tantrum when you were a child. We all did, yelled and kicked our feet when we didn't get our way. Our parents threw tantrums when they were children. And as parents they gave in when it suited them to do so."

Theresa swallowed. "You've spent some time thinking about this, then."

"It's been occupying my mind lately."

"But this has nothing to do with you and India. It doesn't signify, anyway. I know what happened that night. You don't."

"Your brother and Amelia wanted to stay overnight at Reynolds House, because the Reynolds children were their age. You were what, three years younger? And you wanted to go home. Were you asleep when the coach overturned?"

"Yes, but I know what happened, for heaven's sake. Stop talking about it."

"If your parents had waited fifteen more minutes, you would have been asleep regardless of whether they listened to you or not. Do you think they didn't know that?"

"But I screamed for my doll! I threatened to run home if they didn't take me!"

He shook his head. "*That* doesn't signify. They wanted to return home, and you provided the excuse."

A tear plopped onto her hand, and she wiped it on her gown. She wanted to yell that it *was* her fault, as the rest of her family knew, whether they'd forgiven her for it or not. And she wanted to vomit, because she'd heard very similar arguments from Leelee and Grandmama Agnes and she'd dismissed them, but damned Tolly James made her listen to him, and he made sense.

"It's not true," she finally rasped. "And you're mean to attempt to try to distract me from your story by telling me mine."

"It's not a distraction." He sat heavily in the chair by the window. "Your guilt gives you something in common with me, but it's an illusion. I'd rather have you run now than later. Because India *was* my fault."

That stopped the additional protest Theresa had been about to make. "You think after you tell me what happened to you, I'll realize we have nothing in common after all?"

He avoided her searching gaze. "I just . . . you don't need to keep punishing yourself, Tess."

"And you do?"

"I've recently been called a liar and an incompetent coward. Fifteen men have only me to speak for them. I intend to do so. And it won't be pleasant."

The door rattled. "Colonel? The maid's looking for Miss Tess," Lackaby called.

Tolly looked at her. He expected her to leave, she realized. A few days ago she would have done so. Today, though, Bartholomew James seemed to be saying precisely what she'd wanted—needed—to hear for years.

She turned around and opened the door. "Please tell Sally to wait for me in the kitchen."

"I can do that. There's, ah, a lack of a chaperon in here. Should I, ah, come in? I don't embroider, but I could polish boots."

But she didn't want a chaperon. Neither of them could speak as freely as they had been with a chaperon present. Theresa frowned. "I will give you five pounds if you will find somewhere out of the way to polish boots and tell everyone later that you were in here."

The valet grinned at her. "Would an hour suffice?"

"Yes, I believe so."

He bent down and picked up the pair of boots sitting just inside the door. "Be good to him, miss," he whispered. "The next few weeks won't be."

She closed and latched the door again, then joined Tolly by the window. "You'd best begin telling me your tale," she said, sitting in the chair opposite him. "We only have an hour."

Unexpectedly, he snorted. "You arranged for us to be alone for an hour, and you want to spend the time talking?"

"I want to know what happened."

Pushing upright, he put his hands on either arm of her chair and leaned over her. "The problem with that, sweet Theresa, is that when I'm close to you, I can't seem to think of anything but you." He kissed her, tilting her chin up and molding his mouth to hers until she moaned.

She reached up, sliding her arms around his neck.

Just as he said, when they were together, everything else fell away. Even the realization that he was *still* not telling her what she wanted to know—even that didn't matter. Not when they had only an hour.

Using the chair's arms, Tolly muscled himself down onto his good knee, the other leg bent only slightly and angled to one side. It still looked like it hurt. Leaning forward, she followed him down so that their faces were nearly level.

"If you stay, Tess, you will not be able to put this chapter into any booklet on proper behavior."

Theresa touched his face. "Today I'm trying out a new path," she breathed, shivering all over. "A bit of impropriety."

He untied the ribbon at the waist of her gown. "A great deal of impropriety." Sitting back just a little, he curled a loose strand of her light-colored hair around his finger. "You make me feel human again, Tess. Alive. And you're safe with me. I swear it." Slowly he drew her in for another kiss. "I promise it, and I don't generally make promises any longer."

"You make me feel alive, Tolly," she whispered back. That was it; when she set eyes on him, when she chatted with him, her heart beat faster, she smiled more easily, even her steps felt lighter. And it had been at least thirteen years since she'd felt so . . . carefree.

When Alexander had kissed her—well, she couldn't even remember what it had felt like. But it hadn't felt like this. Bartholomew slid his hands slowly up her legs, her skirt lifting beneath his fingers.

"Tolly?" she said in a breathless voice that didn't much sound like her at all.

His palm brushed the inside of her knee. "Yes?"

"If I asked you to stop, would you?"

Amber eyes gazed at her from only inches away. "I'll tell you what. You come down here with me, and I'll leave stopping up to you."

With that he sat down, scooting backward on the floor midway between the chair and the bed. Then, still watching her, he untied his cravat and cast it aside, then one by one opened the buttons of his waistcoat.

Theresa couldn't get enough air into her lungs. Everywhere his fingers went, her mind followed, imagining that it was her touching him and undressing him. *It could be, stupid.* All she needed to do was sink down onto the floor. What the devil was she waiting for? After all, he couldn't very well chase her down if she decided to run.

Not that she wanted to run. Tolly lowered one shoulder, then the other, and pulled his coat from his shoulders. A slight smile touching his wicked mouth, he removed his waistcoat, as well.

"Shall I continue?" he asked. "Or would you care to join me?" His gaze stroked boldly down the length of her, then lifted again to her mouth. "Come here, Theresa," he whispered, his voice a low rumble that went all the way through her.

This was the moment. The moment she could choose whether to stay in her safe, bright, proper garden, or climb over the fence to see what life might offer. And over *this* fence there waited a handsome, battle-hardened man who had been creeping into her heart for weeks. Since the moment they'd met.

Taking a deep breath and holding it, Theresa slid

down from the chair and sank onto her knees. "Are we going to be completely naked?"

His lips curved. "Ideally."

"Then you should have your boots off." She clasped the heel of his right boot and tugged. It pulled loose, and she set it down aside. "I'll be careful with the other one."

Tolly cocked his head, leaning back on his elbows. "I know you will. And I'll be careful with you, sweet Theresa."

Of course he would be. She'd never had a single second of hesitation about that. She trusted Bartholomew James. It was the rest of the world and their opinions where she had her doubts.

Pushing against the top of his calf, she pulled the heel of his left boot. With a slight wince that he swiftly hid, Tolly shifted just a little and the boot came free.

"Well done. I told you that you have the makings of a fine valet." His smile deepened. "Come up here and kiss me."

Low excitement and arousal coursing through her, she glided up over him as he sank back flat onto the floor. Theresa lowered herself along his chest and touched her mouth to his. Tolly slid his arms around her back and shoulders, pulling her closer still. Slowly she relaxed against him, her world narrowing to where they touched, hips, breasts, and mouth. He felt warm, even through their clothes.

His hands lowered to her bottom and he gently squeezed, in a way that felt very good and very naughty. Then he began pulling the hem of her gown up toward his hands. Nerves fluttered through her again. "You should be naked first," she decided.

"Then get to work," he returned, amusement in his voice. "I can't do everything."

"Well, I've never done this before, so you'll have to excuse me."

He shifted again, taking her hands and placing them on the bottom folds of his fine linen shirt. "And I never thought to do this again."

That made her hesitate. When they'd first met, he had conducted himself like . . . like a dead man. He said she made him feel alive. Until now she hadn't realized that he meant it literally. It was a very powerful feeling. Letting out her breath again, she slipped her hands beneath his shirt and pushed upward, unfurling like a cat as her palms caressed warm, soft skin and hard muscles beneath.

Bartholomew groaned softly, lifting his shoulders a little and raising his arms so she could pull the shirt off over his head. With her hands on either side of his shoulders she sank down to kiss him again. This was absolute heaven, and she wanted more. More, more, more.

"As you wish."

She hadn't even realized she'd spoken aloud until he answered her. Tolly fiddled with the front of his trousers, tickling against her stomach, then lifted both her and his hips to shove his trousers down.

"I'm naked now," he announced, kissing all along the base of her jaw until she felt like nothing but a mass of aroused, lightning-tipped nerves. And she had her gown, her shift, and her shoes on. With a very handsome, very naked man beneath her. She shifted her hips, feeling the large, hard . . . thing pressed against her. And she wanted to see him.

Theresa rolled off his right side, her legs tangling in her disheveled skirts. "Oh, my," she whispered, looking down past his hips.

"Turn around," he said with a deepening grin, and made a spinning motion with his forefinger. "I don't want to tear off any buttons."

Buttons. Oh, yes, her dress. Reluctantly lifting her gaze, she turned away. Tolly sat up behind her, and as she pulled his trousers the rest of the way off and then slipped off her shoes, he unbuttoned the back of her gown.

Pushing the material forward, he kissed the nape of her neck. "Can you put your hair up on your own?" he asked, his voice not quite steady.

"No. It took Sally twenty minutes to pin it up this morning." And she'd been so impatient to be gone to James House the entire time.

"Then I won't take it down," he breathed, sounding wistful. "This time."

His kisses continued along her shoulders, inch by inch as he bared her skin. She turned and caught his mouth for another kiss, their tongues dancing as she moaned helplessly. "This is very nice," she breathed.

Bartholomew pulled her arm to turn her back to face him. With his help she freed her arms from the dress, and he lowered it to her waist. "Very nice," he echoed, brushing the backs of his fingers across the outside of her breasts and then drawing them closer and closer until he dragged his thumbs across her nipples.

She gasped, jumping at the sensation. With a low sound, Tolly shifted her onto his lap. "Up," he said, pushing her dress down her hips.

Theresa lifted up, and a moment later she was as naked as he was. More naked, because he had a bandage around his left knee. With anyone else she would have been embarrassed—mortified, but Tolly seemed so . . . fascinated with her that she was too occupied with trying to remember his every touch, his every breath, that the thought didn't even occur to her except in passing.

"What should I do?" she asked, shivering again as a palm covered her breast.

"Whatever you want. I, for example, intend to do this." With a glance up at her from beneath his thick eyelashes, he dipped his head, his soft, warm mouth closing over her other breast.

She dug her fingers into his ragged, mahogany-colored hair, throwing her head back as his tongue flicked across her nipple. *Oh, good heavens.* No wonder this wasn't considered proper behavior. She didn't feel at all proper. What she did feel was wild and wanton and very, very naughty. If he could put his mouth on her, she supposed she could do the same to him. In a moment, of course. She had no intention of stopping him as he turned his attention to her other breast.

When he went after her mouth again, she pushed against his shoulders. She couldn't possibly have budged him if he wanted to stay put, but he gave in and lay down flat on his back again. Mostly flat. The very interesting bit in the middle wasn't at all flat.

She kissed his mouth, then trailed her lips down

his throat as he'd done with her, feeling his pulse and the faint stubble of beard beneath her touch, then the irregular pattern of the scar at the base of his neck. He jumped a little, but she kept kissing him. In a moment she felt him relax again. Now that she had something to compare it to, she could swear that she almost felt as drunk as she had last night—only more euphoric, less weighty. Floating, almost.

"Straddle me," he growled, lifting up to catch her mouth with his again.

Oh my, oh my. Shivery and nervous again, she did as he asked, placing her knees on either side of his hips, that interesting part of his she'd most recently discovered brushing the inside of her thighs with a warm insistence that had her panting.

"Tolly."

He sat up, putting them eye to eye. "I want to do this right for you," he said, his fingers trailing across her skin as though he couldn't help touching her. "But I'm a bit hampered at the moment."

"Are you? I hadn't noticed."

"No, I don't suppose you would." Bartholomew kissed her again, one hand on her face and the other dipping breathlessly between her legs. "Follow me," he murmured, drawing her down on him. "And not to make another excuse, but you'll more than likely enjoy this more every time after this."

"This is very nice."

He smiled. "Just don't yell, or we're both in trouble."

Carefully she sank down on him, feeling the tip of his very large member sliding up inside her. The sensation was . . . indescribable. Why would this make her yell?

Tolly put both hands on her hips. "There are better ways to do this," he continued, "but I'm bloody well not willing to wait." Slowly he pressed his hips forward, pulling her down on him at the same time.

She felt resistance, then sharp pain. Before she could yelp, Tolly kissed her, muffling the sound. Theresa doubled her fists, clenching them against his shoulders. He kept very still, and after a moment the pain began to fade, replaced by . . . "Good God," she muttered, arching her back.

"Mmm-hmm. Move with me." Tolly pulled her forward, impaling her more fully. Rocking back and forth, clinging to him, she couldn't even speak as he filled her and retreated a little, only to return with a rhythm that had her moaning in time.

Holding her around the hips again, he increased his pace, his heated gaze nearly as arousing as his body moving inside hers. The muscles across her abdomen tightened, bringing her closer and closer to the edge of something she couldn't describe, but abruptly needed desperately. Faster and faster, deeper and deeper, and then she gave way. With a keening groan that didn't even sound like her everything went white and hot and pulsing all around Bartholomew.

Bending his head against her shoulder, he held her hard against him, his breathing as ragged as hers. When he lay back again, he brought her with him, and she sank, completely spent, against his chest. And she'd thought riding horses the most delightful thing ever. Clearly though, she'd discovered something even better.

"Are you well?" he asked into her hair, his arms loose around her, keeping her warm and close.

"Yes. That was . . . extraordinary."

"I wanted that with you. I needed it, I think."

She lifted her head to look at him. "Because I make you feel alive?"

Bartholomew nodded. "Yes. And because I *am* alive. I forgot that for a time."

Slowly and gently she ran her fingertip along the scar on his throat. He closed his eyes, but this time he didn't flinch. It was a gesture of trust and surrender—and she realized that she was very likely the only person he'd ever surrendered to. "Tolly," she whispered, sinking into his embrace again, "thank you. For trusting me."

His grip around her tightened a little. "All I can say to that, Tess," he murmured, "is that I am likewise honored." Tolly's chest rose and fell beneath her cheek. "And speaking of trust," he said slowly, "I think I can tell you now. About India."

Chapter Sixteen

"When a gentleman converses, a lady must listen, giving every indication that she finds his conversation interesting, his wit sparkling, and his company incomparable. Between you and me, she is lucky to find genuinely present one of the three, with two being a surprise, and all three something of a miracle."

A LADY'S GUIDE TO PROPER BEHAVIOR, 2ND EDITION

He still didn't want to tell her. But Theresa had shown her trust in him in the most telling way possible, and he needed to repay that very great honor.

Her being there meant his plans had to change. Whether she intended to risk just one moment of impropriety or not, as Bartholomew buttoned his trousers and hauled himself to his feet, he knew he was looking at his future wife. And the prospect filled him with fear and excitement, apprehension and affection all at once. He meant to do right by her, but in the past he'd failed at that task miserably. And he was about to tell her all about it.

And he'd already cheated; he'd meant it when he said he would stand by her, but this seduction had happened because he had a very good idea that after this she wouldn't be too keen to stand by him. Having her only once would be torture, but not having her at all would be worse than death.

"Are you going to keep looking at me, or are you going to talk?" she asked, looking very content sitting in his most comfortable chair and wearing nothing but her shift. She may have hesitated for far too long about her behavior, but she seemed very easy with her decision now. He hoped she wouldn't regret it overly much.

"I'd been in India for the past three and a half years, since the end of Bonaparte. I'm fairly fluent in Urdu, and so my commander, General Osprey, sent me out frequently to deal with local matters."

Still barefoot, he limped to the window and sank one haunch against the deep sill. He felt more like pacing, but after the several exertions of the morning, his leg literally wouldn't stand for it.

"All along we'd heard rumors of the Thuggee, how they would find men traveling on the road far from home, offer to keep them company, and then strangle or stab them to death in the night, dispose of the corpses, and make off with their belongings. Because the men were so far from home, it would be months sometimes before anyone even noticed they were missing. And by then, all traces would be gone."

"It's very clever," she commented quietly. "Horrific, but clever."

"The consensus at Fort William was that the Thuggee stories were exaggerated. After all, if they were so deadly and never left any survivors, who was carrying the tales? At any rate, four or five units would go out twice a week to patrol the roads and make the locals feel safer. Frequently the local Punjabis would hire us to escort them from their homes to Bombay or Delhi. It was good money, and fairly easy work, and it made for friendly relations with the natives.

"I received orders to escort Aadi Surabhi, the eldest son of the local zamindar—chieftain—to Delhi. Aadi and I were about the same age, and we got on well." They'd been friends, but dwelling on that fact wouldn't change the outcome of the story any. "Ten days in, we caught up to a group of monks traveling in the same direction. They said they'd heard that the Thuggee were operating in the area, and they asked if they could camp with us." He shrugged. "There were only eight of them, and together with Aadi's men we were fifteen."

"A logical decision."

He sent her a brief, grim smile. "I thought so at the time. They were jolly fellows. The group's elder had a fondness for tobacco, and he was really quite funny. He was called Parashar, after one of the Hindu saints. I liked him, as well. Another three days saw us into some very rugged country, and I kept scouts out looking for any signs of ambush."

Bartholomew took another slow breath. "As we made camp, the monks began talking about some sort of celestial event that evening. They were all quite excited, and delighted to see that the sky looked to be clear." He glanced at her, taking in her rapt expression, then looked away again. "Do you know why they were so interested in the sky?"

"No."

"Because they could sit beside us, pointing up. When we looked skyward, they threw the garrotes around our necks to strangle us. It was all very quiet at first, just them breathing and us flailing about a little. Then the others came out of the brush. Apparently they'd been following us for three days, and knew when the attack would take place."

"My God."

"I managed to reach my boot knife before a third man could come in to pin my arms. I stabbed him, and broke away. Then I grabbed for my pistol and started shooting."

"Tolly," she breathed, horror in the sound.

"They outnumbered us at least eight or nine to one. We had guns, but most of us never got to them. I remember being stabbed in the side, with a half dozen of them hanging on me and trying to drag me down again. One group of them was digging through our damned supplies while others were still murdering my men. I must have passed out, and when I opened my eyes I was being dragged up to an old well. I could see them tossing in my men, along with Aadi, his people—everyone. I kicked free, grabbed a rifle, and shot Parashar."

"Good for you."

"A bit late to do any damned good. I dropped him, but someone else put a bullet through my leg. They must have been angry with me, because I was rather thoroughly punched and kicked before they dropped me into the well. I remember falling for what seemed like a very long time. The landing at the bottom wasn't so bad—until I realized that it was the bodies of my men, my friends, that had cushioned my fall.

"By searching them, I found another pistol, three knives, and a flint, along with a small bit of water in a canteen." He closed his eyes for a moment, but the images were too close, things he would never tell her about the look of dead eyes gazing at him and the sound of the flies and the smell.

"I don't know how long I was down there, but by using the knives I finally climbed my way out again. Since the Thuggee thought we were all dead, they hadn't bothered to hide their trail, and with the help of a pony I stole, I found it fairly easily. And I remembered that one of the crates we'd been toting had been full of explosives." He turned to gaze out the window. "I don't think any of them survived that. One of the horses did, and I hauled myself over the saddle. When I came to again, I was at one of the local villages being pulled out of the saddle by another of our patrol units. You know the rest."

He heard her stand up. A moment later her hand touched his shoulder. "Look at me."

Bartholomew looked up into her gray-green eyes. "Are you going to tell me that it wasn't my fault? I knew about the rumors, I knew the danger of allowing strangers into camp, but I thought Parashar was amusing. I jested with him. I shared my tobacco and my supplies with him. I gave the order to allow him and his men to join us." And even with all that, at times he thought the worst thing he'd done was to survive.

Theresa leaned down and kissed him. She shone

so bright after the months he'd spent in darkness. Touching her felt almost too close to joy—joy he no longer had any right to.

"I am glad that you lived, Bartholomew James," she whispered, her tears wetting his cheeks. "We never would have met, otherwise. And what happened to you can't be allowed to happen to anyone else. If you'd died, the next group of travelers might already have met up with Parashar and been killed."

Straightening, he leaned down past her for his shirt. "Don't let Lord Hadderly hear you say that."

"I don't think I like Lord Hadderly or his East India Company very much." She ran a palm down his back, her touch both soothing and arousing at the same time. He tried not to flinch when her fingers paused at the jagged scar left by the dagger they'd driven in just below his ribs, but he couldn't quite manage it. "You're alive for a reason, Tolly. Tell me you believe that."

He shrugged again, pulling his shirt on over his head and straightening from his slouch. "I suppose I should have known I could rely on the Company's greed to give me a purpose, but it doesn't sound all that noble."

"It doesn't have to be noble. It just has to be done."

If she'd said anything more comforting, he wouldn't have tolerated it. In all likelihood, though, she knew that. She did seem to have a knack for cutting to the heart of the matter. Arousal spiraled through him again. Bartholomew caught hold of her hand and drew her around to face him.

"You are an unusual woman," he murmured, taking her face in his hands and kissing her again.

He couldn't seem to get enough of her. "And once you realize what a fix I'm likely to be in, you'd do well to run the other way."

"I already know what a fix you're in." She brushed hair out of his eyes. "If you hadn't . . . if you hadn't survived that attack and returned to London, do you think I would be marrying Montrose?"

"You're not marrying him. He's too pretty."

She squinted one eye at him. "I'm being serious."

"Ah. Then I don't know if you would be marrying him."

"He's asked me three times in two years, and mentioned it at least a half dozen times more. Alexander is—well, he's perfect. I am not perfect. And so no, I would not be marrying him under any circumstances. Or anyone else, I imagine. Why do you think I made Michael promise to settle an income on me regardless of my marital state?"

Her skin was so soft and so warm. Sliding the arm of her shift down her shoulder, he followed the trail with his mouth.

"Tolly, are you listening to me?"

"Yes." He pulled her arm free of the shift, turning his attention to her bared right breast. "You're not marrying Montrose." He flicked his tongue across the nipple, then took her breast into his mouth.

Theresa sank against him. "That's not . . . oh, heavens . . . that's not the . . . the point of what I was saying."

He pulled her other arm free. "Is it not?"

Arching her back, she presented him with a lovely view of her breasts as he dipped down for the other one. His cock twitched in response, more than ready for a deeper acquaintance with her however much his leg ached. In part he was surprised that she hadn't hit him or pushed him away. But even after hearing his tale, she still wanted him. And that was the headiest thought he'd ever had.

"Tolly, how do we—how do I—You make me happy. And I'm not certain I de—"

"You're not certain you deserve to be happy," he finished. "The feeling is very, very mutual." He wanted to remind her that her guilt was her own invention, but then she would say something about how he couldn't have known what would happen to his men, and she was wrong. And then he wouldn't be able to bury himself in her again, and at the moment he thought he might go mad if he didn't.

Holding her against him with one hand, he swiftly unfastened his trousers and freed himself with the other. Taking her down with him, he half fell into the comfortable, overstuffed chair. "Theresa," he whispered against her mouth, lifting the hem of her shift up around her waist.

Pulling her back against his chest, he stroked between her thighs, parting her folds with his fingers. She was damp for him. With a gasping moan that nearly did him in, Theresa lifted up and then sank down on him, around him.

Bartholomew held his breath at the tight, heated sensation as he filled her. This was where he wanted to be. No bloody past, no uncertain future. Here. Now. With Theresa. Splaying his hands over her breasts, he sat there with her until he couldn't stand the growing anticipation and her wriggling any longer and began lifting his hips hard and fast against her.

Her breathing grew faster and shallower, and then she clenched her hands over his as she came around him. *Perfect*. Only when she began to relax again did he allow himself to find his own release deep inside her.

As his breathing slowed to normal again, he kissed her ear. "I think I owe Lackaby a raise for finally doing as he was asked."

Theresa leaned back against his chest. "If all proper chits knew about this, London would fall into anarchy."

He chuckled. "That would be a sight."

She twisted to look at his face. "What are you going to do?"

"First, we need to dress. I have no idea how long that damned valet will stay away."

"You're the one who undressed me again," she said, standing and wiggling her hips until the skirt of her shift fell back around her ankles. "And don't attempt to change the subject."

Reluctantly he buttoned his trousers again, then caught his waistcoat when she tossed it over her shoulder to him. "I went to Wellington this morning. Originally I was going to break into the Horse Guards to find the names of any other soldiers who have survived attacks in India, and then demand a trial to settle the issue of my supposed cowardice and incompetence. I would likely lose, but I would be very vocal about it."

He saw her shiver. "Tolly, if they convicted you of cowardice, you could hang."

"Yes, I know. But at the least everyone would be discussing the Thuggee instead of dismissing them as a rumor."

"You can't do that. You have to find another way."

For a long moment he sat, watching her pull on her dress. Almost magically she seemed once more to become the proper chit he'd first encountered—except that the buttons going down her back were undone and her skirt a bit wrinkled. "You came to see me this morning," he finally said. "That has instigated a change of my plans."

"Please tell me that you still mean to do something."

"Doing nothing would make the least bit of a stir," he returned. And it would certainly be easiest on her. He motioned her closer, then stood to button the back of her pretty green and yellow muslin walking dress. "But I have a duty to several dead men." Tolly took a deep breath. "I also now have a duty to you."

"I am not a du . . ." She stopped, opening and closing her mouth again. "I won't lie, Tolly. The idea of being looked at sideways makes me uneasy. But I wasn't jesting when I said I meant to take a new path. And if anyone has a legitimate reason for making a stir, it's you."

He kissed the nape of her neck. "I will be as cautious as I can. Wellington's sending over some notes. I'll see what he has to say before I plan my next move." Bartholomew stepped back into his boots, wincing again as he jarred his left knee. "What shall we say we've been up to with Lackaby as our witness?"

"Leave off your coat," she said. "We won't have to conjure any lie, because I'm going to cut your hair."

A shiver of uneasiness ran down his spine, but he pushed it away. She'd more than proven that she trusted him, and he certainly knew now that he could trust her. "That was your plan all along, wasn't it?"

She grinned. "Yes. I seduced you so that you would let me tame that lion's mane of yours."

"Very devious." As she turned away for her shoes, he grabbed hold of her wrist. "I want to make certain one thing is clear."

Theresa lifted her chin. "What is that?"

"You are with me. You are not marrying Montrose or anyone else. Call it a seduction or a courtship or whatever pleases you, but we are together."

Swiftly she lifted on her toes to kiss his mouth. "Yes. We are together. You and me."

"Then cut my damned hair. And make me look handsome; apparently I have a great many opinions to sway in my favor."

"Well, I'll do my best, but handsome? It might be a bit much to hope for."

He laughed. Whatever was coming for him, after today it would find him a changed man. And not simply because he was getting a haircut.

"Tell me you'll come to Essings this year for the pheasant hunting."

Chuckling, Adam, Lord Hadderly nodded. "I'd been hoping you would invite me, Crowley. I would be delighted."

As they left the House of Lords for their luncheon recess, Hadderly continued his rather dull conversation with the Earl of Crowley. Hadderly always did that, found one fairly undemanding fellow to serve as a barrier between him and the members of the peerage who had second or third sons or nephews who wanted administrative positions with the East India Company.

It was a damned nuisance, though on occasion acquiescing to the right request from the right lord had managed to sway a vote or two in his favor. And then there were lords like Crowley who wanted to move closer to the center of Society's most prestigious inner circle. And the pheasant hunting at Essings was rumored to be excellent.

At the bottom of the steps he caught sight of one of his clerks. The man waved furtively, clearly trying to gain his attention but not attract anyone else's. Keeping his expression unchanged, he excused himself from Crowley.

"What is it, Mr. Peters?" he asked, taking his clerk's arm and continuing on with him.

"Colonel James called at Apsley House this morning, my lord."

Hadderly scowled. "Wellington served as Governor-General of India. He is not going to do anything to jeopardize his standing. The man wants to be prime minister."

"James stood in front of His Grace's carriage and forced it to stop or run him down. Wellington went out and spoke with him. I couldn't hear what they discussed, but Colonel James looked . . . satisfied."

"Wellington does admire men with spleen." He took a breath. "Well. We'll just have to keep a closer eye on our crippled colonel, then. Take what assistance you need, Mr. Peters. I don't like surprises."

The clerk inclined his head. "I'll see to it, my lord."

Bartholomew James by himself was merely a nuisance on his way to becoming a disgraced, discontented soldier. The more ridiculous he could be made to look, the better. After all, it was James's damned injuries and his reputation as a competent, level-headed officer that had caused the latest round of Thuggee rumors in the first place.

But if he looked to be gathering allies or evidence, then he would have to be dealt with. Millions of pounds in imports and profit were not to be jeopardized. Not for anything.

Theresa stood back to do a slow circle around her masterpiece. Well, not a masterpiece, perhaps, but Tolly James *was* hers. Every delicious amber-eyed inch of him.

"Well?" he asked, lifting an eyebrow.

"It's still a bit long, if ye ask me," Lackaby commented, moving around them on the small terrace and sweeping the dark, mahogany hair into neat little piles.

"I like it a bit long," she said, stopping her circuit in front of Tolly. She wanted to kiss him, but settled for brushing her fingers across his temple.

"It's a damned good thing I have sheet over me," he murmured, leaning into her caress.

Her cheeks heated, and she dropped her gaze involuntarily to his lap before she could recover herself. Today had been the most extraordinary day of her life. And all she'd had to do to arrive there was set aside thirteen years of guilt and every one of her preconceived ideas about propriety and proper behavior.

And in return she'd declared her resolve to stand with a man who intended on making more of a stir than she ever would have imagined for herself. And of course having the sex, as he called it, with Tolly, which in her opinion compensated for any number of other ills, past or future.

"Well, your brother is coming through the door," she whispered back, "so . . . control your urges."

"You are my urges."

Lord Gardner stepped onto the small terrace, Amelia and Violet with him. "Tess, you've performed a miracle," the viscount announced, grinning. "Well done."

"I hope you don't think my troubles with the East India Company will vanish simply because my hair is combed."

"What I think is that at least you don't look like an escapee from Bedlam any longer. I count that in our favor."

"Very nice, Tess," Amelia seconded, no sign of suspicion or censure in her gaze.

No one knew, then. No one suspected that she and Tolly had actually been alone and naked in his bedchamber. Well, no one but Lackaby, and she'd already developed an odd affection for the stocky, barrel-chested valet. He seemed to be the only one other than she who could stand up to Tolly.

"Thank you," she said aloud. "I did what I could."

"Come shopping with us now, will you?" Leelee pursued. "If we're to attend the Tomlin-Reese soiree tonight, I would like some new lace. Silver, I think, to match the blue and silver of my gown."

"You're going to the party tonight?" She looked at Tolly.

He nodded. "It was suggested to me that being reclusive would not help my cause."

"Suggested by whom? I would like to thank this person." And to discover who it was Bartholomew had finally decided to take advice from.

Tolly glanced at her, then threw off the sheet. "A friend."

Ah. More than likely the same friend with whom he'd stayed when he'd first returned to London. The one he'd claimed was a female. Jealousy stabbed at her. "And is this 'friend' planning to stand by you at the Tomlin-Reese soiree, as well?"

This time his gaze stayed on her. "I don't know. Are *you* going to attend?"

"Yes. I think I will."

A slow smile curved his mouth. "Then perhaps you should go shopping with Amelia and Violet." Tolly looked her up and down.

Warmth spread through her. If she didn't go, she would more than likely stand about mooning after him for the rest of the day. And then someone would notice. She was actually somewhat surprised they couldn't tell just by looking at her.

And she was mooning after him right now. Squaring her shoulders, she handed the scissors over to Lackaby. "Let's go shopping, shall we?"

Since she already had the barouche with her, they elected to take that over to Bond Street to look for lace. She sat facing backward, while Amelia and Violet sat opposite her. Her cousin and cousin-in-law were very chatty, and from what she gathered at least part of their high spirits was because Tolly seemed to be in a good mood.

Theresa studied Amelia's face as she giggled over

something with her sister-in-law. Leelee was married. Lord and Lady Gardner had done what . . . she and Tolly had done. And yet, she couldn't detect any outward differences in her cousin and dear friend. Hopefully that meant she was safe from discovery, as well.

Not until they had entered the second shop in a row looking for just the perfect silver lace did Amelia take her arm. "I don't know Tolly well," she said quietly, sending a glance at his younger sister ahead of them, "but he seems quite taken with you."

"Does he?"

"He looks at you all the time. And when he notices someone looking at him, he glances away, like he doesn't want anyone else to know."

Oh, my. "He's very interesting," she conceded.

"And the uproar that he's looking to cause? It makes *me* a bit nervous. I can't imagine what you—well, I can't imagine. Will you stand beside him tonight?"

Even a few hours ago that question would have left her uneasy and nervous. Well, it did still. It made no sense to deny that. The difference was in her own heart. She felt . . . strong inside.

Whether it was because she believed Tolly's interpretation of her parents' death or because she found it inspiring that Tolly's tragedy hadn't stopped him from fighting, the old fear of being caught doing something wrong wasn't quite so keen. But then, standing with Tolly felt like something right.

"I intend to, yes," she said aloud. Theresa forced a smile. "And you know Grandmama will be thrilled, because she's never liked Lord Hadderly."

"'Hadderly and those blasted big dogs of his,'"

Amelia growled, doing a very fair impression of their grandmother. "I do find it interesting that she faults him for his dogs rather than for his politics."

Theresa laughed. "At this moment I'm feeling quite a fondness for cats, myself."

"What about Montrose?" Amelia leaned closer to Theresa. "He'll want to know whether you are standing by Tolly because of his relationship to me, or because you like him."

"I don't think any of that is Alexander's business."

"He will think so."

"Well." Theresa considered her answer for a long moment. "Alexander has been asking me the same question for better than two years. I suppose I owe him an answer, whether he will like what I have to say or not."

Amelia clutched her closer still. "Has Tolly offered for you, then?" she asked, obvious excitement making her voice shake.

"No, he hasn't." Nor was he likely to while plotting a battle with the East India Company. But men had been chasing her since she turned eighteen. There was a reason none of them had caught her. They all knew her as the chit she'd sculpted—the perfect and proper one. They were after a nonexistent woman.

Tolly knew who she really was, and he liked her. Not despite of what had happened, or even because of what had happened, but just . . . her. She smiled.

"Something has definitely happened to you, Tess." Amelia squeezed her arm, then released her as they reached the display of dyed lace. "You said it had, but half the time you don't say what you're thinking." She held up a length of silver, eyeing it critically in the light from the window. "This time, all I know is that you seem happy, which makes me happy."

"Then at this moment," Theresa returned, "we're all happy." Tonight, after the first sideways glances and the scowls from Montrose that all might change. Of course, she'd already changed a bit, herself. It was definitely going to be an interesting evening, and in a way she was even looking forward to it. Her second test of courage—only with the results much less pleasurable than the first one had turned out to be.

Chapter Seventeen

"I have heard endless debates over whether it is better to stand at the side of a dance or to accept an invitation from an imperfect gentleman and take to the floor. I find it best to keep in mind that the gentleman may be thinking the same thing about me. And I like to dance."

A LADY'S GUIDE TO PROPER BEHAVIOR, 2ND EDITION

Well?" Lackaby prompted, glancing up from the red and white officer's coat he had spread across the table.

Bartholomew flipped another page of Wellington's—or rather Wellesley's, back then—India journal. "Good God, the man drones on," he muttered. "Dinners he attended, the entire guest list, the cleverest bits of conversation, supply timetables, weather, the food he ate for breakfast, th—"

"And the Thuggee?" the valet interrupted. "I know Arthur heard tales, because I did."

Cursing under his breath, Bartholomew turned another page, then another. "Arthur likes facts."

"Yes, he always was a bit of a foot-in-the-mud," Lackaby mused, turning the coat over and running a polishing cloth over the buttons.

"But why would he even bother with loaning me his journal if there's nothing in here?"

"I don't know."

"That," Bartholomew retorted, "isn't helpful."

He'd been looking through the damned thing for an hour, though it had swiftly become clear that a quick glance through such densely packed bits of facts and information would never net him anything. He was beginning to think that Wellington couldn't possibly remember what he had or hadn't said in his journal, because he recorded every nonsensical thing imaginable.

In another ten minutes Stephen would begin conjuring reasons that Amelia and Violet should remain home tonight—which they more than likely should. But as of this morning he'd had to alter his plan. He was no longer going to throw himself into the whirlwind and damn all consequences. Now he intended to survive to the end, hopefully with some semblance of a reputation. For that he needed his family, he needed some way to spread the word and make it credible without damning himself, and he needed Theresa Weller. Without her, he had no reason to stay alive at all.

"Time we got ye dressed for battle."

Nodding, Bartholomew turned another page. "Finally," he muttered.

"You found something?"

"Yes. A rumored Thuggee attack on a group of travelers." He read on. "Damnation. No survivors.

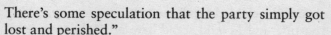

There's some speculation that the party simply got lost and perished."

"Can't tell you how many times I've heard that blasted story." Lackaby carried over his well-polished black Hessian boots. "If ye ask me, as many fellows as they say got themselves lost in the wilds of India, they all must be standing two deep."

"You make a good point." Bartholomew stepped into his right boot, then held his breath and clenched his jaw as the valet pushed and twisted to get his foot into the left one. "If there are no Thuggee, then where the devil have five or six thousand people vanished to over the years?"

"If I was Lord Hadderly, I'd ask which five thousand you might be referring to. Who says anybody's missing at all?" Lackaby commented.

"True again, being that more natives than Englishmen have vanished. Rather than ruminating over what we can't prove, let's be more productive, shall we?"

"I knew three fellows, went out to Delhi on leave and were never heard from again. They were tried for desertion in absentia. One of em, Evers, he might have found some pretty Urdu chit, but Willis and Smythe, they were good men and married. Their families had to live with them being called deserters. Sad business."

Tolly looked at Lackaby as his valet shook out the uniform coat. "Yes, it is sad. Four of mine were married. The others had parents and siblings. I wrote too many letters."

"Arthur wrote letters, too."

Halfway to his feet, Tolly sank back again. "Did you see any of them?"

Lackaby cleared his throat. "I suppose we can keep chatting and I could stand here all night waiting to help you get your coat on, but I'd rather be hunting after them sugar desserts at the soiree."

Bartholomew shook himself. "You know you're supposed to be serving me at the party—not eating sweets." He stood up, and Lackaby helped him pull on his formal military coat, medals and all. Medals and honors that he now rather detested, but they did help prove the point that he wasn't some idiot whose family had purchased him a commission beyond his abilities.

"I don't take 'em when anybody's looking."

"Ah. Carry on, then." Pushing back against the uneasiness that would likely always be present, he lifted his chin to let Lackaby finish fastening up his coat. "Is your reluctance to talk about Arthur's correspondence out of loyalty to the man, or because you think he would deny ever attributing a soldier's death or disappearance to the Thuggee?"

The valet scowled. "A bit of both, I reckon. But if I know Arthur, and I do, he won't do anything to counter what the East India Company's said. And the Company's already stated that the bastards don't exist."

"I agree," Tolly said slowly, sending a last glare at Wellington's journal. "He loaned me this damned thing because at worst he thought I would find someone else who'd be willing to come forward without involving him."

"Or at best because Arthur thought you wouldn't find anything and you would stop going about charging into the street in front of his coach."

That made at least as much sense, damn it all. "We're back to the beginning, then."

"Breaking into the Horse Guards? In a wheeled chair?"

"I reckon I could still set you on your arse if need be, Lackaby. You're to be helpful, remember?"

"Aye, Colonel."

"I do have someone making a discreet inquiry with the War Office, but I haven't heard anything yet."

"Hmm."

"Hmm, what?" Tolly retorted, frowning.

"I don't want to be set on my arse."

Bartholomew blew out his breath. "Out with it."

"I'm just wondering how much blunt the Company puts into the pockets of your discreet friend, is all. Perhaps that's why you haven't heard anything."

And he'd thought he was the cynical one. Wealthy as Sommerset was, it was entirely likely that he had ties to the Company. "I'll look into that this evening," he said.

"Do as you will, Colonel." Lackaby finally stood back. "There. You look fine enough to march before old King George himself. I dare anyone to not be impressed with you." The valet picked a fleck of dust from one shoulder. "She'll be impressed, for certain."

Bartholomew scowled. "None of that. And my appearance has never much influenced Theresa one way or the other."

All day he'd barely been able to put two seconds together where he hadn't thought about Theresa, her voice, her touch, her soft skin and warm mouth and the way she'd squared her shoulders before she'd announced that yes, she meant to stand with him. The

proper chit who hadn't been able to behave properly
in his company. He meant to ask Amelia for a look at
Tess's booklet. If nothing else, it would remind him
how fortunate he was that he had somehow escaped
being lumped in with the general pile of gentlemen
who were courting her. Whether she felt lucky to
have met him or not, he didn't know.

"She ain't the mistress sort, Colonel."

Bartholomew glared at his valet. "I know that. All
I asked for where Theresa Weller is concerned was
your discretion, Lackaby. Not your observations or
advice. Leave off."

"No offense meant, Colonel. I was just wondering
what your plans might be."

"My plans," Tolly returned, grabbing up his cane
and skirting the wheeled chair, "depend on whether
I'll be tarred and feathered and run—or rolled—out
of London. So if you like seeing Tess about, I suggest
you keep your attention on helping me locate anyone
who's survived a Thuggee attack."

"Yes, sir. Not riding the chair down the stairs this
evening?"

"My dignity seems to be recovering faster than my
knee. So, no. You bring the chair, and I'll bring the
cane."

Thankfully for the sake of his leg, Stephen caught
sight of him before he'd made it to the landing.
"Christ, Tolly," his brother grumbled, taking the
stairs at a trot and slinging an arm around his waist,
"do you have to wear the uniform again?"

"I want the attention," Tolly grunted, stifling a curse
just in time as his sister pranced out of the morning
room and into the foyer. "You look lovely, Vi."

She curtsied. "Thank you, Colonel. The red sash is meant to match your uniform." Violet brushed her fingers across the wide sash at her waist. "I'm showing my support for your cause."

"Damnation," Stephen murmured. "Tolly, do something."

Bartholomew cleared his throat. "You're showing support simply by being there tonight, Vi. The trick is to not directly set anyone's back up. The more everyone is charmed by you, the less they'll be able to say something unpleasant later."

"Then I will be charming. You know I excel at that." She saluted. "They won't know what's hit them."

"Thank you."

Once he and Stephen reached the foyer Bartholomew shrugged free of his brother's grip. Grumbling and complaining, Lackaby and two footmen hauled the wheeled chair down after them. "Your throne, Colonel," the valet panted.

Tolly gestured at the front door, and Graham pulled it open. "Go lash it to the back of the coach, will you?"

"At least I don't have to carry the damned thing to the party on my back," Lackaby grumbled, heading outside.

As the valet left the house Stephen glanced after him. "If you find him too insufferable, Tolly, I'll look for someone else for you."

"No need. Lackaby and I seem to understand one another."

"Good, then."

Stephen seemed rather pleased with himself, and Bartholomew let him have his moment. He hadn't precisely been pleasant when his family had arrived back in London. And with anyone other than Theresa and Lackaby standing with him, he was fairly certain he wouldn't be as relatively civilized as he was now.

Their party arrived before the Wellers, though it was entirely possible that Tess or her brother or their grandmother or all of them together had decided it would be best if they didn't attend. Her absence, though, divided his attention between the circulating crowd and the main ballroom doors.

"Colonel James."

He looked up to see a man ten or so years his elder and wearing a very similar uniform, down to the gold and white epaulets on their shoulders. "General Mayhew." Pushing to his feet, he saluted. By the strictest interpretation he was retired from the military, but he'd chosen to wear the uniform tonight. And he didn't want any new rumors of improper conduct attached to him.

"You're a disgrace, James, looking for attention with your men lying dead somewhere."

"Not somewhere, General. My men are in India," he returned coolly, very aware that everyone around them was listening to the conversation. "We pulled them out of the well the Thuggee had thrown all of us into. Unless you think they all jumped in on their own."

"That's your story. I've seen and heard nothing to substantiate such nonsense."

"I'm not surprised, since the evidence lies beyond your well-lined pockets."

A low snicker came from somewhere behind him,

and General Mayhew's already ruddy face went beet red. "That is inexcusable," he sputtered.

"You're the one who began an argument with a cripple," Bartholomew said easily. "Didn't you realize you'd look either a buffoon or a bully?" He saluted again, then deliberately resumed his seat. "Good evening, General Mayhew."

As the general stalked away, muttering to himself, Stephen returned carrying two glasses. He handed over one of Scotch whiskey. "That was a bit savage, wasn't it?"

"My original plan would have been fisticuffs."

"Not that I'm complaining that you've decided to alter your tactics, then," his brother returned, "but why have you done so?"

His breath stilled. Without looking he knew Theresa was in the room, and he knew she approached. "Her," he said quietly, finally turning his head.

"Her?"

Stephen continued speaking, but Bartholomew had no idea what he was saying. All his attention focused on the petite young lady with gray-green eyes and hair the rich color of morning sunshine. Tonight she'd chosen to wear a full silk gown of emerald green, stones of the same color at her throat and dangling from her ears and left wrist.

Liquid heat and desire flowed through him, its ferocity stunning. He wanted her, immediately. For a heartbeat he wondered whether she would regain her senses and walk right past him, but he stood again anyway.

She stopped, gazing up at him. "Good evening, Tolly," she breathed, her voice not quite steady.

Good God, he wanted to touch her. Digging his fingertips into the outside seams of his trousers, he inclined his head. "You took my breath away, just then," he returned.

"Good. I didn't dress up for nothing, you know." She smiled.

A moment later her brother and grandmother walked up behind her. Lord Weller looked agitated and as though he was doing his best to hide that fact; he knew, then, that Tess would be much better off elsewhere. The dowager viscountess, though, was practically beaming as she looked from her grand-daughter to Tolly. At least someone approved the match—whether it would be possible ever to make a match, or not.

"There's Harriet," Lord Weller said, gesturing across the ballroom. "We should go say hello."

Theresa shook her head. "I'm staying here."

"You can't do that, Troll," her brother said more quietly. "No one's even asked for your dance card."

While the deep, possessive part of Bartholomew was rather pleased to hear that she'd apparently fore-gone everyone in favor of him, the more logical part knew that she couldn't be happy with any of that. "Tess," he said with a grin, "the phrase 'stand by me' wasn't actually meant to be literal. And I know you love to dance."

"That doesn't signify."

"Yes, it does."

Her brow lowering, Theresa folded her arms across her lovely chest. "No, it doesn't."

Violet looked from one of them to the other. "Tolly said I should be as charming as possible, to make it more difficult for anyone to say later that they don't like us," she said. "So I am going to dance with everyone, beginning with the most frown-faced gentleman I see."

Theresa's mouth twitched. "Well, I will wager you a lemon ice, Violet, that I find a more frown-faced man than you."

With a giggle, Violet nodded. "That is a wager, then, Tess." She curtsied. "Excuse me. I must go find someone unpleasant."

"Thank you, Tess," Bartholomew murmured, brushing a finger against her skirts. "Save a dance for me, will you?"

"That was the idea, originally," she said wryly. "Now, I'll see what I can manage." With a swish of her emerald gown, she strolled away.

"I hope you know what you're about," Stephen whispered. Then he walked off, presumably and hopefully to keep an eye on their sister.

Violet didn't have the experience or the skill at turning every conversation into something amusing and charming that Tess did. Bartholomew didn't like the idea of either of them looking for trouble on his behalf, but clearly there wasn't much he could do about it.

A finger tapped his shoulder. Starting, Bartholomew twisted his head to look up. "Lord Weller," he said, relaxing a fraction.

Theresa's brother eyed him speculatively. "I never thought it would be you," he finally said, "though in retrospect it makes sense. Whatever you do, don't force her into a scandal. Please."

"I never thought it would be her," Bartholomew

responded. "I will do my best to keep her clear of this. She is rather stubborn, however."

"Yes, I know." Michael smiled reluctantly. "I keep hoping this will all be good for her." He drew in a breath. "Just so you know, I've given Montrose my permission to court her."

Bartholomew clenched his jaw. "I wasn't going to ask."

"Well, you have my permission, anyway. One rebellion at a time." With a nod, Michael took his grandmother's arm and they strolled off, as well.

And so at the moment the total number of people physically standing by him was zero. Except for Lackaby. "What do you think?" he asked over his shoulder.

"I think we'd be better off closer to the table with the sweets on it."

"Any more helpful observations?"

"Mayhew's a git. Glad you told him off. But his opinion doesn't count for much."

"I agree. It's a start, at least." Bartholomew blew out his breath. Sitting here at the fringes wouldn't do much good. Aside from that, he didn't have much of a view of the dance floor. "Wheel me over to the refreshment table, will you?"

"Oh, God bless you and keep you, Colonel."

"Shut up."

Theresa wondered how hard one's heart had to beat before it actually erupted from one's chest. She must be fairly close to that point. It would have been so much easier to remain at home this evening. And she would never have been able to look at herself in the mirror again if she'd done so.

She hadn't been in the ballroom when General Mayhew had confronted Tolly, but she'd heard about it. And even if that particular frown-faced gentleman was much more important in his own mind than in anyone else's, if she could get him to dance with her, everyone at the Tomlin-Reese soiree would notice. And *that* would help Tolly.

"Tess."

Dash it all. She swirled around as though she wasn't at all surprised. "Alexander. You look very handsome this evening."

Lord Montrose took her hand and bowed over it. "I don't even have the words to describe you, Tess. You are a goddess."

"Those words seem quite nice, actually." She smiled.

"Then you're not angry about the . . . time line I've set?"

Good heavens, she'd actually forgotten about that. She pulled her fingers free. "As it turns out, the one week to—how did you put it—decide whether I'm too much of a coward to be seen with Tolly James? That won't be necessary. I don't mind being seen with him. I *like* being seen with him, actually."

Alexander frowned, the expression drawing his exquisitely arched eyebrows downward. "He's not a wise choice for you. It's no secret that you don't like a stir, Tess. And he is at the center of a whirlwind. Or he will be, if he doesn't stop wearing that damned uniform and cursing at generals."

"Oh, but he looks very fine in that uniform," she

cut back, still smiling, but beginning to back away.

"Don't be foolish. I apologize about the ultimatum. Take your time. I'll wait for you. Just stand back from him before you . . . before you ruin yourself."

Ha. He had no idea. And that realization made her feel unexpectedly powerful. "Don't waste your time on me, Alexander. We would never suit."

"I happen to think we would suit quite well. You're smitten with him. Luckily for you, I'm patient. If you haven't realized that by now, look back over the past two years. I'll stand back a bit. But don't make yourself foolish. That reputation you've guarded so carefully is what makes you so attractive. I want a respectable woman for a wife, and for the mother of my heir."

She backed away another step. "You're very understanding, my lord."

"I'm twenty-eight years old. I've looked. You're the one I prefer. Don't ruin it."

"Excuse me, Alexander. I'm looking for someone."

"First give me a place on your dance card. I said I would stand back, but that doesn't mean we shouldn't dance."

He actually made it sound fairly reasonable. "I'll give you a country dance."

"A waltz."

"A quadrille."

"A waltz. You know there are to be two."

With a sigh, flattered at his persistence if nothing else, she handed over her card. Sending her a satisfied grin, he wrote down his name and handed it back.

"Thank you. I'll see you then."

She supposed she couldn't blame Montrose for disbelieving that she'd set her sights on Tolly. At first look, Colonel James *was* all wrong for her. He was direct, could be sullen and rude, had a huge scandal looming over his head, and couldn't dance. Yet he'd drawn her from the moment she'd set eyes on him. He'd told her his story, and in doing so had shown her her own tale in a different light. He stood up for what he believed in, even knowing full well it could cost him his reputation. And that it could cost him a future with her. And she loved him for that.

Theresa stumbled, nearly tripping over her own hem. *Love.* She loved Bartholomew James.

For heaven's sake. It made so much sense. She didn't think she'd ever even thought the word before in connection with any of the men who'd been pursuing her. None of them made her feel as though she was on fire, burning from the inside out.

She turned around. Tolly sat in the wheeled chair he detested, Lackaby handing him another drink and pretending not to eat a sugared strawberry. Warmth slid through her muscles as she gazed at the colonel. Her colonel.

And to think at first she worried that his unpredictability and sharp tongue would goad her into saying or doing something improper. Theresa smiled a little. The something improper had turned out to be the most thrilling, exciting, and life-altering moment of her life.

For the first time since the death of her parents she felt . . . free. And strong. And worth more than her manners. She might have picked a better time and place for such a revelation, she supposed, but on the other hand, the timing might very well have been perfect.

Smoothing her skirt, attempting to draw her scattered thoughts back in, she turned back toward her target of choice. General Mayhew wore a uniform nearly identical to Tolly's, but aside from their employment the two men had almost nothing in common.

"General Mayhew," she said aloud, pasting on her best, most practiced smile.

The square-shouldered, frown-faced officer looked around at her. "Miss Weller." He inclined his head, but the baby-frightening expression on his face didn't alter a whit.

"I was wondering if you had a partner for the next quadrille," she said smoothly. A waltz might have been more effective, but as Montrose had said, there were only two. Alexander had claimed one, and the other was for Tolly. From now on he would always have a waltz, whether he would ever be able to dance one with her or not.

"Is this a jest?" Mayhew returned. "Or another chance to insult me? I am not a fool, Miss Weller. I've seen with whom you are friendly."

"You're referring to Colonel James, I presume. My dear cousin Amelia is married to his brother, you know."

"So in truth you dislike him and are only friendly due to familial obligation? Really, Miss Weller. As I said, I am not a fool."

Theresa deepened her smile. "I was about to say that Tolly and I have become friends, but that I in no way thought that would make you and me into enemies. I am not so fierce, am I, General?"

With clear reluctance he inclined his head. "I concede that point to you, Miss Weller. Did you seek me out as an apology for James's abominable behavior?"

"I sought you out because you are frowning. No one should frown at so delightful a party." She pulled her dance card from her reticule. "So will you frown, or will you dance?"

"Humph." He took the card from her fingers, wrote down his name and returned it to her. "If you mean to leave me standing, I will be very unhappy."

"I try not to leave anyone standing during a dance."

Returning the card to her reticule, she walked off in the direction she'd briefly glimpsed Harriet. There. She'd managed to secure a dance with the frown-faced gentleman, and she hadn't had to lie in order to accomplish it.

She caught her friend by the arm as Harriet strolled by. "Oh, you should always wear pearls, Harriet. I don't know why, but they make your eyes positively sparkle."

Harried hugged her. "I've missed you, Tess. No one hands out better compliments than you."

Chuckling, Theresa returned the embrace. "You are easy to compliment."

"You are the stunning one tonight." Harriet looked her up and down. "This isn't for Montrose, is it?"

"It's for me."

"So Amelia's brother-in-law and his account of the Thuggee doesn't trouble you? I thought all the muttering I've been hearing would have you running the other way."

Theresa's smile faded. "So you think I'm a coward, too."

"What? No! That's not what I meant." Harriet clutched her hand, making the emerald on her wrist spin and sparkle. " 'A lady does not involve herself in politics or military matters except to privately support a male family member in his own endeavors.' That's from your b—"

"My booklet." She'd forgotten about that. Theresa glanced again at Tolly across the room to find him gazing back at her. She sighed, her heart trembling.

A Lady's Guide to Proper Behavior, as far as she knew, had been read by at least half the ladies in this room—though most of them had no idea that she was the author. She absolutely would never have published it except anonymously. But she'd just realized something. She'd had no idea what she was talking about. The second edition of her *Guide* needed to be amended in order to take something else into account. Love.

Chapter Eighteen

"Tradition and custom say that we as females are better fit to watch the great events of the world than to participate in them. This may be true; I don't know. What I do know is that at times action is required, and that sometimes the best man for an undertaking is a woman."

A LADY'S GUIDE TO PROPER BEHAVIOR, 2ND EDITION

Bartholomew was beginning to wish he'd kept his damned mouth shut. No, Theresa didn't need to physically stand beside him all evening, but he much preferred her there to where she was currently—dancing in the arms of Lord Montrose.

She'd also managed a quadrille with General Mayhew, which actually hadn't annoyed him nearly as much and had gained her the admiration of Violet. But Mayhew was an enemy, easily catalogued and easy to deal with. Montrose was more complicated.

"I still know some lads," Lackaby muttered from behind him. "It'd be my honor to see the marquis there accidently shipped off to join the Royal Navy."

Bartholomew studied Theresa's face. She was so damned good at being charming that seeing through her mask was nearly impossible, but as far as he could tell she was strictly being polite. "Not necessary," he returned in the same tone, rubbing his chin with his thumb and forefinger. "Though that may change."

"Aye."

Bartholomew nodded, his gaze still on the waltzing couple halfway across the room. "Whatever comes of this, thank you, Louis."

"If ye want to thank me, stop trying to sack me. And don't call me Louis."

"I can likely guarantee one. But not both." With a grin, Bartholomew glanced toward the door again, to see a tall, broad-shouldered man with dark hair and steel gray eyes stroll into the ballroom. *Finally.* "Wait here," he said, pushing to his feet and reaching for his cane.

The Duke of Sommerset, unlike many of the other high-ranking peers in London, did not seem to travel with a band of sycophants and other hangers-on. In fact, most the times Bartholomew caught sight of the duke, he was alone. As he was now, thankfully.

Once His Grace arrived at an event, however, the scene was very like Moses gathering the faithful. Bartholomew pushed through a group of chattering young ladies, rendering them momentarily speechless, and stopped in front of the duke. "Your Grace."

"Tolly. Is it my imagination, or is your leg improving?"

"Have you made your inquiries at the War Office?" Bartholomew asked, speaking in a low voice.

Sommerset's expression went flat. "Not here."

"I am running out of time, Sommerset. If you can't get me answers there, I'll go and look for them myself."

"I said, not here." The duke took a breath, glancing toward the dance floor as the waltz ended and a cotillion began. "Come to the club tonight after midnight. *Then* we'll talk."

"Yes, we will."

The duke faced him, and Tolly straightened from his three-legged stance to stand at his full height. Eye to eye, they glared at one another. "You *will* address me properly in public, Colonel," Sommerset finally stated, his voice low and even.

"Then yes we will, Your Grace."

Sommerset nodded. "Much better."

A moment later the usual hangers-on began to arrive around them, and Bartholomew slipped away without much notice. Apparently chatting with a duke outweighed avoiding a liar in the eyes of the *ton*. That didn't even surprise him. Not any longer.

"The way I figure it," Montrose said from close behind him, "you don't want to be labeled either a coward or a liar. So what are you going to do, look for other attack survivors and see if they'll defy the East India Company for you?"

Bartholomew slowed. "What the devil do you care what I'm about?"

"I don't, really. Though I do favor you beginning a battle—a war—with anyone but me."

"If that's meant to provoke me, it's a fairly feeble attempt."

The marquis put a hand over his heart. "*I* don't want to provoke you. I'm glad to see you alive and in less than stellar form." Montrose indicated the cane. "Apparently at the moment you're just helpless and harmless enough to attract female attention. Begin a scrap, and your attractiveness disappears."

Ah, so that was what this was about. "Female attention, or a particular female's attention?" he queried. "You're jealous. Now you look more familiar to me."

"Say whatever you like, James. Just remember that I'm willing to offer you help in your battle. Unobtrusively, of course. I doubt you'll find many more allies." Turning his back, Montrose strolled away again.

Well, that was interesting. And in a sense, it was encouraging. Tess had clearly informed her premiere beau that the situation had changed. She'd spoken publicly about—what? About her affection for him? About her decision to stand with someone to whom she was nearly related? About her decision to stiffen her spine and step forward? It could be any of those. *Damnation.*

He turned around. "Montrose."

The marquis stopped his retreat. "What?" he asked, facing around again.

"Just to be clear, she's mine."

"This evening, perhaps. Tomorrow? Well, we'll see, I imagine. The race isn't run yet."

As the marquis left him standing there again, Lackaby appeared with the chair. "Here ye are, Colonel."

"I really don't like that man," Tolly said, taking a seat and stifling his responding sigh.

"I heard there's a navy ship leaving Northampton day after tomorrow," Lackaby said conversationally.

"Headed for Tahiti and the Pacific. It'd be a year or more before he managed to make his way back here. If he were to be aboard, that is."

"Don't bloody tempt me. Over there, if you please. And stop eating where everyone can see you."

He motioned toward where Stephen stood with his bride, both of them smiling and looking happy—more than likely because he'd been on the other side of the room. Bartholomew scowled. If there was a way to make his point without pulling his family into scandal, he would do it. But he needed them now. They helped tie him back to the *ton*, to respectability. And for Theresa's sake, that was where he needed to be. At the end of this, he needed to be respectable enough to offer for her.

Once the next dance began, easing the crowding of the rest of the ballroom just a little, Bartholomew had the valet push him up to his brother and sister-in-law. "You aren't dancing? I hope that's not on my account."

Amelia smiled. "*I'm* not dancing on account of a new pair of shoes that looked darling but aren't at all practical. *He's* not dancing in protest of my not dancing."

"Ah. Have you heard anything interesting?"

"No one's saying much about you to us," Stephen commented. "Lady Weller—Grandmama Agnes—did say that Lord Hadderly more than likely employs the Thuggee to line his own pockets."

"Not fond of Hadderly then, is she?"

Leaning closer, Amelia hid a smile behind her hand. "Lord Hadderly raises very large dogs. My grandmother is obsessed with cats."

Well, under the circumstances, he would even accept feline alliance. "I'll remember that," he said aloud. "No large dogs."

"What about you?" Stephen asked. "I saw you talking with Sommerset. If anyone outside the Company has contacts in India, it's Nicholas Ainsley."

"I don't know if he'll cooperate or not," Bartholomew hedged, hoping his brother wasn't the only one to notice him speaking with Sommerset. The more pressure he could put on the duke to assist him, the better.

"And Montrose? What did he want?"

"He offered his assistance."

"What?" Amelia exclaimed. "He's in purs—I mean, he and . . . I would never have expected that."

"I know quite well that he's offered for Tess," he returned. "He seems to think my ruination will aid his cause."

"That's devious of him." His sister-in-law scowled.

Bartholomew, though, shrugged. "He wants Theresa. I can hardly fault him for that. Though I do mean to best him in it."

Because he was looking for it, he saw the shadow cross Amelia's face, the doubt that he could possibly be what Tess wanted. After all, apart from whatever wreck might come of his reputation, he couldn't even dance.

If he lost to the lies of the East India Company, clearly he would lose everything. And any reason to continue fighting. In that instance, perhaps he might find employment in America. He could still ride, after all, and he was a better than fair shot. Anywhere but

England would do, he supposed. Or India. That left a great, wide, empty world if . . .

He shook himself. *This* was his second chance. Before he'd met Theresa, he hadn't thought to look for one. He hadn't thought he deserved one. The damned Company had sparked a fire in him, but it was Tess who'd sent it into an inferno. Even if he didn't deserve this, he bloody well meant to fight for it—for her—anyway.

"Excuse me, Colonel," Theresa's soft voice came from just beyond Amelia, "but I believe this is our waltz." She stepped around her cousin, emeralds glinting in the chandelier light.

For a moment all he could do was gaze at her. *His.* Until the world came crashing down around his ears, Theresa Weller was his. And whatever happened, he meant to take full advantage of every moment of it. "So it is," he said aloud.

He stood again, offering his free arm to her. "Might I suggest a limp through the garden?"

Warm fingers gripped his sleeve. "That would be delightful," she said, a smile in her voice. "I need to practice my limping."

"Very amusing." They headed out the nearest door that opened onto the terrace. She almost seemed to float beside him, all grace and beauty next to the limping, three-legged wreck that was he. "I want to kiss you, Tess." Bartholomew stopped to face her the moment they were out of sight of the ballroom windows. "I want more, actually," he continued, unable to keep the low growl from his voice, "but a kiss will do me for the moment."

"Well, then," she whispered, and lifted up on her toes.

He closed his eyes at the soft touch of her lips to his. Time seemed to stop there in the Tomlin-Reese garden. Cupping her face with his free hand, he deepened the kiss, the warmth of her seeping into his bones, into his soul.

Slowly she lowered herself onto the ground again. "You are very distracting," she murmured, her gaze still on his mouth.

"Me? Have you looked at yourself lately?" He smiled. "I saw you dancing with Mayhew," he said. "You've won the lemon ice, I think."

She chuckled. "I detest him, but he dances well enough. And he refused to say anything kind at all about you. Something about your gall in disputing the claims of an enterprise that's made Britain great."

"Hmm. And to think, all I've done is get shot in the knee and not die. Wait until I actually have evidence to support my view."

"Have you found someone, then? Anyone to corroborate the danger of the Thuggee?"

"Not yet. I'm to meet someone tonight. Hopefully I'll learn something useful, then."

"Who?"

"I can't tell you."

She frowned. "If you can't even meet with this person publicly, how large a chance is there that he'll say anything you can actually use to help us?"

He sighed, running his thumb along her lower lip. She'd said "us." "Not much. But it's a chance."

"I've been thinking about that," she said, twining her fingers into the sleeves of his red coat. "If no one else comes forward, perhaps you might write a book."

Bartholomew frowned. "A book? What the devil for?"

"It's just a thought. But everyone's read the newspaper, if not the East India Company's actual report. And then they see you, claiming to have been attacked but not providing anyone else to join their experience to yours. And they don't know any of the details of what happened to you."

"You're the only one who knows," he muttered. "You and my commanding officers. I have no desire to advertise my mistakes, Tess."

"And what will happen to the next colonel who escorts a group of locals somewhere and is befriended by a jolly old monk who doesn't want to travel alone? Especially if no one is allowed to breathe a word to that colonel about the Thuggee?"

The jolly old monk was dead, and so were most of his men. From what Bartholomew had been able to discover, though, Parashar's assassins had only been one clawed finger of the insidious beast called Thuggee. And Tess was absolutely correct; the other side of the East India Company's attempt to increase trade and travel to India was that everyone would think they were safe.

Soldiers would look for pickpockets and ham-fisted highwaymen, not pleasant fellows who befriended them and then slaughtered the entire trusting party en masse for their money and belongings. The murderers and their victims would all vanish—the killers back into the hills to wait for the next group of well-heeled travelers, and the dead into the dirt or deep dry wells or some lost, rocky ravine never to be seen or heard from again.

"Tolly?"

He blinked, then leaned down and kissed her again, hard and deep. "I'm very glad I met you, Theresa Weller. If nothing comes of tonight, I think I'll try my hand at writing a book. I should be able to make it hair-raising enough that the East India Company can say whatever they wish. People will be afraid, and they will be wary."

"It's not a perfect solution, you know," she returned. "It might save lives, but not your reputation. The questions will be whether you wrote the book for profit, or if it's full of lies just to save your own reputation, or worse yet, if you just intentionally wrote a novel."

"A novelist? I shudder at the thought." Tolly favored her with a hopefully encouraging grin. "I suppose the reasons won't matter, as long as it's read." Inside the ballroom, the waltz ended. She would have her next partner waiting for her. Letting her go, though, was another matter entirely. His heart skipped a beat. Silently Bartholomew tilted her chin up with his fingers. "What about you, though?"

"Me? This isn't about me, Tolly."

"Yes, it is. Could you . . . could you tolerate life with a crippled, disgraced novelist?"

Theresa felt all the blood leave her face only to rush forth again, roaring in her ears. She tried to string together a logical line of thought—what she'd thought to make of her life, what had changed since she'd met Tolly—but everything crashed together in her skull, a mishmash of fears and guilt and well-hidden hopes and dreams. She pulled in a hard breath, trying to steady herself. "Are you asking—"

"My apologies," he interrupted, grabbing her shoulder before she could back away. "That was shabby of me."

Then he wasn't asking? "Make up your damned mind about what you intend to say before you speak to me again," she snapped, jerking free of him.

"That's why I apologized," he retorted, cutting off her retreat with apparent ease, despite his bad leg. "Asking something that . . . important shouldn't be done so badly that you can't decipher what I'm saying."

She glared at him. "And?" she prompted, trying to ignore the furious pounding of her heart.

"I can't kneel," he said quietly, dropping his cane and taking both of her hands in his.

"I don't care."

"No, you don't, do you?" he murmured, his gaze mesmerizing even in the dim, flickering torchlight. "I have to put a condition on this," he continued after a moment. "If everything collapses and I end up arrested, I won't hold you to anything. I know your sensitivity to—"

"Ask me the question, will you?" she broke in again, beginning to wonder whether he would talk himself out of it. If the question he was attempting to ask was the one she wanted to hear, that was.

"When I returned to England," he said slowly, "I had already given myself up for dead. You are my miracle, and I can't imagine any sunrise without you in my life." He cleared his throat. "Would you do me the very great honor of marrying me, Theresa?"

Now *that* was a proposal. "Before I met you," she returned, "men followed me about because I'm wealthy and had impeccable manners. I wouldn't have married any of them, because they wanted someone I wasn't."

"And?" he prompted, much as she had a moment ago.

"And then you brought me back to life, Tolly. I love . . . I love you. And it would be *my* honor—and my pleasure—to marry you."

For a long moment he just stood there, gazing at her. Then Tolly wrapped his arms around her waist and lifted her into the air. "Thank you," he whispered, kissing her. "Thank you."

Theresa flung her arms around his neck. She wanted to thank him back again, but between the kissing and the laughing, she couldn't muster enough breath even to speak. Then abruptly she was tumbling to the ground, Tolly swearing and then twisting her around so that he went down beneath her.

"Apologies," he grunted, wincing even as he continued to grin at her.

She steadied herself across his thighs, still holding on to his shoulders. So many people were angry or about to be angry at him, it didn't seem fair that all on her own she could add a dozen thwarted beaux to the list. "We shouldn't say anything about this."

Tolly tilted his head at her. "If you're ashamed of me at this moment, the next few weeks are going to be intolerable," he said carefully, his amber eyes going distant. "Perhaps you should change your answer."

"That's not what I meant," she retorted. "Montrose,

Henning, Lionel Humphreys, Henry Camden—they'll all be out of sorts. You don't need more enemies."

"Ah." His expression eased. "Nor do you." Reaching back, he found his cane. "Help me up, then, and we'll keep this our secret. For the moment." Slipping his free hand to cup the nape of her neck, he kissed her again. "Though I mean to remind you on every possible occasion."

Thank goodness. "I do hope so." Standing, Theresa straightened her skirt and then offered him a hand. He nearly pulled her over, but between her, the cane, and a nearby tree trunk he managed to climb to his feet again. "Who are you meeting tonight?"

He glanced sideways at her before offering her his arm. "I'll tell you tomorrow, if I can. It's a bit of a sticky situation."

"You can trust me, you know."

"I know that. It's not my secret to keep."

"Oh." Leaning into his arm while they still had the privacy of the garden, she walked with him back toward the terrace. "It's a matter of honor, then."

"Somewhat. I owe this person a favor."

"Is this the person with whom you stayed before you returned home?"

His jaw tightened. "I wouldn't have you be less bright than you are, but you're going to have to be patient. And stop asking so many damned questions tonight. I just proposed to someone, and I'm a bit . . . disconcerted."

Theresa laughed. "Good. I was beginning to think you were Achilles, with your knee your only vulnerable spot."

"Achilles," he repeated, grinning back at her. "I like that."

"Hmm. You would."

The moment they stepped back into the ballroom, the noise and smells and sights rushed back in on her. Compared to this, the garden seemed a veritable Eden. Her partner for the cotillion was pacing the side of the dance floor, looking for her, and with a sigh she squeezed Tolly's arm and left him.

"There you are," Lionel said, scowling as he looked past her at Tolly. "Not still lending an ear to that fool, are you? You know they're saying that he led his men into the wilderness, got lost, and then was the only one to find his way out."

She kept her charming smile carefully on her face. "You never fail to make me laugh, Lionel. Though I'm not certain the stabbing, strangling, and shooting deaths of eight soldiers should be the subject of a jest. I'm certain the soldiers' families don't think it's amusing."

He stammered. "They found his men?"

"Of course. Didn't you read the newspaper when he returned? His commanding officer praised his courage and intelligence. It's just a shame now that his brave deeds fall contrary to the East India Company's pocketbooks."

"Yes," he said uncertainly, following her onto the dance floor and taking her proffered hand. "A shame."

As she turned and dipped and hopped in time with the music, she kept half her attention on Tolly. Most people who passed by ignored him, or even went out of their way to pretend not to notice him. He was definitely a striking presence, but also a very direct one. No, this time she had the advantage. She had spent years learning precisely how to be the most charming. And everyone knew that more snakes had been caught with a smile than with a sword point. Or some saying like that, anyway.

But that very realization worried her where Tolly was concerned. He'd been too hurt to be easy on anyone. And if this mysterious person he was to meet felt the same, things could get very dangerous. Which left her, she supposed. A very nervous, very unskilled, very loyal her.

Chapter Nineteen

"Men are stubborn creatures who make unilateral decisions they claim are for the best—which means, the best for *them*. I will wager that for every time a man says something is 'for the best,' you will find a better solution. Then make him think the new solution is of his own making, and you will have much more successful results."

A LADY'S GUIDE TO PROPER BEHAVIOR, 2ND EDITION

Tom hadn't been happy to be roused from sleep well after midnight and sent to saddle Meru, but if Sommerset was feeling secretive, Bartholomew had no intention of hiring hacks and attracting attention both by his limp and his person if the rumors had begun to spread outside the circles of the *ton*.

The leather cuff he tied around his leg wasn't the most fashionable accessory, but he'd never much cared about that. And the support it provided more than made up for the wrinkling of his trousers. Of more interest was the way the binding didn't hurt quite as much as it had the last time he'd worn it, and the way he had to lash it tighter. That meant both that the swelling in his knee had gone down, and that the break was beginning to heal.

In his imagination, it meant that perhaps one day he might be able to walk normally again, and that sometime in the unforeseeable future he might be able to waltz with his wife. *His wife.* He couldn't quite believe that she'd said yes. He hadn't even planned to ask her until he'd resolved this damned mess, but out in that garden with her dressed all in emerald and her eyes shining like twin stars, he hadn't been able to resist. *And she'd said yes.*

Most of the *ton*'s parties were ending at this hour, and the street rang with the sound of hooves and tack and carriage wheels. Bartholomew took a deep breath. Since he'd returned home to James House, the only time he'd ever been truly alone was when he'd been asleep—and he hadn't been alone there since India and the nightmares he'd brought back with him, so that hardly counted.

In all that time, though, he'd *felt* alone no matter who surrounded him—unless it was Theresa. During the mess he'd made in India and the careless way he lived his life before that, he must have done at least one good thing. Otherwise he couldn't explain why he deserved her.

Sommerset must have alerted his stable that a guest would be arriving, because Harlow came jogging around to the front of the house the moment Meru set hoof on the front drive. "Colonel," the groom said, moving around to take Tolly's weight as he stepped to the ground.

Bartholomew, though, waved him back. "I'll give it

a try," he said, swinging down right leg first. Thankfully Meru knew by now to tolerate all sorts of nonsense, and the gelding didn't even flinch as he grabbed onto the cantle to steady himself. By God. He made it to the ground and onto his feet by himself, for the first time in nearly a year.

"Well done, sir," the groom said, grinning.

Tolly inclined his head as he freed his cane from its restraining straps. "Thank you."

He considered pounding on Sommerset's front door, because this time his business concerned the man rather than his Adventurers' Club. But the duke also represented his best chance at finding a fellow survivor. Angering him for no damned reason other than contrariness didn't strike him as being very wise. And he was attempting to be wise. Wiser.

Pulling the club key from his pocket, he limped to the half-hidden door and let himself inside. It was crowded tonight; nine men sat about the room, four of them at the same table and playing faro. "Welcome back, Colonel," Gibbs said, coming forward. "A drink?"

"No, thank you. Where's Sommerset?"

"He'll be down in a moment. You might wish to go have a seat by the inner door."

The inner door. The one that led into Ainsley House proper and out of the Adventurers' Club. He hadn't been inside the duke's private residence since the day he'd been invited to join Sommerset's odd little mix of outcasts. With a brief nod to the footman, he limped across the room.

"In the nine months since Sommerset began this,"

damned Easton's voice came from one of the tables, "not a one of us has been asked to leave the club. What do you think of that, Colonel?"

Bartholomew ignored him. This place had helped keep him alive when he'd first returned to London, and it would be worse than a shame if the duke decided he didn't deserve to take his ease behind its walls any longer. But at the same time, he had other concerns, and he couldn't turn from the path he'd chosen without losing something. He might lose it all anyway, but he'd discovered a reason to take a chance.

The inner door opened. The Duke of Sommerset stood there, taking in the occupants of the room. Then he angled his head toward the inside of the house. "In here," he said, barely sparing Bartholomew a glance.

"Goodbye, Colonel James!" Easton called, chuckling.

"Sapskull," Sommerset muttered, closing and locking the door once Tolly limped through it.

Bartholomew took a breath, reminding himself to keep his temper in check. "Thank you for agreeing to see me to—"

"Do you think I meant to give you my word and then do nothing?" the duke interrupted.

"It had occurred to me that you might have stronger ties to the East India Company than to a troublesome member of your club."

The duke glared at him. "'Troublesome' is a damned good description. I knew how much money this could potentially cost me before I made the offer to assist you. Now stop impugning my honor and sit down before you fall down," he said, leading the way past the stairs and into a small sitting room.

"Does all that mean you have information for me?" Bartholomew asked.

"Have some bloody patience, will you?" Sommerset snapped.

"I was called a coward by General Mayhew this evening. It made me angry."

"Mayhew's a fool," another male voice stated.

At the sound of an additional speaker, Tolly looked toward the back of the room. "Ross," he exclaimed, unable to keep the surprise from his voice.

Major-General Anthony Ross stood at the far side of the fireplace, his expression supremely somber. "Tolly."

Ironic as it seemed that Bartholomew wore his uniform while the serving officer was in dark civilian clothes, under the circumstances it wasn't that surprising. "You're Sommerset's source at the Horse Guards?" Tolly asked aloud.

"I am no one's damned spy," Ross snapped. "I tried to call on you days ago. You wouldn't see me."

"I—"

"After the report became public, I couldn't very well go looking for you. When Sommerset mentioned his friendship with you, I asked him to set up a discreet meeting."

Tolly finally took a seat in one of the sitting room's comfortable chairs. "I apologize, Anthony. I haven't been very social since my return."

Ross cleared his throat. "Understandable. But you saved my skin in Belgium, and I wanted to repay the debt. It's too late now to warn you about the East India Company's report, but I can at least tell you that Hadderly consulted with the Horse Guards before publishing. *You* are the only known English survivor of a reputed Thuggee attack. Don't look for allies at the War Office, Tolly. We've been warned against aiding you."

For a long moment, Tolly looked at him. "Why? I've served honorably for ten years."

"Because there is a shortage of wars at the moment," Sommerset put in, leaning on his elbows over the back of a chair. "In order to keep itself financially and politically . . . useful, the army has to ally itself with the Company. It's business, Tolly. But I wanted you to hear it from Major-General Ross, since you seem to think I have ulterior motives."

"I owe you an apology as well, Your Grace."

"Yes, you do. I would have been rather surprised—and disappointed—however, if you weren't suspicious of everyone."

Apparently the circle of people he trusted was beginning to grow again despite everything that had happened. And for that he owed Theresa another debt of gratitude. "Then what do you suggest I do now, Your Grace?"

"Talk to the army. Persuade them that their soldiers knowing about the Thuggee threat is vital to continued commerce in India. They may not do anything publicly, but within the ranks it may save lives."

"But not my reputation." And he needed his reputation in order to enable him to marry Theresa.

"The Company will never admit to a danger they can't control. They would lose millions of pounds.

Compared with that, a few dozen soldiers and a few hundred natives disappearing now and then is justifiable." The duke glanced at Ross, who looked grimmer by the moment. "In my opinion, the best you can hope for is convincing the Horse Guards and then going north for a few months until the next scandal erupts in Town."

"And stop wearing your uniform," the major-general added. "Because while I believe you, a great many of my fellows prefer to believe the Company, and they find you genuinely . . . offensive."

"I actually don't care if the commanders who are deserting me are offended by my actions. And I'm not going anywhere."

"I don't think you have a choice."

"I am engaged," Bartholomew said stiffly. "And I expect you to keep that to yourselves, the same way I'm keeping your . . . assistance to myself. But I'm not about to drag her into disgrace."

Sommerset gazed at him speculatively. "The chit who had you thinking about dancing?"

"Yes."

"Damn."

The duke spoke so quietly that Tolly wasn't certain he was meant to hear the curse. But he did, and he knew what it meant. Sommerset saw no way around this. In order for the East India Company to remain successful in India, any stories of the Thuggee needed to be suppressed. And while he might have some success in convincing the army to at least keep their soldiers informed, none of that would be public knowledge. People would continue to vanish, and his reputation would remain where it was—damaged and crumbling further as his leg healed and he lost what sympathy his injury gained him.

He cleared his throat. "Someone suggested that I write a memoir of my experiences in India."

Sommerset paused, then took a seat. "A memoir with the idea of publication."

"Yes."

"You would be denting a great many pocketbooks. Including mine."

"And my word as a senior officer with the War Office, Ross put in."

Bartholomew let the hard jolt of tension flow into his shoulders. He couldn't outrun anyone, but he had a very hard cane in his hand, and he knew how to use it—and the rapier hidden inside it. "Is that going to be a problem?" he asked slowly.

The duke looked away for a moment, clearly running scenarios through his head. "No," he said finally. "Not from me."

Ross shook his head. "I had friends in your unit as well, Tolly. They shouldn't be forgotten."

"But I suggest you do this secretly," Sommerset continued. "And quickly. The longer it takes, the more likely someone who isn't willing to sit by is to discover it. And by that I mean anyone with ties to the Company. Which might be almost anyone, these days."

"Danger doesn't precisely trouble me." Bartholomew stood, keeping his weight balanced just on the chance that one of the men wasn't as accepting of this plan as he pretended.

"Whose idea was this? Do you trust him?"

"Her. Yes. I trust her."

The duke stood as well. "Wait here a moment, Ross. I don't want to risk you two being seen together." He opened the door and led Tolly back toward the club entrance. "Let me know when you think it's ready to be looked at. Several other club members have been published, and I know one or two honest publishers who won't sell your information to the East India Company." He stopped, blocking the way. "You may be comfortable with danger, Tolly, but there are those around you who aren't."

"I'll manage." When he straightened, he and Sommerset were eye to eye. "I saved Ross's life. He owes me a good turn. But I'm trusting you, Sommerset. And in the past trusting people hasn't done me well. If I see trouble and it looks like it's come from here, I won't wait for an explanation."

"Generally people don't threaten me in my own home, Colonel." The duke unlocked the door. "Under the circumstances, I'll let it go. Yes, some of my wealth comes from the East India Company. Not all of it. And not enough for me to harm someone I consider a friend." He offered his hand.

Bartholomew hesitated, then shook hands with the duke. The man had already saved his life, and his leg. He hoped he'd become a better judge of character in the past year, because yes, he did consider Nicholas Ainsley, the Duke of Sommerset, a friend. And the duke had already described himself as such to Ross.

"Contact me if you need assistance. But do it discreetly."

"I will. Thank you."

"You're welcome. And keep Miss Weller close; she seems to have some rather brilliant ideas."

Of course if anyone knew which lady had caught his eye it would be Sommerset; he rarely seemed to miss anything. "I intend to."

"Can't we go home now, miss?" Sally asked, bundling herself tighter in her shawl.

Theresa kept her steady gaze out the hack's window. "Not until Colonel James reappears," she said.

They'd been stopped just down the street from Ainsley House for nearly thirty minutes. Whatever his business there, and she suspected that the Duke of Sommerset must be his secret contact, he hadn't used the front entrance. Rather, he'd disappeared through a door halfway down the front of the house and well hidden by an archway covered with vines.

It was definitely peculiar. And now that she had an additional reason to worry over Tolly, she was very glad she hadn't stayed at home and waited to see what might come of tomorrow. And if she didn't see Colonel James reappear in the next twenty minutes, she was going in after him.

He could escape this, if he wanted to. He could leave the country, or go somewhere far from London where no one had heard of the Thuggee or his service in India. But he would go a disgraced man, and he could never return without being seen as the same. Bartholomew *could* do that, and could more than likely live with the consequences. But he wouldn't. And that was because of her.

"Miss Tess, it's very late," Sally muttered miserably. "If anyone in the household was to wake and see you gone, there would be the devil to pay."

"Hush, Sally. If everything goes as it should, we'll

be home again without ever having left the hack, and no one the wiser."

"Colonel James will not like you spying on him, you know."

"Colonel James will never know that I'm spying on him," she retorted in a low voice. "And I'm only making certain he's safe."

A few weeks ago she wouldn't have been able to imagine herself riding about Mayfair in the middle of the night. She wouldn't have been able to imagine any reason dire enough to justify such a breach of propriety. Now, though, she was beginning to wish she'd left Sally at home so that she could perhaps attract Tolly's attention and they could find a way to sneak him into her house, or her into his. It didn't matter, as long as she had another chance to be alone and naked with him.

Finally Tolly reappeared, collecting his lovely gray gelding Meru from a waiting groom and swinging back into the saddle. It was far too dim to make out his expression, but at least he seemed well and whole—or as whole as he'd been when he'd gone inside.

"Duck," she whispered, pulling Sally down beside her to the rather sticky floor of the hack.

A moment later someone knocked high up on the hack's door. "I can see you down there, you know," Tolly's voice came.

She straightened. From the back of his horse Tolly sat looking in at her. Now she could read his expression—but she still wasn't certain whether he was amused or annoyed. "Hello," she ventured.

"What are you doing out here?" he demanded,

keeping his voice low and sending a glare at the driver when he started mumbling something.

"You said you were going out to meet someone in secret. I was worried."

"So you came out here to protect me."

"Well, yes."

Tolly leaned sideways, grasping the bottom of the hack's open window with one hand. "Come here."

Theresa scooted up against the door, covering his hand with hers. She stood, leaning into the opening to kiss him. Warmth crashed through her again, dispelling the evening's chill with one hard beat of her heart.

Sally gasped. "Miss Tess! You can't!"

Slowly Theresa straightened again. "That was nice."

"Only nice? I'll have to work harder next time." He glanced up at the driver again. "Take them to Charles Street. I'll ride along with you just to be certain you arrive home safely."

"Just to be certain?" she repeated, smiling.

"And to tell you that you're brilliant." He grinned back at her. "And that I'm apparently about to become a novelist, after all."

Arthur Peters ducked back around the corner as the hack and Colonel James on his horse passed by. Once they were well out of sight he returned to his own horse and the two men waiting with it.

"Anything?" one of them, Mr. Williams, asked.

"Several things. Follow James and Miss Weller to make certain they aren't going anywhere but their respective homes."

"We're watching a chit, now?"

"This one, we are. And be glad you're going after her; I have to go wake Lord Hadderly."

It was becoming a very crowded and foul kettle of fish. Middle-of-the-night meetings with the Duke of Sommerset, a secret attachment of some sort with Miss Weller, and something about a novelist. He might well be setting himself up for a thrashing, but Lord Hadderly didn't like secrets. And this smacked of several very large ones.

She'd followed him. Bartholomew kept pace with the hack as it turned onto Charles Street and up to the foot of the Weller House drive. Theresa, until very recently obsessed with propriety, had sneaked out of her house in the middle of the night. And she'd done it because she was worried about him.

The notions of trust and betrayal had consumed him for the past year, but he hadn't stopped to think that Theresa trusted *him*. And Sommerset trusted him. How and when had this happened?

"Promise me that you're going straight home, Tolly," Tess whispered as she stepped down from the hack.

"I promise." He reached down for her hand, wishing he could risk dismounting on his own, but fairly certain his knee wouldn't tolerate any more of that tonight. "I want you in my bed, Tess," he breathed, twining his fingers with hers.

"I want to be there."

"Miss Tess," the maid said, hurrying up to them, "we must go inside."

She nodded. "I'm calling on Amelia tomorrow. Perhaps I'll bring some writing tablets."

"You should stay away from me," he countered, still gripping her hand. "Sommerset is of the opinion that if word of my intentions gets out, things could get very nasty. And there's absolutely no reason for you to be caught up in that."

Her shoulders rose and fell, and he abruptly realized he wasn't certain whether he wanted her to agree with him or not. Her safety was of course paramount, but he felt like a better person when she was with him.

"Don't forget," she said with a clearly forced smile, "I've already published a booklet. I may be of some assistance."

"Tess."

"Don't try to make me stay away, Tolly." A tear ran down her cheek.

God. He would give her the moon, if she only asked him for it. "Come if you wish, then. I'll leave it to you." Reluctantly he released her fingers. "But now go inside. It's cold."

"I didn't notice."

"Oh, I did, Miss Tess." The maid took her arm and began half dragging her mistress toward the front door. "Please, miss. Before someone sees."

It was far too late to keep Theresa from being ruined, but at the moment the two of them—and Lackaby—were the only ones to know it. For her sake, he wanted to keep it that way.

Once she was inside the house and the door quietly and safely closed, he clucked to Meru. At the corner he slowed a little, making a show of adjusting his stirrup while he took in the two riders hiding in the shadow of the large oak trees there. For a brief moment he considered confronting them, but at night and unarmed but for his boot knife and the cane rapier, he decided against it. And he wanted to make certain that they followed him home rather than staying close to Weller House.

Sommerset had warned him that things would get more dangerous. He just hadn't expected it to begin already.

"What do you think?" Bartholomew stood back from the billiards room curtains the next morning and looked out over the street.

Lackaby moved up to the other side of the window. "This one looks tougher than that fellow last night. And he's better at hiding himself in plain sight."

Bartholomew nodded. "Hopefully the Company is just trying to avoid being taken by surprise."

"By what? You suddenly decide to run for prime minister?"

"I don't know. But as long as they don't know we're watching them, I suppose we have the advantage."

"It doesn't feel that way."

No, it didn't. "For the moment keep this to yourself."

Lackaby left the window, passing by the billiards table with a longing gaze. "Who would I tell? The grooms? The butler? They ain't much in the way of military assistance."

Bartholomew limped after the valet. "No, they aren't. Which is why I don't want to involve them."

"Aye. I've never heard of winning a campaign by writing a book before, but I suppose we'll find out."

"Just remember that we're not discussing any

books, either. Only Stephen knows." And that had been quite the conversation earlier that morning. Surprisingly, though, his brother had finally agreed that this seemed the best solution.

"Only Lord Gardner and you and me and Miss Tess, you mean." Lackaby sent him a sideways glance as he hefted Bartholomew's arm over his shoulder to help him down the stairs. "She does know what you're about, I assume."

"Yes, not that it's any of your damned business."

"Aye, Colonel."

Gripping the balustrade to stop them both on the landing, Bartholomew pushed his valet back a step. "I take that back. If anything does go wrong, you have one duty—see that Theresa Weller is safe and protected. Is that clear?"

The valet drew himself up for a crisp, precise salute. "Yes, sir."

"Good. And thank you."

"I only hope you can write, or all this will be for nothing."

"Get me down the damned stairs, Louis."

"You're a cruel man, Colonel."

"You have no idea. And settle in; this is going to be a siege." Privately he hoped he could put the swirling nightmares in his mind into some sort of coherent order, as well, and that he could do it quickly. Because the longer it took him to save his reputation, the more likely the East India Company would be to discover what he had planned.

Chapter Twenty

"A lady will keep the secrets of her friends no matter the temptation, which is why one should be very careful in choosing friends to begin with. The difficulty is deciding when a confidence must be broken, and whether the consequence is worth the loss of the friend you've betrayed."

A LADY'S GUIDE TO PROPER BEHAVIOR, 2ND EDITION

You're off to see Amelia again?"

Theresa stopped halfway out the front door of Weller House. "Yes, Grandmama. I may stay for dinner, but I'll send word to let you know." She headed out again, Sally on her heels.

"What about the Brewster recital?"

"I've sent my regrets."

"Just a moment, Tess." Grandmama Agnes hurried down the staircase. "For ten days now you've been running out the door to James House. Do you think I haven't noticed that you've canceled every afternoon engagement this week? Not to mention that a dozen men have come calling without you even sending your regrets for not being home to receive them."

"I miss my cousin," Theresa offered.

"And what about Colonel James? He has nothing to do with this, I suppose?"

Theresa blushed. "You know a lady never calls on a gentleman. It's not at all proper."

Her grandmother grinned. "But a lady does call on her cousin at a home where a very handsome bachelor also happens to reside." With a cackle, Agnes pulled a bonnet from the rack by the front door. "I miss Amelia, myself. Ramsey, I'll be at James House if anything should arise. I may stay for dinner, but I'll send word."

With a smile, the butler sketched a bow. "I'll inform Lord Weller when he returns from Parliament."

"Yes. He may wish to join us. Good thinking, Ramsey."

"Thank you, my lady."

Theresa stifled a frown as she found herself following her grandmother out to the carriage. She'd been hoping to finally manage some time alone again with Tolly. With Sally, Lackaby, and Lord Gardner all hovering about, plus Violet attempting to wheedle out of her brother what he was scribbling all the time and Amelia pestering both her and Lord Gardner for the same information, Tolly had barely managed to kiss her a half dozen times in ten blasted days.

Now today she would likely have to spend all day sitting about and chatting with Leelee and her grandmother. *Damnation.* She already felt half ready to combust. Every night she dreamed of being in his embrace, and every morning she couldn't wait to see him.

"Spending the day with my two dearest girls," Grandmama Agnes said with a smile, patting Theresa on the knee. "Oh! Perhaps we should go have luncheon with Lady Primstead. She mentioned that her Lady Duchess is going to have kittens. That cat has the most pretentious name, but she does have very pretty eyes."

"Yes," Theresa agreed, attempting to keep the smile on her face, "that sounds delightful. I do think I might stay behind. Colonel James has been reluctant to . . . exercise his leg, but I seem to be able to goad him into taking a walk."

"You goad him into it, or he likes to spend time in your company?"

Theresa let out a sigh. "It's complicated."

Agnes snorted. "Complicated is good. And your old grandmama isn't quite as daft as you think. Is he as fond of you as you are of him?"

"Am I that obvious?" Theresa asked, a small measure of relief running through her.

"I'm very crafty." Agnes's smile softened. "If not for that blasted Hadderly getting everyone to think that Colonel James lied about the attack that killed his men, I would be hoping to hear about a match. Under these circumstances, however, I'm very proud that you have remained his friend."

Oh, she was very much more than his friend. "Thank you for saying that, Grandmama."

"You're welcome. And I won't force you to accompany Amelia and me to luncheon."

"Thank you again."

Agnes patted her on the knee again. "I hate to say this, because I haven't seen you so happy in a very long time, but be a little cautious, my love. I would hate for you to finally give your heart to someone only to discover that you can't tolerate his circumstances."

With a nod, Theresa hugged her grandmother's arm. "I'm very lucky to have you, Grandmama."

"Yes, you are. And don't you forget it."

Considering that she hadn't bothered to discover whether Amelia would even be home or not, Theresa was very pleased to find her cousin in the small James House garden, cutting flowers. "Leelee!" she exclaimed, pushing back her abrupt guilt that she'd spent nearly every minute of the past ten days at her cousin's home and had barely exchanged a dozen words with her.

"Tess! And Grandmama!"

"We're here to take you to luncheon," Agnes announced, hugging her granddaughter. "Or I am."

Leelee looked over at Theresa. "Ah. He's upstairs, in the east sitting room. Again."

"Thank you," Theresa said, with a grin she couldn't help.

"If you know what he's doing up there, I wish you would tell me. I don't like being barred from entering rooms in my own house. Particularly when my cousin goes wherever she wishes."

"I—" Theresa closed her mouth again. Instead of attempting to explain something she couldn't, she flung her arms around Amelia in a tight hug. "It's all to help," she whispered in her cousin's ear. "I'd tell you if I could."

"That's what Stephen keeps saying." Amelia grimaced. "Oh, go on. What are daisies compared with Colonel Tolly James?"

She didn't wait for another invitation. Leaving Sally behind in the garden, she hurried up the back stairs, past Tolly's bedchamber, and up to the closed door marking the east sitting room. She knocked. "Tolly? It's me."

Silence.

Then, a heartbeat later, she heard chair legs scraping against the wooden floor, and the distinctive thump of a cane. The key on the inside of the door turned, and the handle lifted. The door cracked open, and a hand, fingertips stained black with ink, reached out to circle her wrist. Then he pulled her inside and closed the door behind them.

"Hello," he said, pushing her back against the closed door and kissing her.

She flung her arms around his shoulders, kissing him back. After better than ten days of being so close and barely able to touch, he felt so warm and solid and delicious that she wouldn't have cared if Lackaby was in the room next to them.

A heartbeat later she turned her face away a little. "Lackaby's not in here, is he?"

"I banished him for incessant pacing." Tolly rested his forehead against hers. "I'm very glad you didn't listen to me when I said you should stay away." Slowly he kissed her again, teasing at her mouth until her heart pounded and she could barely breathe.

"I'm . . . I'm not here to distract you, you know," she managed, groaning as his hands lowered to her hips, pulling her up against him. She could feel his arousal between them, and her knees went weak.

"You're not distracting me," he returned, shifting his attention to her bare throat and jaw. "You're saving me from pitching myself out the window."

"Tolly!" She shoved his shoulders. He retreated all of an inch, but at least he stopped kissing her long enough that she could think. "There is to be no pitching out of windows."

"It was just an expression." He ran a hand through his dark, disheveled hair. "I am not a writer. Lackaby keeps yelling at me to add more adjectives, and Stephen says I'm too brutal."

"What happened was brutal."

He nodded. "And I want it out of my mind for just a damned minute or two."

Theresa reached between them to loosen the knot of his cravat. "Then perhaps I can be of some help, after all."

Tolly smiled, the expression sensual and wicked and just for her. "I was hoping you would say that." With a click he turned the key again, locking the door.

"I don't know how much time we have," she said, untying his cravat and pulling it free. "Sally will come looking for me, and my grandmother's here, as well."

"Then we'll have to hurry." He pulled her fingers away from his waistcoat. "Don't bother with that."

"But—"

His mouth took hers again. "If I don't have you now, Tess, I cannot guarantee my sanity."

They sank onto the floor in such a tangle of limbs

and clothes that she could barely tell where she stopped and he began. Where before he'd been slow and gentle and careful, clearly he had more urgent things on his mind today. He grabbed her skirt in both hands and yanked it up around her waist. Then he turned her onto her back, leaning over her for another burning, openmouthed kiss.

Somehow he managed to kneel between her thighs, keeping his weight on his good knee. Swiftly he unfastened his trousers and shoved them down. Theresa felt wild, wanton, and she couldn't tear her eyes from him, from his large, aroused manhood. She ached for him, and she couldn't imagine any clearer evidence that he wanted her. Badly, apparently.

"Theresa," he murmured, settling his body over hers.

"Now, Tolly. Please."

He angled his hips forward, sliding inside her. Theresa gasped, wrapping her ankles around his thighs as he thrust into her again and again, harder and faster until she couldn't breathe, couldn't even think. Abruptly she shattered, throbbing, clinging tightly to his shoulders.

"Oh God," she moaned. "Oh God."

His pace increased as he gazed down at her, amber eyes glinting. "Mine," he rumbled, sinking down to kiss her again. "Say you're mine, sweet Theresa."

"I'm yours, Bartholomew James," she managed, tangling her fingers into his hair.

With a groan he came, holding himself hard inside her. Theresa slid her arms around him as he lowered his head to her shoulder. Both of them breathing hard, they lay there tangled on the floor together.

"I feel better now," she breathed, smiling.

Bartholomew lifted his head again, grinning back down at her. "Not a great deal of finesse, but I have to agree." He kissed her soft mouth again. "The next time I intend to very slowly remove all your clothes and then lick every bare inch of your skin."

"That sounds very nice, too."

"Nice has nothing to do with it." With an even more wicked grin he sat up beside her. "And now I'm going to be disappointed if someone *doesn't* come knocking at this door almost immediately."

Chuckling, Theresa climbed to her feet. For heaven's sake, she hadn't even removed her shoes. She lowered her skirts again, smoothed at them, then dragged the writing chair over for Tolly. "I almost threw my own grandmother out of the carriage this morning because I thought I would miss seeing you."

With a stifled groan, Bartholomew hauled himself to his feet. Straightening, he fastened his trousers again. All morning he'd been distracted with thinking of her—though in truth he had been distracted by thoughts of her for weeks. At least now he would survive through the day.

Moving as swiftly as he could, he unlocked the door again, shoved it half open, and pushed his chair back to the desk where he'd been sitting for the past ten days. As he passed Theresa, though, he couldn't help pausing for another kiss.

"How far have you gotten?" she asked, pulling another chair up beside him.

"I've finished with the section about that last patrol of mine. And I prefaced it with various accounts I'd heard about the Thuggee before that." He picked up his dipped pen, then set it down again. "Frankly, not much else about my time in India is anything worth writing about. And even less worth reading about, I think."

She frowned. "I think it's fascinating."

"You are unique." He glanced at the page again. "The idea is have as many people as possible read *this*." He lifted the thin stack of papers. "Not to make me known as a great writer. And an entire book, I'm afraid, will only prove that I'm more adept at riding and shooting than I am with pen and paper."

For a long moment Theresa gazed out the window. "You said Sommerset had contacts with the publishing houses."

"Yes, but dull is dull, my love. No matter how—"

"Does he have contacts with the *London Times*?"

Bartholomew looked at her. "You mean I should serialize the story?"

"Or print it all at once as an editorial. It doesn't matter, after all, if everyone knows it's your opinion, because that is all you mean for it to be."

He smiled. "Have I mentioned lately how brilliant you are?"

She shrugged, her gray-green eyes dancing. "It never hurts to say it."

"You, my dear, are brilliant."

"Thank you."

Slowly he gathered up the stacks of papers that littered the desk and the window sill. "If all I need is a very widely read editorial, I'm nearly finished." He handed her one of the two stacks. "In fact, I would be honored if you would read it and give me your

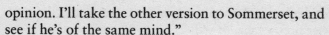

opinion. I'll take the other version to Sommerset, and see if he's of the same mind."

"Now?"

"I want to marry you, Theresa." He stood. "I have no intention of stalling about with this—unless you've changed your mind." It physically hurt to say it, but he absolutely was not going to trap her into anything. Never. "Just tell me, and I—"

She smacked him in the shoulder. "Stop that. I wouldn't be here now if I'd changed my mind."

"I just wanted to hear you say it." He leaned down and kissed her again.

"Thank God I'm not Lady Weller," Lackaby said from the doorway, "or I'd be needing my smelling salts about now."

"Shut up, Lackaby." Bartholomew glanced over his shoulder at the valet. "Go have Meru saddled. I'm going out for a bit."

"You have a book to write, Colonel. You told me to tie you to that chair if you couldn't sit in it on your own any longer. And I am a man of my word."

"I may be finished."

The valet blinked. "Beg your pardon, but not even the goddess Kali could write that fast, and she has four hands."

"A slight change of plan, which I am not going to waste time discussing with you. My horse."

Blowing out his breath, Lackaby left the room again. Bartholomew turned back to Theresa. "I need to go get my leg brace. Will you stay here until I get back from Ainsley House?"

She nodded, her fingers clutching the pages he'd

given her and an alluring mix of worry and hope on her pretty face. "I will."

"And no following me," he added. "And no telling anyone where I've gone. Sommerset wants as little public involvement as possible."

"I know that. I'm only . . . I don't want to begin hoping yet. If Sommerset still thinks a full-length memoir would serve you better, then—"

"Then I still have a great deal of work to do. But it will all end the same." Picking up his cane, he limped up in front of her. "With you and me together."

Theresa stood, sliding her arms up his chest and then around his neck. "Then I'll just begin hoping now, after all," she whispered, and kissed him.

He kissed her back, the warmth, the life of her, sinking into him. "You've even got me hoping, now."

She grinned against his mouth. "Good. And Tolly?"

"Hmm?"

"Don't forget your cravat."

He blinked. Thank God it had been Lackaby barging in, after all. Using his cane to scoop up the cloth, he continued toward the door. "And by the way, thank you."

"For what?"

"For saving my life." He smiled at her. "I'll be back shortly. Keep your fingers crossed."

"I will."

He met Lackaby climbing the stairs again, and tossed him the neck cloth. "Where did you learn to tie a knot?" he asked, stopping to let the valet fix the garment.

"You said I'm to mind my manners, Colonel, so I'll

only smile and ask if ye want any company, wherever it is you're going."

"No. Just keep an eye on our friend outside. Hopefully he'll follow me, in which case I may have a bit of a delay losing him. But I think we both know I can manage that."

"I've seen you ride, Colonel. What about Miss Weller?"

"She's staying here. Keep your other eye on her."

"Yes, sir."

As he expected, the moment he left the James House drive, the watchful fellow outside stopped sketching whatever he was pretending to draw and swung up on his own horse. Good. The further this mess stayed from his Tess, the better.

"Go, Meru," he urged, leaning lower in the saddle and surreptitiously touching the satchel slung over his shoulder. Tess had a less scratched-out copy, but he damned well didn't want this one getting loose and flying about Mayfair. Not until he was ready for it to do so.

Immediately the gray broke into a gallop. In the crowded streets the pace was nearly impossible to maintain, but he didn't mean to have to keep it up for long. Swiftly they dodged around a milk wagon and whipped around a corner, then fell in ahead of a half dozen coaches and turned the other direction.

In ten minutes he would have found himself hopelessly lost, if not for the fact that he'd spent every summer of his youth in Mayfair and its environs. Finally he slowed Meru to a more respectable pace, cut through St. James's Park to put another dozen riders between him and the fellow he hadn't caught sight of in two twisted miles, and then headed off to Grosvenor Square and Ainsley House.

If the fellow had any wits he would return to James House. Lackaby would keep watch, and as long as Tess and the other ladies were inside, there was nothing to worry over.

He trotted onto South Audley Street, and pulled Meru to an abrupt halt. A half dozen riders stood ranged across the narrow boulevard, blocking him. Behind him another four riders closed in, his original pursuer badly out of breath, but among them.

Well. This was one thing he hadn't considered—that they already knew where he was going. His last thought as something hard cracked across the back of his head was that Tess would be waiting for him, and that he hoped she wouldn't blame herself for his death.

Chapter Twenty-one

"How many of us have gazed at a man and thought, 'yes, him,' only to have him pay his attentions to someone else? And how many of us have sighed and waited for some other gentleman to come forward? All I wish to ask is, why? Why not strike up a conversation? Why not determine for ourselves whether 'he' is the one? Why leave it to fate?"

A LADY'S GUIDE TO PROPER BEHAVIOR, 2ND EDITION

Michael and Lord Gardner arrived at James House together. Theresa looked up from reading Tolly's account of the Thuggee attack as her brother and the viscount entered the sitting room. "What is it?" she asked, reading the tense look on her brother's face.

"Some daft bastard proposed a resolution condemning any soldier who claimed to have been attacked by the Thuggee," he said, glancing about the room. "Which is apparently one soldier in all of England."

"Where's Tolly?" Stephen asked, his expression

even more angry. "We put the issue down for now, but it's bound to arise again. I thought he should know."

"He's gone out to see someone," she stated, feeling a bit self-conscious sitting in the room Tolly had occupied for ten days and reading his private scribblings. "He asked me to look over this."

"And how is it?" Lord Gardner shifted, looking as though he wanted to read through it, himself.

"Frightening. Your brother has a very matter-of-fact way of stating the most horrific of occurrences." He actually wrote the way he spoke, and though it wasn't full of the adjectives Lackaby claimed it needed, it was brutal and forthright. And very convincing.

"What is it?" Michael asked, frowning as he looked from one to the other of them.

Oh, heavens. Michael hadn't been included in their little circle of conspirators. If there was anyone else they could trust, however, it was her older brother. She took a breath. "Tolly looked for other survivors, someone to corroborate his story, but he couldn't find anyone. The only other way we could think of to help him regain his reputation was for him to write about his experience. And it's a secret; don't say anything to anyone else."

"That's fairly brilliant," Michael said after a moment. "Is that why you've been scampering over here every day? To help him write his memoirs? That's a bit different than your booklet on proper behavior, isn't it?" He paused. "Unless there's anything you'd care to tell me. Is there?"

He couldn't possibly have guessed. "Not at present."

Stephen left the sitting room. "Come downstairs with us. Amelia and Grandmama Agnes are just sitting down for luncheon."

"I thought they were going out to secure a new kitten."

"Good God," Michael muttered.

"Let's find out, shall we?" Lord Gardner motioned them toward the stairs.

Theresa sighed. She would much rather have remained in the sitting room to finish Tolly's writings, but she was a guest in the James home. Holding the papers against her chest, she led the way out to the garden terrace where Violet had joined the other two ladies and the footmen were setting out fruit and thinly sliced ham.

It all seemed so . . . peaceful. In the spring, shortly after Leelee and Stephen had married, they'd had luncheons exactly like this one at least once a week. Everyone chatted, said witty things to one another, and they hadn't a care in the world—at least not one they discussed.

How things had changed. For the first time in years she felt . . . free, able and ready to move forward with her life. No more being pleasant and polite simply because she was terrified to be otherwise, and no more telling her suitors she simply wasn't ready to marry when in reality she never would be. The only thing missing from luncheon today was Tolly.

"What do you have there?" Amelia finally asked in the middle of the general conversation, indicating the papers at her elbow.

"Just something Tolly asked me to read," she said, keeping her tone breezy. "Pass me the butter, will you?"

"Is that what he's been doing in the sitting room?" Violet took up, leaning sideways to eye the papers. "Writing?"

"What did you think he was doing?" her brother replied with a grin. "Painting lead soldiers?"

"Well, I had no idea, did I? No one tells me anything these days. All I hear is what other people are saying about Tolly. I nearly punched Sarah Saunders in the nose yesterday because she said that her uncle said that once Tolly climbed out of his wheeled chair, no one would want anything to do with him at all."

"Your brother is a very brave man," Theresa said quietly. "And hopefully very soon everyone will realize that."

"I hope so," Violet stated emphatically. "Because I may not be able to restrain myself for much longer." She indicated the papers. "Could I read that when you're finished?"

"No," Theresa and Stephen said in unison.

"Well."

Clearing her throat, Theresa reached over to grip Violet's fingers. "You will be able to read it, but it's not quite finished yet. And what it says is . . . awful. I think Tolly will want to talk with you about it first."

His younger sister sighed. "Very well. Where is he, anyway?"

"He had an errand. He should be back soon."

By three o'clock, however, Tolly still hadn't returned. Tess had read through his account twice, and written a half page of her own notes and a few possible adjectives. She was glad she'd suggested the newspaper editorial; he'd been correct in thinking that the story was so powerful, putting it into the middle of a long account would only dilute it.

Stretching, she stood and walked to the sitting room window again. He'd ridden to Ainsley House to speak with the Duke of Sommerset. She assumed that Sommerset would read the other copy of the paper, then decide whether he agreed that it was enough by itself or would be better in a longer, even-handed memoir. And then he would either provide Tolly with contact information for the *London Times*, or he wouldn't.

It would take some time, of course, but it had been four hours. Unless Sommerset was completely illiterate, which she knew he wasn't, they should have finished their discussion already. Or if Sommerset hadn't been home, Tolly should have returned. Her heart stuttered. What if Sommerset had simply dismissed the story completely? That would leave them out of ideas to rescue Tolly's reputation. And where might he have gone, if that were the case?

Oh, dear. Trying to keep herself calm, she headed out to find Lord Gardner. He and Michael were in the billiards room, in the middle of a game. "Excuse me," she said, "but if Tolly were . . . upset about something, where would he go?"

Stephen set down his billiards cue. "What do you mean, 'upset'?"

"I mean that he should have been back by now."

"Perhaps it would help if you told me where he went, Tess."

For a moment she looked from her brother to her cousin-in-law. As far as she knew Tolly had only spoken about Sommerset to her because she'd followed him to Ainsley House. No one else knew. But how long was she supposed to wait before she did something? Six hours? Eight?

Quietly she closed the door behind her. "He rode to Ainsley House. Sommerset has allied himself with Tolly, and agreed to assist with the publication. Tolly wanted his opinion on publishing in the newspaper rather than taking the time to write an entire book."

"And you think Sommerset turned him down?"

"I don't know. All I know is that he's been gone for better than four hours. I've read everything through twice, had luncheon, made notes, and had time to worry."

Stephen and Michael glanced at one another. Whatever it was they were communicating, she didn't like it. Worry deepened into fear.

"What?" she demanded.

"I'll have our horses saddled," Stephen said, moving past her to open the door again. "You wait here with Amelia and Violet and your grandmother."

"No. I'm going with you."

"You're not dressed for riding, Tess," Michael pointed out. "Stay here."

"No." She pushed past them as they hurried down the stairs. "Leelee!"

Her cousin appeared from the drawing room. "Goodness! What is it?"

"I need to borrow your horse."

"Certainly. What's amiss?"

"Nothing," Stephen put in. "We'll be back shortly."

Graham the butler pulled open the front door just as they reached the bottom of the stairs. Theresa abruptly stopped as she saw the figure in the doorway. Her relief, though, almost immediately slid into annoyed frustration. "Alexander? What are you doing here?"

Lord Montrose sent a glance at the butler, then moved past him into the foyer. "I've been calling at Weller House for nearly a week," he said in a low voice. "I finally realized that you must be here."

"Well, yes, I am. But I'm about to lea—"

"I need to speak with you."

Cupping her elbow in one hand, Michael moved around her. "Five minutes," he said, following Stephen out the front door and around toward the stable. "Or we're leaving without you."

Scowling, she backed into the morning room. "This way," she said, gesturing Alexander to follow her.

"Is something amiss?" he asked, glancing back toward the foyer.

"Just a bit of an errand. What may I do for you?"

"I want you to come and see Montrose Park," he said. "If you agree, I'll arrange for a house party. Bring any of your friends you like. But I think once you see the estate of which you could be mistress, any hesitation you have about marrying me will be erased."

Oh, dear. "Alexander, I don't want to leave London during the Season."

"Not even for me?"

"Not for anyone. Now if you'll excuse me, I need to g—"

"This is about Colonel James, I suppose?" he interrupted, his eyes cool.

"What makes you say that?"

"Because he's the only gentleman in residence whom I haven't seen, and he's the one who seems to infatuate you."

Infatuate, obsess, trouble, stir—so many words at the moment. "I really can't speak to that, but excuse me."

"I'll ride with you."

Halfway through the door, she paused. "No, you won't."

"You can hardly stop me. And if this has something to do with him confronting the East India Company, I'd prefer not to miss it." He sent her a grim smile. "Though I have to admit that my own hopes more than likely run contrary to his."

"Tess!" her brother's voice came from outside.

"Come along then," she decided, turning her back on him.

"Miss Tess!"

For heaven's sake. She sent a quick glance up the stairs at Lackaby as the valet charged into view. "Later, if you please," she snapped, and hurried outside.

"No, miss," the valet countered, actually catching her arm. "Now."

"Unhand her," Montrose ordered, his tone highly affronted.

Theresa, though, had seen the look in the valet's eyes. "What is it, Lackaby?"

"I'm to keep my eyes on you, Miss Tess," the valet said.

That caught her attention all over again. "Why?"

"I, ah, it was my orders, miss."

Clearly there were too many blasted secrets in this group. Scowling, Theresa grabbed him by the arm and pulled him onto the drive. "Why are you to keep your eyes on me?" she demanded. "The truth. Now."

"When the colonel asks why I gabbed to you, you have to tell him that you threatened to sack me or something."

"Yes, very well."

By now Stephen and Michael had reached them again, both of them scowling. The valet looked as though he would rather be eating bugs, but he nodded. "The last fortnight or so, someone's been . . . hanging about the house. Outside. Colonel James figured it was the Company, trying to find out if he meant to do anything to counter their report on the Thuggee."

"What?" Stephen asked, fury darkening his features.

"The fellow followed the colonel, which is what he figured, but he wanted me to be sure you was safe, Miss Tess."

Stephen motioned at a groom to dismount. "You're coming with us, then, Lackaby. Now."

Theresa wanted to gallop to Ainsley House, but in the late afternoon the Mayfair streets were choked with carriages and riders paying visits or returning visits. And in the middle of it, her, the former princess of propriety, riding to the house of a bachelor duke in the company of three gentlemen and a valet.

They were met in the Ainsley House drive by a pair of grooms, who moved up swiftly and professionally to take charge of the horses. Stephen led the way up the shallow front steps and pounded on the front door. Ideally Tolly himself would meet them, saying he'd just been on his way back home and what the devil were they all doing there looking for him.

The door opened, revealing a tall, angular man in crisp red and black livery. "Good afternoon," he said politely.

"Is the Duke of Sommerset in?" Stephen asked, clearly impatient to be inside.

"His Grace is currently unavailable. May I inform him that you came to call?"

"It's rather urgent," Tolly's brother replied. "Please tell him that Lord Gardner and Lord Weller are here, looking for Colonel Bartholomew James." Behind him, Alexander cleared his throat. "And Lord Montrose," he added.

"As I said, my lord, His Grace is currently unavailable. I will be honored to deliver any message or letter to him when he is—"

"Is my brother here?" the viscount demanded.

"I am not at liberty to speak of or for anyone but His Grace. The—"

Theresa backed away as Michael joined in the argument with the butler. Silently she walked down the side of the house to the vine covered archway and the plain door beneath it. This was how Tolly had entered and left the house before. Perhaps he'd done so again today.

Taking a breath, she tried the handle. Locked. Considering the raised voices at the front door, Stephen and the others still weren't having any luck gaining either entry or answers. And she wanted—needed—to know where Tolly was, and if he was well. Balling her fist, she knocked on the door.

Silence.

He'd gotten in somehow the last time, and in the middle of the night. She knocked again, waited, and then pounded. Still nothing. "Open this door," she called, feeling rather silly, "or I shall scream so loudly that all Mayfair will come running to investigate!"

The door opened.

A stout, broad-shouldered man stepped into the opening, blocking her view of the inside. "This is a private entrance," he said stiffly. "Please use the front door."

Before he could shut the door again, Theresa stuck her foot in the way. "I am looking for Colonel Bartholomew James. He came here at eleven o'clock this morning, and he was expected back home hours ago. Is he still here?"

"I have no idea why you would think that anyone would be here at the side entry to Ainsley House, miss. Please call at the front d—"

Theresa took a deep breath to scream. Almost immediately another hand reached around the first fellow and yanked her inside, slamming the door closed behind her. "Unhand me at—"

"You are not supposed to be here," the Duke of Sommerset growled, still gripping her arm hard.

Despite her abrupt uneasiness, part of her was immensely relieved. "Your Grace. I'm looking for Colonel J—"

"I heard you the first time." His gray eyes hard as steel, he dragged her back from the door. "Sit down."

As he released her, she sat down hard in a chair. For the first time, she looked around her. A dozen tables and thrice that many chairs lay scattered across a wide, open floor, a comfortable sofa and more well-padded chairs at the back of the room in front of a fireplace. Books lined the back walls, and two tall, narrow windows overlooked the lovely Ainsley House garden, with a billiards table and a pianoforte beneath them.

Several of the chairs were occupied, with a half dozen or so men all staring at her and none of them looking very happy to see her there. "What is this?" she asked.

"None of your business," the duke returned, sitting opposite her. "What makes you think your Colonel James would be here?"

Whoever these men were, Tolly likely wouldn't appreciate them knowing his business. She sat forward in her chair so she could lower her voice. "He came here to bring you some . . . reading material," she said quietly. "Please don't assume I'm a fool. All I want to know is if he is still here, or when he left."

Sommerset gazed at her for a long moment. "I haven't seen him today," he said finally.

Her heart stopped. "But he came specifically to ask your opinion on a newspaper editorial approach," she hissed, clenching her fists. "Your Grace, he left James House before eleven o'clock this morning."

He didn't move, but she had the abrupt sensation that a great sleek panther had come awake. "You're certain he came here?" he asked in a low voice.

"Positive. He brought a draft of his account. We thought that—well, that doesn't matter now. I have four men pounding at your front door at this moment trying to reach you. Perhaps your butler turned Tolly away, too."

"My butler would not have turned Tolly away." With a low curse he stood, offering her a hand up. "Come with me."

Swiftly he led her across the length of the room and through another door that led into what looked more like the inside of a very wealthy gentleman's home. "What was back there?" she asked again, indicating the other room.

"A refuge. Pray don't mention it. You've come through the servants' entrance. Is that clear?"

"Yes, of course."

A moment later they were in the foyer, and he gestured for his butler to stand aside. "This way, gentlemen," he said.

"It's about damned time," Stephen snapped, then noticed Theresa. "How did you manage to break the siege?"

"I came in through the servants' entrance," she said. "His Grace says Tolly never arrived here this morning."

They entered a large sitting room, but Theresa, at least, couldn't remain still long enough to join the men in the chairs. He'd never arrived. Somewhere between James House and Sommerset's residence, he'd . . . vanished. Where? And why? It had to have something to do with the man watching James House, but what, precisely?

"How long have you been assisting my brother with this damned East In—"

"What are you doing here, Montrose?" Sommerset interrupted.

The marquis sent a quick glance at Theresa. "My interest is in Miss Weller. But whatever my personal feelings about Colonel James, I'm not some villain. If he's missing, I will do what I can to assist."

"Then you will also be expected to keep several confidences. I don't want to threaten you and thereby lessen the impact of your . . . selfless behavior, but I think you know what I can do to you if I am betrayed."

"Yes, well, if you threatened everyone I would feel a bit better, but I understand. And I agree."

With a nod, Sommerset gave the men a swift review of their literary plans and why they'd decided to keep it all a secret. Privately Theresa didn't see why they needed to waste time with explanations, but at the same time if she refrained from interrupting they would finish with the nonsense more quickly.

"Have you heard any stirrings from the East India Company?" Michael asked, his own expression growing grimmer by the moment. "Any indication that they know what's afoot?"

"I haven't heard anything," Sommerset replied.

"If they know anything, then they'll know not to inform you," Theresa stated, gazing again out the window.

"True enough."

"Lackaby, tell him about the man watching James House," she ordered.

It was *men*, as the valet explained it, apparently taking turns and none of them familiar to either Tolly or Lackaby. Why hadn't Tolly told her? Theresa shook herself. She would be very happy to have the opportunity to yell at him later.

"So where do we begin looking?" she asked, facing

the men once more. "Because I'm finished with chatting about who might know what."

"Determining who might know what," the duke returned, "is the best way to figure where Tolly might be."

"The East India Company," Lord Gardner ground out, his jaws clenched, "seems to be our one and only suspect. What would they do with my brother?"

"Kill him, I would imagine," Sommerset answered.

Theresa froze, her blood turning to ice and her heart stopping. "No," she whispered, everything going numb.

Her brother grabbed her as her legs gave out. "Damnation, Sommerset," he growled. "My sister is in love with him, if you haven't noticed. Show some decency."

"No," she said, fighting her way upright again. "Decency won't help Tolly. What if we made it known that there is another copy of his account out there? Surely they wouldn't harm him if doing so would give his story credibility."

Thankfully no one mentioned aloud that her plan would only work if he wasn't dead already, but she knew they all had to be thinking that. She was. Instead, Sommerset rose. "You are a very bright young lady." He pulled open the door. "Have Khan saddled. Now."

"Yes, Your Grace," the butler returned, hurrying out of the foyer.

"What's your plan?" Tolly's brother demanded.

"This little parade is going to call on Lord Hadderly and inform him of exactly what Miss Weller suggested. The sooner the better." He looked over his shoulder, his gaze remaining on Theresa. "I recommend that you return home."

"And I recommend that Lackaby return home, so if Tolly reappears someone will know where to come and inform us. If there's a hunt, I'm going to be in on it."

And if something had happened to Tolly James, she would wither away and die. But before that, she would make damned certain that what he meant to accomplish, happened. No matter what.

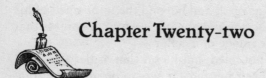

Chapter Twenty-two

"It is my hope that you will read this booklet and see it not as rules, but as a friend—someone else's opinion to consider, but not necessarily with which to agree. I, for one, have found that my original printing held many errors which I have hopefully since corrected. But without the errors, I daresay I might not have found my way."

A LADY'S GUIDE TO PROPER BEHAVIOR, 2ND EDITION

Bartholomew kept his eyes closed for several minutes after he regained consciousness. Appearing more or less dead had saved him once before, and he wasn't about to discard that strategy now.

Distant sounds touched his ears: a dog barking, several voices yelling as they hawked wares, the heavier sound of a coach or a cart. He seemed to be still in London, and close to a thoroughfare of some sort.

He was sitting upright, his arms aching and numb, and his neck stiff. Slumped into a chair, then, his arms bound behind him. Experimentally he flexed his good knee, and his leg remained immobile. Legs tied as well, then. A quick twitch of his jaw told him that he was gagged, and beyond the faint smell of his own blood he could make out a damp mustiness that conjured the image of a cellar.

His head pounded, but he set that aside. The devil knew he'd been injured far worse before. Anything short of being shot and cast into the bottom of a well seemed survivable by comparison. Especially now, when he had another reason to survive. If whoever had snared him had had any intelligence or courage at all, they would have killed him outright.

Something scuffed very close to him. At least one other person in the room. He took a slow breath in through his nose, since his mouth was covered. Best get on with it, then. Slowly tensing his muscles, he made a show of rocking his head and moaning.

"He's coming around," a low male voice said. "Go tell him."

Footsteps tromped away and then up what had to be stairs. They were definitely in a cellar, then. Bartholomew opened his eyes and lifted his head.

"This is a fine idea," a tall, slightly pot-bellied man said, hefting the brace they'd obviously removed from his leg. "Hold the bones and muscles steady so you can still ride."

He was dressed like a gentleman, but not a nobleman—a clean linen shirt and fairly inexpensive-looking waistcoat and long jacket, with a simply knotted cravat at his throat and five shilling boots on his feet. A clerk, then, like the pair who'd followed him back from Sommerset's house the night he'd discovered Theresa also there spying on him.

More boots thudded on the stairs again, somewhere

behind him. The cellar itself was well insulated, with the faint scent of cork and wine now coming to him as his companion moved about. Considering that he'd already concluded he was in some well-appointed gentleman's wine cellar, seeing Lord Hadderly come around into his line of vision wasn't even surprising.

"You're a damned nuisance, Colonel," the earl said. He lifted a stack of papers in one hand. "Seems as though we've met at just the right moment." He glanced beyond Bartholomew's shoulder. "Turn him around."

Two men took the seat and back of the chair and dragged it around a hundred and eighty degrees. Several racks of wine lined the walls, and what looked like a spare set of dining room chairs stood half-covered under a sheet. There were seven of them; he apparently rated the eighth. And they were fairly sturdy looking things, too.

Hadderly strolled into view again. "You've placed me in an awkward position, you know," he said conversationally. "I'm responsible for a great amount of commerce. Money, employees, even the stability of England all fall under my purview.

"Did you ever think," he continued, "that if you hadn't survived that so-called attack, we might have been able to invent some heroic end for you and your men? Saving natives from a flood or a fire, or some such thing. One thing I know you didn't do, however, is this." He shook the papers in his hand.

"We've already had to create one report simply because of your continued presence. That in itself cost the Company over a hundred pounds, and that doesn't even take into account how many wealthy young men waiting for adventure and a place to invest might have been frightened away from India and the Company by you. That's enough of a loss."

He walked over to the small lead and iron stove in the corner opposite the dining room furniture, squatted down, and lit the newspaper and tinder inside. Once it was burning well, he rolled up the pages of Bartholomew's India account and one by one pushed them into the fire.

When he'd finished, Lord Hadderly straightened again. "That's one part of the problem eliminated. I don't suppose you'll tell us if you have any copies of that lying about."

Tolly didn't make a sound. It wouldn't serve any purpose that would aid him, and he had absolutely no intention of doing anything to point a finger at Theresa. Hopefully she was still at James House, and hopefully Lackaby was keeping a close eye both on her and on the house in general.

"Very well," the earl continued. "Make yourself comfortable. We have a few things to determine, and since you've made a nuisance of yourself by appearing at soirees and reconciling with your family, someone will notice you've gone missing. They might point at the Company, and we can't have that. So I suppose we'll have to start a rumor or two about you . . . despairing of ever recovering the reputation you threw away by lying about the Thuggee. Once that's all sorted and we settle on a nice, remote place to put you under the ground, well, we'll be back to things as they should be."

Ah. At least it was just business. In a sense, that

had been the Thuggee philosophy, as well. How else could they pretend friendship and then strangle the very men with whom they'd shared a meal thirty minutes before? Money, profit, greed. He hadn't needed to travel all the way to India to find that.

"There is one thing, though." Hadderly walked up to him and jerked the cloth from around his mouth. "If you simply tell us whether you've left any further copies of that thing lying about, I will give you the opportunity to write a last note to your family. A chance to bid them farewell. Wouldn't that be worth something? You could tell your sister that she's not to blame, that it's for the best if you disappear. And that lovely Miss Weller who's been spending so much of her time at James House. You could add a word for her. Wouldn't it be lovely, to have such a pretty creature shed a tear at your demise?"

Bartholomew settled a calm stare on the earl. "When I kill you," he mused coolly, "is there any sentiment you'd like for me to convey to *your* loved ones? I thought I should ask now, since you'll be coughing blood and shitting yourself after I stab you in the throat."

Hadderly blinked. "You're a very violent fellow, aren't you?"

"Yes."

More feet tapped on the stairs. "My lord, you're needed upstairs."

The earl nodded, backing for the stairs. "Put the gag back in his mouth. I doubt he'll be so brave without an audience, and I don't want him screaming."

"Yes, my lord."

"And stop fooling with that damned thing, Mr. Peters." Hadderly grabbed the leather knee brace out of the clerk's hands and trotted up the stairs.

Thankfully they left him facing the front of the cellar as Mr. Peters yanked the gag up again and made certain it was tight around his mouth. Because with his back to them, he could work on the knots binding his hands. Violent man or not, he knew something about pain. And about how to put it aside when the need arose.

And considering that Hadderly had named both his sister and Theresa, nothing was going to stop him from getting his hands on the earl and choking the life out of him. It might be just business for the earl, but for him it was about his life. And his heart, which for him equaled the same thing.

If Theresa hadn't been worried out of her mind, the sight of four very fit, quite handsome young men flanking her would have been enjoyable, if not outright amusing. Of course one of them was her brother, but Michael hardly resembled the good-natured, teasing muggins who called her Troll and chuckled at the number of suitors she'd gathered.

Considering that Sommerset's butler had very nearly succeeded in keeping them at bay, she was rather glad that His Grace had joined the hunt. She doubted there was a servant in England who wouldn't admit him into a house. Lord Hadderly's man hadn't so much as batted an eye before showing them into a sitting room off the foyer.

Sommerset walked over to stand beside where she

waited by the window. "Do you know Hadderly?" he murmured.

"We've been introduced. I stay well away from him because my grandmother loves cats, and Hadderly breeds dogs."

His jaw twitched. "Does Hadderly know of his lack of popularity with the Weller family?"

She wondered why that mattered, but if they had to wait, she supposed he was doing her a service by distracting her for a moment. "He doesn't seem to notice much that doesn't directly concern him."

"Ah, you're wrong about that, Miss Weller. He notices far more than he sees himself, because he has people watching on his behalf."

"You mean the men Tolly saw watching James House report to Hadderly?"

"That's only a guess, but given what I know of him, I wouldn't be at all surprised. I say this because I intend to confront him fairly directly. I leave it to you to notice what I cannot. Tolly has several times mentioned your skill at observation. Can you do this?"

She nodded once more. "Now that I know how directly he may be involved, I don't intend to blink," she whispered fiercely.

"Neither do I."

The sitting door swung open, and the Earl of Hadderly strolled into the room. "Your Grace, my lords, Miss—Miss Weller? My goodness. What brings you all here and looking so serious?"

"My brother is missing," Stephen said. "Considering his recent return from India and the way his claims dispute the official stance of the East India Company, we thought to come here."

"And in very large numbers." His expression concerned, Hadderly motioned for them all to sit. "Let me assure you that whatever our 'stance' as you call it, in the past Colonel James has served the Company well and honorably. If there's anything I can do, you must tell me."

Sommerset left Theresa's side, walking forward to sit on the couch directly across from where Hadderly had taken a seat, himself. The earl looked as impeccably-dressed as always, cravat neat and conservatively tied, his coat well fitting and padded at the shoulders to disguise any imperfections in his posture. Whether he was involved with this horror or not, she didn't like him. She never had, really, however amusing her grandmother's venom toward him was.

"Did you ever read the report taken from Colonel James's account?" the duke asked smoothly, his tone less confrontational than Tolly's brother.

"I don't know that there ever was an official report," Hadderly returned. "Not one where he was interviewed by his commanding officers, anyway. I of course read the independent one submitted by his superiors to Lord Hastings in India." He glanced at Stephen. "I don't know what merit discussing that would have on finding the colonel today." He sat forward. "Do you have no idea where he might have gone? A friend, or a fellow officer's home? I do know that our report has made things a bit . . . difficult for him."

" 'Difficult'?" Stephen repeated forcefully.

"Please, Lord Gardner. I don't mean to make things worse. I'm genuinely trying to help you here."

"Why?" the duke asked.

Hadderly blinked. "I beg your pardon, Your Grace?"

"I said, 'why'? Colonel James gone means one less man to dispute your Company's stance, as Lord Gardner calls it. Why do you wish to assist us in finding him?"

"Well, he's a fellow nobleman. Whatever might have become of him, or whatever he may have . . . done to himself, I think it's important to find him."

"Ah. So you favor suicide."

"For God's sake, Sommerset," Stephen growled, his face white. "I don't need to hear such nonsense, and neither does Tess."

"No," Theresa protested. "I want to hear of any and every theory and possibility." She didn't, but she did want him to be able to follow his line of questions with Hadderly. She knew the man to be unpleasant unless he was intentionally attempting to be charming. Today, unless she was greatly mistaken, he was being deliberately charming.

"What would you suggest, then, Your Grace?" Hadderly said, frowning. "I don't want to dwell on the worst possibility, but in all honesty this is a man who staked his reputation on a story that is now known to be untrue."

"Hmm. Do you think that a man with a close-knit family would take his own life?" Sommerset went on, crossing his legs at the ankles and apparently completely unconcerned with the topic at hand. Theresa was relieved that he'd spoken to her beforehand; even Montrose looked rather dismayed at the duke's sangfroid. "A man in pursuit of a young lady?" He motioned over his shoulder in her direction.

"Please, Sommerset. Of course such a man would take his own life. How else to save his family from being dragged into scandal with him? And this young lady is known to have several suitors. Lord Montrose, you're one of them, aren't you?"

Alexander nodded. "I am."

"Well. A possibly hopeless pursuit, then."

Theresa took a deep breath, beginning to wish she was a man so that she could punch this very annoying earl in the nose. "Not hopeless, my lord," she said aloud. "As a matter of fact, Colonel James and I became engaged nearly a fortnight ago. We are to be married."

All eyes in the room turned to look at her. Of all of them, only Sommerset didn't look surprised. In fact, he sent her a brief smile and a nod. "Congratulations, then, Miss Weller." He faced Hadderly again. "This does put a bit of a wrinkle in your theory, doesn't it?"

Hadderly frowned at her, then returned his attention to Sommerset. "Not a theory, Your Grace. A possibility. One of many, clearly. And I have to ask, considering that Miss Weller's news is clearly a surprise both to her brother and to Colonel James's, do you think you have any idea at all where he might be? You seem to know very little about him, begging your pardon."

A pair of Hadderly's cat-menacing wolfhounds trotted into the room, nuzzling up to their master and wagging their tales. As the men continued their debate over where Tolly might have gone and why, she watched the dogs. Personally she had nothing against the animals, but they were very slobbery looking and had large teeth.

One of them was carrying a leather toy in its teeth, strips hanging off it and reaching nearly to the floor. No, not strips. Straps. Theresa sat forward again. *Dear heavens.* Her fingers shaking and her heart even more unsteady, she stuck her hand out toward the beast. "Come here, boy," she cooed, knowing she recognized that leather mess even before she could logically have been sure of anything.

"I will be happy to loan you a dozen of my own men to search, if you think . . ." Hadderly trailed off, his gaze meeting hers and then lowering to his dog. The earl shot to his feet. "Titan. Come here, boy," he ordered sharply.

The wolfhound turned around. Theresa wanted to yell that she knew where Tolly was, knew who had him, but she needed to be certain. Holding her breath, she lunged forward, snatching the leather out of the dog's mouth.

"Miss Weller!" the earl roared. "Leave my dog alone. And give me back his damned toy."

The leather brace was sticky and malformed, but she recognized it. And the brass buckles Tolly used for fastening it around his knee. Standing up, she jabbed it in Hadderly's direction. "This is Tolly's leg brace," she shouted, her voice shaking. "What have you done with him? Tell me! Tell me!"

The earl advanced on her, then stopped short as Sommerset grabbed him around the throat and backed him up again. "You heard Miss Weller," he murmured, ignoring Hadderly clawing at his forearm. "Where is Colonel James?"

"You're all mad," the earl croaked. "The fool killed himself. Accept that, and move on."

Theresa ran to the door and out into the main part of the house. "Tolly!" she yelled. "Bartholomew James!"

"Tess, slow down," her brother ordered, grabbing her by the arm.

"He's here." Tears ran down her face, but she didn't care. "Michael, they had him here. What if they've—"

"We'll find him. I promise you."

Stephen came pounding up behind them, Montrose on his heels. "The cellar," Lord Gardner panted, pointing. "This way."

They wound down the hallways toward the back of the house. A half dozen servants and menacing looking men fell back, out of the way, as they advanced. Theresa would have fought them all single-handedly if she had to. He had to be well. Surely Hadderly wouldn't have harmed him. Not until he could finish spinning his ugly little tale about suicide.

Just outside the kitchen Stephen put his shoulder against a door and shoved it open. The men pushed past her, charging down the stairs, and leaving her to follow behind. Inside, sprawled on the floor with another man slumped beside him, was Tolly.

"Tess," he said, ignoring everything else.

She flung herself forward, falling into his arms. "Thank God," she sobbed, digging her hands into his jacket. "Thank God."

He wrapped his arms around her, holding her close. "You came to rescue me again," he whispered, burying his face in her hair.

Theresa straightened a little. He had an ugly bruise

over one eye, dried blood trickling down from the cut there. "Again?"

"You rescued me the moment I set eyes on you. You were all I could think of. I love you, Theresa. So much."

"So very much," she whispered back.

"Come on, Tess," Michael said, taking her beneath the arms. "Off the floor."

She didn't want to let go of Tolly, but he couldn't have been easy there on the floor with everyone towering over him. Stephen hefted him up onto the second stair. "You seemed to be doing a fair job of rescuing yourself," Lord Gardner noted, pulling a knife from his boot and cutting the rope that remained around one of Tolly's forearms. Both of his wrists looked raw and torn, but from his smile he didn't care.

Sommerset stepped into the doorway above them. "All is well, I presume?" he asked, looking down at them.

"Yes. Thank you, Your Grace." Stephen looked near tears, himself.

"Thank Miss Weller. She figured it out before I did." He moved aside. "Montrose, might I impose on you to keep watch on Hadderly while I pay a visit to Lord Liverpool? This will take some delicacy."

Goodness. Now the prime minister was involved. Before Alexander climbed the stairs, Theresa took his hand. "Thank you," she said, and kissed him on the cheek.

The marquis gave a brief smile. "I said I wasn't the villain of this piece." He glanced at Tolly, then back to her again. "Not the hero, either. He's still a crippled former soldier, you know. And I'm still a marquis. I'll wait for a time. Just in case."

"He can wait until hell freezes over," Tolly rumbled, taking her hand and drawing her down across his legs. "You're mine."

"I love you, Tolly," she whispered, leaning into his shoulder. "And I don't care who knows. I *want* everyone to know."

"We do, now," Michael said wryly. "Let's get everyone back to James House, shall we?"

Once Tolly climbed to his feet she wrapped her arm around his waist to help him climb the stairs. "You're certain, Theresa? No regrets?" he murmured.

"Never."

The rest of the Season flew by in a flurry of parties and wedding preparations and abrupt, unwanted hero worship for Tolly. Once the *London Times* published his editorial and Lord Hadderly mysteriously left London for the West Indies, everyone seemed to forget that they'd once refused even to speak to Colonel Bartholomew James.

"Tess, you look so pretty tonight," Harriet said, greeting her as she walked into the ballroom of Garrity House, her grandmother and Michael on either side.

Theresa kissed her friend's cheek. She felt pretty. And she felt happy; in fact, her face hurt some evenings, she'd been smiling so much. "You look lovely yourself, Harriet," she returned. "Doesn't she, Michael?"

Her brother lifted an eyebrow, then sketched an

elaborate bow. "You do indeed, Miss Silder. Have you a waltz to spare?"

Harriet blushed. "I happen to have one, yes."

Theresa's dance card filled nearly as swiftly as it used to when half the men present were pursuing her. She'd never expected that they would still wish to dance when she didn't have a dowry to offer, and when she'd actually begun speaking her mind when the mood struck her—which it did more and more often.

The best part of the flurry of balls and soirees—all of them demanding their presence once the wedding announcement had appeared—was the one dance she always saved for Tolly. It was always the first waltz of the evening, and their quiet, kiss-filled walks in gardens or along terraces or in someone's ill-used library were absolutely the only things that gave her the patience to wait for a formal, proper wedding. Otherwise she was half certain she would simply have moved into James House to live with him in sin.

Tonight, however, by the end of the quadrille with Francis Henning, Tolly still hadn't appeared. She frowned. Where the devil was Bartholomew? He'd said he would attend tonight, whatever he thought of crowds and of the fickle-mindedness of people who could shun him one moment and celebrate him the next.

"Theresa."

With a start, she turned around. "Tolly," she said, smiling. *Thank goodness.*

He sat in his wheeled chair, Lackaby behind him. "Did you save me a dance?"

"I did." She always would. Always. "What shall we do this evening?" She had several ideas, but she couldn't precisely mention those in front of the valet. "The Garrity House garden has a lovely fish pond, I hear."

"Does it?" Tolly slowly pushed to his feet, then took a step forward. And another. It took a moment for her to realize that he'd left his cane behind, and that he was barely limping at all. "What shall we do this evening, my love?" he repeated, gazing down at her as he took her hand and brought it to his lips. "I think we should waltz."

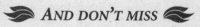